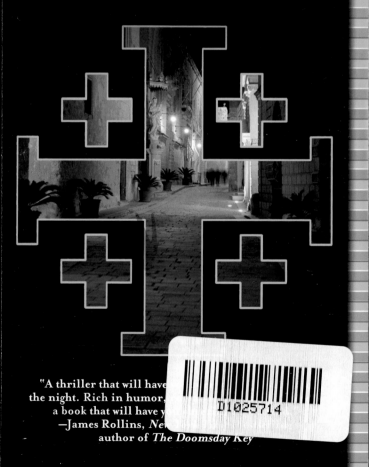

...and for whoever possesses it,
the most dangerous.

D1025714

ARK *of* FIRE

ARK *of* FIRE

C. M. PALOV

BERKLEY BOOKS, NEW YORK

THE BERKLEY PUBLISHING GROUP
Published by the Penguin Group
Penguin Group (USA) Inc.
375 Hudson Street, New York, New York 10014, USA
Penguin Group (Canada), 90 Eglinton Avenue East, Suite 700, Toronto, Ontario M4P 2Y3, Canada
(a division of Pearson Penguin Canada Inc.)
Penguin Books Ltd., 80 Strand, London WC2R 0RL, England
Penguin Group Ireland, 25 St. Stephen's Green, Dublin 2, Ireland (a division of Penguin Books Ltd.)
Penguin Group (Australia), 250 Camberwell Road, Camberwell, Victoria 3124, Australia
(a division of Pearson Australia Group Pty. Ltd.)
Penguin Books India Pvt. Ltd., 11 Community Centre, Panchsheel Park, New Delhi—110 017, India
Penguin Group (NZ), 67 Apollo Drive, Rosedale, North Shore 0632, New Zealand
(a division of Pearson New Zealand Ltd.)
Penguin Books (South Africa) (Pty.) Ltd., 24 Sturdee Avenue, Rosebank, Johannesburg 2196,
South Africa

Penguin Books Ltd., Registered Offices: 80 Strand, London WC2R 0RL, England

ARK OF FIRE

A Berkley Book / published by arrangement with the author

PRINTING HISTORY
Berkley edition / December 2009

Copyright © 2009 by Chloe Palov.
Internal artwork by Jeanne Chitty.
Front cover illustration copyright © by 3DI Studio. Stepback photograph copyright © by Feraru/
Nicolne/Shutterstock. Cover design by Richard Hasselberger.
Interior text design by Laura K. Corless.

ISBN: 978-0-425-23146-3

BERKLEY®
Berkley Books are published by The Berkley Publishing Group,
a division of Penguin Group (USA) Inc.,
375 Hudson Street, New York, New York 10014.
BERKLEY® is a registered trademark of Penguin Group (USA) Inc.
The "B" design is a trademark of Penguin Group (USA) Inc.

PRINTED IN THE UNITED STATES OF AMERICA

10 9 8 7 6 5 4 3 2 1

To Ria Palov for keeping the faith.
And Steve Kasdin for taking a chance.

The author would like to express thanks to Jeanne Chitty for the exquisitely rendered artwork.

CHAPTER 1

His movements slow and deliberate, the curator ran his finger-tips over the small bronze coffer, lightly grazing the incised Hebrew letters. A lover's caress.

Holding his breath, he opened the box.

"Claves regni caelorum," he whispered, entranced by the relic nestled within the box. Like Eve gazing upon the forbidden fruit, he stared at the twelve polished gemstones anchored in an ancient gold setting.

The keys to the kingdom of heaven.

Dr. Jonathan Padgham, chief curator at the Hopkins Museum of Near Eastern Art, reached into the coffer, carefully removing what had once been a gem-encrusted breastplate. *Once.* Long ago. More than three thousand years ago, by his reckoning.

Although bits and pieces of the gold scapular still precari-ously clung to the setting, the relic was scarcely recognizable as a breastplate, the chains that originally secured the gem-studded shield to the wearer's body having long since van-ished. Only the stones, set in four rows of three, gave any indication as to the relic's original rectangular shape, the breastplate measuring some five inches by four.

"That's some real bling-bling, huh?"

Annoyed by the disruption, Padgham glanced at the curly-haired woman engaged in placing a digital camera on a tripod. Not for the first time, he wondered what possessed her to pair black leather motorcycle boots with a long tartan skirt.

A cheeky grin on her face, Edie Miller stepped over to his desk, bending her head to peer at the relic. Since immigrating to "the land of the free," he'd come to realize that American females were far more brazen than their English cousins. Ignoring her, Padgham arranged the breastplate on a square piece of black velvet, readying it to be photographed.

"Wow. There's a diamond, an amethyst, and a sapphire." As she spoke, the Miller woman pointed to each stone she named. Padgham was tempted to snatch her hand, afraid she might actually touch the precious relic. A freelance photographer hired by the Hopkins to digitally archive the collection, she was not trained to handle rare artifacts.

"And there's an emerald! Which, by the by, happens to be my birthstone," she continued. "What do you think that is, about five carats?"

"I have no idea," he said dismissively; gemology was not his strong suit. Hers either, he suspected.

"How old a relic do you think it is?"

Barely glancing at the plaid-garbed magpie, he again replied, "I have no idea."

"I'm guessing *really* old."

To be certain, the age of the breastplate was punctuated by a very large question mark. So, too, its provenance. Although he had an inkling.

Again, Padgham ran the tip of a manicured finger over the engraved symbols that adorned the bronze coffer in which the breastplate had been housed. He recognized only one word—

יהוה

—the Hebrew tetragrammaton. The unspeakable four-letter name of God. It had been placed on the coffer as a talisman to ward off the curious, the covetous, the carnivores who gobbled up ancient relics like candy-coated Sweeties.

How in God's name did an ancient Hebrew relic end up in Iraq, of all places?

Although the museum director, Eliot Hopkins, had been

very hush-hush, he did let slip that the relic originated in Iraq. Padgham, an expert in Babylonian art, had been entrusted by the old man with the initial evaluation of the bejeweled breast-plate. He'd also been cautioned to keep mum. Padgham was no fool. Far from it. He knew the relic had been bought on the black market.

Risky business, the purchase of stolen relics. In recent years a curator at the renowned Getty had been brought to trial by Italian prosecutors for having knowingly purchased stolen artifacts. The black-market antiquities trade was a billion-dollar business, particularly with the unabated pilfering of Iraqi relics and Babylonian art popping up all over the place these days. Many in the museum world turned a blind eye, jaded enough to believe that they were preserving, not stealing, ancient culture. Padgham concurred. After all, had it not been for European art thieves, the world would have been deprived of such treasures as the Rosetta stone and the Elgin Marbles.

"There's too much backlight falling on the relic. Do you mind if I adjust the window shades?"

Padgham drew his gaze away from the relic. "Hmm . . . no, no, of course not. This is your arena, as it were." He pasted a smile on his face, needing the woman's cooperation. He'd been ordered not to show the relic to anyone on the museum staff. It was the reason why he was conducting his preliminary evaluation on a Monday, when the museum was closed to the public and no staff were on the premises. Of course, the photographer didn't count; the woman was a freelance contractor who didn't know a breastplate from a bas-relief. *Who would she tell?* As far as he knew, aside from the two guards in the museum lobby, they were the only two bodies afoot.

A flash of light momentarily illuminated the dimmed office.

"Looks good," the photographer remarked, reviewing the image on the camera display. She deftly popped a blue plastic card out of the camera. "I'll just snap a backup copy. No sense having four gigabytes of internal memory if I don't use it." No sooner did a second flash go off than she gestured to the bronze coffer. "Do you want a shot of the metal box as well?"

"Is Queen Anne dead?" Then, catching himself, he added in a more congenial tone, "If you would be so kind."

Padgham stood aside as the photographer repositioned the tripod. Contemplating the beautiful relic, he worriedly bit his lower lip. As curator of Babylonian antiquities, he'd been given custody of the breastplate because it'd been found in the deserts of Iraq. The museum director assumed he'd be able to put flesh to bone, to derive the four Ws of provenance: who, where, when, and why. To Padgham's consternation, those answers eluded him. The breastplate was most definitely of Hebrew derivation, and his knowledge of the ancient Israelites was sketchy at best. Thus, the reason for the digital photograph.

As fate would have it, an old Oxford chum, Caedmon Aisquith, was currently in Washington on a publicity junket for his newly released book, *Isis Revealed*—one of those faux histories that purported to expose the arcane secrets of the long-buried past. That sort of esoteric conspiracy theory was all the rage. Never one to gawk at the proverbial gift horse, upon reading the newspaper review he immediately rang up Aisquith, renewing their acquaintanceship. Surprising, really. Last he'd heard, old Aisquith had absconded to the continent, taken his inheritance, and opened an antiquarian bookshop on the Left Bank. Drinking Beaujolais and banging French tarts; the man should have his head examined.

Although they hadn't set eyes on one another in nearly twenty years, Aisquith had agreed to meet him later that evening for drinks. Hoping to pique his interest—and in the process glean some kernel of information about the mysterious Hebrew relic—he intended to e-mail Aisquith the digital photographs. A true Renaissance man with an encyclopedic knowledge of ancient history, Caedmon Aisquith would, hopefully, be able to shed some much-needed light.

As with the freelance photographer, Padgham did not deem the secrecy clause set down by the museum director applicable to his Oxford chum.

"All finished," the photographer announced. Popping open the digital camera, she removed the memory card and handed it to him.

He stared at the minuscule piece of stored data. "And what I am supposed to do with *this*? I asked you to take a photograph."

"And I did just that. There's your photograph. On the memory card." She stuffed the digital camera into her pocket, her outlandish garb topped by a khaki-colored waistcoat.

Cheeky cow, Padgham thought, frustrated. Although he was only forty-two, he often felt as though the modern world and all its technical sleights of hand were passing him by at a dizzying speed.

As she dismantled the tripod, Padgham repeated his question. "What am I supposed to do with this?"

"You're supposed to download it to your computer. Once you do that, you can print it, e-mail it, doctor it up, whatever."

There being no staff available to assist him, Padgham was forced to grovel. "I would be most appreciative if—"

Just as he hoped, she snatched the memory card out of his hand. Bending at the waist, she inserted it into the computer tower under his desk.

Biting back a pleased smile, he pointed to a notepad inscribed with the museum logo. "I would like to send the photographs, via e-mail, to that address."

"Yes, sire. I live to serve."

Padgham turned a deaf ear on her disgruntled mumblings. "You're most kind, Miss Miller."

"You say that only because you don't know me." She seated herself at his carved mahogany desk. "All right, let me get this straight, you want me to send the pics to one C Aisquith at lycos dot com?" When he nodded, she said, "Probably best if we send the photos as jpegs."

"Yes, well, I'll leave it up to you."

She quickly and deftly tapped away on the keyboard. Then, getting up from his executive-style chair, she said, "Okay, I want you to pull up your e-mail account."

"I would be only too happy to oblige." Padgham seated himself at the desk. "What the bloody hell!"

"What's wrong?"

"Are you blind, woman? The screen has gone blank." He pointed an accusing finger at the blackened monitor.

"Calm down. No need to have a conniption. It's probably just a loose cable."

"Hmm . . ." He glanced at the floor-bound computer, then at his Gieves & Hawkes hand-tailored trousers. The problem had but one solution. "Since you so easily diagnosed the problem, would you be a dear and . . . ?"

"You do know that this is *not* in my job description," Edie Miller griped as she scrambled to her knees. There being no room to pull the computer tower forward, she was forced to wedge herself under the desk in order to check the cables. Padgham glanced at the Waterford candy dish on the nearby console, thinking he might offer her a cellophane-wrapped sweet. Recompense for a job well done.

As the woman under the desk silently went about her business, Padgham picked up the ancient breastplate, returning it to the incised bronze coffer.

"Ah, let there be light," he murmured a moment later, pleased that a spark of life now emanated from his computer, the monitor flickering the familiar Dell logo.

Out of the corner of his eye, Padgham saw a third person enter the office.

Surprised to see a man attired in gray coveralls with a black balaclava pulled over his head, he imperiously demanded, "Who the devil are you?"

The man made no reply. Instead, he raised a gun and pointed it at Padgham's head, his finger poised on the trigger.

Death was almost instantaneous. Padgham experienced a sharp, piercing pain in his right eye socket. Then, like the flickering lights on his computer monitor, he saw an explosion of color before the world around him turned a deep, impenetrable shade of black.

CHAPTER 2

"Who the devil are you?"

Pop.

Crash!

Thud.

Those sounds registered on Edie Miller's brain in such quick succession that it wasn't until she saw Dr. Padgham's lifeless body sprawled on the Persian carpet, three feet from her huddled position under the desk, that she realized what had happened.

She stifled a shriek of terror. Like a freight train that had jumped the tracks, her heart slammed against her chest. Hearing a clang above her, she froze, the murderer having picked up her folded tripod from the top of the desk.

In a state of shock, her brain sent a series of urgent messages. *Don't move. Don't speak. Don't twitch so much as a finger.*

Terrified, Edie heeded the commands.

And then her fear turned to joy.

Several seconds had passed since Dr. Padgham had hit the floor, and she was still alive. It was her lucky day. The killer didn't know she was crouched in the knee well under the desk. Covered on three sides by antique mahogany, she was hidden from view. In order to find her, the killer would have to bend at the waist and peer under the desk.

From her low vantage point, Edie saw a pair of gray-clad legs suddenly come into view. At the end of those legs was a pair of tan military-style lug boots. Next to those legs she saw a large masculine hand wrapped around a pistol that had a silencer attached to the end of it. As though she were looking through the lens of a camera, she focused on that ham-fisted hand, noticing the hairy knuckles and the unusual silver ring made up of interconnected crosses. The notion that she and the killer might actually pray to the same God caused her to bite down on her lip, hard, a hysterical burst of laughter threatening to escape.

And that's when the killer did the completely unexpected.

Stepping over Dr. Padgham's body, he set the gun on top of the desk and, bending forward, began clicking away on the computer keyboard. A few seconds later, Edie heard him softly swear under his breath as he yanked open the desk drawer.

He was looking for something.

Edie barely had time to wrap her mind around that thought when the killer reached under the desk and removed the digital memory card from the computer.

She held her breath, praying to God, Jesus, anyone who would listen, that the killer didn't see her. It stood to reason that you couldn't plead with a man who sneaked up on his victims and killed in unpitying silence.

Only able to see the killer from the waist down, she watched as he unclipped a cell phone from his belt. Then she listened, and heard seven digital beeps. A local phone number. He was calling someone in the Washington, D.C., metropolitan area.

"Let me speak to the colonel." Several moments passed in silence before he again spoke. "Sir, I've got the breastplate. I've also got a problem."

The breastplate, she belatedly realized. Dr. Padgham had been killed because of the bejeweled breastplate.

"I'm not sure, but I think the little English homo sent digital photos of the relic to someone outside the museum. I found a tripod on the desk, a memory card with photos of the breastplate, and an e-mail address." Edie heard a sheet of paper being ripped from a pad. "C Aisquith at lycos dot com." A short pause. The killer carefully spelled out the e-mail address. Another pause ensued. "No. I couldn't find the camera . . . Yes, sir, I took care of the guards . . . don't worry, sir, I'll cover my tracks."

Edie heard a digital beep as the call disconnected. She then heard the metallic *whhsh!* of a zipper. The killer was putting the bronze box with the bejeweled breastplate inside some sort of carrying case.

And then he was gone, exiting the office as unobtrusively as he had entered.

Edie slowly counted to twenty before she crawled out from under the desk. Forced to straddle Dr. Padgham's corpse, she took one look at his bloody, mutilated eye socket . . . and promptly threw up. All over the Persian carpet. Not that it mattered; the carpet was already stained with blood and brain matter.

Still on all fours, she wiped her mouth on her sweater sleeve. She'd never liked Jonathan Padgham. But someone else had liked him even less. Enough to kill him in cold blood. Correction. Warm blood. Warm, wet, coppery-smelling blood.

Lurching to her feet, Edie picked up the telephone. Nothing but dead air. The killer had disabled the phone line. With a sinking heart she knew that her cell phone was still plugged into the battery charger on her kitchen counter. So much for calling the cops to come to the rescue. Since the killer "took care" of the two museum guards downstairs, Edie knew she was on her own.

Her goal being to get out of the museum as quickly as possible, she left the office and headed for the main corridor. The Hopkins Museum was housed in a four-story nineteenth-century Beaux Arts mansion located in the heart of the Dupont Circle area, a vibrant commercial and residential district. Once she was free of the museum, help was only a shout away.

Coming to a halt at the end of the hall that led to the main corridor, Edie tentatively peered around the corner.

Oh, God.

Stunned to see the killer, Edie caught herself in midgasp. A behemoth of a man in a gray janitor's suit with a black ski mask pulled over his head was standing in front of the wall monitor attached to a security keypad. In order to gain access to the administration area, every employee, regardless of rank, had to key a personal ID number into the security system, repeating the procedure when they left the admin area. The code activated the lock on the intimidating steel door adjacent to the keypad through which one entered and departed the fourth-floor office suite. The computer system enabled museum security to monitor all employees' whereabouts.

It occurred to Edie that in order to enter the office suite, the murderer had to have had a valid security code to unlock the steel door.

How did he get ahold of a valid code?

It didn't matter. All that mattered was that she was stuck on the fourth floor with a murderer. To get to the elevator, she had to pass through the steel door. Meaning she'd have to wait him out. Once he left the premises, she could escape the building.

Wondering what the killer was doing, Edie watched his supersized hand move across the keypad with surprising dexterity. She knew from experience that it took no more than two seconds to key in a five-digit code and unlock the door, but by her reckoning the killer had been standing in front of the monitor and keypad a good thirty seconds.

So just leave already.

"Fucking shit!' she heard the killer mutter as he removed a notepad and pencil from his breast pocket.

As she watched him scribble something onto the notepad, Edie went slack-jawed. Although the monitor was too far away to verify, she suspected the killer had accessed the computer security log. If true, that meant the name *E. Miller* had just popped up on the monitor. Beside her name would be the exact date—12/1/08—and time—13:38:01—that she had entered the fourth floor. Even more damning, there would be no date or time indicated in the *DEPART* column.

Edie had watched enough crime dramas on TV to know she'd been made.

She had to find a hiding place. Now. This very instant.

Terrified that the Neanderthal in the gray coveralls would somehow home in on her, Edie slowly eased away from the corner. She then ran down the hall, past the office with the sprawled corpse on the floor, grateful for the hideous maroon carpet that muffled her footfalls.

Turning right, she headed down another hall, this one dead-ending at the supply room. Lined with shelving units that were, in turn, stacked with boxes, it would make an excellent hiding place.

Or it would have made an excellent hiding place, had the door been unlocked.

Stymied, she stared at the locked door.

Now what?

If she could get downstairs to the exhibition galleries, she could yank an artifact off the wall, instantly triggering the museum alarm system. The D.C. Metropolitan Police would arrive within minutes. Maybe even seconds, if there happened to be a squad car in the area. But to do that, she'd have to first sneak past Dr. Padgham's killer.

Too faint of heart to give the idea further consideration, Edie spun on her booted heel. As she did, she caught sight of a bright red sign with bold white lettering.

The fire escape.

With renewed hope at seeing the word *EXIT*, Edie rushed down the hall toward that welcoming red light. When she reached the door, she grabbed the bar handle and pushed, bracing herself for what she assumed would be a very loud alarm.

CHAPTER 3

"I think Isis is like the total embodiment of the wise woman. That's why my magick circle practices a devotional ritual to invoke the power of Isis at each full moon."

Caedmon Aisquith glanced at the pierced and tattooed reception attendee, an autographed copy of *Isis Revealed* clutched to her breast.

"Do you by any chance mention the Rites of Isis in your book?"

About to answer in the terse negative, Caedmon caught himself. His American readers tended to fall into two categories: the erudite and the asinine. Not that it mattered, as he'd been ordered by his publicist—who looked on with the stern prerogative of an English headmistress—to treat all questions, no matter how inane or idiotic, with due consideration. Particularly if the questioner had already purchased a copy of his book.

Caedmon schooled his features into an attentive expression. "Er, no, I am afraid there are no magical rituals detailed in the text. However, you are quite correct in that Isis, like her Greek counterpart, Sophia, represents wisdom in all its myriad forms."

Apple polished, Caedmon thanked the young woman for her interest in ancient mysteries and cordially took his leave of her. A private man, he was uncomfortable in the role of public author, finding the meet-and-greet segment of the book signings a tiresome exercise in the fine art of chin wagging—an art form he'd never quite mastered.

His belly ached from the cheap champagne, and his facial muscles ached from the fool's grin he'd been forced to wear since entering the bookshop, so he was actually relieved when his mobile began to softly vibrate; the incoming call was a perfect excuse to turn his back on the nattering group crowded into the diminutive confines of Dupont Books. To lessen his publicist's displeasure, he made a big to-do of raising his mobile to his left ear, silently signaling that he needed to take the call. This being the last leg of a twelve-city tour, they'd had their fill of one another, Caedmon anxious to return to the quiet monotony of pen and ink.

"Yes, hello," he said, always feeling like a bit of an ass speaking into, essentially, thin air.

"Caedmon Aisquith?"

Politely correcting the man's butchered pronunciation of his name, he said, "Who's calling, please?"

The question met with a long, static silence, followed by a distinctive click as the call was abruptly disconnected.

"Bloody hell," Caedmon muttered, yanking the mobile from his ear.. The hair on the back of his neck suddenly bristled. He didn't give out his number. Hit with the unnerving sensation that he was being watched by someone who had no interest in discussing ancient lore or swilling free bubbly, he turned on his heel. Slowly. Calmly. A man with nothing to fear.

Only he knew such posturing was an outright lie.

With training ingrained from the eleven years he'd spent indentured in Her Majesty's Secret Service, he calmly glanced about the bookshop, searching for the face that did not belong in the crowd, the telltale flush, the quick breakaway glance of the guilty. Seeing no suspect characters prowling about, he next glanced out the plate glass windows that opened onto Connecticut Avenue, at the city pavement teeming with holiday shoppers.

Nothing appearing out of the ordinary, he quietly released a pent-up breath.

All quiet on the western front.

Like most men with a price on his head, he didn't know how it would end, if the day just lived would be his last. All he knew was that when the thugs of the Real Irish Republican Army did finally catch up to him, they would see to it that he died a barbaric death, indeed. An eye for an eye, and all that.

Five years ago he had avenged the death of his lover by tracking down an RIRA chieftain and killing the bastard in the streets of Belfast. Such deeds did not go unpunished. Forced to go to ground, he'd spent the last several years living in Paris. He'd spent the time wisely, writing his first book, a treatise on the esoteric traditions of the ancient world. Lulled into a false sense of security, he'd decided against using a pseudonym, foolishly thinking he'd fallen off the RIRA radar screen.

Only now did it dawn on him that that bit of arrogance might cost him dearly.

Ah, the folly of a firstborn son still trying to impress the long-dead father.

He rechecked the digital readout on his mobile, on which the words *BLOCKED CALL* were prominently displayed.

"Why am I not surprised?" he murmured. Again, he scanned the bookstore, certain he was being stalked.

His gaze fell on a volume of Byron propped on a nearby book shelf.

For the Angel of Death spread his wings on the blast.

As the long-forgotten line popped into his head, he bit back a caustic laugh, knowing he'd been that same dark angel. Once. A long time ago.

Still holding the mobile in his hand, he strolled over to his publicist. "My hotel just rang me," he blithely lied, falling back on the lessons learned at MI5. "A bit of a sticky wicket with the billing. Something about my credit card being denied." He pointedly glanced around the bookshop, the tops of the shelves littered with abandoned champagne flutes. "Seeing as how the festivities are winding down, you won't mind if I dash out and take care of it?"

His publicist, a touchy woman with the ironic surname of Huffman, stared at him from behind the frames of her ruby-red spectacles. "Do you need me to call the front desk for you?"

"No bother," he replied with a shake of the head. "I'm a big boy. Although perhaps I should fortify myself before battling the dragon." He picked up a full champagne flute from a nearby tray, ignoring the fact that it had long since gone flat. "Cheers."

Taking his leave of her, the champagne flute still clutched in his right hand, he headed to the back of the bookshop, veering down a hall marked *EMPLOYEES ONLY*. Blatantly ignoring the admonition, he continued until he came to a room stacked with cardboard boxes, the sole inhabitant a lank-haired young man unpacking a shipping crate with the desultory air of an underpaid cog who didn't much care if or when the wheel turned.

Caedmon nodded, acting as though he had every right to be there. "The exit, if you please."

The young man jerked his head at the door opposite.

On the other side of the service exit, Caedmon found himself standing on a cigarette-strewn pavement behind the bookshop, the concrete walls covered in ribald graffiti.

No sooner did the exit door close behind him than he smashed his champagne flute against the wall.

Weapon in hand, he waited.

Come out, come out, wherever you are, he silently taunted, readying himself to do combat with his unseen nemesis.

A full minute passed in tense silence.

Realizing he'd given in to his fears, he derisively snorted.

"The ghosts of Irishmen past," he murmured, tossing the jagged-edged flute to the pavement.

The moment of lunacy having passed, he flipped up the collar of his wool jacket, warding off the cold. He recalled having seen a coffeehouse several blocks away. In dire need of caffeine, he headed in that direction.

Although he knew he was being paranoid, Caedmon couldn't shake the unnerving feeling that an Irish militant who refused to accept the peace had tracked him to the far side of the Atlantic.

Where he intended to settle a very old, yet still outstanding score.

Who else would have had the audacity to ring him on his mobile? As if to say, we can see you, but you can't see us.

CHAPTER 4

To Edie's surprise, no fire alarm sounded. There was only the reverberating clunk of the bar handle as she swung open the exit door.

The killer had disabled the alarm system.

Hit with a blast of cold wintry air, she found herself on the precipice between the open door and an external fire escape that zigzagged across the back side of the museum. Completely enclosed with black chain link, the escape was designed so that only those inside the museum had access to it, keeping vagrants and thieves at bay.

With no time to worry that it was lightly snowing, that she had no coat, or that she was afraid of heights, Edie stepped across the threshold into the caged stairwell as the exit door swung shut behind her. She kept her gaze on the alley below, knowing that if she looked anywhere else but down, she'd get dizzy, maybe even faint. Keeping a white-knuckled grip on the railing, she made her descent. The clanking sound of her boots hitting the metal grate of the steps echoed in the alley below. At the bottom, she opened a cage door, emerging into the alleyway. As with the emergency exit above, the door automatically closed and locked behind her.

Hurriedly she glanced around, disoriented, uncertain which direction to go. Like a weird netherworld, the alley was filled with garbage Dumpsters, SUV-sized air-conditioner condensers, and parked service vans. Against an adjacent building was a tall pile of discarded office furniture; the offices next door had recently been remodeled, and the outdated stuff was still waiting to be hauled away. Given that it was December, every window that looked onto the alley was closed. And because no one wanted a bird's-eye view of big blue trash Dumpsters, the blinds were all pulled shut.

From above her, Edie heard a door suddenly swing open.

The killer had accessed the fire escape.

Not wasting a second, she ducked behind an air-conditioning condenser, praying she hadn't been spotted. If she hurried, she could escape the alley before he reached the bottom rung. But that was a really big *if*. Particularly because she couldn't exit the alley without moving into the killer's line of sight.

That left only one option—she had to hide before he reached the alley.

Keeping to the shadows, she dashed some fifteen feet to the heap of jumbled chairs, their wooden arms and legs jutting into the air at odd angles. Like so many broken bones. As far as hiding places went, it was pretty pathetic. The ungainly pile wouldn't stop a bullet. Or prevent a big, meaty fist from clos-

ing in on her. But it was the best that she could do on short
notice.

Spying a small opening at the bottom of the pile, she got
down on her hands and knees and crawled into the chasm. The
opening was no more than twenty inches high, so she had to
navigate with care. One wrong move and the heap of furniture
could well tumble to the ground. With her underneath.

Unable to crawl any farther into the pile, she came to a halt.
Tucking her legs beneath her body, she made herself as small
as possible. Invisible would have been better. Better because
she knew with a sickening sense of certainty that if he found
her, the man on the fire escape wouldn't hesitate to kill her.

Hearing the rattle of a metal door, she peered through the
jumble of furniture, keeping watch as the killer exited the fire
escape. He'd removed his ski mask, and Edie could see that
he sported a military-style buzz cut. His face mottled with
rage, he looked to be on the verge of a steroid-induced rampage.

In hunting mode, the killer swiveled his head from side to
side, perusing the alley. Edie saw a large bulge at the back of
his waist. *A gun.* The very same gun that had killed Dr.
Padgham.

Methodically, the killer's gaze moved from target to target:
blue Dumpster, green condenser, white service van. And then
his gaze zeroed in on the furniture pile.

*These may very well be the last few moments before my
death.*

Edie envisioned her bleeding body sprawled beneath a
pile of discarded chairs put out for the trash. No doubt, that's
who would find her—the orange-suited guys in the sanitation
department.

Holding her breath, Edie slowly counted backward from ten.

Ten, nine, eight, seven—

The killer's gaze suddenly swung to the other side of the
alley, where a group of recycling bins overflowed with alumi-
num soda cans.

She'd gone undetected.

Surprisingly light-footed for such a large man, the killer

walked all the way down the alley toward Twenty-first Street
before turning around and heading back to the fire escape. As
he did, a police cruiser pulled into the alley from the opposite
direction.

Relieved beyond words, Edie released a pent-up breath.
Opening the door to the fire escape had obviously triggered a
silent alarm, and the D.C. police had arrived to investigate.

Although for some strange reason the killer didn't seem the
least bit perturbed by the sudden appearance of the cop car,
actually raising his hand to flag down the cruiser.

Why would he do that? she wondered. *Might as well an-
nounce that he set off the alarm.*

A few seconds later she had her answer. A uniformed police
officer got out of the cruiser and approached the killer, who removed a duffel bag from his shoulder and handed it to the cop.

The bejeweled breastplate.

The cop was in on the murder.

The cavalry had come to kill her.

"Looks like the op is a go," Edie overheard the cop say as
he took custody of the stolen relic. "We fly to London at nineteen hundred hours."

The killer shook his head. "We've got loose ends dangling.
Someone else was in the museum besides Padgham and the
two guards. The little shit escaped down the fire escape."

A resounding bang ensued as the cop pummeled his fist
against the hood of the police cruiser. "Shit! We're fucked! The
English fag was supposed to have been the only staff person in
the building."

"It gets even worse," the killer said. Reaching into his breast
pocket, he removed the same notepad that Edie had seen earlier. "Padgham e-mailed photos of the breastplate. I notified
the tac team at Rosemont. They're hunting down the person at
the other end of Padgham's e-mail."

Watching the exchange, Edie took slow, deep breaths, willing her cramped legs to stop quivering, her body protesting the
straitjacket confinement.

"This was supposed to have been a simple snatch-and-go,"
the cop muttered.

"And sometimes a mission gets bogged down in the mire. What we need to do is find this fucker—what's his name?—E. Miller and get things tidied up."

Thank you, God. She'd caught a small break. They mistakenly thought she was a man. That's who they would be looking for—a man, not a woman. They also didn't know that Padgham never sent the e-mail. But that wasn't her problem. Her problem was getting free and clear of the alley.

"So far, there's been no calls made to 911."

"When Miller does call, I want to know ASAP."

"Don't worry. I'm on it," the cop said before getting into his police cruiser.

At hearing that, Edie felt the knot in her stomach tighten painfully. If she contacted the police, the killer would know where to find her. And because one of the killer's cohorts—maybe more—wore a police uniform, she'd have no way of distinguishing the good guys from the bad.

More scared than ever, Edie watched as the police cruiser drove away. The exchange ended, the killer walked over to the service entrance of the museum and punched in a code to buzz the locked door open. As if he owned the place, Padgham's killer went inside the museum.

Edie hurriedly backed out of her hidey-hole. Standing upright, she took a big gulp of air. The alley reeked of old urine and rotting garbage, the stench so strong her eyes welled with tears.

Hearing a loud mechanical rattle, she spun on her heel.

Across the alleyway a garage door slowly opened. Meaning she could exit the alley without having to go past the museum.

No sooner did a black BMW emerge from the underground garage than Edie broke into a run. Or at least tried to. Severely hobbled by cramped leg muscles, she awkwardly lurched forward.

The driver turned his head and glanced at her—a wild-haired terrified woman with an ungraceful gait—then just as quickly glanced away.

"Obviously, one of the apathetic multitudes," Edie mumbled under her breath as she dodged into the garage.

Seeing an elevator, she headed toward it. Not until she was safe inside the elevator, the doors closing with a melodic chime, did she permit herself a sigh of relief. Although in actuality it was more like a sag of relief as her body went into an old-lady slump, her legs barely able to support her weight.

A few seconds later, the elevator doors opened onto what looked to be an upscale apartment building lobby. Straight ahead, a pair of plate glass doors beckoned. Overcome with a sudden burst of giddiness, she limped toward those beautiful glass doors with their big beautiful brass handles. Yanking the door on the right side wide open, Edie barely restrained herself from running up and hugging the mailman in the vestibule who was busy inserting mail into rows of identical-looking postal boxes. Instead, she smiled at him. A big, toothy, glad-to-be-alive smile.

Just then, a cab pulled up to the curb in front of the apartment building.

Free at last. Thank God Almighty, she was free at last.

CHAPTER 5

ROSEMONT SECURITY CONSULTANTS
THE WATERGATE COMPLEX

Like a man who'd just been baptized in the cool waters of the Jordan, retired Marine Corps colonel Stanford J. MacFarlane stared at the jewel-encrusted breastplate.

The Stones of Fire.

Arguably one of the most sacred of all biblical relics, third only to the Ark of the Covenant and the Holy Grail.

Mine eyes have seen the glory of the coming of the Lord.

Stan MacFarlane knew from his Bible studies that the twelve inlaid stones had originally been entrusted to Lucifer when he was still God's favorite. After Lucifer's expulsion from heaven, God retrieved the stones and later gave them to Moses, who created the breastplate according to God's specific instruction. Worn only by the Hebrew high priest, the breastplate came to be known as the Stones of Fire. Hidden within the sacred confines of the Jerusalem Temple, the breastplate was plundered by the Babylonians when Nebuchadnezzar's army sacked the holy city in the sixth century B.C. For the next twenty-six centuries, the holy relic had remained hidden in the deserts of Babylon, in what is now modern-day Iraq.

When the U.S. military forces liberated Iraq, Stan had ordered a special-ops team to find the relic. Much to the team's chagrin, someone beat them to the prize. Shortly thereafter, he learned from paid informants that Eliot Hopkins, the director of the Hopkins Museum of Near Eastern Art, had uncovered the Stones of Fire in Iraq. Not about to let the relic elude him a second time, Stan sent his most trusted aide to retrieve the breastplate.

Except his trusted aide had made a very careless mistake.

"'And the serpent cast out of his mouth water as a flood after the woman that he might cause her to be carried away of the flood,'" he hissed to the man who stood at attention in front of him. His temper bridled with a loose slipknot, he stared down the red-faced subordinate. "So tell me, Gunny, how did this Miller woman get away from you? Do you think she hitched a ride on Satan's dinghy?"

The penitent, former gunnery sergeant Boyd Braxton, shook his head. "I told you, sir, I don't know what happened. I didn't even know that she was a woman until I found her purse in the museum."

"The weaker sex, yet still she eluded you." MacFarlane stepped toward the gunnery sergeant, jabbing him in the chest with his finger. "Boy, you're not going soft on me, are you? I hate to think that you've been pussy whipped."

"No, sir. You don't need to worry about that, sir."

"You make certain of it, Gunny. Each and every day, you make certain."

His subordinate properly chastened, Stan MacFarlane stepped back. Such discipline was necessary to keep order in the ranks—a lesson he'd learned during his thirty-one years in the Corps.

A full-bird colonel when he left the service, he'd still be in uniform had his career not been abruptly derailed two years ago by the Pentagon watchdog group Freedom Now! The godless cabal made up of left-wing lawyers and activists had targeted him soon after he'd been promoted to the intelligence office of the Undersecretary of Defense. Hypocrites one and all, they claimed their purpose was to protect religious freedom in the U.S. military. Because of his strict adherence to the word of God, Freedom Now! branded him a religious fanatic bent on converting the whole of the U.S. military to the evangelical faith.

Well, guess what, you godless hippie freaks? It was already happening.

When Freedom Now! caught wind of the weekly prayer meeting he held in the Pentagon's executive dining room, they wasted no time blowing the whistle, somehow getting their lily-white hands on a photo of him standing in a prayer circle with other uniformed officers. The photo made the front page of the *Washington Post*. In the accompanying article, several junior officers claimed that he'd personally harassed them, told them they would eternally burn in hell if they didn't attend the prayer meetings.

The left-wing pundits had had a field day, and the Washington politicos and military-bashers were unwilling to let the story drop. Soon thereafter, he'd been relieved of command.

God, however, worked in mysterious ways.

No sooner did the furor die down than Stan founded Rosemont Security Consultants. In recent years private security firms had become the mercenary might behind the U.S. military; tens of thousands of private fighters had been hired in Iraq alone. With his top-level Pentagon contacts, he was soon making money hand over balled fist. Made up of entirely of former special-ops soldiers, Rosemont numbered twenty thousand strong. As leader of this well-armed flock, Stan had made certain that there wasn't a pluralist or atheist or agnostic among them. Holy warriors, each and every one.

"Sir, what do you want me to do about the woman?"

MacFarlane glanced at his subordinate; the former gunnery sergeant was a member of his handpicked Praetorian Guard. This elite team, which served as his eyes and ears in the nation's capital, was embedded in law enforcement agencies all over the city. Contemplating how best to clean up the mess, he opened the satchel that had been retrieved from the museum and removed a leather wallet. For several seconds he stared at the driver's-license photo of a thirty-seven-year-old curly-haired woman.

"You heard the gunny . . . what shall we do with you, Eloise Darlene Miller?" he contemplatively murmured.

A quick background check uncovered the fact that the Miller woman had been arrested in 1991 for protesting the first Gulf War. In his book, that made her a Chardonnay-sipping left-wing tree hugger. Like the bastards who'd derailed his military career.

Nothing like a "terrible swift sword" to keep an unruly woman in her place.

"Any word on the whereabouts of"—Stan glanced at the name scrawled on a sheet of paper—"Caedmon Aisquith?" A similar background check had turned up a noticeable dearth of information, prompting Stan to order his intelligence team to dig deeper.

"Aisquith managed to slip out of the bookstore undetected. We're keeping a close watch on his hotel, but he's yet to show up," the gunnery sergeant informed him.

"Hmm." Stan MacFarlane contemplatively rolled the silver ring that he wore on his right hand, the intertwined crosses worn smooth over the years. "This man Aisquith is another loose end we can't afford to let dangle."

"I hear ya, Colonel."

"Then hear this." Stanford MacFarlane looked his subordinate straight in the eye so there would be no misunderstanding. "You will search. You will find. And you will destroy."

The order clearly to his liking, the gunnery sergeant smiled. "By day's end, sir."

CHAPTER 6

Feeling like she'd gone fifteen rounds with a heavyweight champ, Edie Miller dragged herself out of the cab. From her skirt pocket she removed a crumpled ten-dollar bill and handed it to the driver. If the dark-skinned man with the turban thought it odd that she'd made him pull into the alley behind her Adams Morgan row house rather than dropping her at the front curb, he gave no indication.

Relieved to be back on familiar terrain, Edie raised a weary hand, letting the cabbie know that no change was necessary. Small recompense for whisking her to safety; the driver of the plum-colored cab had been a godsend. Her Mini Cooper, her purse, and her keys had all been left behind at the museum. But she'd gotten out with her life and the digital camera she'd stuffed in her vest pocket right before Jonathan Padgham had been killed. And that's all that mattered.

What a nightmare, she thought, still in a daze. What a surreal, unbelievable nightmare. The cops were actually in on the murder. Moreover, she had no idea how many people were involved in the gang that had stolen the ancient breastplate. All she knew was that they had no inhibitions about resorting to murder to achieve their objectives. And right now their objective was to "get things tidied up."

Shuddering, she bent down and lifted a long-dead chrysanthemum out of a clay pot. Holding it by the stem, she shook a silver key out of the clump of brown peat moss. With a quick backward glance, she scurried up the patio steps. Unlocking the back door, she stepped inside her kitchen.

Spirulina. Barley grass. Psyllium husks. She took one look at her kitchen countertop and the neatly lined-up containers of vile-tasting health concoctions that were supposed to ensure a long life, and bitterly laughed aloud. Such precautions were a wasted effort if the Grim Reaper, dressed in a gray janitor's uniform, came a-calling.

Although she wanted to stuff her face with Häagen-Dazs ice cream, she couldn't afford the luxury of emotionally collapsing. She had to quickly gather her things and get out. Before they found her. Before they did to her what they'd done to Jonathan Padgham.

Edie snatched a canvas grocery tote from the wooden peg on the back of the kitchen door. Bag in hand, she opened the freezer, removing a box of spinach. Not bothering to open the box, she tossed it into the canvas bag. Having learned at a tender age the importance of keeping a ready cash supply on hand, she always kept three thousand dollars hidden in the freezer.

Money stowed, she grabbed a vintage motorcycle jacket from the next peg. Pulling off her bloodstained khaki fisherman's vest, she stuffed it into the bag. Hurriedly she donned the jacket.

Next she strode down the hall into the small home office she maintained in the front of the house. Yanking open a file cabinet, she thumbed through the dog-eared files until she found the one marked *Personal Documents*. Inside was her passport, her birth certificate, the title to the house, the results of her last Pap smear, and an official copy of her college transcripts. She unceremoniously dumped the contents of the file into the canvas tote bag.

About to head upstairs to gather her toiletries, Edie stopped in midmotion. Peering through the window, she saw a dark blue Crown Victoria pull up to the front of the house. Behind the wheel was the buzz-cut killer. At his side, the dirty cop.

Quickly she ducked away from the window.

They must have found the purse that she'd left in her office cubicle.

Knowing she had only a few seconds to escape through the back door, Edie closed the file cabinet. She then slung the canvas bag over her shoulder and retreated to the kitchen, where she grabbed her BlackBerry out of its charger. She then snatched a set of keys out of the brightly colored ceramic fruit bowl, a souvenir from a fun-filled vacation in Morocco.

Keys in hand, she let herself out the back door, taking a second to lock the deadbolt. She didn't want anyone to know she'd been on the premises. She then tiptoed down the circular staircase that led to the alley below. She paused a moment, listening. She heard Spanish music emanating from the apartment building opposite. But no voices. *So far, so good.*

Not knowing how long her luck would last, Edie sidestepped her neighbor's parked Jeep Wrangler and hurried up the adjoining set of stairs to the same neighbor's house. Garrett was in Chicago on business. He was frequently in Chicago on business. And when he was, she watered his plants and fed his cat. Good friends, they each kept a set of keys to the other's house.

Grateful for the well-oiled lock, she opened the back door and rushed inside, ignoring the huge marmalade cat asleep on the kitchen counter. She then ran down the hall to the living room, taking up a position at the double-hung window that overlooked the street.

Standing in the crease of a full-length velvet drapery, she pulled back the purple fabric a scant half inch, giving herself a sliver of a peephole.

The two men were already out of the Crown Vic, the cop halfway to her front stoop.

Edie held her breath as he banged on the door.

"Open up! D.C. police!"

When he got no response, he banged again.

Then he did exactly what Edie expected him to do—he unlocked her front door using the house keys they'd undoubtedly found at the museum.

Because the two residences shared a common wall, Edie could hear the soft reverberations as the cop charged up her wooden staircase. That was followed of the slamming of several doors. Then he stomped back down the stairs. She wasn't sure, but she thought she heard the back door open. All the while, the killer stood sentry beside the Crown Vic.

A few moments later, the cop emerged from the house, stepping onto the porch.

"She hasn't been here," he announced to his partner, who joined him on the porch. As they stood side by side, Edie could see that the two men were near equal in height, giants the both of them.

"You certain?"

The cop nodded. "Nothing's been touched in the bathroom. I can't imagine a chick hitting the road without her electric razor and makeup bag."

"Fuck! Where the hell is she?"

"Dunno. According to the background search, she has no living relatives and there doesn't appear to be a significant other in the picture."

Edie tightened her hold on the velvet drapery panel, disbelieving what she'd just heard.

They'd done a background check on her. They knew all about her. Her friends. Her family. Or lack thereof. Everything. They held all the cards and she . . . she was about to pee her pants.

Even if she hid out in Garrett's house—and the thought was awfully tempting—she figured that sooner or later they'd come banging on his front door. Not having a key, they'd probably kick it in when no one answered.

"Where the fuck is she?" the killer again snarled.

"Don't worry. We'll find her. Without a wallet, she's not going to get very far."

"Don't be so sure. She got out of the museum, didn't she?"

Smirking, the cop said, "Hey, don't blame me. As I recall, that happened on your watch, not mine."

The killer countered with a glare. Of the two men, he was

definitely the more frightening. "You've got the first watch. I want to know the second the bitch shows up," he growled before stomping down the steps. The cop, relegated to guard duty, stayed behind on the porch.

Moments later, seeing the plume of white smoke emitted from the Crown Vic's tailpipe, Edie let go of the drapery panel.

Time had suddenly become a precious commodity. She rushed into the kitchen, threw open a cabinet door, and grabbed a roasting pan off the shelf. Filling it with dry cat kibble, she placed it on the floor. She then removed a large mixing bowl from the same cabinet, filled it with tap water, and placed it beside the food. She figured it would do until Garrett returned at week's end.

As she locked the back door behind her, she prayed that Garrett had filled the tank in his Jeep before leaving for Chicago. Along with the keys to his house, she had the keys to his wheels. And those wheels were her ticket out of town.

Unlocking the driver's-side door of Garrett's black Jeep Wrangler, she slid behind the steering column. As she did, she slung her canvas tote bag onto the passenger seat. Seeing the big wet spot from the melting box of spinach, she was hit with an onslaught of memories. Of leaving in the middle of the night to escape the landlord. The bill collector. The abusive boyfriend. The junkie in need of a fix. On any given day, those were the bit players in her mother's poorly acted psycho drama.

As if she'd just been dunked in a cold tank of water, the memories crashed in on her. Thirty years had come and gone, and she was still that scared little girl huddled in the backseat of her mother's old Buick Le Sabre.

Her hands violently shaking, Edie stared at the steering wheel. She tried to put the key in the ignition, but couldn't; the metal key repeatedly slid off the steering column. She didn't know how to deal with the fear then. She couldn't deal with it now.

Breathe, Edie, breathe. In and out. Long, slow, deep breaths.

It won't conquer the fear, but it will mask it. Just enough so you can put the key in the ignition switch and start the vehicle.

A lost soul, she obeyed the voice in her head. Breathing deeply, she told herself that she could do this. She could escape the bastards. She'd escaped four different juvenile centers in the span of two years. This was no different.

By the fourth exhalation, she was able to start the Jeep.

She glanced at the fuel gauge.

Thank you, Garrett. I owe you big time.

Driving to the end of the alley, she turned left. Not too fast. Not so slow. She didn't want anyone to later recall having seen a black Jeep Wrangler. As a light snow began to pelt the windshield, she reached over and turned on the wipers, still taking deep measured breaths.

At the corner of Eighteenth and Columbia, she put her foot on the brakes as the light turned red. As though she were an escaped felon, Edie nervously glanced from side to side. On the street corner nearest to the Jeep, a group of Latino men were huddled in front of a check-cashing joint. On the opposite corner, the owner of the quaint Salvadorian café La Flora was busy opening the shades on the plate glass windows that fronted the street. Edie was a frequent patron, having stopped in just that morning for a quick breakfast of frijoles and eggs.

Catching her eye, Eduardo raised his hand in greeting.

Edie reluctantly returned the wave, hoping, *praying*, that if the "police" canvassed the neighborhood, they steered clear of La Flora.

Taking a small measure of comfort in the fact that there wasn't a Crown Vic in sight, she threw the Jeep into first gear and continued down Eighteenth Street. Reaching over, she retrieved her BlackBerry from her tote bag. She needed to contact C. Aisquith; his or her life was in grave danger. She didn't know if he or she was a local. Didn't know anything about him or her. She only knew the mystery person's e-mail address.

God, she hoped C. Aisquith was at a computer. And that said computer was in the near vicinity. Otherwise, what she was about to do would be a colossal waste of time. Something that at the moment she didn't have a particularly big supply of.

Like most city dwellers forced to use their vehicle as an office on wheels, Edie was able to drive, text, and chew gum all at the same time. Her arms draped over the steering wheel, she quickly moved her thumbs over the keypad.

Finished with the e-mail, she pushed the *Send* button.

"He'll think I'm a crazy woman," she muttered, knowing that if the shoe were on the other foot, if she were on the receiving end of that hastily composed message, that's exactly what she would think.

She glanced in the rearview mirror, her line of sight blocked by an orange and white U-Haul van riding her tail.

Startled by a shrill ring tone, she glanced at the BlackBerry in her lap, hesitating, the words *BLOCKED CALL* sending an ominous chill down her spine. Shaking off what she hoped would prove an unfounded fear, she reached for her wireless headset.

"H-hello."

"Ms. Miller, so glad to have reached you," a masculine voice purred in her ear.

Edie didn't recognize the silky-smooth southern accent.

"Who is this?"

"I mean you no harm, Ms. Miller. I'm merely someone who's very interested in your safety and well-being."

Edie yanked the headset away from her ear.

Oh, God.

They'd found her.

CHAPTER 7

Caedmon Aisquith opened the door to the Starbucks and was assailed with the inviting aroma of fresh-ground coffee and cinnamon scones.

The comforts of a civilized life.

Such scents made him forget, at least temporarily, that he inhabited a most uncivilized world. A world where brutal acts of violence took place with chilling regularity.

When it came his turn at the head of the queue, Caedmon ordered a hazelnut coffee, wondering who the devil thought it a clever idea to call the medium serving a *grande*. It always made him think of an insecure bloke discussing the size of his appendage.

Coffee cup in hand, he glanced about the interior, which was jam-packed with small bistro tables, each customer an island unto him- or herself. Spying a favorable-looking islet, he strode in that direction, seating himself next to the window, his own porthole unto the world. This strategic move would enable him to keep an eye on the pedestrian traffic outside the window while monitoring every customer who entered the shop. Although he tried to shake off his earlier unease, he was still troubled by the anonymous phone call that he had received at the bookshop.

Knowing the Irish to be a persistent bunch, he removed his mobile and placed it in clear view on the tabletop. If they made contact again, he would be ready for them.

Christ! To think he was still fighting the old battles after so many years.

Purposefully nonchalant, he dunked his scone into his coffee cup. The rules of polite behavior were not so rigidly

adhered to in the Americas, so he took a bite. Then, acting like
a man totally absorbed with scone and coffee, he surreptitiously glanced out the window. From his vantage point, he had
a view clear across all four lanes of Connecticut Avenue, able
to see the Church of Scientology nestled in the trees beyond.
Idly, he wondered how long Tom Cruise's latest marriage to
Katie—

"Bloody hell," he muttered, catching himself pondering the
inane.

Although pondering the inane was better by far than pondering old memories.

The memory in question had been named Juliana Howe. A
reporter for the BBC, Jules had been a media darling, having
acquired a well-earned reputation for edgy reporting.

As fate would have it, their relationship took seed as a rou-
tine undercover operation. When MI5 caught wind of the fact
that Juliana Howe was in contact with a North African terrorist
cell, they sent him in to assess the situation and track down her
"unnamed" source. Playing the absentminded but sincere
Charing Cross book dealer, Caedmon worked the case for six
months. Like a pastry chef applying layers of icing to a stacked
gâteau, he slowly gained Juliana's confidence over pints at the
Fox and Hound, dinner dates at Le Caprice, and evenings spent
at Covent Garden.

And thus the legend of Peter Willoughby-Jones was born;
Caedmon became the man that an MI5 background check
had indicated would most appeal to the gently bred and well-
educated Juliana Howe.

He also became the intelligence officer who committed the
unpardonable sin of falling in love with his target.

Except the object of his affection knew him as Peter
Willoughby-Jones. Would always know him as Peter Willoughby-
Jones. Because of the nature of her work, the background inves-
tigators at Thames House deemed Juliana Howe a high-level
security risk—meaning he could never reveal to Jules his true
identity.

After the North African cell had been put under lock and

key, Caedmon continued his relationship with Juliana, unable to give her up. He assured his superiors that there was still more intelligence to be gleaned, that being in daily contact with an investigative reporter at the BBC would prove beneficial. When the Real Irish Republican Army detonated a bomb in front of the BBC, his section chief suddenly agreed. But the bloody bastards in RIRA weren't content to stop there. Bent on terrorizing the city of London, they detonated several more bombs that summer.

In the end, their bombs took from him the woman he loved above all others. And because a man who has lost his heart often becomes a heartless bastard, Caedmon took it upon himself to right that horrible wrong.

After he hunted down Timothy O'Halloran, the RIRA leader responsible for the bomb blast, he spent weeks in a pickled state, like an inebriate in a Hogarth engraving. The pain was unbearable. He discovered that killing O'Halloran had not exorcised the demons of that fateful bomb blast; it merely satisfied his need for revenge. But revenge did not bring solace. Nor redemption. It only taught him that he had the capacity to kill.

Not an easy revelation for any man.

When he finally came to his sobered senses, he discovered that MI5 does not burn its own, no matter the transgression. But it does punish them. Demoted to maintaining a safe house in Paris, it was five years before he was discharged from Her Majesty's service. Finally, a free man.

Caedmon glanced at the mobile on the table, recollecting the earlier call.

Maybe he'd been too quick to cut the old ties.

"Rather late, old boy, for such regrets," he muttered, garnering a pointed glance from the horse-faced woman at the next table.

He apologetically smiled. "Don't mind me. I tend to rumble about when lost in thought."

"Glad to hear that I'm not the only one who talks to themself." She met his gaze and held it. An overture.

"Yes, quite." His mobile softly chimed, notifying him of an incoming e-mail. Relieved to have a graceful exit, he picked up the device. "I apologize, but I must attend to business."

"Oh, sure." Blushing all the way to her widow's peak, his neighbor took a sudden interest in adjusting the plastic lid on her coffee cup.

Caedmon accessed his e-mail file. Staring at the log list, he drummed his fingers on the tabletop, having no recollection of giving his email address to anyone named Edie Miller. Although that didn't mean his publicist hadn't given his private e-mail address to someone at a book signing. Assuming that to be the case, he opened the e-mail rather than delete it outright.

His eyes narrowed; the missive was not what he thought it to be.

From: Edie Miller
To: caisquith@lycos.com
Date: 12/01/08 02:16:31 p.m.
Subject: DANGER!!

urgent I meet w u @ NGA cascade café TODAY will wait until closing your life in danger mine 2
ps im not crazy

edie103@earthlink.net

"Indeed," he murmured, reading the postscript.

CHAPTER 8

Edie Miller replaced the wireless headset in her ear.

She wasn't going to run. She wasn't going to hide.

She was going to play dumb.

"My safety and well-being? Um, gee, I have no idea what you're t-talking about. I'm doing just fine." Her voice noticeably warbled; bravado was slow in coming.

"Come now, Ms. Miller. Let's not play games with one another," the caller replied, seeing right through her ploy. "We both know that you were at the Hopkins Museum earlier today."

Her hands began to shake as the Jeep swayed out of its lane.

Surrender, Dorothy. Now. Before the little winged monkeys get to you.

A UPS truck to the left of her laid on the horn, causing Edie to swerve back into the correct lane. Hitting the turn signal, she navigated the Jeep into the inner lane of Dupont Circle.

Back burner. That's where she needed to put the sudden blast of fear.

"Of course I was at the museum," she replied, the best lies being those fashioned from the truth. "I'm at the museum every Monday. It's the only day of the week that I can take photos of the collection. But you already know that." She dramatically sighed, hoping she sounded like a whipped and defeated cog. "Linda in payroll has been threatening for weeks to sic the auditor on me for not clocking out when I leave the museum. I know. I know. Really bad habit. Guess you guys in auditing finally caught up to me, huh?"

"Is it also your habit to exit the museum via the fire escape?"

"Oh, gosh . . . *bus-ted.*" She nervously laughed, the lies fast mounting. "All these smoke-free buildings make it hard for us addicts to get our nicotine fix."

"And what of your purse? You left it on your desk. Is that also another of your bad habits?"

Edie braked to avoid hitting a ridiculously long stretch Hummer limo that hogged two lanes of traffic. "Yeah, well, what can I say? *Absentminded* is my middle name."

"According to your driver's license, your middle name is Darlene. Lovely picture, I might add. But then I've always had a weakness for curly-haired maidens."

Edie racked her brain for a response, fast running out of lies.

Determined not to end up like Jonathan Padgham, she injected a big dose of faked incredulity into her voice. "*You* have my wallet? Thank God. I was wondering who— You will be a dear and return it, won't you? It'd be such a pain to have to cancel all my cards."

"No need to worry . . . I've already taken the liberty of canceling your credit cards. I've also cleaned out your checking and savings accounts. My, my, what a thrifty little miser you are. You've hoarded away nearly thirty thousand dollars."

They'd cleaned out her accounts. How in God's name did they get the security codes to—

The dirty cop. He would have access to God knows what records. Her cell phone number. Her social security number. Every Big Brother computerized database under the sun.

"I'd be happy to give you a reward for returning my purse," she said, scrambling for a foothold, a limb, a scraggly root, *anything* she could hold on to. "I'd also appreciate if you didn't let payroll know that I cut out of my shift a couple of hours early. I had a killer headache and—"

"'Thou shall not lie!'" the caller barked into her ear. A half second later, as though he had just reined in his runaway temper, he calmly said, "Entertaining though they are, I'm beginning to grow weary of your lies, Ms. Miller."

"Lies? What lies?" When that met with silence, she said, "Look, you've got me confused with another woman in the lineup." When the silence lengthened, she said, "That was a joke." *As in, people with something to hide are not capable of cracking a joke.*

"A mailman in the apartment building behind the museum, believing he was performing an act of civil defense, identified you from your D.C. driver's-license photo. You see? We know everything about you, Ms. Miller. We also know that you were at the museum, on the fourth floor, when Dr. Padgham met his unfortunate end."

Unfortunate end? Was he being for real? Jonathan Padgham's brains were blown clear out of his head. Talk about wiping the toilet bowl clean.

"Who are you?"

"Who I am is unimportant." Then the caller's voice dropped a scary octave. "Perhaps at this juncture I should mention that you can run, but you cannot hide."

Edie looked in the rearview mirror.

SUVs. Late-model sedans. Taxis and delivery trucks of every stripe.

But no Crown Vic.

And no D.C. police cruisers.

She decided to call his bluff.

"Word of warning, fella. When you're trying to threaten a woman, overused clichés usually don't inspire a whole lot of fear. As for threats, here's one right back at you . . . call me again and I will not *hesitate* to go to the FBI. Normally, I'd call the cops, but I figure I wouldn't get out of the precinct alive. I can just hear the news broadcast now. 'Edie Miller, the victim of an unfortunate accident, slipped on a recently mopped floor at D.C. police headquarters, cracking her skull.' What do you think? Does that sound about right?"

"I'm certain that the FBI is much too busy tracking jihadist terror cells to take your call, let alone give you the time of day."

"Ah, but like you said, I'm the sole surviving witness to a brutal execution. One that involves a well-organized art ring," she added, laying all her cards on the table. "I think the suits at the FBI will be only too happy to spare me a few minutes of their time."

"How do you know we haven't infiltrated the FBI?"

She didn't. And the cocky bastard knew it.

"What do you want from me?"

"Merely to talk. To clarify the situation so as to alleviate your unwarranted fears. I have very deep pockets, Ms. Miller, and would be only too happy to triple the balance in your two bank accounts."

Yeah, right. Something told her she'd never see a dime of the promised blood money.

Accelerating, she jerked the Jeep over one lane. Then another, exiting the traffic circle at Mass Avenue.

"You want to talk? Fine. Here's the only thing I have to say to you—" Although it was hard, she dragged out the silence for several seconds. Then, her voice at screech level, she screamed, "Go to hell!'"

Pulling the wireless headset out of her ear, she flung it in the direction of the tote bag.

Shaking—not like one leaf, but a whole pile—she kept her eyes glued to the road, the familiar equestrian monuments passing in a blur as she drove around Scott Circle and under Thomas Circle. She then turned right on Eleventh, drove a few blocks and made a left-hand turn onto Pennsylvania. In the distance loomed the U.S. Capitol.

The snow started to fall a bit heavier. Driving on autopilot, she turned up the defrost.

At Fourth Street, she turned right; the East Building of the National Gallery of Art was on her left, the West Building on her right. Not bothering to signal, she made a sharp turn into the circular drive next to the museum, pulling the Jeep into the first available parking spot she could find, right behind a snow-covered Lexus. It was a primo parking spot, mere steps from the museum entrance. It also required an NGA-issued parking decal.

"So sue me," she muttered. It was snowing and she didn't

have time to find a legal parking space; the Mall was crowded despite the foul weather.

Yanking the keys out of the ignition, she tossed them into her tote bag and got out of the Jeep. The National Gallery of Art was the most public place she could think of to hide. One of the largest marble buildings in the world, it exuded a sense of strength and security. Not to mention there were guards every-where. Tons of 'em. As she rushed toward the oversized entry doors of the West Building, she tried not to think of the two dead guards back at the Hopkins.

Opening the glass door, she glanced at her watch. Two-thirty. The museum would be open for another two and a half hours. Enough time to figure out her next move. Hopefully, C. Aisquith had received her e-mail and was on his or her way to the museum.

At the front guard station, Edie opened her tote bag for in-spection; the guard gave the contents only a cursory glance. If he noticed the box of spinach, he gave no indication. Edie slung the tote bag back on her shoulder, unimpressed with the museum's post-9/11 security measures.

Well acquainted with the layout, having spent hours perus-ing the museum's collection since first moving to D.C. nearly twenty years ago, Edie rode the escalator down one flight to the underground concourse that connected the two wings, east to west. Passing the Henry Moore sculpture at the base of the escalator, she headed into the museum gift shop. The muffled echo inside the concourse was nonstop. People chatting. Peo-ple talking on cell phones. People waxing poetic about the beautiful boxed Christmas cards. The commingling of all those voices was a comforting sound, reassuring Edie that she was finally safe.

Reaching the Cascade Café, the museum's version of a food court, she took up a position next to the gushing waterfall that gave the café its name. Enclosed behind a giant screen of glass, pumped water continuously flowed over a wall of cor-rugated granite. One story below ground, the protective glass wall was the only source of natural light in the concourse; Edie could see the wintry gray sky above.

For the next fifteen minutes, she carefully scrutinized every museum patron who entered the concourse. Teens garbed in Gap. Ladies-who-lunch garbed in Gucci. Museum staff garbed in drab gray. Everyone. And then she saw him: a tall redheaded man, fortyish, who had about him a discernible air of self-assurance. From the cut of the clothes—expensive navy wool jacket, cream-colored cable-knit sweater, black leather shoes paired with blue denim jeans—she pegged him for a European.

The redheaded man came to a stop in the middle of the crowded concourse. Turning his head, he glanced at her, held her gaze, then looked away.

Edie stepped away from her post and purposefully strode toward him. Having spent a summer selling timeshares in Florida, she wasn't afraid of approaching strangers.

The redheaded man swerved his gaze back in her direction, a questioning look on his face.

"C Aisquith at lycos dot com?"

He nodded, blue eyes narrowing. "And you must be Edie one-oh-three at earthlink dot com. I would normally say 'Pleased to make your acquaintance,' but given the dire content of your electronic missive, that may be a bit premature." Like Jonathan Padgham, he had a cultured English accent. "I'm curious. How did you recognize me? There must be a hundred people milling about."

"Lucky guess," she replied, shrugging. "That and the fact that you have the same British 'I'm so superior' air about you that Dr. Padgham had."

One side of the man's mouth quirked upward. "Had? I can't imagine old Padge has changed all that much."

Edie swallowed, the moment of truth having arrived much too abruptly.

"I said 'had' for a reason . . . he's dead. Jonathan Padgham was killed a little over an hour ago. And just my luck, I'm the only witness to the murder."

CHAPTER 9

". . . And if they find us, we're both going to wish we'd had the foresight to prepurchase a headstone and burial plot."

For several moments Caedmon Aisquith stared at the paranoid, Pre-Raphaelite beauty standing before him. Like a raving-mad maestro, she used her hands to punctuate the nonsensical words issuing from her chapped, bloodstained lips.

"Why contact me? Why not go to the authorities?" He spoke calmly, not wanting to tip the scales from *raving mad* to *stark-raving mad*.

"Because 'the authorities' were in on the kill, that's why. As in dirty cops and FBI infiltrators. They mistakenly believe that Dr. Padgham sent you an e-mail right before he died," she answered, clearly unable to speak in coherent sentences. "That's why they want to kill you. And trust me, killing you would be child's play for these guys. Like the Grim Reaper pulling the Energizer Bunny right out of the ol' top hat."

"Mmmm." He wondered if she had taken some sort of hallucinatory drug.

"Is that all you have to say?"

"I could say that you have a penchant for mixed metaphor."

"Look, I'm dead serious. Emphasis on the word *dead*, just in case you're too dense to get the message. You still don't believe me? Fine. I've got the proof right here."

"Indeed."

She began to rummage through the tote bag hanging off her leather-clad shoulder. Peering inside, Caedmon caught sight of what looked to be a manila file folder and a box of frozen vegetables.

It was plain as a pikestaff; the woman was absolutely bonkers.

With a determined look on her face, she removed a khaki-colored waistcoat from the tote bag and brandished the garment in front of his face. "I was wearing this when Dr. Padgham was murdered. When I had to crawl over his body"—her chest visibly heaved—"that's his blood smeared on the front of my vest."

"May I?" Caedmon touched the bloodstain, surprised to discover that it was wet.

Were it not for the still-damp bloodstain and the faint smell of vomit, he would have dismissed the woman outright. Instead, he removed his mobile phone from his breast pocket.

"What are you doing?" Edie Miller frantically grabbed him by the arm, preventing him from raising the mobile to his ear. "If you call the police, we're as good as dead."

"If you would be so kind as to unhand me, I'm going to ring Padgham." *And, hopefully, get to the bottom of this lunacy.*

"Be my guest," she muttered, releasing her hellion's grip.

He let the phone ring five times, disconnecting when an automated message began to play.

"It appears that the old boy has turned off his mobile."

"Wrong!" Edie Miller screeched at him, garnering several sideways glances from passersby. "The old boy is lying under his desk in a pool of his own blood."

Worried that she might continue to draw unwanted attention, he motioned to the cluster of nearby tables. "I'm willing to hear you out, provided you keep calm. Understood?"

She nodded, actually managing to look contrite.

"Very well, then. Do be seated while I get us some coffee. Unless, of course, you prefer tea."

"No. Coffee is fine." She glanced at the nearby espresso bar. "A cappuccino would be better."

"Duly noted. I won't be but a moment."

Like an obedient child, she shuffled over to a small bistro table adjacent to the espresso bar. Seating herself in a chair, she removed the tote bag from her shoulder and clutched it to her breast. Though the mass of dark brown corkscrew curls was her crowning glory, it was the deep-set brown eyes that drew and held his attention. Attenuated by straight brows, the combination gave her a somber, almost sad air wholly at odds with her forceful personality. And wholly at odds with her eccentric attire: a black leather motorcycle jacket, clunky black boots, and a long purple and red tartan skirt.

"God help me for coming to the crazed damsel's rescue," he muttered under his breath. Mistakenly thinking her e-mail had something to do with his earlier suspicions regarding an RIRA reprisal, he'd decided at the last to don his armor and go to battle. He couldn't have been more off the mark.

After placing his order for a cappuccino and a hazelnut coffee, he removed several notes from his wallet and handed them to the cashier. Moving away from the queue, he grabbed sugar packets, dairy creamers, plastic stirrers, and paper napkins, stuffing them into his jacket pocket. A few seconds later, a coffee cup clutched in each hand, he made his way to the bistro table.

"Not knowing how you take your coffee, I rather overdid it." He plunked the treasure trove onto the middle of the round table.

His noticeably subdued companion reached for two of the sugar packets. "I always sweeten the deal with a couple of sugars," she remarked, snapping the paper packets to and fro as she spoke. Ripping them open, she poured the contents into her cup. "You know, it's just occurred to me that I don't even know your first name."

"Caedmon," he replied, watching her brow wrinkle when she heard the Old English moniker, the unusual name his father's way of making a man of him, forcing him to face the bully boys at a tender age.

"I thought the English were all tea drinkers."

"Rumor has it I'm something of an iconoclast." Opening a creamer, he poured a dollop into his cup. That done, he began the inquiry. "How is it that you came to witness this *supposed* murder?"

"You're a hard sell, aren't you? Although I suppose if the boot were on the other foot, I would be as well. To answer your question, I'm a freelance photographer at the Hopkins Museum. That's how I came to witness the murder." About to raise the cup to her lips, she suddenly lowered it to the table. "Before I tell you what happened, I need to know in what capacity you knew Dr. Padgham," she abruptly demanded, her lack of subtlety disarming.

"We played cricket together at Oxford. As so often happens with youthful friendships, we eventually lost touch with one another. When Padge learned that I was in Washington on the last leg of a book tour, he rang me up. Suggested we meet for drinks. Talk over old times, that sort of rubbish. Satisfied?" When she nodded, he said, "It's now your turn, Miss Miller."

"A month ago I was hired by Eliot Hopkins to photograph and digitally archive the entire museum collection. I work on Mondays because that's when the museum is closed to the public."

"Enabling you to take your photographs unimpeded," he intuited.

"Exactly. But today was unusual."

"How so?"

"Dr. Padgham was in his office. He's *never* in the office on Mondays."

"Was there anyone else in the museum?"

"Per usual, there were two guards downstairs in the main lobby." She shot him a penetrating glance. "You're following all this, right?"

"Yes, yes," he assured her. "Please continue."

"Sometime around one thirty, Dr. Padgham called and asked if I would come upstairs to the administration offices."

"Why did he do that?"

"He wanted me to take some photographs for him. I got the idea that he was working on some kind of special project. That's why he was in the office on his day off. Obedient minion that I am, I went up to the fourth floor and took the photos." As she spoke, Caedmon detected a note of sarcasm in her voice. "I was about to leave Dr. Padgham's office when a cable came loose on his computer. Dr. Padgham conned me into climbing under the desk to tighten the connection."

Caedmon nodded. "Now *that* sounds like the Padge I know and love."

"You *knew* and *loved*. I told you, he's—"

"I know, he's dearly departed. No need to belabor the point."

"No need to be so crabby," she countered, proving she was no shrinking violet. "Anyway, I was still crouched under the desk when a man walked into Dr. Padgham's office and shot him in the head point-blank." As she spoke, her hands began to tremble. She wrapped both of them around her cup. "He was killed instantly. The killer had no idea that I was under the desk . . . that I witnessed the whole thing."

Caedmon stared at the curly-haired beauty sitting across from him, resisting the urge to pull her to him, to calm the fearful quiver that had traveled from her hands to her entire upper body.

"How did you get away?"

"I climbed down the fire escape. I was hiding in the alley when I saw the killer approach a D.C. cop. And *this* is where the story takes a turn for the worse." She looked him in the eye, her gaze disturbingly direct. "The killer and the cop were in cahoots with one another."

Cahoots?

By that, he assumed the two men were in collusion.

"Did these two men see you hiding in the alley?"

"No. But it didn't much matter because the killer had already accessed the museum security logs. That's how they found out that I was in the building at the time of the murder. That's why they're looking for me."

"Would you be able to identify the assailant?"

"Murderer," she corrected. "And, no, I didn't see his face. He wore a ski mask. By the time he took off the mask, he was too far away to get a good look-see. Although he sported a military-style buzz cut. And he was big. Really, *really* big. Steroid big," she added, using her hands to indicate height and

width. If her measurements were to be believed, the killer had
an improbable shoulder span of some four and a half feet.
"That's all I can remember."

"I see."

"Wait!" she exclaimed, cappuccino spilling over the brim
of her cup as she excitedly jostled the table. "He wore an unusual silver ring on his right hand." Opening her tote bag, she
removed a sheet of paper. "Do you have a pen?"

He wordlessly reached into his breast pocket, obliging her
request. Pen in hand, she drew an intricate pattern. Tilting her
head to one side, she reviewed her handiwork before sliding
the sheet of paper in his direction.

"Sorry, I'm a photographer, not an artist."

Caedmon examined the drawing, instantly recognizing the
pattern.

"How interesting . . . it's a Jerusalem cross. Also known as
the Crusader's cross. The four tau crosses represent the Old
Testament." He pointed to the larger of the crosses. "And the
four Greek crosses the New Testament. You're certain this is
the symbol that was on the, er, killer's ring?"

She nodded. "Is that significant?"

"It was to the medieval knights who conquered the Holy
Land," he informed her, well acquainted with the topic, having
had an interest in the Knights Templar when he was at Oxford.
An obsessive interest, as it turned out, one that ultimately cost
him his academic career. "In the twelfth century, this particular cross served as the coat of arms for the short-lived Kingdom of Jerusalem. Although the European knights—" He
self-consciously cleared his throat. "I apologize. I'm rambling.
Do you recall anything else?"

Edie Miller sucked her lower lip between her teeth, enabling him to see that she had slightly crooked front teeth. And plump beautiful lips.

"No, sorry. But you do believe me, don't you? About Dr. Padgham being murdered?"

He shook his head, uncertain what to make of her fantastical tale. "Why in God's name would this masked man kill Jonathan Padgham? Padge was as harmless as the proverbial fly. Annoying, at times, I admit, but utterly harmless."

She stared at him, long and hard. As though he'd just asked a fool's question.

"He was killed on account of the stolen relic."

"'Stolen relic?' This is the first that you've made mention of a relic."

A confused look crept into her eyes. A second later, shaking her head, she said, "Oh, God, I'm sorry. So much has happened. I'm getting everything mixed up. Like my brain is starting to short-circuit."

Shock. She was beginning to go into shock. Again, he was tempted to pull her into his arms. Although her travails might be imaginary, her fearful panic seemed real enough.

"Drink some more coffee."

She gulped down the last of her cappuccino. Seeing a faint brown smear on her upper lip, he unthinkingly picked up a paper napkin and wiped the smudge clean. Then, guiltily aware of the trespass, he crumbled the napkin into a ball, tossing it onto the table.

"Dr. Padgham was in the process of sending you a digital photo of the relic when he was killed."

"A digital photo? Why would he have done that?"

Opening her tote bag, she removed a camera. "He didn't say. As a back-up, I-I saved the photograph on the camera's internal memory. Here—" She shoved the camera at him. "That's the relic that was stolen."

Holding the camera within a few inches of his face, Caedmon examined the digital photo, as through a glass darkly, disbelieving what he was seeing.

His breath caught in his throat, her outlandish story suddenly making perfect sense.

"Bloody hell . . . I don't believe it. I absolutely don't believe it," he whispered, unable to draw his gaze from the photo.

"I take it from your stupefied expression that the relic is valuable enough to steal."

"Most assuredly."

"And how about killing? Is it valuable enough that someone would kill to obtain it?"

He lowered the camera, keenly aware that Edie Miller was in very grave danger.

"Oh, I think a great many people would kill to obtain the fabled Stones of Fire."

CHAPTER 10

There will be in these last days many deceivers and false prophets and many who will follow them: For many deceivers are entered into the world.

With reverential care, Boyd Braxton closed the gilt-edged book and replaced it in the glove compartment. The Warrior's Bible, leather bound and emblazoned with the Rosemont Security Consultants emblem, had been personally given to him by Colonel Stanford MacFarlane. And though he was in a beaucoup hurry, the colonel always said that it was important to give the Almighty his due.

Reaching under the Bible, he removed an official police permit and placed it on the dash of the Crown Vic. The permit gave him the right to park anywhere in the city. It didn't matter that he wasn't on the Metropolitan Police force. He looked like a cop. And he drove a cop car. No one would think twice.

Parked directly in front of him, covered in a light layer of newly fallen snow, was a black Jeep Wrangler. Just as he figured, no sooner did he leave her pad than the bitch crept out of her hidey-hole.

"Stupid cunt," he muttered, getting out of the Crown Vic. Walking over to the Jeep, he slapped a magnetic tracking device on the metal underbelly. He could now monitor the vehicle's every move on his cell phone, the tracking device programmed with an automatic call-out feature.

"You, bitch, damned near cost me my job," he muttered as he walked toward the museum.

And being Colonel Stan MacFarlane's right-hand man at Rosemont Security Consultants was a job he took real seriously. Just like he'd taken his stint in the Marine Corps real seriously. A former jarhead, he still wore his hair high and tight, having served fifteen years in the Green Machine. Now he served Stan MacFarlane. If it hadn't been for the colonel, he'd be eating institutional slop and lifting weights alongside the brothers in the state penitentiary. No chance of parole.

Juries didn't look kindly upon gunnery sergeants who'd murdered their wife and child.

A lot like that dark day four years ago, he'd fucked up royally today at the Hopkins Museum.

But soon enough, he'd make it right, proving to the colonel that he was still a hard charger. That he was still worthy of his trust. That he was still a holy warrior.

Swinging open the glass door that fronted the Fourth Street Entrance, Boyd entered the National Gallery of Art.

Beautiful. Not a metal detector in sight. The Ka-Bar knife and Mark 23 pistol would pass undetected.

Like he was a cop on official business, he strode over to the guard station. Which was a joke because the guard station didn't amount to much more than a cloth-covered table manned by a pair of rent-a-pogues. Opening the flap of his leather coat, he removed a very official-looking Metropolitan Police badge.

"Is there a problem, Detective Wilson?" the gray-haired guard inquired, straightening his shoulders as he spoke.

"I'm looking for someone. Have you seen this woman?" Boyd held up a photograph of one Eloise Darlene Miller.

The guard reached for the pair of reading glasses hanging from his neck. After several seconds of careful scrutiny, he said, "Yeah, not too long ago, as a matter of fact. If I'm not mistaken, she headed down to the concourse."

Never having been inside the National Gallery of Art, Boyd glanced around the cavernous marble-walled lobby. "Where's the concourse?"

"At the bottom of the escalator," the guard said, pointing to the other side of the hall. "You want me to alert the museum security team?"

"No need. She's not dangerous," he assured the guard. "We just need to ask her a few questions." Returning the photo to his coat pocket, Boyd headed toward the escalator.

At the bottom of the escalator, he took note of the white sculpture, unimpressed.

"If that's art, I'm Pablo Pick-my-ass Picasso," he muttered. The sculpture looked a lot like the molar he'd once knocked out of a drunken swabbie's head. For years he'd kept that tooth as a good-luck charm, a souvenir of his first bar fight of any real note.

Entering a dimly lit gift shop, Boyd saw that the place was overrun with people pushing wheelchairs, people dragging toddlers, and people yakking on cell phones. Everyone he looked, people were mindlessly meandering about, like so many lost sheep. *Perfect.* No one would later be able to recall who did what when; large crowds were the best camouflage a hunter could have.

As he passed a stack of cards with a Nativity scene, he made a mental note that this might be a classy place to do his Christmas shopping. Not that these godless people would even know the meaning of Christmas. Or any other event described in the Bible. Nowadays people put a popular spin on the Word of God, forgetting that biblical text was not subject to New Age feel-good interpretations.

Only a deluded fool would paraphrase the Word of God.

The colonel had taught him that. The colonel had taught

him a lot of things since that day four years ago when he'd ordered him to get down on his knees before the Almighty. Never having prayed before, Boyd had been wary, but once he got over the initial embarrassment, he discovered it was an easy thing to beg God's forgiveness. And just like that, in one life-altering moment, he was forgiven all of his sins, past and present. The bars, the brothels, the brawls, all forgiven. So, too, the murder of wife and child.

Although it was a daily struggle, he tried mightily to be a perfect holy warrior. He didn't drink. Didn't smoke. Kept his body a temple unto the Lord. He wished that he didn't cuss, but as he'd entered the Corps at age seventeen, that was proving a hard habit to break.

Always room for improvement, he thought as he left the gift shop and entered the food court.

Coming to a standstill, he scanned the chow hall.

She was here, somewhere in the crowd; fear made a person stand out, having an energy all its own. Its own stink, as it were. Like a bull's-eye, her fear would lead him right to her.

But first he had to cover his ass.

Catching sight of a tall, big-gutted custodial worker lackadaisically pushing a yellow bucket on wheels, Boyd knew he'd found his man. For ten years, his father had pushed a similar bucket. Which was why Boyd knew that custodial workers of every stripe were invisible to the rest of the world. Most people didn't favor them with a polite hello, let alone a sideways glance. Pleased that the op was going so smoothly, he followed the janitor through a door marked *Custodial Staff.*

In fact, he was thinking about his daddy—a mean, drunken bastard till the day he died—when he cold-cocked the unsuspecting janitor, knocking him to the floor with one well-aimed punch.

Not believing in chance occurrences, Boyd recognized the fortuitous appearance of the janitor for what it was—a gift from God.

CHAPTER 11

"Since its creation some thirty-five hundred years ago, the Stones of Fire have cost the lives of countless individuals."

"Including Jonathan Padgham," Edie pointedly remarked, not in the mood for any more of Caedmon Aisquith's sidestepping.

"Sadly, I am inclined to agree with you."

"Well, it's about time. Most people, if you tell them that their life is in danger, are willing to give you the benefit of the doubt."

His red brows drew together. "And why is *my* life in danger? I understand why this masked killer would be searching for *you*, since you did, after all, witness Padge's murder. But I have no involvement whatsoever in this nefarious plot."

"Think again, C Aisquith at lycos dot com. The killer mistakenly believes that Dr. Padgham e-mailed you photos of the relic." Edie jutted her chin at the camera still clutched in his hand.

Caedmon studied the camera for several seconds, a thoughtful look on his face. "That can only mean one thing . . . the thieves don't want anyone to know of the relic's existence. Since the discovery of the Stones of Fire would have made international headlines and set biblical scholars a-twitter, we must assume that the relic came to be at the Hopkins Museum via the back door." Wearing a pensive expression, he slowly shook his head. "'The perfect treasure of his eyesight lost.'"

"Are you saying what I think you're saying, that the relic was smuggled out of its country of origin and sold on the black market?" When he nodded, Edie said, "Well, that would explain why the breastplate isn't listed in the museum's permanent collection. Since I'm archiving the collection, I have the master list of every ancient whatnot owned by the Hopkins. The breastplate was most definitely *not* on the list. Why did you call it 'the Stones of Fire'?" she abruptly asked, beginning to suspect that he knew more than he'd so far let on.

Caedmon Aisquith removed his gaze from the digital photo. "The name was first coined by the Old Testament prophet Ezra. Actually, the relic has been known by quite a few names. The ancient Hebrews called it the Urim and Thummim. There are also several biblical references to the Breastplate of Judgment or the Jewels of Gold."

"The Stones of Fire. The Urim and Thummim. These names tell me nothing. I feel like the elevator doors just opened on the ground floor of the Tower of Babel."

"Perhaps I should retrace my steps." Caedmon pushed his empty coffee cup to the side and positioned the camera in the middle of the table, enabling her to clearly see the photo of the jewel-studded gold breastplate. "Bearing in mind that everything I am about to say is mere speculation, I believe that this relic"—he pointed to the image on the digital camera—"or *askema*, as it is known in Hebrew, may have been the actual breastplate worn by the Levite high priest when he performed the sacred temple rituals. What makes the breastplate utterly priceless is the fact that it was created by Moses himself as directed by God. So although it's not his actual handiwork, the breastplate is the actual design of God."

Edie, who had been silent up until this point, stubbornly shook her head. "But I saw it with my own eyes. It was just . . . just an old breastplate. You don't really believe that *that* was designed by God?" She tapped the camera display for added emphasis.

"Who am I to dispute the Old Testament prophets? The Bible is inundated with naysayers struck down by the wrath of God." The droll remark left Edie in some doubt as to whether Caedmon Aisquith actually believed what he'd just said.

"Since all that remains of the original breastplate are twelve stones and a few bits and pieces of gold, how can you be so sure it's is the real deal?"

"The relic would be easy enough to authenticate, given the detailed description in the book of Exodus. Conceived as a square design, it was originally composed of laced pieces of gold linen, inlaid with twelve stones set in four rows of three." Grabbing the same sheet of paper she'd earlier used to draw the Jerusalem cross, Caedmon sketched out a design. "Based on the account in Exodus, I believe the breastplate would have looked something like this." He turned the sketch in her direction.

"As you can see, my artistic talent is rudimentary at best. Be that as it may, each of the twelve gemstones possessed a divine power. In the first row there was a sardius, a topaz, and a carbuncle . . ." As he spoke, Caedmon carefully wrote the name of each gemstone. "In the second row, an emerald, sapphire, and diamond . . . in the third row a ligure, an agate, and an amethyst . . . and finally, in the fourth row, beryl, onyx, and jasper. Rather gemmy, don't you think?" He smiled slightly, making Edie realize that he was a handsome man. She didn't usually go for redheads, but there was something uniquely appealing about the man sitting across from her. And, of course, the accent didn't hurt.

She glanced back and forth between the digital photo and penned sketch, suddenly able to see how beautiful the relic must have been eons ago. "Is there any significance to the fact that there are twelve stones?"

"It's highly significant," Caedmon replied. "The number twelve symbolizes the completion of the sacred cycle. In the Torah, or the first five books of the Old Testament, it's written that the twelve stones represented the twelve tribes of Israel. Just as each tribe had a unique function, the Levites being of the priestly caste, for instance, so, too, each of the twelve stones symbolized a hidden truth or virtue."

"Since emeralds are my birthstone, I know that they symbolize immortality."

"Rather ironic, what with the relic mysteriously appearing after so many centuries of being hidden away, supposedly lost forever." The awestruck expression that Edie had seen when Caedmon first looked at the photo returned. "If the relic can be authenticated, it would be a truly astounding discovery, the Stones of Fire having disappeared from the pages of the Bible several thousand years ago."

She sat silent. Somewhere in the museum café Chinese food was being served; Edie could smell stir-fried vegetables and soy sauce. She swallowed back a queasy knot.

"According to biblical scholars, the breastplate disappeared during the Babylonian— Are you all right?"

"No, I feel—" About to tell a lie, she instead said, "I'm scared, hungry, and exhausted. Take your pick."

"Would you like something to eat?" He gestured to the pastries and desserts on the espresso bar.

"I'll pass on the dessert. But if you wouldn't mind getting me another cappuccino . . . ?"

"I'd be only too happy."

Excusing himself, Caedmon got up from the table; Edie followed him with her gaze. Although he spoke with a proper English accent and possessed a proper English name, albeit an antiquated one, Caedmon Aisquith's red hair, blue eyes, and tall height fairly screamed of a Scot in the woodpile. A really smart Scot, Caedmon Aisquith was a one-man brain trust. That intelligence was admittedly a turn-on, the mind being the sexiest organ a man could possess. Had she and the strangely named Brit met under different circumstances, she could easily envision herself asking him out on a dinner date.

When Caedmon returned, setting a steaming cup of cappuccino in front of her, Edie smiled her thanks.

"Tell me, when you gazed upon the Stones of Fire, did you notice anything extraordinary, or strange, or even mystical?"

She gave the question a moment's consideration. "No. Should I have noticed something out of the ordinary?"

"Difficult to say. Biblical scholars believe that once garbed with the breastplate, the high priest could foresee the future, as though the hand of God had momentarily pulled back the curtain of time."

"So then the breastplate was used as some sort of divination tool?"

"Only secondarily. The primary function was that of a conduit between the high priest and God." Caedmon paused a moment, letting the factoid sink in. Or maybe he was considering how much he should divulge. Decision evidently reached, he continued. "Specifically, the high priest used the breastplate to control and harness the divine fire contained within the Ark."

About to take a sip of her cappuccino, Edie lowered her cup to the table.

"The Ark? As in the Ark of the Covenant?"

"None other."

CHAPTER 12

. . . blessed be God Most High, who has delivered your enemies into your hand!

"Praise be, praise be," Boyd Braxton whispered as he recited his favorite Bible passage. Finished buttoning the dark blue janitor's shirt, he unzipped the pair of cheap polyester pants and tucked in the shirttails. Then, not willing to mess with his juju, he cupped his balls. "You're the man, B.B. You are the man."

He'd been out of boot camp only a few weeks when his

mess buddies had taken to calling him "B.B." As in *Big Bang*. As in the fact that he could outdrink, outfight, outfuck any man in the unit. The fighting part landed him in the brig more times than he could recall, Boyd damned with his father's murderous temper. The colonel said his temper was a cross he had to bear. Like Jesus lugging a hundred and ten pounds of lumber all the way to Calvary. It was a daily struggle. Sometimes he took the day. Sometimes the day took him.

A quick glance at the name badge sewn on the front of the matching blue jacket indicated that the black man sprawled at his feet was named Walter Jefferson. Blood seeped from his head and dribbled from his snot box; the janitor had broken his nose when he hit the deck.

"Sorry 'bout that." Boyd snickered, figuring it'd be a couple of hours before the man came to. Since the colonel had been adamant that everything be by the numbers—i.e., no more screwups—he'd taken the extra precaution of stuffing a dirty rag into the janitor's mouth. Then, trussing him up like a big Butterball turkey, he'd secured his hands and feet with a belt. He'd fucked up at the Hopkins Museum, but this time there would be no more dumb-ass boot mistakes.

Removing his pistol, Boyd popped the mag. Fifteen rounds. He only needed one to kill the Miller broad, but it was always a good idea to have extra ammo. Just in case.

His movements quick and steady, he screwed a silencer onto the end of the barrel.

Locked and loaded, he shoved the Mark 23 into the small of his back, the janitor's jacket hiding the telltale bulge. He jammed a leather scabbard next to the pistol; the Ka-Bar knife was his backup weapon of choice. Silent but deadly, a Ka-Bar could slice and dice a man in less time that it took to say howdy-do. Or a woman—Boyd having killed more than one bitch in his time.

Suited up, he grabbed the mop handle and steered the yellow bucket toward the closed door of the janitor's supply closet. Gray water sloshed up the sides, forcing Boyd to slow his stride. Opening the door, he rolled the mop and bucket across the threshold. Then, covering his tracks, he reached for the keys dangling from his belt. It took a few tries, but he found the right one, locking Walter Jefferson safely inside. That done, he hid his rolled ball of clothes, including his leather jacket, under a nearby bench.

Approaching the crowded concourse, he surveyed the jabbering horde of touristos. Again, he thought that they'd make good cover; his plan was to kill the Miller bitch, chuck the untraceable gun into the bucket of water, and get his hairy ass out of the building before anyone realized what had happened.

Pushing the yellow bucket, Boyd could see that no one paid him any mind. Like he'd figured, he was just a big blue custodial ghost.

Perfect. He loved when everything came together.

'Cause God help him, he knew what it was like when the fucking floor gave way. When you were sinking in quick shit without a buoy in sight.

That's how it was back in '04 when he'd returned from his first deployment in Iraq.

Fallujah.

What a fucking shithole.

Every night he woke up in a cold sweat. One night he actually pissed the bed. If his wife, Tammy, so much as brushed her bare leg against his, he'd bolt upright out of the bed, reaching for his M16. Except he didn't have his combat rifle at the ready. Didn't even have a damned sidearm; Tammy refused to let him bring a loaded anything into the house on account of Baby Ashley. Six months old, Baby Ashley cried all night long. Just like those fucking raghead babies in Fallujah. One night he couldn't take it any longer: Ashley bawling for a milk titty. *Couldn't the brat just shut the fuck up?!* With each ear-piercing scream, the pounding inside his skull got louder. And louder still.

And then everything went eerily quiet, Ashley's screams muffled with a pillow.

Just like that baby in Fallujah.

That's about the time his wife ran into the room, jumped on his back, and actually sank her teeth into the side of his neck, the bitch going for his jugular. He'd had no choice but to fling the rabid cunt off his back. She hit her head on a nearby rocking chair; the blow pretty much killed her on the spot. Not knowing what to do, he'd telephoned Colonel MacFarlane. Like he was his own flesh and blood, the colonel took care of everything, giving him an airtight alibi, making it look like a robbery gone bad. The local police bought the story. Even the dickheads at the *Daily News* bought it; the local paper speculated that it was one of a series of local robberies committed by strung-out junkies looking to make some quick cash. *Unfortunate Tragedy Befalls War Hero.*

The colonel said the same thing. Except he went one step further. He said God understood what it was like to be a warrior, to come home from a hard-fought battle only to have to fend off the devil.

Colonel Stan MacFarlane was a great and good man, and Boyd owed him. Big-time. Not just for saving his ass, but for showing him the Way. For leading him into God's fold. And when the little dick bastards at the Pentagon drummed that great and good man out of the Corps, Boyd went with him.

Pushing the yellow bucket, Boyd scanned the crowd, his nose twitching at the faint smell of stir-fried chink food.

The Miller bitch was here. Somewhere in the jostling crowd.

Soon enough he'd find her. And when he did, it'd be like shooting ragheads in a rain barrel.

CHAPTER 13

". . . The story of the Ark of the Covenant is an operatic drama played out on the stage of the biblical Holy Land," Caedmon continued in answer to Edie Miller's question.

"'Operatic'? Don't you think you're laying it on a bit thick?" his companion sardonically remarked.

"Not in the least. As you undoubtedly know, the Ark of the Covenant, or *aron habrit* in Hebrew, was an ornate chest that was roughly four feet long, two and a half feet wide, and two and half feet high"—as he spoke, Caedmon spanned his hands first in one direction, then the other, approximating the proportions in midair—"inlaid with hammered gold. But what you may not know is that the Ark of the Covenant was constructed *exactly* like an Egyptian bark."

"Like the gold boxes that I saw last year at the King Tut exhibit, right?"

"Right down to the gold rim on the lid and the winged figures which adorned the top cover. Furthermore, the Egyptian bark and the Ark of the Covenant both had the same purpose: to contain their respective deities."

Her brow furrowed. "But I thought the Ark of the Covenant was a container for the Ten Commandments. What are you saying, that the Ark of the Covenant was some kind of magical God-in-the-box, like in that movie *Raiders of the Lost Ark*?"

Caedmon chuckled, amused by the question. "Just as the sacred Egyptian bark contained the might and majesty of Aten, so, too, the Ark of the Covenant contained the power and glory of Yahweh. And once contained, the only means by which to control all that cosmic power was for the high priest to shield himself with the Stones of Fire."

Raising her steaming cup to her lips, Edie took several moments to digest what he'd just said. As she did, Caedmon surveyed the throng of museum patrons. Nothing appeared out of the ordinary; his eyes took passing note of a man pushing a wheelchair-bound octogenarian, a custodian pushing a yellow bucket, and a harried mother pushing a covered pram. Briefly he noticed two youths, one fuchsia-haired, the other a tiger-stripe, locked in a passionate embrace in front of the massive glass wall that fronted a cascading waterfall.

"Okay, we know what happened to the breastplate; it was confiscated by Nebuchadnezzar, hidden in Babylon, and recently rediscovered and smuggled out of Iraq," Edie said, drawing his attention back to the table. "But what happened to the Ark of the Covenant?"

Ah, a woman after his own heart, the topic long a favorite of his.

"At some point after the construction of Solomon's famous temple, the Ark of the Covenant disappeared from the pages of the Bible. Whether it was captured, destroyed, or hidden, its current whereabouts are unknown."

She folded her arms across her chest. "Yeah, well, I seem to recall you saying the same thing about the Stones of Fire, but the breastplate managed to mysteriously turn up. And because of it, you and I are now in serious danger."

Out of the corner of his eye, Caedmon noticed that the custodian pushing the yellow bucket had suddenly broken ranks and was headed in their direction.

Odd that the man was wearing military-style combat boots.

Even more odd that the man was built like a Bristol rugger bugger.

He was big. Really, really big. Steroid big.

Recalling Edie's earlier description of Padgham's killer, Caedmon felt a prickly sensation on the back of his neck.

"I am beginning to concur with your assessment," he murmured, his eyes still trained on the custodial giant, watching as the man removed his right hand from the mop handle and reached behind his back.

In that instant, Caedmon saw the flash of a silver ring.
In the next instant, he caught the dark flash of—
He squinted, bringing the object into focus.
Bloody hell! The man had a gun!

CHAPTER 14

There being no time to think, Caedmon shoved the bistro table aside and hurled himself at Edie Miller, flinging both of them to the floor in one strong-armed motion.

The bullet struck the upturned table and ricocheted off the stone top. With his female companion in tow, he scooted behind a nearby column. The second bullet went *ping!* as it struck a metal planter less than a meter from their huddled position.

A woman in the crowd frantically screamed.

A man gruffly shouted, "He's got a gun!"

Yet another man yelled, "It's a fucking terrorist!"

Several other people joined the chorus, a cacophony of fear.

Not waiting for the third bullet, Caedmon went on the offensive. Stretching his right arm, he placed his hand on the back of a wheeled busboy's cart parked to the side of the column. With a mighty heave, he propelled the cart forward. Dirty plates, stacked in a plastic tub on top of the cart, crashed to the floor. A smashing diversion.

Catching sight of the motion, the gunman spun on his heel, reflexively firing a third round. The bullet hit the sheet of clear glass that contained the cascading water fountain; the safety glass shattered on contact. Almost immediately, water gushed into the concourse.

Chaos quickly ensued, people running pell-mell in every direction.

Armor-piercing bullets, Caedmon thought, horrified. The man was using bloody armor-piercing bullets.

Edie, flattened beneath the weight of his body, shrieked in his ear. Raising his head, Caedmon scanned the panic-stricken crowd, searching for the armed behemoth.

The gunman was nowhere in sight. All that remained was the yellow bucket, a wooden mop handle protruding from its murky depths. He'd fled the scene. Or he'd moved to a different firing position. Either way, they had but mere seconds to escape the concourse.

He pushed himself to his knees, yanking Edie off the floor as he did so.

"What's happening?" she asked in a strangled voice.

"Padgham's murderer has just paid his respects."

"Oh, God! We're not going to get out of here alive!"

Suddenly concerned that he might soon have a hysterical woman on his hands, Caedmon roughly grabbed her by the shoulders. "We *will* escape. But only if you remain calm and do *exactly* as I say. Understood?" When he received no answer, he shook her. Hard. "Understood?"

She nodded. Satisfied with the mute reply—her input unnecessary and unwanted—he surveyed the damage. The frenzied swarm, some running, many crouched on the concourse floor, had become a shouting, screaming mass of collective hysteria. A Bosch painting come to life.

Caedmon directed his gaze first one way, then the other, determining how best to navigate through the melee. To the right was a tunnel-like hallway. To the left was the adjacent gift shop. With its dimmed recessed lighting and numerous display counters, the gift shop offered the best cover. Grabbing Edie by the hand, he ran in that direction.

"Where are we going?" she demanded, huffing as she kept pace with him.

He sidestepped around a museum employee who was actually attempting to direct the frenzied horde, much like a traffic cop directing motorists after a crash-up.

"We're going as far from the madding crowd as possible," he informed her, having to shout to be heard over the din. Spying a black trench coat hanging from a countertop, the owner having abandoned it in the rush to escape, he grabbed it as they ran past. He then dodged behind an oversized column. Out of sight, he came to a halt.

"Quickly! Put this on!" Unceremoniously, he shoved the coat at his companion's chest.

"Why would I want to—"

"Your outfit is preposterous. As such, it makes an easily discernible target."

Removing her tote bag from her shoulder, somehow managing to have kept the bag on her person during the rumpus, Edie shoved her arms into the trench coat. "With your red hair, you kind of stick out yourself."

"Point taken." As he spoke, Caedmon plucked a knit cap from a bespectacled Asian teenager who ran past, too terrified to do anything other than keep on running. Having lived through several RIRA terrorist attacks on London, Caedmon knew that chaos had a way of making even the most truculent uncharacteristically pliant. He shoved the green cap with the gold-lettered emblem that read *PATRIOTS* onto his head. Cap donned, he reached over and yanked the two sides of the much-too-big trench coat across Edie's waist, hurriedly cinching the belt around her.

Camouflaged, he led them through the gift store in a zigzag pattern, the most difficult for the human eye to follow. Hand in hand they darted from sales counter to column to yet another sales counter.

A few seconds later they emerged into a well-lit antechamber that housed a Henry Moore sculpture. Quickly, Caedmon assessed their three choices: escalator, lift, or staircase.

Always execute the least likely maneuver, that being the only way to escape a determined enemy.

A lesson well learned at the hands of his MI5 masters. Caedmon grabbed Edie by the shoulder, spinning her toward the stairs.

"But it's quicker to take the escalator."

"Quicker, perhaps, but far more dangerous."

Side by side, they ascended the steps, the staircase deserted, unlike the crowded escalator on the opposite side of the antechamber, people packed onto it like frantic sheep being led to slaughter.

At the top of the stairs, they found themselves in a large vestibule where two matched bronze pumas stood sentry. On the far side of the vestibule the lift opened and a half dozen owl-faced patrons hurriedly spilled out. A few feet away, he sighted the public facilities marked with their respective male and female symbols. Just beyond the pumas was the Fourth Street lobby; the area was a veritable mob scene, with frantic museum goers running to and fro and harried guards attempting to corral them through the exit door.

Like doomed fish in a glass bowl.

Easy pickings for a hungry cat.

Having evaluated the situation, Caedmon grabbed Edie by the hand and dragged her toward the WC. Shoving his shoulder against the swinging door, he pulled his companion into the ladies' loo.

"What are you doing?" she screeched, the shrill sound echoing off the stark white tiles.

"Saving your life, I daresay."

"But you're a man! You're not allowed in here!"

Ignoring her, he scanned the facilities.

Six stalls. Five sinks. No occupants.

He pushed open one of the middle stall doors.

"Did you hear me, Caedmon? I said that you're not allowed—"

"Do calm down, will you?" He shoved her inside the stall, following on her coattails. "And while you're at it, lower your voice. Getting into a dither will only make things worse than they already are."

An adamant look on her face, she continued to protest the trespass. "But this is the ladies' room."

"Precisely why I chose it over the little boys' loo. Mind you, it's only a guess, but I seriously doubt our testosterone-driven assailant will think to look for us in here; the word

Ladies will act as a natural deterrent. For the moment, at least, we're safe."

"Not to mention cramped like peas in a porcelain pod," she muttered, awkwardly twisting her upper body as she straddled the toilet; the stall was barely wide enough to accommodate one person, let alone two.

After locking the stall door, Caedmon removed a visitors' guide from his coat pocket, having picked up the map when he first arrived at the museum.

"Now what?"

"Now, we figure out how best to outwit our nemesis." Unfolding the map, he held it in front of his chest. Edie, forced to stand on tiptoe, peered over his shoulder. "According to the map, there are five possible exits from the museum."

"The nearest exit is no more than fifty feet away. That being the one we just passed." Reaching over his shoulder, she jabbed her index finger at the nearby exit. "Right there. The Fourth Street exit. My Jeep is parked outside the door. We can be out of here in seconds. As in 'Gentlemen, start your engines.'"

Caedmon negated her suggestion with a brusque shake of the head. "I have reason to suspect you were followed to the museum. Which means the Fourth Street exit will undoubtedly be manned by either the gunman or an accomplice. Our point of egress should be the most distant exit from our current position."

She grabbed him by the upper arm, awkwardly turning him toward her. "Are you crazy? You're talking about the Seventh Street exit!" she hissed in a highly agitated whisper. "That's all the way on the other side of the National Gallery of Art. It's three city blocks from where we're at right now. If you think that's a good plan, you're totally insane!"

"Ah, I see my reputation precedes me."

His mind made up, he refolded the map and replaced it in his breast pocket. Not bothering to ask permission, he searched the pockets of Edie's pilfered trench coat. Discovering a black canvas rain bonnet, he handed it to her.

"Here, put this on."

"Unh-uh." She shook her head, brown curls buoyantly

bouncing about her shoulders. "You might not care if you get a case of head lice, but I—"

"Don the cap," he ordered, thinking her adamancy yet again misplaced. "Head lice can be cured with a bit of medicated shampoo. Resurrection is trickier to manage. As I speak, the gunman is searching the museum for two targets: a redheaded bugger and a curly-haired maiden. Trust me. We have danger in spades."

"Not to mention hearts, clubs, and diamonds," she muttered, stuffing her curls into the canvas bonnet.

"Much better," he said, nodding his approval. "Come. We've tarried long enough." He unlocked the stall and swung it open.

Edie stared at him, refusing to budge, her obstinacy now replaced with a look of fearful dread.

"Do you think we've got a chance of getting out of here alive?" she whispered.

Rather than make an empty promise he might not be able to keep, he said, "We shall find out soon enough."

CHAPTER 15

A fiddle fuck.

That's what he had on his hands, a goddamned fiddle fuck.

Uncertain how things turned so bad so quickly, Boyd Braxton shoved his arms into his black turtleneck sweater. The unconscious Walter Jefferson was still sprawled on the floor of the janitor's closet. Having retrieved his bundle of clothing from where he'd earlier stowed it, he'd returned to the closet, needing to reconnoiter. In a big-ass hurry, he yanked his black pants over the top of the blue pair he already wore. He didn't give a rat's ass how he looked. He just needed to *not* look like a janitor. Too many people had seen a janitor firing into the crowd. No way in hell would he be able to get out of the museum decked out like some numbnuts custodial worker.

He shoved the Ka-Bar and the Mark 23 into his waistband. Next he checked his cell, the phone programmed with a preset number to immediately warn him if the tracking device was activated.

He heaved a sigh of relief; the Jeep was still parked out front.

The bitch was in the museum. He could make this right. Wherever the bitch went, he would follow.

Yanking open the door of the janitor's closet, he stepped across the threshold; the museum concourse was directly across from his present position.

Quickly he scanned the area. *Blown-out glass. A couple of overturned tables. Some broken plates.* The concourse was all assholes and elbows as people frantically sloshed across the wet floor, water having gushed from the fountain when the plate glass shattered. A sobbing woman in a tight-fitting suit, hobbled by a pair of stiletto heels, limped past. Boyd nearly gagged in her wake; the broad was doused in more perfume than a Bangkok whore.

Through the hole in the glass, he heard the blare of at least a half dozen police sirens. Any second, the place would be swarming with cops.

No sense looking for the Miller bitch; he already knew she'd fled the concourse, having earlier caught sight of her and that redheaded bastard heading toward the gift shop.

Just who the fuck was he, anyway?

Obviously, the guy was a player. He had to be. Nobody had reflexes *that* quick unless he'd been trained. Maybe the redheaded bastard worked for a law enforcement agency. Whoever he worked for, it meant trouble.

Boyd strode over to where the Miller woman had been sitting and snatched a sheet of paper off the floor.

"Shit!"

On the sheet of paper were two hand-drawn sketches: one a drawing of the relic he'd earlier stolen from the Hopkins, the

other the Jerusalem cross that he and every other man at Rosemont Security Consultants wore on his right ring finger.

As he continued to stare at the piece of paper, he caught
sight of a Muslim couple; the wife wore a hijab and was hurriedly pushing a baby stroller as the kid bawled its head off.
The couple stopped a few feet away from where he stood. The
woman peered into the stroller, the kid bawling even louder.

*The bawling baby in the back room was gonna give away
their position. There was a sniper in the building across the
street and dozens of raghead fuckers prowling the streets of
Fallujah in Toyota pickups, RPG launchers at the ready. If the
brat didn't stop bawling, he and his men were gonna end up
hanging from a streetlight with no head and no balls. Burnt
toast.*

*Boyd strode into the back bedroom. "Hey, Fatima, shut the
fucking brat the hell up!" he hissed.*

*Wrapped in a big black chador, she stared at him. Like he
was a freakin' Martian or something.*

*Well, fuck that shit! He was sick and tired of getting his ass
shot at for these ungrateful, godless people.*

*Lunging forward, he slashed the black-swathed woman's
throat. Then he grabbed a pillow off the bed and shoved it over
the bawling brat's face.*

The piece of paper in Boyd's hand began to shake as his
head suddenly exploded in a corona of pain.

Babies crying. Women crying. Everybody and their fucking
Uncle Tom crying. Christ, you'd think he'd killed somebody.
Like this was a goddamned war zone or something. *This* was
nothing. A minor public disturbance. A custodial worker gone
postal. Except this time around, nobody got killed.

And that was the problem. Somebody was supposed to
have ended up dead.

Kill 'em. Kill 'em all. God will know his own. Isn't that what
the colonel always said?

Still staring at the Muslim couple and their screaming baby,
Boyd reached behind his back, his hand curling around the gun
grip. Slowly he slid the Mark 23 from his waistband. *Papa,
Mama, and Baby Bear.* One, two, three.

No sooner did he pull the gun free than his cell phone vibrated against his breastbone.

Boyd shoved his piece back into his waistband. Turning his back on the Muslim couple and their screaming brat, he reached for his cell. The digital display read *RSC*. Rosemont Security Consultants.

"Fuck."

It was the colonel calling for a status report.

Feeling like Joe Shit the Ragman, he depressed the *Answer* button. Since the colonel hated what he referred to as *circumlocution*—what Boyd and everybody else with a twelfth-grade education called *beating around the bush*—he didn't bother with the pleasantries. Instead, he simply said, "We've got a problem, sir. The target escaped, the place has turned into a three-ring circus, and the cops have just arrived."

The statrep met with a moment's silence; Boyd braced himself for a world-class ass chewing.

"Is the Miller woman still on the premises?" the colonel asked, his calm tone of voice taking Boyd by surprise. Usually this kind of fuckup would meet with a wrath second only to that of God Almighty.

"I believe so, sir. Her Jeep is still parked out front. I found a sheet of paper with two drawings: one of the relic, the other a Jerusalem cross. And one other thing, sir"—he hesitated, knowing the colonel would break his balls but good—"she's hooked up with somebody. A tall guy with red hair. I'm not altogether certain, but he may be a player. What do you want me to do, sir?"

Another silence ensued. In the background, Boyd heard the muffled strains of several voices, the colonel having put him on the speakerphone. Then he heard what sounded like a file folder being opened.

"Gunnery Sergeant?"

"Yes, sir."

"Stand by for further instruction."

CHAPTER 16

Colonel Stanford MacFarlane took a moment to review the dossier just handed to him. Turning his back on his chief of staff, he discreetly removed his reading glasses from his breast pocket. He despised weakness of any sort, particularly in himself. Though he was physically fit, there were days when he felt each and every one of his fifty-three years.

Adjusting the reading glasses on his nose, he glanced at the file. With his contacts inside the intelligence office of the Undersecretary of Defense, he'd managed to finagle a full dossier on one Caedmon St. John Aisquith.

He examined the photo attached to the upper right-hand corner with a paperclip. *Red hair. Blue eyes. Fair complexion.* He next glanced at the physical particulars. *6'3½". 190 lbs.* It stood to reason that Aisquith was the tall guy with red hair seen with the Miller woman at the National Gallery of Art.

Next, he skimmed the personal background material. *DOB 2/2/67. Eton. Queen's College, Oxford. Master's Degree in Medieval History. Recruited MI5—1995. Formal resignation— 2006.*

MacFarlane's shoulders sagged ever so slightly, as though weighed down with a heavy load.

Why now, God? Why this impediment with the prize so close at hand?

Still clutching the file folder, MacFarlane walked over to the sliding glass door behind his desk and pulled it open, stepping onto the balcony. A gentle snow fell upon the midday traffic that ebbed and flowed ten stories below on Virginia Avenue, the busy thoroughfare made heavenly with the covering of pristine white flakes. To his left he could see the majestic gray spires of the National Cathedral high atop the city; to his right, the majestic white spire of the Washington Monument.

God first. Country second.

Words to live by.

A credo to die for.

Again, he glanced at the file folder. MI5 was Britain's elite secret service branch. As such, the agency safeguarded Britain's national security. *Regnum Defende.* Defend the realm.

How did the Miller woman make the acquaintance of a former British intelligence officer?

The dead curator had been a Brit. Perhaps he'd arranged the meeting.

But why? And how was it that Aisquith and this woman knew about the Stones of Fire and the Jerusalem cross?

MacFarlane didn't like having more questions than answers.

With Armageddon near at hand, why would God—

It was a trial, he suddenly realized, the weight lifting from his shoulders. A trial to prove his worthiness to the Almighty. To prove that he could indeed be trusted with God's great plan. *Shadrach. Meshach. Abednego.* Like those holy men of old, he, too, was being tested by God.

MacFarlane glanced at the beautiful gray spires in the distance, offering up a quick prayer of heartfelt thanks, grateful for the opportunity to prove his worth unto the Lord. Closing the file folder, he stepped back into his office. He punched the big blue *Speaker* button on his telephone console.

"You listen up, Gunny," he said without preamble. "I'm sending in a five-man team, one man to be posted at each museum exit. ETA two minutes. You stay with the Jeep. Edged weapons only. I want Miller and Aisquith in zippered bags before the new hour strikes. You hear me, boy?"

"Yes, sir," Boyd Braxton replied. "But what if . . ." MacFarlane could hear the confidence leach from the other man's voice. "What if the two of 'em manage to slip past us?"

Although gung-ho and loyal to a fault, the former gunnery sergeant lacked decision-making skills. Such men made good followers and even better fodder, but were poor leaders.

"To ensure they don't escape, I want you to rig the Miller woman's vehicle."

"I hear ya, sir!" Braxton exclaimed, his confidence clearly regained.

"Keep me posted."

CHAPTER 17

Edie and Caedmon emerged from the ladies' room. As they did, a loud alarm blared overhead; the teeth-jangling sound was accompanied by a continuously repeated recorded message. Surreally calm, the disembodied voice stated the obvious. *"The museum alarm has been activated. Immediately make your way to the nearest exit lobby. Thank you."*

"You heard the man. He said 'the nearest exit lobby.' That would be the one right over there." Nudging her companion in the ribs, Edie pointed to the Fourth Street lobby on the other side of the vestibule, which was jam-packed with people clamoring and jostling as they headed toward the oversized glass doors.

Intractable, Caedmon simply said, "I think not." Grabbing her by the upper arm, he pulled her toward the staircase on the right.

"What are you doing?"

"We're going to take the stairs to the upper level of the museum."

Jerking her arm free, Edie stared at him.

The main floor of the museum? Was he nuts? They'd have to navigate their way through umpteen art galleries and a couple of sculpture halls.

She shook her head, vetoing the idea. "It'll be faster if we stay on the lower level of the museum. The main floor will be a mob scene."

"Yes, I assume that it will be. However, a mob scene will serve us well if the beast should, again, rear his ugly head."

Refusing to budge, Edie folded her arms over her chest. "How many times have you visited the National Gallery of Art?"

"This is my maiden voyage." Again, Caedmon took her by the arm, his grip this time noticeably more firm. "Though you are no doubt well acquainted with the museum floor plan, you are also suffering from delayed shock. Not the best frame of mind for making a decision."

"Look, I may be losing it, but I still have a mind of my own."

Ignoring her last remark, Caedmon pulled her toward the staircase. As they ascended, Edie twice stumbled on the steps. Twice Caedmon had to catch hold of her before she took a nosedive.

At the top of the steps, she turned to him. "Now what?"

Rather than answer, Caedmon strode toward an abandoned wheelchair with *Property of the NGA* stamped across the brown leather back support. Her eyes narrowed as he took hold of it by the handles and wheeled it toward her.

"Bum in the chair," he brusquely ordered.

She balked. "Two fumbles does not an invalid make."

"The gunman will be searching for a female yea high." Holding out his hand, Caedmon raised it parallel to the top of her head. "The gunman will not be looking for a wheelchair-bound woman."

"How do I know that—"

"Seat yourself! Before I put a bloody boot up your Khyber!"

Edie did as ordered, belatedly realizing that she was doing a first-rate job of antagonizing the very man who had earlier saved her from a gunman's bullet. At great risk to his own life.

Craning her head to peer at him, she said, "Look, I'm sorry for being a bitch. I'm just . . . really, really scared." And unaccustomed to relying on anyone other than herself. Particularly for her safety and well-being. Over the years, too many people had let her down.

"You have every right to be frightened," Caedmon replied, once more the courteous Brit. Unlocking the brake, he shoved the wheelchair forward.

Edie removed the tote bag from her shoulder and clutched it to her chest. Inside its canvas depths were cash, car keys, and passport. Everything she would need to escape this madness.

As Caedmon navigated his way through the crowd, she realized that the wheelchair was an inspired idea; the horde parted before them like the Red Sea parting before the Israelites. Admittedly, she'd been leery of Caedmon's plan to take the long route through the museum. Maybe his plan, like the wheelchair, would prove a good call after all.

Within seconds they had passed the American painting gallery, eclipsing George Bellows's famous pair of boxers in a darkly hued blur.

A few seconds after that, they entered the East Court Garden and the cloying, humid air inside the cavernous space. Even more cloying were the winged cupids astride a giant scallop shell dead center in the middle of the courtyard, water merrily tinkling over their chubby feet. Caedmon veered to the right, bypassing the fountain. As he wheeled the chair around the columned perimeter, Edie caught sight of a homeless man sound asleep in a wrought-iron chair, oblivious to the alarm and automated message blaring on the PA system.

Exiting the courtyard garden, Caedmon increased his speed as they traversed the long, barrel-vaulted sculpture hall. On either side of her, Edie saw familiar flashes of color in the adjoining galleries—Toulouse-Lautrec, Renoir, Inge—the history of nineteenth-century French art reduced to a colorful blip.

Straight ahead of them, like mighty old-growth trees in a virgin forest, loomed the huge black marble columns of the main rotunda.

"We can exit at the rotunda," she said, turning in her seat to look at him, clasping her hands together in a beseeching gesture.

Her proposal met with a whirring silence, the wheelchair advancing full speed ahead.

It's like entering one of Dante's lower circles, Edie thought as they entered the domed rotunda a few seconds later. Everywhere she looked, swarms of people were haphazardly congregating in undulating lines that meandered in the direction of the main entrance. In front of the exit doors, a handful of uniformed guards quickly patted down every museum patron before permitting them to depart the premises. Edie assumed they were searching for the armed gunman.

"It would appear that all roads lead to Rome," Caedmon remarked as he steered the wheelchair away from the disorderly crowd.

Like the courtyard garden they'd earlier passed through, the rotunda was jungle humid on account of all the potted plants. Afraid Padgham's killer might be lurking in the vicinity, Edie tucked her chin into her chest, making herself as unobtrusive as possible.

No sooner did they clear the rotunda than Caedmon took off running.

Bronze sculptures. Flemish still lifes. Della Robbias.

Famous works of art passed at such a dizzying speed, Edie feared she would upchuck the contents of her stomach.

"Slow down, will ya? You're giving me a bad case of motion sickness."

If Caedmon heard her, he gave no indication, the man fast proving himself a well-spoken hard-ass.

Having covered three-fourths of the distance of the museum in less than two minutes, Caedmon wheeled her into the West Garden Court, a mirror image of the courtyard at the opposite end of the museum. Swerving sharply to the left, he somehow managed to maintain control as the chair took the turn on two rubberized wheels.

A few seconds later, Edie could see the marble wall that marked the end of the main hall.

"Quick! Put on the brakes!" she screeched, a full-length statue of St. John of the Cross standing sentry directly in front of her. She grabbed hold of the padded arms and held on tight as Caedmon brought the wheelchair to an abrupt halt mere inches from the stern-faced saint.

"Bloody hell." He turned his head from side to side. "There's supposed to be a lift at the end of— Ah, yes, there she be, starboard bow." Caedmon rolled the wheelchair to the elevator that was tucked away to the right of them.

Edie reached out and pushed the button; the metal doors instantly slid open. With no room to turn the wheelchair around, she sat facing the back wall of the elevator. Within moments, they'd be free of the museum, via the Seventh Street exit located on the lower level.

Readying herself for the last cavalry charge, she opened her tote bag. Quickly, she rummaged through it, her hand bumping against the now soft-sided box of melted spinach.

"What are you doing?"

Edie spared Caedmon a quick, upward glance. "I'm searching for the car keys."

"Driving your vehicle would be ill-advised."

Placing her arm over the back of the chair, she twisted her upper body so she could look him in the eye. "You're kidding, right? The Jeep is our only means of escape."

"How do you think the gunman found you? I'll warrant it was no mean guess."

"Maybe it was an educated guess. And let us not forget about the old lucky guess," she retorted. Then, realizing how childish she sounded, "Okay, he followed me here. But I can promise you that he won't be following us when we leave. I know this town like the back of my hand. Trust me, Caedmon. I can get us out of here."

She watched as he mulled over her proposal. He was tempted; she could see it in his eyes.

"There's a back service alley one block away at Federal Triangle. If we're being followed, it's the perfect place to lose a tail."

The elevator door opened with a melodic *ping*. Caedmon backed the wheelchair out of the elevator and turned it toward the Seventh Street lobby, where the scene was almost identical to what they'd witnessed in the rotunda.

Seeing all the hustle and bustle, the mass confusion, the absolute chaos that reigned within the marble-walled space, Edie breathed a sigh of relief.

The end was in sight.

CHAPTER 18

Holding a museum map in front of him, Boyd Braxton re-checked the exits.

He had Sanchez on the Mall exit, Harliss at Constitution, Napier across the street at the East Wing, Agee manning the Fourth Street exit, and Riggins posted at the Seventh Street exit. Experienced war fighters, one and all, each of 'em was equipped with a Ka-Bar knife and two ID photos: one of a dark curly-haired bitch and the other of a tall redheaded bastard. *And the best part?* To the man, they were decked out in D.C. police uniforms. Given that the National Gallery of Art was swarming with every badge the city could rustle up, no one would give them a second glance.

The op in play, Boyd secured a communications device to his right ear, enabling him to speak to all five of his men. "You've got your orders: take out both targets. Edged weapons only. We want this to go down swift, silent, and deadly."

"Copy that, Boss Man," Riggins replied, speaking for the group. An expert at close-quarter fighting, Riggins knew how to wield a knife with lethal proficiency. Better yet, he *enjoyed* wielding a blade. Close-range combat appealed to a particular kind of warrior: the kind who liked to look his victim in the eye when he went in for the kill.

"Okay, boys and girls. Let's go have some fun," Boyd said, grinning, confident that this time there would be no more fuck-ups. "And don't forget . . . we go with God."

"Amen, brother." This from Sanchez, a former Army Ranger and Afghanistan vet well experienced in slaying the godless.

As he headed toward the Fourth Street exit, Boyd glanced at the ring he wore on his right hand; the cluster of silver crosses was a constant reminder that he and his men were soldiers in God's army. Holy warriors not unlike the crusaders of old. The colonel often spoke of the men who, a thousand years ago, went forth to conquer the Holy Land. *Hugues of Payens. Godfrey of Bouillon. Yves of Faillon.* Boyd felt a kindred link to those knights of old who fought with a sword in one hand and a Bible in the other. The sword he had great experience with, having spent fifteen years in the Corps. The Bible was new to him; his old man had not held the Good Book in very high regard. In fact, Joe Don Braxton hadn't held much of anything except a bottle of Old Crow. And he'd held that damned near every night. Rumor had it there was a half-drunk fifth of bourbon clutched between Joe Don's thighs the night he drove his Dodge pickup into a stand of poplar trees.

Approaching the museum lobby, Boyd jutted his chin at the Rosemont man standing sentry near the coat room; Agee was a good man to have in a tight fix. The silent greeting was returned with an innocuous nod.

Not about to stand in line, Boyd slid his hand into his coat pocket and removed a leather wallet. Flipping it open, he thrust the D.C. Metropolitan Police badge at the same guard he'd tinned when he first entered the museum.

"Detective Wilson," the guard said by way of greeting. "Hell of a mess we've got on our hands, huh?"

"Just another day in Sin City. Anyone get a look at the bastard who fired the shots?"

"As a matter of fact, one of the museum patrons was able to videotape some of it on his cell phone."

Hearing that, Boyd froze.

Within hours his face would be plastered on BOLOs, You-Tube, and all of the major news outlets.

"Glad to hear it," he replied, his facial muscles taut with a fake smile. "Keep up the good work"—he glanced at the man's name badge—"Officer Milligan." He had no idea if security guards were addressed as *Officer*, and at the moment he didn't much care. The fake grin replaced with a grimace, he headed for the plate glass doors, shoving aside a couple of jabbering tourists.

Once outside, he came to a standstill, his booted feet planted on the cobbled stone driveway that fronted the entrance. Ignoring the two-way traffic jam of human bodies—badges heading into the museum, touristos heading out—he raised his head to the gray sky above. And prayed. *Hard.*

Dear Lord, help me make this right.

Boyd didn't want to let down the colonel. He owed everything he had to Colonel Stan MacFarlane. Sometimes, when his mind wandered, he liked to imagine that the colonel was the father he never had but always wanted. Stern, but fair. Righteous. A man who'd never hit you unless he had just cause.

Like a soothing balm, the gently falling snow cooled his brow, its big fluffy flakes sticking to his eyelashes, his lips, the tip of his nose. It put him in mind of the first time he'd ever seen the snow fall from the sky during a tour of duty in Japan. A backwater kid from Pascagoula, Mississippi, he'd only seen winter snow on celluloid. He well remembered standing there, a bad-ass, two-hundred-thirty-pound jarhead, sorely tempted to lie down, flap his arms and legs like an epileptic, and make angels in the snow. Come to think of it, it'd been snowing the day he made his first kill. A Jap with an attitude had accused him of stiffing on the sake bill and had followed him into the alley, attacking him from behind while he took a piss. He killed the slant-eyed shitbird with a backward jab of the elbow, ramming his nose all the way into his skull. A ruby-red bloodstain on virgin white snow. *It had been a beautiful sight.* Like a silk-clad whore spreading her legs for a li'l game of peekaboo.

Reinvigorated, the blood pumping through his veins fast and furious, Boyd straightened his shoulders as he strode past the black Jeep Wrangler. The colonel said that God was a fine

one for testing the faithful. Maybe that's what all this fiddle
fucking was about—he was being tested.

If that was the case, *bring it on!*

He was up to the challenge.

Sticking the key in the trunk of the Crown Vic, he opened
it and removed a drawstring pouch. Inside the ditty bag were
two spare cell phones, coiled wire, duct tape, and a small block
of C-4. Everything he needed to make things right.

CHAPTER 19

Glancing at the plate glass doors that fronted the Seventh
Street museum exit, Edie figured the headline story on the
local newscast would be "Gunman Goes Berserk Inside the
National Gallery of Art." Particularly since the Channel 9 and
Channel 4 news vans had just pulled up outside the museum
and a bevy of technicians were hurriedly unloading their camera equipment.

As she continued to observe the action on the other side of
the exit door, it appeared that a great many people were unloading equipment from the back of official-looking vehicles.
EMTs unloading stretchers. Firefighters unloading axes and
water hoses. D.C. police unloading orange traffic cones. The
museum had become a scene of industrious purpose—patrons
exiting one door, first responders entering through another.

Still seated in the wheelchair, she sat quietly as Caedmon
rolled her over to a large Chinese vase set inside a wall niche.

"Time for milady to exit her carriage."

Edie hurriedly extricated herself from the wheelchair, her
legs so wobbly she unthinkingly grabbed the Qing dynasty
vase to keep from falling.

Caedmon wrapped an arm around her shoulders, gently removing her hand from the priceless objet d'art. "Steady as she goes," he whispered in her ear. "Deep breaths will slow your heart rate. Leastways, it always works for me."

She nodded her thanks, surprised by the admission. Though she barely knew him, Caedmon Aisquith seemed to have been born with the proverbial stiff upper lip. No deep breaths required.

"Given the well-orchestrated attack, we must assume that our adversaries will attempt to track our movements via electronic transactions." Removing his billfold from his pants pocket, Caedmon peered into the worn brown leather. "I'm afraid that my assets are somewhat paltry. Seventy-five dollars U.S. and three hundred euros. How much do you have?" he bluntly inquired.

The question caught Edie off guard. Her eyes suspiciously narrowing, she said, "I have three thousand dollars. What's it to you?"

"I say! You must have cleaned out your bank account."

"In a manner of speaking," she mumbled, unwilling to elaborate.

"Very well, then. I suggest we assume two aliases, Mister and Missus Smythe-Jones, or some such rot, and check into a hotel."

"The two of us? In a hotel?" Edie had given no thought as to what would happen once they left the museum, having assumed they'd go their separate ways. She'd come to the National Gallery of Art only to warn him of the danger, not to hook up with him.

Although she supposed there might be some truth in the old adage about safety in numbers.

"Yes, a hotel," Caedmon reiterated. "I don't know about you, but I'm in dire need of a soft bed and a stiff drink."

"Bed and booze. Okay, I'm in."

Caedmon motioned to the throng of people lined up to exit the museum. "Shall we join the multitude?"

As they approached the line of people being searched by museum guards, Edie surveyed the crowd of museum goers, most of whom were excitedly chatting about what they'd seen, what they knew, or what they'd heard.

She nudged Caedmon in the arm. "Did you hear what that man just—" She stopped suddenly, catching sight of a familiar face out of the corner of her eye.

It was the dirty cop she'd seen in the alley behind the Hopkins Museum.

"To your left! It's the killer's cop buddy!" she hissed out of the corner of her mouth.

Without so much as turning his head, Caedmon swerved his gaze to the left. "The bloke with sandy blond hair?" When she nodded, he said, "Did he catch sight of you at the Hopkins?"

"No. But they have my driver's license photo. They know what I look like."

"Right."

An absentminded look on his face, Caedmon patted his breast pocket, giving every appearance of a man searching for a pen or a pair of reading glasses. It took a moment for Edie to realize that he was very carefully casing the joint, his eyes moving from left to right and back again.

"In a few seconds there's going to be a frightful stampede toward the door," he said in a low voice, taking her firmly by the upper arm as he spoke. "Be ready to run for your life."

Edie nodded, knowing he spoke literally, not figuratively.

"Good God!" Caedmon suddenly boomed in a loud, forceful tone of voice. "There's the gunman! That man standing by the elevator doors!"

At hearing Caedmon's commanding voice—which sounded an awful lot like a trained Shakespearean actor bellowing about kingdoms and horses—every head in the lobby abruptly turned.

A second of shocked silence ensued.

Then, in a tremendous burst of explosive energy, the façade of order gave way, there being utter disorder in the ranks.

Like rats jumping ship, the museum patrons closest to the plate glass doors rushed outside. All four museum guards and every policeman in sight charged in the opposite direction toward the elevators.

   That being their cue, Edie and Caedmon ran to the door,
elbowing their way to the head of the pack.

   Several seconds later, they burst free of the building.

   "Hurry!" Caedmon ordered, taking her by the hand as he
descended the portico steps that fronted the museum. "I suspect we fooled everyone save the man searching for us. What
is that across the street?" He pointed beyond the traffic jam of
news vans and patrol cars to the grove of leafless trees on the
other side of Seventh Street.

   "That's the outdoor sculpture garden."

   "And in this direction?" He pointed toward Constitution
Avenue.

   "Federal Triangle."

   "Am I correct in thinking there's a tube station near at
hand?"

   "There's a subway station a couple of blocks away. On the
other side of the Archives."

   "Right." Still holding her by the hand, Caedmon scurried
past a coterie of beat cops attempting to hold back curious
onlookers with a flimsy strand of yellow crime scene tape.

   "In case you've forgotten, my Jeep is parked—"

   "Not now!"

   Knowing their first prerogative was to escape the sandy-
haired cop she'd seen in the lobby, Edie held her tongue. They
could hash out the specifics of the escape plan once they were
free and clear of the museum.

   Breaking into a run, they crossed Seventh Street, Caedmon
leading the way to the sculpture garden. Through the sparse
foliage Edie saw a steel sculpture on the right and a bronze
sculpture on the left. Ahead of them was an outdoor skating
rink, where a trio of skaters gracefully glided across the smooth
ice, blissfully ignorant of the pandemonium on the other side
of the street.

   Still leading the way, Caedmon skirted to the right of the
rink, turned right yet again, then made a sharp left. For a man
unfamiliar with the city, he was doing an excellent job of maneuvering them through the garden maze.

It wasn't until they emerged onto Constitution Avenue, some two blocks from the Seventh Street museum exit, that Caedmon slowed his pace.

Her lungs burning with the frigid December air, Edie came to a grinding halt, unable to catch her breath. When Caedmon put a steadying hand on her shoulder, she instinctively hurled herself at his chest.

"That c-cop would have killed— If you hadn't— We would be—" She burrowed her head into his shoulder, fear causing her thoughts to incoherently smash together.

Caedmon wrapped his arms around her. "*Ssshh*. It's all right. We're out of danger," he murmured, his breath warm against her cheek.

It took a good half minute before her breathing returned to something approximating normal. Self-conscious of the fact that she'd thrown herself at him, Edie pulled free from Caedmon's embrace.

"Better?" he solicitously inquired. Other than the fact that his eyes had turned an iridescent shade of cobalt blue, he showed no outward sign of exertion.

Doing a good imitation of a bobble-head doll, she warily nodded. Warily because she could hear the blare of sirens in the near distance. A police net was being thrown around the National Gallery of Art. If the net was extended, they might yet be ensnared.

She glanced at her watch. Unbelievably, no more than fifteen minutes had passed since the three shots had been fired in the museum concourse. The expanse of lapsed time seemed both longer and shorter, as though time had sped up and slowed down all at once.

"I don't know about you, but I feel like I just got sucked into a killer cyclone, with houses, cows, and farm fences spinning all around me."

"I feel much the same." One side of his mouth quirked upward. "Certainly, this was not how I envisioned spending my afternoon."

"I hear you." Still embarrassed by her earlier show of weakness, she wiped several wet flakes from her eyelashes. The snow had slowed to a desultory smatter, its wispy flakes blowing on a cold westerly wind.

From where they stood, the National Archives kitty-corner to them, they had an excellent view in either direction of Constitution Avenue. Spread along the famous thoroughfare were familiar citadels of sanity—hot dog vendors, concession stands, T-shirt-packed kiosks. Tiny punctuation marks haphazardly placed between ponderous block-style buildings.

Deciding to take charge, Edie turned to the right, intending to backtrack to her parked vehicle.

She'd taken no more than a step when Caedmon grabbed her by the elbow, preventing her from taking that all-important second step.

"Where do you think you're going?"

"We discussed this already. I'm going to the Jeep. Are you in or are you out?"

"Though there are advantages to having a vehicle at our disposal, there are certain disadvantages that must be considered."

Desperate to get back to the Jeep, that being the quickest means of escaping the madness, she straightened her shoulders. No easy feat given that she was bundled in a leather jacket and an oversized trench coat. "On the count of three: rock, paper, scissors."

His copper-colored brows drew together in the middle. "I beg your pardon?"

"You heard me. Since there's just the two of us, we can't put it to a vote. So, instead, we'll use rock, paper, scissors to decide. You guys do that in England, don't you?"

"I am familiar with the hand game. In fact, it was invented in the mid-eighteenth century by the Comte de Rochambeau as a means to settle—"

Edie held up a hand, stopping him in mid-discourse.

"More information than I need to know." Sick and tired of being the follower rather than the leader, she met his gaze head-on. "On three."

In unison, they each moved a balled right fist through the air.

CHAPTER 20

A cold wet rain fell upon the heath.

A line straight out of a Victorian novel, Caedmon moodily thought as he pulled back the drawn hotel curtain. Except it wasn't a heath; it was an asphalt car park bounded by eight-foot-high brick walls and a twelve-story office building directly opposite.

"My, my, what a posh life we lead," he muttered, releasing the rubber-backed curtain and stepping away from the window. Since paper beat rock, they'd left Washington via the subway, checking into a Holiday Inn across the river in Arlington, Virginia. That was two hours ago and he was still trying to muddle his way through the calamitous chain of events that had landed him in this monochromatic hotel room with its uninspiring view.

He glanced at his companion. Edie Miller was coiled in a ball on one of the double beds, her mouth slack, her eyes unfocused. His gaze lingered a few impolite moments; Caedmon thought she looked like a dahlia curled in the frost.

In dire need of a refreshing punch, he strolled over to the serving counter, the room equipped with a coffeepot, a microwave oven, and a diminutive refrigerator. He uncapped a green bottle, having purchased Tanqueray and tonic at the wine and spirits shop down the street.

"What are you doing?" A drowsy expression on her face, Edie lifted her head from the pillow.

"I thought I'd mix myself a G&T."

The dahlia instantly revived. "Make mine a double."

Tumbler in hand, he walked over to the bed. As though mocking their dismal plight, the ice cubes merrily clinked against the sides of the glass. "Sorry, but the bartender is fresh out of limes," he said, handing her the half-full tumbler.

Swinging her bare feet over the side of the bed, Edie unlimbered into a seated position, the tumbler clasped between her hands. "The AWOL lime is the least of our worries."

"Indeed."

Safe for the moment, Caedmon suspected that they were being hunted by a very determined adversary. And though the adversary had possession of the prize, the Stones of Fire having been stolen from the Hopkins Museum, their enemy was very keen to erase all traces of the theft.

But why?

The question had been plaguing him for the last two hours. Neither he nor Edie Miller could identify Jonathan Padgham's killer. Nor did they know the current location of the bejeweled breastplate.

So why launch a bloodthirsty manhunt?

The manhunt implied that their foe did not want it made public that after several thousand years, the fabled Stones of Fire had been rediscovered. If true, it spoke to motive. Clearly, their foe had an ulterior purpose for stealing the breastplate, one that had nothing to do with plunder and profit.

Lost in thought, he belatedly realized he'd depleted his glass.

Careful, old boy. You've already slain that dragon.

Needing to pace himself, Caedmon set his tumbler on the dresser. Drink was a tempting mistress, one that beckoned when he least expected it.

Bare feet still dangling over the side of bed, Edie looked at him, her expression forthrightly quizzical. At a loss for words, he returned the stare, enjoying the sight of long brown curls framing her face and shoulders in a riotous halo. Admiring a woman's attributes was one of those simple pleasures that made a man momentarily forget stress and strife; he lowered his gaze. Like chapel hatpegs, her nipples were visibly prominent through the thin fabric of her silk pullover, Edie having removed her bulky jumper.

"Is something the matter?"

Caught with his hand in the biscuit tin, Caedmon quickly glanced at the telly on the other side of the room. His cheeks warm with color, he picked up his depleted G&T and made a big to-do of swirling the ice cubes clustered in the bottom of the glass.

Damn the woman for being so keenly observant. And so blunt in expressing those keen observations.

A sudden knock at the door sparked their joint attention.

"You don't think . . . ?"

"No, I do not," he replied, striding toward the locked door. A quick glance in the peephole confirmed what he already knew—the bellhop had arrived. A fortuitous interruption, the room awash with sexual tension.

Come now. What did you expect, checking into a hotel room with a lovely American woman?

Unlocking the door, he greeted the bellhop with a courteous nod as the young man handed him a paper bag emblazoned with the Holiday Inn logo. Before taking custody of the bag, Caedmon reached into his trouser pocket and removed several crumpled notes. The exchange made, he closed and locked the door.

Awkwardly smiling, still conscious of the earlier misstep, he hefted the white bag in the air. "I come bearing gifts, compliments of the establishment."

Edie patted the mattress. "Sit yourself over here and let's see what's in the gift sack."

Uncertain what to make of the invitation, he obediently complied. He knew that in the aftermath of a bum-clenching terror, each person acted differently. Some turned to alcohol, some turned to drugs, and a good many turned to sex. Caedmon preferred the first, had never been interested in the second, and wasn't altogether certain how he felt about the latter. While he found Edie Miller attractive, he in no way wanted to take advantage of the situation.

He dumped the contents of the bag onto the bed. "One tube of toothpaste, two toothbrushes, hand lotion, shaving cream, razor, and, alas, only one comb. I'm afraid we'll have to share."

"I'm kinda getting used to sharing."

Caedmon assumed the offhand remark had to do with the fact that the room had been paid with a soggy hundred-dollar bill that had come from her "spinach fund." Concerned that their electronic transactions would be monitored, he had imposed a moratorium on all credit cards. Certain his room at the Churchill would also be monitored, he phoned his hotel and asked that they gather his belongings and put them in storage until such time as he could collect them. He'd also rung up his publicist, informing her that he was catching a late-night flight back to Paris. If asked, she would lead the inquisitors astray.

"Would you mind . . . ?" Edie toggled her glass back and forth, silently indicating that she needed a refill.

"Not in the least." Getting up from the bed, Caedmon walked over to the makeshift bar on the other side of the room. Along the way he collected his own glass.

The silence unnerving, he busied himself with mixing the drinks. Rightly concerned that he might cross the invisible line, and equally worried his companion might be receptive, he went easy on the gin. With his font of small talk dried up, he wordlessly handed Edie a replenished glass.

"Cheers," he said, clinking his tumbler to hers.

"Actually, more like 'Tears,' don't you think?" Her demeanor glum, Edie listlessly raised the tumbler to her lips.

"For myself, I prefer taking the 'glass is half-full' approach to all of this."

"Don't you care that your friend was murdered?"

"Of course, I care," he retorted, not wanting to have this conversation with a woman he barely knew. "However, experience has taught me that the pain will only worsen if I permit myself to wallow in it."

"Is that what I'm doing, wallowing?"

"No, you are not wallowing. Wallowing is when one forgoes the tonic water." As well he knew. Hoping to lighten the mood, he said, "His pet name for me was 'Mercuriophilus Anglicus.'"

"I assume that you're referring to Dr. Padgham."

"Padge could never recall anyone's forename."

"Probably because he was too caught up in his own self-importance." No sooner did the words escape her lips than Edie slapped a hand over her mouth. "God, that was horrible! I'm sorry." Then, laughing, "Did I mention that I'm a mean drunk? So, what does *Mercurio Blabbityblop* mean?"

"It means the English Mercury Lover."

Still smiling, she lifted a brow. "Hmm, sounds kinky. Do I really want to know the story behind your strange moniker?"

Enjoying the silly game, he feigned indignation. "I can assure you that the story is not nearly as racy as you presume. It so happens that alchemical mercury suffuses all of creation. In ancient times, it was thought to be the secret essence of the All in all things."

She drew a long face. "Oh, puh-*leeze*. There must be a class you guys take at Oxford where they teach you how to pontificate to us little people."

"Are you always so frank?"

"Not always." Her brown eyes mischievously twinkled. "I do have to sleep."

Caedmon threw back his head and laughed, her offbeat humor growing on him.

"You know it's crazy," Edie said, suddenly serious. "All of this murder and mayhem happening because of an old breastplate."

He walked over to the striped wingback chair situated on the far side of the bed and seated himself. "The Stones of Fire are much more than 'an old breastplate.'"

"You said something about the breastplate being designed by God and manufactured by Moses."

"So claim a good many biblical scholars."

"Come on. You don't really think that the breastplate was divinely inspired?"

"Actually, I think the breastplate has a far more"—he paused, not wanting to offend her religious beliefs—"*complex* pedigree than that contained within the pages of the Old Testament."

"*Really?* What exactly do you mean by 'complex'?" Drawing her legs onto the bed, she curled them beneath her bum. "I thought it was pretty straightforward: Moses would don the breastplate in order to control the—how did you phrase it?—the 'cosmic power' contained within the Ark of the Covenant."

"Which raises the question . . . where did Moses learn such a feat? I have long suspected that Moses was not only an Egyptian, but a trained magician in the pharaoh's court."

"Moses, the man who led the Jews out of bondage and commanded the ragtag Hebrew tribes as they wandered the wilderness for forty years? *That* Moses was an Egyptian magician?"

He nodded.

"You know what I think, Mr. Caedmon Aisquith? I think you've eaten *way* too much paste. For starters, the Egyptians were a bunch of pagans. They had—what?—like a couple hundred gods."

"Not nearly as many as all that," he quietly corrected, well aware that the theory he was about to propose would scandalize many a churchgoer. "Would it surprise you to learn that the ancient Egyptians were the first people to practice monotheism? Known as Atenism, for several decades it was the state religion, the pharaoh Akhenaton officially declaring that Aten was the only god in the heavens." Leaning forward, he propped his forearms on his thighs; the point he was about to make was key to his argument. "Aten was not the supreme god; Aten was the *only* god. Furthermore, I believe that Moses, or Tuthmoses as he was known in the Egyptian high court, was not only an avid follower of the Aten religion, but he fused the beliefs of Atenism to that of the fledgling Hebrew faith."

Edie stared at him, saucer-eyed. "What are you saying, that Yahweh and the Egyptian god Aten were one and the same?"

CHAPTER 21

Unwilling to tread those murky depths, Caedmon purposefully equivocated. "I am merely saying that there are areas of overlap between the two religions."

"Such as . . . ?"

"Such as the Ten Commandments, which are suspiciously similar to the behavioral mandates put forth in the Egyptian Book of the Dead, a work that predates the biblical Exodus. And let us not forget circumcision, an unusual practice to say the least. Did you know that circumcision was a ritualistic procedure among the Egyptian royal family and their attendant court? Other similarities include the stricture against graven images, a hereditary priesthood, the sacrifice of animals, and the use of a golden ark to contain the might and majesty of what can only be called a very jealous god." His case made, Caedmon folded his arms across his chest. "Would you not agree that such similarities give one pause?"

"Yeah, well, right now I need to pause and catch my breath because I'm still grappling with Moses being an Egyptian magician." Edie took a noisy slurp of her G&T, loudly chomping down on an ice cube. "I'm sorry, Caedmon,.but I'm having a hard time buying off on Judaism descending from some long-lost Egyptian religion."

"I am not speaking of Judaism as it is practiced today, that being a religion primarily created in the sixth century B.C. during the Babylonian Captivity. I am speaking of the Hebrew religion as it was practiced from the time of the Exodus up until the Babylonian Captivity, a span of roughly seven hundred years."

"So, which came first, the worship of Aten or the worship of Yahweh?"

"Ah, the 'chicken or egg' conundrum. In the same way that Roman religious practices influenced early Christianity, I believe that the enslaved Jews in Egypt influenced, and perhaps even inspired, the worship of Aten. The Old Testament makes mention of Moses having been instructed in 'all the wisdom of the Egyptians.'"

"What exactly does that mean, 'all the wisdom of the Egyptians'?"

The question immense in its scope, Caedmon thoughtfully considered his reply. "The prescribed Egyptian education included the study of crystals and metals, necromancy, and the art of divination. Knowledge that Moses put to good use when creating the fabled Stones of Fire."

"But I saw the breastplate with my own eyes. It was just"— she shrugged—"twelve jewels and some bits of old gold."

"Yes, but it's those very jewels that give the Stones of Fire its immense power."

"Okay, I'll nibble. What's so special about those twelve jewels?"

"Allow me to preface my answer by saying that gemstones are not the inert, inanimate objects that most people assume them to be. Indeed, gemstones, as well as crystals, are energy conduits. In Asian cultures, such energy is known as *chi*."

"I have a girlfriend who's into crystals. She swears that if you hold a crystal long enough in your hand you'll soon feel a vibratory pulse. Personally, I consider that awfully New Agey."

"Not if you consider the fact that crystals are used to boost radio waves in a process known as piezoelectricity. In a similar process, the ancients used gemstones and crystals to both generate and enhance energy. A high priest steeped in the mysteries of ancient Egypt, Moses used his vast knowledge of gems and crystals when creating the Stones of Fire. I would even go so far as to say that the breastplate is nothing less than a form of ancient technology, each stone specifically selected for its unique vibratory properties."

At hearing that, Edie snorted. "You're kidding, right? I'd hardly call an old breastplate a technological wonder."

"Ah, but that's exactly what the breastplate was, and perhaps still is—ancient technology. Just because the word *Sony* isn't stamped on it doesn't make it any less sophisticated than the mobile phone in my breast pocket," he countered, patting said pocket. "The Stones of Fire, even by twenty-first-century standards, is state of the art."

She mulled that over for a paltry half second before uttering a noncommittal, "Huh."

Reaching across to the nightstand that separated the two double beds, Edie grabbed a pink and white bag of Oreo cookies. Using both hands, she ripped it open, slid free a tray of factory-packed, chemical-laced brown biscuits, and offered him one.

"No, thank you," he politely demurred.

Her lips curled in a come-hither smile. "Ah, come on, Caedmon. Try it, you'll like it."

Realizing how easily Adam had been swayed, he took a crème-filled biscuit.

"Quite tasty," he remarked a few seconds later.

With a twist of the wrist, Edie unscrewed the two halves of her biscuit. Then, to his utter surprise and lurid fascination, she proceeded to lap at the white cream with her tongue. "Okay, let's suppose for argument's sake that Moses was a member of the Egyptian priesthood. Why would he lead a bunch of Hebrew slaves out of Egypt?"

"Your question presumes that the Jews, and only the Jews, left Egypt."

"Well, who else would have gone with them?"

"All those in grave danger of losing their lives." He let that sink in a moment before saying, "Specifically, the entire court of Akhenaton."

She lowered her cookie. "Come again?"

"What you must understand is that when the pharaoh Akhenaton imposed a monotheistic faith upon the inhabitants of Egypt, it was nothing short of a religious revolution. Not unlike the furor that ensued when Martin Luther put nail to paper. Suddenly, overnight, the pantheon of familiar gods and goddesses—Isis, Set, Osiris—were rendered null and void."

"I'm guessing that what some considered a new religion, others considered an out-and-out heresy," Edie correctly surmised.

"Indeed. When Akhenaton died, the practitioners of the old religion swooped down upon the royal court. And with a vengeance, I might add, all traces of Akhenaton and Aten wiped clean from the annals of Egyptian history."

"What happened to those Egyptians who still believed in Aten?"

"They fled Egypt in the dead of night. A vast migration of slave and nobility."

"Well, that would explain the passage in the book of Exodus where the Hebrew slaves supposedly took 'jewels of silver and jewels of gold' with them when they fled Egypt. I mean, how the heck did a bunch of slaves get that kind of treasure trove?"

He nodded, surprised that she was so well versed in scripture. "In truth, it was not the Hebrew slaves who possessed such wealth, but rather the Egyptian nobility who accompanied them on their flight."

"Moses leading the way to the Land of Canaan."

"So I believe."

"While it makes for the greatest story never told, I still need more proof before I chuck away years of Sunday school indoctrination." She glanced at the electric alarm clock on the nightstand. "Time for the six o'clock newscast," she announced, lunging off the bed.

Aiming the remote at the telly, she hit the power button. A suited woman sporting a blond bob appeared on the screen.

"In a scene reminiscent of the pandemonium that struck Washington in the wake of 9/11, museum goers at the National Gallery of Art came under terrorist fire earlier today when a gunman began shooting a loaded firearm into the underground concourse area."

As the news broadcaster read her script, a grainy video of the "pandemonium" appeared on the screen, the footage clearly shot by an amateur hand. And a shaking hand at that, there being a decidedly frenetic quality to the captured images. To Caedmon's relief, neither he nor Edie was visible in the video.

Slack-jawed, Edie turned to him. "They've got it all wrong . . . it wasn't a terrorist attack." Reaching for the remote, she quickly changed channels.

"The shooting spree in the museum's concourse was part of a well-coordinated terrorist attack, with a car bomb detonating yards away from the Fourth Street entrance. No fatal casualties were reported, although several emergency workers suffered severe burns."

"Oh, God," she murmured as she watched the accompanying video of the smoldering blast site. Then, her eyes filled with tears, she turned to him. "That's the Jeep. The same Jeep that I wanted us to—"

"Don't say it," he roughly ordered, equally jarred by the charred wreckage being shown on the telly. "By a fortuitous stroke of luck, we escape the demon."

"That's crap and you know it! They're not going to stop until they find us." She shoved a balled fist against her mouth, her eyes glued to the television screen.

In silence, they watched the remainder of the news broadcast. Edie muted the volume when the sports segment aired.

"Don't you think it's odd that there was no mention of Padgham's murder? There are three dead bodies at the Hopkins Museum, yet there's no mention of it on the nightly news."

"I presume the bodies haven't been discovered."

She shook her head, negating the suggestion. "On Mondays, the cleaning crew arrives at four o'clock. Why didn't they—" She gasped. "Oh, God! Maybe they killed the cleaning crew." Spinning on her heel, she made a grab for the telephone. "I'm going to make an anonymous call to the D.C. police and inform them that Dr. Padgham and the two security guards were—"

Striding between the two beds, Caedmon yanked the phone out of her hand.

"What are you doing?"

"In this day and age, it's impossible to be truly anonymous," he matter-of-factly informed her. "We already know that the local police force has a tainted officer in their midst. If you contact the authorities, you may inadvertently lead the enemy—"

"Right to us." Grim-faced, Edie sank to the bed.

"I have a far better suggestion."

"Unless it involves a magic wand, I don't know how you're going to make things better."

Knowing its source, he ignored the sarcasm. "I propose we do a bit of cyber sleuthing. High time we meet the enemy." He removed his wool jacket from the back of the wingback chair.

"But we don't have a computer."

"True, but the bloke downstairs at the front desk seemed amiable enough."

CHAPTER 22

"Boy, you don't know your dick from a stick!" Stanford Mac-Farlane railed at his subordinate.

Just like his son, Custis. Had he lived, Custis would be twenty-eight years old this month. But Custis was no longer among the living, the weak-kneed snot having—

MacFarlane shoved the thought to the backwater of his mind.

The framed photographs had been removed, the name Custis Lee MacFarlane stricken from the family bible. No sense regurgitating the past. It was over and done with. Mortal man could affect nothing save the here and now. And then only if it was in God's purview to do so.

"What was running through your gourd, Gunny, detonating that wad of C-4 without the Miller woman being in the vehicle? This operation was supposed to have been swift and silent, not a blind man's game of grab-ass."

"Sir, the explosives were rigged to go off when the engine was started. I had no way of knowing the C-4 would detonate when the tow truck hooked the—"

"Well, you should have known! And how is it that Aisquith and Miller eluded six, count 'em, six men trained in urban warfare?"

"I don't know how they got the slip on us, sir."

Hearing that, MacFarlane was sorely tempted to ram his knee into his subordinate's crotch. Penance for his sins. Instead, he strode over to his desk. A hardbound book, *Isis Revealed*, lay in plain sight on top of his in-basket. He snatched the book in his hand, waving it in front of the gunny's face.

"Are you saying that the man who wrote this pack of lies outsmarted six of Rosemont's finest?" He'd earlier had one of his assistants purchase the book; a hunter needed to know the nature of the beast before he laid his traps.

"He's good, sir. That's all I know. Riggins is fairly certain they slipped through the Seventh Street exit."

MacFarlane wasn't fooled by the Brit's bravado. No doubt Aisquith and the Miller woman were holed up somewhere, trying to figure out their next move. They were afraid, uncertain whom they could trust. He had carefully cultivated that mistrust when he earlier spoke to the woman. The mess at the Hopkins Museum had been swept clean and the fiasco at the National Gallery of Art attributed to a rogue terrorist. But all that could change if Ms. Miller gave a statement to the police.

He dismissively tossed the book into his in-box, his gaze momentarily landing on the book jacket photo of a red-haired man in a tweed sports jacket.

There was a special place in hell for men who blasphemed the teachings of the one true God.

Soon enough, the ex-operative turned faux historian would know the meaning of terror; Aisquith was playing with a fire that could not be extinguished.

As the silent seconds ticked past, Boyd Braxton wordlessly stared at him, a *Help me, I'm drowning* look on his broad face. It put him in mind of the night that the gunny murdered his wife and child—a boot mistake committed in a moment of unchecked rage. MacFarlane had used the calamitous event to bring the sobbing, baby-faced gunnery sergeant to God. He'd done good work that night, having made a promise not to turn his back on the man who now stood before him.

Ass chewing administered, Stanford MacFarlane pointed to the parquet floor. "On your knees, boy. It's time you begged the Almighty's forgiveness."

A look of relief on his face, the gunnery sergeant obediently dropped to his knees, his head bowed in prayer. Glancing downward, MacFarlane could see the crisscrossed scars that marred his subordinate's skull. Remnants of a sinner's life, the scars were undoubtedly the result of a broken beer bottle making contact with Braxton's head.

Stepping back, giving the other man the space he needed to make his peace with God, he walked over to the shipping container on the other side of the room, the Stones of Fire packed and ready for transport. Acquiring the breastplate had been the preliminary step in a much larger operation. A means to an end. The end being the cleansing of all perversion, all licentiousness.

Like ancient Egypt, America was headed down the path of destruction, the world no different now than it was in the days of the pharaoh. Plague upon plague had been sent upon the godless pagans, none immune save the God-fearing Moses and his Hebrew entourage. So, too, this epoch would see God's might as never before, his "terrible swift sword" striking down the false prophets, the feel-good TV shrinks, the prosperity gurus. Those who did not heed the warnings of the Old Testament prophets would discover firsthand how God judges sin.

With so little time left, America must have a revival of repentance, the nation having strayed from the tenets of God's word as transcribed by the prophets. A course correction was needed. Holy warriors were needed.

MacFarlane walked over to the framed map that hung behind his desk. Starting at Washington, D.C., he cast his gaze due east. To Jerusalem.

"Oh, holy city of Zion. God's glittering jewel," he murmured. "God said the Temple shall be rebuilt . . . and so it shall." Rejuvenated, he turned away from the map. "Rise to your feet, boy, and start acting like the man of God that you are."

As Braxton shoved himself upright, a disembodied voice came over the telephone intercom. "They just brought Eliot Hopkins into the waiting room, sir."

Pleased, MacFarlane turned to his subordinate. "Show the museum director into the office. And make sure you give him a hearty Rosemont welcome."

CHAPTER 23

"How is it that you know so much about Moses and his Egyptian roots?" Edie inquired as she and Caedmon waited for the computer to boot up.

The hotel night clerk, a good-natured student at the nearby George Mason School of Law, had given them access to a computer in the back office. More a storage alcove than a true office, the room was stacked with plastic bins and boxes. Sitting side by side at the computer, Caedmon in the lone swivel chair, Edie perched on a bin, they were there to cyber sleuth. Although what Caedmon thought he'd find was a mystery to her.

"For a brief time, I dabbled in Egyptology while an undergraduate student at Oxford," Caedmon said in response to her question. "That was before I became thoroughly infatuated with the Knights Templar and jumped ship, as you Yanks are prone to say."

"The Knights Templar? Yeah, I can see that." Volunteering a personal tidbit of her own, she said, "I've got a master's degree in women's studies."

Broadly grinning, Caedmon winked at her. "Nearly as obscure a course of study as medieval history. And this business with taking the digital photographs at the Hopkins Museum?"

"A girl's got to make a living somehow."

Enjoying the flirtatious banter, she wondered if anything would come of it. Because of the near miss at the National Gallery, they'd decided against separate rooms. *Would he put the moves on her once the bed covers were turned down?* Imagining what that might be like, she stared at his hands, admiring the raised pattern of veins. She'd seen those hands before. In Florence on Michelangelo's *David*.

Admittedly intrigued by the brainy, street-smart man with the masculine hands, she decided to pry the lid a bit higher. "Earlier today you said something about being on a book tour."

"I recently wrote a book about the Egyptian mystery cults. Which permits me to put the word *author* on my curriculum vitae."

"That would make you—what?—a historian?"

Caedmon keyed in the logon code given to them by the front desk clerk. "Actually, I prefer to think of myself as a rehistorian."

"Last time I looked, that particular word hadn't made it to the pages of Webster's."

"Nor the Oxford English Dictionary. But seeing as there's no word to accurately describe what I do, I was forced to improvise."

"And just how does a rehistorian differ from your standard garden-variety historian?"

"An historian gathers, examines, and interprets the material evidence that remains from the near and distant past," Caedmon replied as he pulled up the Google home page. "In contrast, a rehistorian reveals that which has remained hidden from view, scholarship and speculation going hand in hand."

She smiled. "Well, you did lay claim to being an iconoclast."

"So I did. But enough about me." Leaning forward, he retrieved the pad of blank notepaper lying on top of the desk, the Holiday Inn logo stamped across the top border. He then removed a pen from his breast pocket. "I want you to tell me every pertinent detail you can recall from your earlier ordeal."

"You mean at the Hopkins Museum?" When he nodded, she propped her chin on her balled fist, the memories admittedly convoluted. "Well, I already told you about the ring with the Jerusalem cross. But what I didn't tell you is that right after he murdered Dr. Padgham, the killer called someone on his cell phone. I counted seven digital beeps, so it had to be a local call."

Caedmon scribbled the words *D.C. phone call* on the pad of paper.

"And I remember that the killer said something about going to 'London at nineteen hundred hours.'" Edie bracketed the last five words with air quotation marks. "Or maybe that was the cop who mentioned London. I'm not sure. Sorry. I don't remember. No! Wait!" Excited, Edie slapped her palm against the desktop. "The killer mentioned a place called Rosemont."

"Let me make certain that I have this correct: D.C. phone call, London nineteen hundred hours, and Rosemont." When she nodded, he ripped the sheet of paper from the pad.

"Now what?" Edie scooted the green bin closer to the desk so she could better see the computer monitor.

"Now, we delve into the abyss."

Edie nudged him in the arm with her elbow. "Thanks for that bit of heightened drama. Like I wasn't scared enough already."

Caedmon glanced first at his arm, then at her face. For several seconds they wordlessly stared at one another, two strangers drawn together by a trio of seemingly unconnected clues.

As she continued to gaze into Caedmon's blue eyes, Edie detected a fire. A passion. But for what, she had no idea. History. Religion. The occult sciences. Hard to tell.

The first to break eye contact, Caedmon typed the words Rosemont + D.C. into the search field. "Since the London reference is too vague, we'll start with this."

"You know, I remember the good ol' days when everyone used to have what was quaintly referred to as a 'private life.'"

"Yes, little did Orwell imagine that Big Brother would come in the guise of a desktop computer."

"Looks like we've got a hit," she exclaimed a half second later, pointing to the computer screen. "It's a Wikipedia entry for Rosemont Security Consultants." Quickly, she scanned the brief description. Then, baffled, she turned to Caedmon. "Rosemont is some sort of security firm headquartered in Washington."

Caedmon clicked on the entry. To her dismay, only one scant paragraph appeared. Caedmon hit the *Print* button and the HP printer whirred to life.

Edie read the particulars aloud. "'Founded in 2006 by former Marine Corps colonel Stanford MacFarlane, Rosemont is one of several security consulting firms created in the wake of the Afghan and Iraqi conflicts. Specializing in security consulting, stability operations, and tactical support, Rosemont has security contracts in twenty-two nations worldwide.'" As the information began to sink in, Edie's shoulders slumped. "A security consulting firm . . . that's a polite way of saying that Rosemont specializes in mercenaries for hire."

"So it would seem." Caedmon typed a new entry into the search field. "Damn. Rosemont Security Consultants doesn't maintain a Web page. Although I shouldn't be surprised, given that such companies prefer to operate out of the public eye."

"You know what this means, don't you? It means that we're not dealing with one or two armed bad men. We're dealing with an entire army of—"

"We don't know that," Caedmon interjected, still the voice of reason. "Padgham's killer may simply be in the employ of Rosemont Security Consultants. It in no way implies that the firm had anything to do with Padgham's murder or the subsequent theft of the Stones of Fire."

Suddenly recalling something she'd failed to mention, Edie threw her right arm into the air, waving it to catch the teacher's attention. "One last premature leap, okay? I remember that the killer asked to speak to 'the colonel.'" She snatched the printed sheet of paper out of Caedmon's hands. Turning it toward him, she underlined the first sentence of the Wikipedia entry with her index finger. "It says here that the man who founded Rosemont Security Consultants is an ex–Marine colonel by the name of Stanford MacFarlane. Do you think there's a link? That this might be who the killer called on his cell phone?"

"Possibly," Caedmon replied, obviously not one to leap without looking. He quickly typed the words Stanford + MacFarlane into the search engine. A dozen entries popped up, most of them dating to the year 2006.

"That one," Edie said. "The *Washington Post* article dated March twentieth."

Caedmon clicked on the entry.

In silence, they both stared at the photograph that accompanied the front-page story: a group of military officers, some in dress uniform, some in combat fatigues, linked arm in arm, their heads reverentially bowed.

Edie read the headline aloud. "*Pentagon Top Aide Conducts Weekly Prayer Circle.* And according to the photo tagline, that guy in the middle with the thinning gray buzz cut is Colonel Stanford MacFarlane. I think you better—"

"Righto," Caedmon said, hitting the *Print* button.

As the page printed, they silently read the article. Edie's gaze zeroed in on the last paragraph.

"'Found guilty of violating military regulations regarding religious expression, Colonel MacFarlane was officially relieved of his duties as intelligence advisor to the Undersecretary of Defense. In a news conference held late yesterday, Colonel MacFarlane announced that he intended to operate a private security firm specializing in defense contracts while continuing his ongoing work in the religious organization Warriors of God.'

"MacFarlane may have had a fall from grace, but it appears he bounced into a very lucrative career running a security contracting firm." She derisively snorted, the story a common one in D.C. "Talk about a golden parachute. Last I heard, there's tens of thousands of these armed paramilitary types running around Iraq, most of them ex–Special Forces."

"Even more worrisome, Colonel MacFarlane probably maintains his high-level contacts within the Pentagon. The man did, after all, work for the Undersecretary of Defense."

"I have no idea who's on his Christmas list. All I know is that MacFarlane has at least one inside man working for the Metropolitan Police force. If we go to the authorities, MacFarlane will find us." Edie despondently stared at the newspaper article. "Religious fanatics . . . not good. Try searching for this 'Warriors of God,' will ya?" She tapped her index finger against the computer screen.

A few seconds later, Caedmon found MacFarlane's Web page, the domain address none other than www.warriorsofgod. com. It featured a scathing rant against homosexuality.

"Did God not make Jonathan Padgham as he made you and me?" Caedmon softly whispered.

"Do you think that's the reason why they killed Dr. Padgham, because he was a homosexual?"

A sad look in his eyes, Caedmon slowly shook his head. "No, I don't think that was the reason why they killed Padge. Although in another place, and at another time, that might have been sufficient reason to take his life. But it wasn't the reason this day."

Edie took several deep breaths, opened her mouth to speak, then found she had nothing to say. The day's events had unraveled in such a helter-skelter fashion, she didn't know if she'd ever be able to untangle the skeins.

"While some might dismiss that"—she jutted her chin at the computer screen—"as your run-of-the-mill hateful chatter, it scares the bejesus out of me."

Having had her fill, the diatribe bringing to mind her own religious upbringing, Edie turned away from the computer. Her grandfather had been a hardcore evangelical Christian, fervently believing that the Bible was a literal transcription. From God's mouth to the prophets' ears. And like those towering figures of the Old Testament, Pops had been a rigid taskmaster, daily force-feeding his family an ultraconservative brand of hellfire and eternal damnation. Unable to bear it, her mother had left home at age sixteen. Edie lasted a bit longer, beating a hasty retreat on her eighteenth birthday, managing to escape via a full scholarship to George Washington University. The day she boarded the northbound Greyhound bus was the last day she spoke to her maternal grandfather, Conway Miller.

For the first couple of months, she'd made a halfhearted attempt to keep in touch with her gran, but when the letters were returned, unopened, she got the message. She'd not only left the family, she'd left the flock. She had officially been branded a nonperson. It was another fifteen years before she stepped foot inside a church. The congregation at St. Mattie's was an eclectic mix of female priests, gay deacons, and multiracial couples. People of all stripes and colors, joined together in mutual joy. A blessed gathering. Edie didn't know if it was a form of rebellion against the religion of her youth, but she loved attending Sunday service at St. Mattie's. No doubt, Pops weekly turned up the dirt above his gravesite.

"It would appear that Stanford MacFarlane is the kingfish in a very murky pond," Caedmon said, drawing Edie's attention back to the computer screen. "In my experience, men consumed by a burning hatred, who cloak themselves in God's love, are the most dangerous men under the heavens."

"Just read the newspaper. Religious fanaticism is a global phenomenon."

"Which raises the question . . . why did a group of fanatical Christians steal one of the most sacred of all religious relics?"

Edie turned to Caedmon, shrugging. "I have no idea."

"Nor I. Although I am keen to uncover the answer."

CHAPTER 24

Outside the hotel room window the day had dawned, damp and cold. No glimmer of sunshine to cast even a smidge of false hope. Through the leafless trees Edie stared at the snaking procession of headlights, the early-morning motorists lost in an enviable world of undone Christmas shopping, overdue bills, and holiday office parties.

She sighed, her breath condensing into a cloudy smudge as it struck the plate glass window.

"All is not lost," Caedmon said from behind her, his voice taking her by surprise.

Edie turned to face him, unaware that her glum mood had been so obvious. "Then why am I having so much trouble finding an answer that makes any sense? I don't know about you, but I tossed and turned all night trying to figure out why an ex–Marine colonel, who now owns and operates a mercenaries-for-hire contracting firm, would have had Dr. Padgham murdered?" She held up her hand, forestalling an objection. "I know. In the world of biblical artifacts, the Stones of Fire are out there. But did they have to go and—"

Hearing a thud, Edie rushed over and unlocked the door to their hotel room, snatching the just-delivered, complimentary copy of the *Washington Post* off the doormat. Door closed and relocked, she quickly flipped through the newspaper, ignoring the front-page story regarding the terrorist attack at the National Gallery of Art. Instead, she searched for a headline, a photo, a story tucked away in the Metro section, anything regarding a triple homicide at the Hopkins Museum.

"There's nothing in the paper . . . how can that be? Surely by now someone has found Dr. Padgham and the two dead security guards." She tossed the newspaper onto her unmade bed.

"It's been less than twenty-four hours since the murders were committed," Caedmon calmly reminded her. He had just showered and shaved, which explained why he was half dressed, his red hair matted to his skull. Attired as he was in a white muscle-man tank, Edie could see that he had broad shoulders and a lean, rangy build.

"Yeah, but the night shift should have found the bodies. The guards are supposed to make the rounds of the museum every thirty minutes. And I know for a fact that Linda Alvarez in payroll arrives at the museum at seven o'clock sharp. She has to walk right past Dr. Padgham's office to get to—" Edie stopped, hit with a sudden thought. "Once they access the computer logs at the museum, the police will know that I was at the museum when Dr. Padgham was murdered. Which makes me a fugitive."

One side of Caedmon's mouth quirked upward. "Hardly a fugitive."

"Well, okay, a person of interest. Isn't that what they call them on cop shows?" She peered at her mussed reflection in the wall mirror. Feeling the sting of tears, she turned her back on Caedmon, worried the dam might burst.

Since yesterday afternoon she'd been fighting the onslaught, and, truth be told, she was tired of fighting. Tired of being strong. She just wanted to curl up in her unmade bed, pull the pile of stiff covers over her head, and cry her eyes out. But she couldn't. She barely knew Caedmon Aisquith and if she scared him off, she'd be left to fend for herself. Like she'd had to do so many times before. When she was a kid, her mother used to leave her untended for days on end.

"I'm sorry for getting all emotional on you. I just—" She sank her teeth into her lower lip, struggling to hold back the tears.

As she stood there, her back still turned to him, she heard Caedmon pad over to where she stood. Then she felt a warm hand on her shoulder.

"There's no need to be ashamed of your emotions."

"Easy for you to say . . . you're a redheaded pillar of strength."

"Not true." Gently he turned her in his direction, pulling her into his arms. Because he stood somewhere in the neighborhood of six foot three, her head perfectly fit into the niche of his freckled shoulder.

Edie closed her eyes, drinking in his warmth, his solidness. It felt so good to be held in his arms. Good in a way that made her think of the sleepless night just passed. *How many times had she been tempted to climb out of her bed and get into his?* Too many to count.

Worried she might give in to those wayward urges, sex being the best balm of them all, she extricated herself from his arms.

"I need to call the Hopkins and find out what the heck is going on," she said, striding over to the desk that was wedged between the TV armoire and the dresser drawers.

"Given that we're very much in the dark, I think that's a wise idea. Although make no mention of what you saw or witnessed yesterday at the museum."

Nodding, Edie dialed the main number for the Hopkins Museum. When prompted by the automated phone system, she keyed in the four-digit extension for the payroll department. Hearing a perky voice answer, "Linda Alvarez. How may I help you?" Edie motioned Caedmon to silence.

"Hey Linda, it's Edie Miller. I'm sorry for pestering you so early in the morning, but I really screwed up my time card yesterday . . . oh . . . really? Huh."

Edie placed her palm over the handset, whispering, "According to Linda, I never clocked in yesterday. But I know for a fact that I did."

She removed her hand from the phone. "Silly me, huh? You'd think after all these weeks I'd be able to get it right. I, um, was in and out so quick that I guess I forgot to—" Caedmon mouthed the words *Ask for Padgham.* "Is Dr. Padgham in his office by any chance? He asked me to take some photos for a special project and I was just . . . oh, gosh, that's terrible. Well, um, since he's not at the museum, would you be a dear and walk down the hall to his office for me? I spilled a cup of coffee all over his Persian carpet and I just wanted to make sure the cleaning crew took care of— Yeah, he is a bit of a priss, isn't he? Thanks, Linda."

Again, Edie placed her palm over the handset. "You're not going to believe this. She claims that Dr. Padgham's longtime partner was killed yesterday in a hit-and-run accident and that Dr. Padgham flew to London to take care of the burial arrangements."

Caedmon's blue eyes narrowed. "They're trying to make it appear that Padge is still among the living. My, my, what a tangled web we weave."

A finger to her lips, she again motioned him to silence. "That's great. Well, I, um, gotta run. Thanks a million, Linda. I'll catch you later."

Edie hung up the phone, stunned.

"What did she say about the bloodstained carpet?" Caedmon prompted.

"Per Linda Alvarez's eagle eye, there's no stain on Dr. Padgham's carpet. No bloodied bits of brain matter. No noxious pile of vomit. Nothing but a beautifully vacuumed Persian carpet." Edie pulled out the chair in front of the desk and plopped into it. She glanced at Caedmon's reflection in the wall mirror. "It's a cover-up. A huge, wipe-the-slate-clean cover-up."

"Since the last thing that the thieves want is for the police to become involved, they'll undoubtedly devise an accident for Padge in London. No one on this side of the Atlantic will question Padgham's sudden death except to say that it was a tragic misfortune he didn't see the lorry in the roundabout."

"I think they killed Dr. Padgham's partner."

"More than likely they did," Caedmon replied, his crisp accent noticeably subdued.

"How in God's name did the thugs at Rosemont pull off such a well organized cover-up?"

Caedmon seated himself on the edge of the bed. "With inside help, I dare say. Who captains the ship?"

"At the Hopkins? That would be the museum director, Eliot Hopkins."

"Call him. Set up a meeting for later this morning."

Edie cast him a long, considering glance. "Tell me why exactly I want to set up a meeting with the museum director?"

"In the hopes that Mr. Hopkins will spill some gilded beans."

"You're a fine one for wishful thinking. I can't think of a single reason why Eliot Hopkins would agree to meet with us, let alone give us the straight scoop."

"Try coming at the problem from a different angle. Why would the venerable Mr. Hopkins agree to participate in the theft of a relic he already owned?"

"That's easy. Insurance fraud. He intends to collect on the policy."

"But I suspect that the Stones of Fire was purchased on the black market."

"Meaning the relic wasn't insured," Edie said, beating him to the punch.

"Ergo, Eliot Hopkins had nothing to do with Padge's murder. But I believe he had something to do with the subsequent cover-up."

"But why cover up the murder? It doesn't make any sense."

Still sitting on the edge of the bed, Caedmon crossed one jeans-clad leg over the other. "What would happen if the authorities discovered that the director of the Hopkins Museum knowingly purchased a stolen relic that was smuggled out of its country of origin?"

"In addition to a hefty fine, Eliot Hopkins might be sentenced to prison."

"And in the process, his reputation and good name would be ripped to shreds. All of which makes Eliot Hopkins a very weak link."

"And you want to find out who's yanking his chain," Edie said, the reason for the proposed rendezvous suddenly making sense. "I'm guessing it's the guys at Rosemont. Probably what's-his-name, Colonel MacFarlane. Who else could it be?"

Rather than answer, Caedmon stretched out along the length of the bed, reaching for a tourist map on top of the nightstand, the map part of the welcome-to-your-cookie-cutter-room package. Unfolding the map, he spread it on his lap. "The National Zoo, the National Cathedral, or the Lincoln Memorial. Which of these are you the most familiar with?"

"The zoo," she answered, wondering where he was headed. "It's only a few blocks from my house. When the weather is nice, I like to power-walk it."

Caedmon refolded the map. "Then the National Zoo it is. Tell Mr. Hopkins to be there at ten a.m. Sharp. Do be sure to add that. When dealing with thieves and murderers, it's always best to speak with authority, that being the only way to subjugate a schoolyard bully."

"That or kick him in the nuts," Edie muttered as she reached for the phone.

CHAPTER 25

GEORGETOWN

Eliot Hopkins slowly hung up the telephone.

Just as the monsters at Rosemont Security Consultants had correctly predicted, Edie Miller had initiated contact.

The first piece of a very complicated puzzle had fallen into place.

He sighed, a long, drawn-out breath that was equal parts regret and pain. Regret because he was fond of the quirky and

offbeat Ms. Miller. Pain on account of the cracked rib he
nursed, courtesy of a muscled behemoth with a misplaced
sense of civility, the fiend having grinned and said "Howdy-do"
after administering the unexpected blow. The men of Rosemont wanted his cooperation. And they'd gone about gaining
it in a most primitive fashion.

Why negotiate when one can use fists and threats to achieve
the same end?

Glancing at the imposing John Singer Sargent portrait that
hung above the mantel, Eliot thought he caught the hint of a
smirk on his great-grandfather's stern visage, the coal magnate
having put down more than one strike with clubs and bullets.
Unlike Andrew Carnegie, who suffered from a guilty con-
science, Albert Horatio Hopkins never lost a single night's
sleep worrying about the plight of the men who earned him his
immense fortune. A true Hun, Albert Hopkins raped the West
Virginia mountains of its minerals and raped the people of
their dignity.

Long live King Coal.

Although he was the great-grandson of Albert Hopkins, he
was, also, and more important to his mind, the grandson of
Oliver Hopkins. In his day and age—the feel-good, anything-
goes frenzy before the big crash—Ollie Hopkins had a well-
deserved reputation as a ne'er-do-well adventurer. Turning
his back on the family business, he instead supped with African chieftains, rode wild horses with Mongolian warriors,
and explored the licentious world of the harem with Arab
potentates.

Along the way, he spent a king's ransom searching for the
relics of the Exodus.

As a young boy, Eliot would sit for hours at his grandfather's knee, enthralled by the exciting tales that rivaled the
adventure books of his youth. His particular favorite had been
the time that his grandfather, disguised as an Ottoman Turk,
had tunneled into the bowels of the Temple Mount, only to be
discovered by Sheikh Khalil, the hereditary guardian of the
Dome of the Rock. Chased through the streets of Jerusalem by

an angry mob, his grandfather made his getaway in a hijacked motor yacht harbored in the port of Jaffa.

Considered a wastrel by his father, Oliver was eventually disinherited. Penniless when he died, Oliver left his favorite grandson the fruits of all his labors—an immense collection of artifacts and relics mined over the course of some fifty years. The collection became the cornerstone of the Hopkins Museum of Near Eastern Art, the museum founded in homage to the man who'd given Eliot the only familial affection he ever knew.

His grandfather also bequeathed to him a magnificent obsession . . . the Stones of Fire.

It'd taken decades of dangled carrots and very large bribes, but he finally found it.

Only to lose it in the blink of a jaded eye.

Had he been a religious man, he might have thought it God's punishment for daring the unthinkable. Certainly, he'd been a fool to entrust Jonathan Padgham with the holy relic. But the man had been an expert on Near East antiquities, and Eliot needed to verify that what he'd found in the sands of Iraq was in fact the fabled Stones of Fire.

Blinded by his obsession, he never considered that there were others even more intent on finding the treasures of the Bible. Men unfettered by the rule of law.

Wearily, Eliot rose to his feet. There being no time to ponder the ethics of the situation, he walked over to a paneled door on the far side of the rosewood library. He pressed a hidden latch and the door swung open. He turned on the light in the small, windowless room. In turn, he surveyed each glass case, his collection of antique weaponry a private passion. Out of respect for his thirteen-year-old daughter, Olivia, who had an unnatural fear of guns, he kept his collection out of sight.

Pausing in front of a velvet-lined case, he briefly considered the Colt revolver once owned by the gunslinger Buffalo Bill.

In the end, he settled on the World War II–era Walther. The handgun of choice for the German SS.

Over the years, he'd dealt with greedy dealers, ruthless brokers, and pompous curators. Last night was the first time he'd come face-to-face with religious zealots, the interaction shocking. One could not reason with such men, for they served but one master.

One could only acquiesce.

CHAPTER 26

"Do you think we're being followed?" Edie asked, glancing into the side mirror of a parked car.

Caedmon waited until the cross light at Connecticut Avenue turned yellow. Then, cinching his hand around her elbow, he hustled her across the street toward the main entrance to the National Zoo on the opposite side of the intersection. A few seconds later they passed the two bronze lions that stood guard at the gated entrance.

"If we are being followed, our pursuers have successfully faded into the proverbial woodwork."

Edie shivered, the previous day's snow having turned into a chill-laden drizzle. She moved closer to Caedmon, the two of them huddled beneath a black umbrella they'd purchased en route. Passing the Visitor Center, she peered at the 180-degree reflection cast by the bank of glass doors. No surprise that the zoo grounds were eerily deserted; animal watching was not a big draw in December. But then, they weren't there to see the sights. They were there to meet with the man who'd illegally purchased the Stones of Fire, setting into motion yesterday's brutal train of events.

"Does your family live in the area?" Caedmon conversationally inquired. Throughout their subway ride from Arlington, he'd maintained a steady stream of pleasant chitchat. On to his tricks, Edie assumed the light fare was more for her benefit than his—Caedmon's way of alleviating her all-too-obvious dread. Little did he know that personal questions elicited a similar response.

"Um, my mother and father were both killed in a boating accident off the coast of Florida," she answered, the lie well honed from twenty-five years of sharpening. Approaching the Small Mammal House, she gestured to the walkway on the right, the zoo grounds a maze of pathways that wound through what was surprisingly hilly terrain. "It was Labor Day weekend and a drunk in a speedboat rammed right into them. I was only eleven years old when it happened."

Usually she embroidered the tale, going into great detail as to how the nonexistent boater only had to spend two years in prison. But today, for some inexplicable reason, she felt guilty about the fabrication. Although why she should feel any guilt was a mystery. Shame, yes. Guilt, no. After all, it wasn't her fault that her father was listed on her birth certificate as *Unknown* or that her mother had been a junkie, never able to lose her taste for smack. When her mother OD'd, Edie had been forced to spend two and a half years in the Florida foster care system. A kindhearted social worker had taken an interest in her case, going the extra two miles to track down her maternal grandparents in Cheraw, South Carolina. Edie never spoke of the thirty nightmarish months spent on the foster care merry-go-round. Not to anyone. Some things a person couldn't, or shouldn't, share with another human being.

Seeing a vaporous cloud approach, Caedmon waited until a red-faced man decked out in winter Lycra jogged past. A few moments later, he solicitously took her by the elbow, steering her clear of an icy patch. "Who took care of you?"

"Oh, I, um, went to live with my grandparents in South Carolina. Pops and Gran were great. Really, really great," she said with a big fake smile. Uncomfortable with the lie, she feigned a sudden interest in the leafless shrubbery planted along the low-slung retaining wall. Winter had its claws dug deep; the nearby trees and plantings were covered in a crystal shroud. Most of the animals had taken to ground. As they passed the tamarin cage, there wasn't a primate in sight.

"South Carolina . . . how interesting. One would think you'd have a more pronounced accent. And you've been in Washington for how long?"

Wishing he'd cease and desist, she said, "It's coming up on the twenty-year mark. What anniversary is that? Crystal? I'm not sure."

"I believe that would be china," he replied, intently watching her out of the corner of his eye.

Edie cleared her throat, wondering if she'd laid it on too thick about Pops and Gran. As happened with all new acquaintances, she feared that he was on to her.

Hearing a branch suddenly snap, Caedmon momentarily paused as the silence filled with several unidentified screeches. Evidently satisfied that the noises were not man-made, he said. "I'm curious . . . why did you get a degree in women's studies?"

"Why do you want to know? You're not a closet chauvinist, are you?"

"Not in the least."

Satisfied with his reply, Edie shrugged. "Since someone else was footing the bill for my education, I studied what interested me. At the time I was interested in the role of women in American society." What she didn't tell him was that, given her background, she wanted to find out why women made the choices they did. "I had an internship at a nonprofit, but because of budget constraints it didn't pan into a paying gig. Luckily, I found gainful employment at a downtown photo shop." At the time she hadn't known squat about photography, having charmed her way into the job. But she learned quickly, enamored with the way that photography could be used to manipulate the real world, to erase the ugliness.

"And how long have you been working as a photographer?"

"Gees, what are you, a Spanish inquisitor?" Edie retorted, determined to end the personal interrogation. "You know, I usually love the zoo, but today it's got creepy written all over it."

Caedmon slowed his step as they wound their way through what looked to be an impenetrable chasm, with huge buff-colored boulders, a full story in height, lining the pathway. She wondered if the man at her side was thinking what she was thinking, that this would be an excellent place for a gunman to hide.

A few moments later, they emerged from the stone-lined walkway and approached the caged hillside set aside for the Mexican wolves, the designated meeting place with Eliot Hopkins. To the right side of the outdoor exhibit, a lone man bundled in a wool topcoat sat on a park bench, a cup of Starbucks coffee clutched in his gloved hand.

"There he is," Edie said in hushed whisper, fearful her voice might carry. "I don't know about you, but I fully intend to give the SOB a grilling."

At hearing that, Caedmon jerked his head in her direction.

"What? Why are you looking at me like that? It's called good cop/bad cop."

Grabbing her by the upper arm, Caedmon drew her to his side. "Now is not the time for us to be out of step with one another," he hissed in her ear. "We merely want to tickle the man."

"Yeah, before we move in for the kill."

CHAPTER 27

"Figuratively speaking," Edie amended.

"I most certainly hope so." Concerned his companion may have watched too police dramas on the telly, Caedmon tightened his grip on her arm. Like a harried parent with an unruly child.

Surreptitiously, he glanced to and fro. Rock-laden, treed, and hilly, the surrounding terrain could easily camouflage a hunter on the prowl. Attired in her red and purple plaid skirt, Edie made an easy target. Although warning bells did not yet toll, they did tinkle, the place having about it a sinister air.

As they approached the bareheaded man seated on the park bench, Caedmon closed the black brolly he'd been holding aloft, the wintry rain having dwindled to a mere spit. He hooked the curved handle on his bent arm.

"A most interesting place to meet, betwixt and between these two beautiful creatures of prey," Eliot Hopkins remarked, slowly rising to his feet. He gestured first to the lone wolf that warily prowled the fenced hillside beside them. Then he pointed a gloved hand to the bald eagle perched aloft on the opposite hillock. "Did you know that the eagle has been a symbol of war since Babylonian times?"

With his thatch of wavy white hair, patrician features, and ruddy red cheeks, Caedmon thought Eliot Hopkins a grandfatherly-looking man. Dressed in English tweed, he could have passed for a country squire. A harmless dolt who, if prompted, could natter for hours on end about shifting weather patterns and the breeding of Leicester Longwool sheep.

"How about canning the bullshit," Edie retorted, ignoring his earlier admonition. "Because of you, and your boundless greed, Jonathan Padgham is dead! And don't give me any bunk about him going to London to take care of funeral arrangements. I know what happened yesterday at the museum."

"Jonathan's death is most unfortunate and, I am sad to say, entirely my fault," the museum director readily confessed, a morose look in his rheumy gray eyes. "I had no idea that Jonathan was in danger. Although once the deed was done, I had no choice but to assist in the cover-up."

"I'm curious as to how you became involved with such a bloodthirsty gang of men," Caedmon remarked. "You don't strike me as running in the same circle."

Smiling ever so slightly, Hopkins nodded. "Shortly after I acquired the Stones of Fire I was approached by a private consortium interested in buying the breastplate at an exorbitant price. When I refused to sell the relic, the consortium resorted to blackmail, demanding that I relinquish custody of the breastplate or they would alert the SAFE organization."

Edie nudged him in the arm. "Who or what is SAFE?"

"Saving Antiquities for Everyone is a nonprofit group that monitors the international trade in stolen or secretly excavated antiquities."

"And that would have created quite the public scandal," she correctly deduced. "So why didn't you give the consortium the Stones of Fire? Why take the risk of being exposed?"

"I called their bluff, knowing full well that if SAFE became involved, the consortium would lose all chance of getting their hands on my precious relic. A tragic miscalculation, as it turned out."

"Proving that one cannot trump the devil," Caedmon muttered, infuriated that the deadly game had cost an innocent man his life.

"I can assure you that if I knew several weeks ago what I know now, I would have—"

"Oh, puh-*leeze*!" Edie interjected. "You sound like someone running for public office." She folded her arms over her chest, a stern headmistress in black leather. "I just don't get it. Why would this so-called consortium resort to cold-blooded murder to get the Stones of Fire? It's just a bit of gold with twelve gemstones."

A drawn-out pause ensued as the museum director evidently debated whether to answer. "In and of itself, you're probably correct," he finally replied. "But when used in concert with that other holy relic, the Stones of Fire become a conduit to God. Thus making them a prerequisite for the larger prize."

. . . that other holy relic . . .

. . . a prerequisite for the larger prize.

Caedmon's mouth slackened, the realization hitting him like a fist to the belly.

"I don't believe it . . . they're actually going after the Ark."

"The Ark?" Edie's gaze ricocheted between him and Eliot Hopkins. "As in the Ark of the Covenant?"

"None other," Hopkins confirmed.

Still in a state of shock, Caedmon pressed harder. "How do you know that the consortium is searching for the Ark?"

"I know because *I* was searching for the lost Ark. Two days before the theft at the museum, my Georgetown home was burglarized. Imagine my surprise when the only thing stolen was my research notes. For some thirty years I've hunted down clues, sent excavation teams into remote areas of the Middle East, continuing the work my grandfather began but could not finish."

"Good God! Do you mean to say that you're Oliver Hopkins's grandson?" Considered by scholars to be daft as a brush, Oliver Hopkins spent a fortune searching for the Ark of the Covenant during the early part of the twentieth century—to no avail; the wealthy adventurer barely escaped the Holy Land with his head intact.

"I came considerably closer to finding the elusive jewel in the biblical crown than my grandfather did. And in so doing, I knew that if I was to avoid the curse of Bethshemesh, I had to first find the Stones of Fire."

Edie derisively snickered. "The curse of Bethshemesh? Who are you, a character in an Indiana Jones movie?"

"Hardly," Caedmon replied, the conversation about to darken several shades. "The punishment for accidentally touching the Ark of the Covenant was a very painful and instantaneous death, Yahweh having a beastly temper. That said, in the book of Samuel, a cautionary tale is recounted about the city of Bethshemesh, where Yahweh indiscriminately slaughtered fifty thousand of the residents as punishment for the handful of men who, seized with curiosity, dared to peer inside the Ark."

"Jesus," she softly swore. "God did that?"

"Elsewhere the Bible speaks of the Ark leveling whole mountains, parting rivers, annihilating enemy armies, and destroying fortified cities. Those who doubted the Ark's power often found themselves covered in cancerous tumors or painful burns," he informed her, knowing that most people preferred their God sanitized, the ugliness of the Old Testament swept under a heavenly carpet.

"It sounds more like a weapon than a religious artifact."

"The Ark of the Covenant was, to use the modern parlance, a weapon of mass destruction, enabling the ragtag Israelites to conquer the Holy Land. Shielded with the Stones of Fire, the high priest could channel and control all of that explosive energy."

"Thus making the Stones of Fire a 'prerequisite' to finding the Ark of the Covenant."

Having stood silent, Eliot Hopkins rejoined the conversation. "Now do you see why I'm convinced that my mysterious consortium is intent on hunting bigger game? Think of the power contained within that precious gold chest. The Ark radiated divine power and might. And if one had a mind to communicate with the celestial spheres, the Ark could summon forth angels and even manifest the Almighty himself."

The enraptured expression on Eliot Hopkins's withered visage belonged to that of a man obsessed. Caedmon knew the look well, having once been an obsessed man himself, his fascination with the Knights Templar having bordered on the fanatic—which was why, long years ago, he'd been ousted from Oxford.

"A lot of people would say that the supposed power of the Ark was nothing but a fanciful myth used to entertain the Hebrews who gathered around the evening campfire," Edie argued.

"And there are those who claim that God is dead. I, however, am not one of them."

"So, what happened to the Ark? Was it plundered? Was it lost? Or was it destroyed?" Edie asked in rapid-fire succession.

Eliot Hopkins lifted his wool-clad shoulders in an eloquent shrug. "The pages of the Old Testament don't give so much as a hint. We know only that Moses constructed the Ark in the fifteenth century B.C.; five centuries later, King Solomon built a lavish temple to house the Ark; and sometime prior to the construction of the Second Temple in 516 B.C., the Ark vanished, seemingly into the dust of history."

"Surely, there's a theory or two to explain its disappearance," Edie persisted.

"Most biblical historians concur that there are five probable scenarios to explain the Ark's disappearance," Caedmon replied, beating the older man to the starting gate. "The first of these concerns Menelik, King Solomon's son with the Queen of Sheba. Those who adhere to that particular theory have postulated that Menelik stole the Ark from the Temple around 950 B.C. and took it to Ethiopia, where it resides to this day."

"And let's not forget the theory put forth in *Raiders of the Lost Ark*," Edie said, smirking. "You know, that the Ark is in Egypt."

"A valid theory, as it turns out. Its adherents believe that a few years after Solomon's death, the Ark was raided by the Egyptian pharaoh Shishak and taken to his newly constructed capital of Tanis. Then there are the three remaining theories, which involve the Ark being plundered by the Babylonians, the Greeks, or the Romans, take your pick."

"And I did, painstakingly considering each of those theories in turn," Eliot Hopkins informed them. "As you may or may not know, there are nearly two hundred references to the Ark in the pages of the Old Testament. Most of those references concern the time period between the Hebrew exodus from Egypt and the construction of Solomon's Temple. All of which led me to surmise that the Ark of the Covenant disappeared shortly after Solomon built his famous temple."

Proving herself a sure-footed student, Edie said, "Then the Ark was either stolen by Menelik or plundered by Shishak."

"I know for a fact that the Ark does not reside in Ethiopia," the older man quietly asserted.

Hearing that, Caedmon deduced that Eliot Hopkins had very deep pockets. The political situation in Ethiopia was dicey, to say the least; Obtaining permission to mount a thorough search would have been bloody expensive.

"So that means Shishak stole the Ark and it's buried in the pharaoh's tomb."

"Not necessarily," the older man said in reply to Edie's deduction. "Some years back, during a trip to the Middle East, a group of Bedouin traders told me a most fascinating tale of an English crusader who, en route between Palestine and Egypt, discovered a gold chest buried in the Plain of Esdraelon amid the ruins of what had once been an Egyptian temple."

"I've heard this story," Caedmon murmured, hit squarely with the ghostly specter of his Oxford days.

"Careful, Mr. Aisquith. In this game, a little knowledge can be a dangerous thing." Eliot Hopkins smiled, a kindly man offering a sage word of advice. "If you are familiar with the tale, then you undoubtedly have guessed at the final resting place of the Ark of the Covenant."

Refusing to take the bait, Caedmon went on the offensive. "Why are you being so forthcoming with us? For years you've gone to great lengths to keep your pursuit of the Ark a secret, and I'm at a loss to understand your sudden burst of loquaciousness."

Grimacing, the museum director slid his gloved hand inside his wool topcoat. "Because it is inconsequential whether you know or don't know."

"And why is that?"

Eliot Hopkins removed his hand from his coat, a German-made Walther pistol clenched in his fist. "Because I have been ordered to kill you."

CHAPTER 28

With only a wolf and an eagle to bear witness to their deaths, Caedmon affected a calm he didn't feel. "I say, old boy. That's not very cricket of you."

"You're a fool to think you can get away with murdering us," Edie hissed, tacking her vessel in an entirely different direction.

One side of Eliot Hopkins's mouth lifted in a rueful half smile. "Killing you and your charming companion will be the least of my crimes."

"You're actually going to kill us in cold blood all because of some religious artifact? Gold stuff! That's all it is."

"None of the biblical artifacts mentioned in the Bible can compare with the Ark of the Covenant," Hopkins whispered, the gun unsteadily wavering in his gloved hand. "The Ark contains the majesty and glory of Yahweh. It alone could inspire or destroy a nation."

"Or a man," Caedmon murmured, the Ark about to claim its next two victims.

Raising the gun a few inches higher, Hopkins pointed it at Edie's chest. "I do hope you will forgive my actions, but if I don't comply with their orders, they'll kill my daughter."

"'They' being your mysterious consortium, aka the Warriors of God."

Despite her brave façade, Caedmon felt the tremble in Edie's shoulder. Although he was tempted to put a comforting arm around her shoulder, he refrained. Instead, he said, "I can see to it that no harm comes to your daughter."

"Olivia presently attends boarding school in Switzerland." As he spoke, tears welled in Eliot Hopkins's eyes. "My hands are tied. I have but one child. She alone is my hope for the future. My legacy."

"I can contact Interpol," Caedmon pressed, using the only gambit he had to play. "Within the half hour your daughter will be placed in protective custody."

"Entrust my daughter to strangers more than four thousand miles away?" The museum director wearily shook his head. "You ask the impossible."

Refusing to surrender, Caedmon pressed a bit harder. "Yesterday afternoon, in your museum, Jonathan Padgham was senselessly slain. Let us stop this madness before anyone else is killed."

"I can't stop the madness," the older man croaked, barely audible. "I am truly sorry. I have no choice but to—"

Quite unexpectedly, a lion roared in the distance, a deep-throated bawl that rumbled through the leafless trees and echoed off the ice-laden boulders. The stentorian bellow momentarily distracted the elderly angel of death as Eliot Hopkins nervously glanced about.

Caedmon had no way of knowing whether it was divine intervention or a bit of serendipity. He only knew it was the moment to act. Before the window slammed shut.

Carpe diem, he silently invoked, his thighs, buttocks, and biceps all tightening as he yanked the closed umbrella from where it hung on his forearm, hurling it like a spear. That done, he shoved Edie out of the line of fire, pushing her behind a massive cement trash receptacle. He watched as the umbrella hit its mark, the stainless steel tip hitting Eliot Hopkins square in the chest.

Stunned by the force of the unexpected blow, Hopkins dropped the handgun to the pavement, where it skittered along the icy surface.

About to retrieve the gun, Caedmon stopped in his tracks as a bullet whizzed past in the wrong direction, slamming into Eliot Hopkins's heart and killing him on impact.

There was a sniper on the hillside!

It had been a setup. None of them was to have left the zoo alive.

Knowing that in combat, he who hesitates is lost, Caedmon lurched behind the trash receptacle, using his body to shield Edie's quivering backside.

"I'm beginning to think that 'the land of the free' means free to shoot and kill," he muttered against her ear.

"He's on the hill, above the bald eagle, isn't he?"

Caedmon nodded, knowing they'd been followed by a professional assassin, the man's movements so smooth, so subtle that he'd tracked them into the zoo, then faded into the landscape. If they showed themselves, he would expertly fire two kill shots. Men trained to kill at a distance did so without remorse or regret, the action no different than breathing.

Edie peered at him from over her shoulder, a stricken expression on her face. "Please tell me that you've got a plan."

"I don't," he truthfully replied. Although he had better come up with a plan bloody quick. They had only a few seconds before the sniper readjusted his gun sights.

Briefly he considered lunging forward and retrieving the Walther pistol. Just as quickly, he rejected the idea, certain he'd take a lead bullet to the head for his troubles.

"May I take a peek inside your tote?" he asked, tugging on the canvas bag she had clutched to her midsection.

Edie wordlessly complied, opening the tote for his inspection. With no time for niceties, he riffled through the bag's contents, removing her khaki-colored waistcoat.

"Perfect." Reaching beside him, he grabbed a fistful of snow.

"What are you doing?"

"Weighting the garment so I can toss it through the air. If we're lucky, the sniper will see the sudden motion, take aim, and fire. The ruse won't gain us more than a few precious seconds, but that's all the time we'll need to get our arses behind those rocks." With a lift of the chin, he indicated the jumble of boulders some twenty meters from their current position.

If she had misgivings, and no doubt she did, she kept them to herself.

A brave woman, indeed.

Hoping the venture didn't prove deadly, Caedmon quickly

tied the ends of the waistcoat into a knot, securing the icy ball
of snow. Silently mouthing the words *On three*, he counted to
two before tossing the waistcoat through the air. A perfectly
bowled cricket delivery.

There being no time to observe the arc and descent of the
makeshift decoy, Caedmon snatched Edie by the hand. Bending at the waist, making himself as small a target as possible,
he charged toward the clustered rocks. Behind him, he heard a
bullet ping off the metal handrail that fronted the Mexican
wolf exhibit.

The ruse had worked.

With Edie in tow, he dodged behind a waist-high boulder.
Assuming a crouched position, they pressed themselves against
the oversized stone.

Quickly, he glanced from side to side. In the hilly terrain
above the bald eagles, he thought he detected a blurred figure
in a black anorak. A deadly specter on the prowl.

"It would be suicide for us to retrace our steps to the main
entrance," he said in a hushed tone, fearful that if they didn't
find another means of escape they would meet the same fate as
the dead museum director.

Edie lifted her head a scant few inches, enabling her to
furtively glance about. Grimacing, she swiped the base of her
palm across the trickle of blood that oozed from a scrape on
her upper cheek. With the same hand, she gestured uphill.

"If we can get to the Think Tank at the top of the hill, there's
a path leading down to Rock Creek. This time of year, the
creek should be low enough for us to cross on foot."

"And the advantage to this escape route?"

"It's the quickest way out of here." Again she swiped at the
scrape on her upper cheek. A blooded huntswoman.

He took a moment to consider the merits of her plan. Although the uphill route would put more strain on lung and leg,
the pavement was hedged with clustered bunches of reedy
bamboo, which would provide excellent cover. If they navigated quickly and carefully, they could remain hidden from
sight. Assuming the sniper had no cohorts with him.

Caedmon deferred to her plan with a quick nod.

Once again snatching her by the hand, he led the way, running toward the uphill fork in the pathway. He considered it a good sign that he heard no whizzing bullets. However, the screeching bald eagle did not bode well, signaling that the sniper was in pursuit.

Midway up the hill, Edie started to lag, her exhalations loud and uneven. There being no time to rally the troops, he yanked her toward him. Letting go of her hand, he slung his left arm around her shoulder, pulling her to his side, forcing her to keep pace with him.

"You can catch your breath once we're free and clear of our assailant."

Propelled, no doubt, by a burst of fearful adrenaline, Edie managed to hasten her step.

A few seconds later, the path leveled out.

"The Think Tank is that stone building straight ahead of us," Edie informed him, pointing to a quaint structure straight out of a Thomas Hardy novel.

Pulling her behind a stacked stone wall that oozed frozen icicles, he surveyed the area. Dismayed, he could see that they'd have to navigate a long stretch of open pavement, with no trees, rocks, or bamboo to obscure their movements.

"There's thirty meters of open terrain between here and the Think Tank. Will you be able to sprint that far?"

She nodded. Then, sinking her fingers into his forearm, "Caedmon, I'm afraid. Really, really afraid."

"No disgrace in that. I'm feeling a bit unmanned myself."

Her brown eyes opened wide. "You're kidding, right? You're like one of those guys in the Light Brigade."

"Yes, well, we know what happened to them, don't we?"

"No, what happened?"

"Nearly half the brigade perished in the ill-fated charge." Not giving her time to contemplate the dire significance of that bit of British lore, he snatched hold of her hand and took off running. His gait the longer, she had to move her legs twice as fast to keep up. A lone zookeeper, attired in wellies and a pair of brown coveralls, rode past in a covered golf cart with several buckets of animal feed lashed into the cargo space with bungee cords.

"I'm halfway tempted to hitch a ride," Edie muttered, huffing heavily as she spoke. Barely able to raise her arm, she pointed to a grotto-like area. "There's the path . . . on the other side of the building."

"Right." He veered in the direction indicated, the path being a set of wood-planked steps that snaked down the side of a very steep hillside. At the bottom of the wooden steps, Caedmon could see a deserted car park.

"Rock Creek is on the other side of the parking lot," Edie informed him between two noisy gasps of breath. "Once we cross the creek, we should be able to hike our way up to Beach Drive, where we can hopefully hail a cab."

Caedmon redirected his gaze beyond the car park. Through a dense grove of leafless tress, he saw a winding creek burdened with tumbled rock. And though he couldn't see it, he could hear a busy motorway on the far side of the ravine, autos speeding along at a fast clip. Somehow, he had his doubts about hailing a cab.

Keeping his reservations to himself, he led the way down the wooden steps.

They made fast time of it down the steps, which were layered in a broad pattern that allowed for an easy descent down the steep hill.

As they neared the bottom, Edie murmured an apology, her heavy-heeled boots repeatedly making a rhythmic thump on the weathered wood.

"It might help if you—" He stopped in mid-suggestion, suddenly picking up the reverberation of an unseen footfall.

He peered over his shoulder, catching a flash of motion at the top of the steps. His visibility impaired by the thick growth of shrubs and trees on either side of the steps, he had no way of knowing if the third party was a zookeeper, a bystander, or a cold-blooded killer.

"We have company," he whispered in Edie's ear, motioning her to silence.

Frantically, she glanced behind her. He wasn't certain, but he thought she mouthed the words *Oh, God*.

A few seconds later, reaching the bottom of the steps, they crossed a paved road. On the left side of the pavement was the deserted car park; on the right, an abandoned greenhouse with sheets of torn plastic eerily waving in the breeze. In between lay a wild hinterland that hadn't seen scythe or blade in many a year.

"This way," Edie hissed, lifting her skirt to knee height as she tramped through the underbrush.

Caedmon fell into step, reaching over top of her head to brush aside hanging limbs and scraggly foliage. Although the brambles and briars caught on hands, face, and clothing, the overgrowth provided excellent camouflage. Caedmon was still unsure who followed them down the steps, the intruder having yet to reveal himself.

Reaching the creek embankment, they came to an abrupt halt.

"Bloody hell," he muttered, surprised to see that the creek was far more than the tinkle of water he'd foolishly envisioned. Instead of a tinkle, a calf-high torrent of water raged past, creating frothy whitecaps as it hit ice-covered rocks. "If we attempt to ford this so-called creek, we'll break our—"

Just then, a tree limb plunged into the water, severed from its parent by a high-speed bullet.

As though pushed by the hand of God, the two of them barreled into the frigid creek, any lingering concerns about the wisdom of crossing the treacherous waters shoved to the wayside.

Within seconds of braving the creek, Edie lost her footing, her arms windmilling in the air as she attempted to regain her balance. Caedmon grabbed hold of her tartan skirt, preventing her from pitching forward. Yanking her upright, he released the fistful of fabric only to shove his hand into her waistband, that being the most expedient way to keep her from lurching into what was fast becoming numbingly cold water. Thusly linked, they sloshed across the aptly named Rock Creek.

"Oh, God!" Edie shrieked as a nearby rock shattered from the impact of another bullet, splashing them both in the face.

Retreat not an option, they emerged from the creek, skirt and pant legs saturated with cold water. Their goal being the nearby motorway, they clawed their way up the embankment.

After one near tumble and an ungainly scramble to keep from falling backward, they reached the top.

In front of them loomed a four-lane thoroughfare with cars whizzing by at forty miles per hour.

"There's a cab!" Edie exclaimed, pointing to a bright yellow vehicle in the distance. "Start waving your arms so the cabbie can see us."

Several feet from where they stood, a bullet embedded itself into the asphalt pavement.

Galvanized into action, Edie ran along the median strip, her arms wildly swinging to and fro. Almost instantly, car horns began to blare, and one motorist rudely gestured as he drove past. Caedmon had no choice but to give chase. Drenched to the knees, with twigs and debris clinging to their garments, they looked like a pair of escaped asylum inmates.

In a reckless show of heroics, Edie stepped into the roadway, frantically hailing the fast-approaching cab.

The driver swerved into a skid, barely managing to brake his vehicle to a screeching halt several feet from where she stood.

Rushing over, she yanked open the back door.

Like a jack-in-the-box, a wide-eyed passenger popped his immaculately groomed head through the opening. With an upraised arm, he prevented her from getting into the vehicle.

"In case you didn't notice, this cab is already taken."

Undeterred, Edie shoved her hand into her tote bag. A second later, she slapped a hundred-dollar bill into the passenger's hand. "Now shut up and move over!"

Cowed into submission, the man obediently slid to the far side of the seat.

CHAPTER 29

"Drop us off at the next corner," Edie ordered the cabdriver, handing him a ten. Still pissed that she'd had to pay a hundred dollars in bribe money to the Beltway bandit, who'd earlier disembarked at a K Street lobbying firm, she grudgingly signaled the driver that he could keep the change.

Having yet to utter a single word, the cabbie stopped in front of McPherson Square; the city park was overrun with homeless men huddled around metal subway grates, their worldly possessions stowed in plastic shopping bags.

No sooner did Caedmon slam the cab door shut than she turned to him. Confused, angered, and more than anything else, terrified, she said, "I can't believe they actually killed Eliot Hopkins."

"Like you, I didn't foresee today's deadly turn of events." Sliding an arm around her shoulders, he led her to one of the vacant benches that rimmed the park. Although they were both soaked to the knee, no one in the park took note of their bedraggled state; more than a few of the benchwarmers were in far worse straits. It was no accident that she'd picked McPherson Square; the downtown park was an excellent place to fade into the city landscape.

"Just as they manipulated yesterday's murder scene at the Hopkins Museum, no doubt Colonel MacFarlane had planned a similar artifice for today's bloodshed."

Edie derisively snorted. "I can see the headlines now . . . 'Love Triangle Turned Deadly.'"

"Or some such tripe." Caedmon's red brows drew together. "I think we're both in need of a fortifying cup of hot coffee," he said, gesturing to the ubiquitous Starbucks, the chain coffeehouse located on the nearby street corner.

"Do you mind if I sit here and wait for you? To be honest, I don't know if I'm capable of putting one waterlogged foot in front of the other."

Caedmon surveyed the park grounds. Not only were there homeless men on nearly every park bench, there were homeless men bundled in sleeping bags, the only thing protecting them from the cold, flat pieces of corrugated cardboard.

"Go on. I'll be perfectly safe. They might look dangerous, but these guys are perfectly harmless," she assured him.

"A bittersweet irony to see so many men living rough while others live in the lap of luxury." He glanced at the nearby Hilton Hotel.

"Yeah, well, unless we can figure out a safe place to lay low, you and I may be reduced to the same plight come nightfall."

"A topic we'll discuss when I return."

Edie nodded, inclined to leave the decision making to Caedmon. Without his quick thinking, she'd be lying in a puddle of her own blood, the second member of the imaginary love triangle. Whether she liked to admit it or not—and she didn't—she needed his protection.

With a backward wave of the hand, Caedmon departed on his coffee run.

"Don't forget the biscotti," she yelled at his backside, the screech earning another wave.

Her legs about to give way, Edie sat down on a vacant park bench. Within moments it began to sleet, pellets of crystallized ice assaulting her person, hitting her on the face, nose, and forehead. She hunched forward, tucking her chin into her chest.

Miserable, she listened to the uneven tattoo of ice striking the wood planks of the weathered bench. With nowhere to run, and fast running out of places to hide, she felt imprisoned in a winter canvas of gray, taupe, and white.

How apropos, she dejectedly thought, her body starting to

go into deep freeze. Her limbs becoming immobile, her thoughts were reduced to a sluggish meander of the nonsensical.

Seeing red instead of winter neutrals, she shoved her hand into her canvas tote bag, retrieving her BlackBerry. Hopefully, she had enough juice to make a local phone call.

She dialed 411.

The days of speaking to a real person a thing of the past, she slowly said, "Rosemont Security Consultants" when prompted by the automated operator. A few seconds later, the same computerized voice recited a seven-digit phone number. Edie hit the 1 key, requesting to be connected.

The call was answered on the first ring. "Rosemont Security Consultants."

Edie was taken aback that the office receptionist was a man, not a woman.

"I want to speak to Stanford MacFarlane," she brusquely demanded, hoping the lackey on the other end picked up on her don't-mess-with-me attitude.

He didn't.

"I'm sorry, but the colonel is unavailable to take any calls at this time. If you would like to leave a—"

"Tell him that Edie Miller is on the line. Trust me. He'll take the call."

The receptionist put her on hold, Edie treated to the annoying strains of elevator music.

Midway into Sinatra's "My Way," the line reengaged.

"Ah, Ms. Miller. What an unexpected surprise." Edie shivered. Stanford MacFarlane was eerily cordial. "I trust that you're feeling—"

"Can the bullshit, MacFarlane. How do you think I feel after watching one of your goons gun down a scared old man?"

"None too well, I suspect. You do know that you're proving a most elusive target." Edie wasn't certain, but she thought she detected a note of grudging respect in his voice.

Disgusted by the thought that she and Caedmon had become some kind of perverted pastime, she said, "I know what you're up to, you sick bastard! Eliot Hopkins told us all about your plan to find the Ark of the—"

From out of nowhere, an unseen hand yanked the Black-
Berry away from her ear.

Craning her neck, Edie was surprised to find Caedmon
standing behind the park bench. In his right hand he held her
BlackBerry, in his left an egg carton carrier of coffee.

Without a word, Caedmon unceremoniously shoved the
cell phone into his jacket breast pocket. Then, acting as though
nothing were even remotely wrong, he handed her a cup of
coffee.

"If I recall correctly, you take two sugars."

Edie's shock turned to outrage.

"Do you know why the British have never rebelled against
the monarchy? Because you're afraid to take action! You're
afraid to say, 'I'm mad as hell and I'm not going to take it any
longer!'"

"Unlike you, I believe that restraint is the better part of
valor."

"Oh, stuff an argyle sock in it, will ya? I'm beginning to
think you love the sound of your own voice."

Caedmon straightened his shoulders, drawing himself to his
full imposing height of six foot three. "Because of your im-
petuousness, we have lost our only advantage. Not only did
you divulge the fact that we know their identities, but you foolishly disclosed the information given to us by the now-deceased
Mr. Hopkins."

"Look, I don't know about you, but I'm sick and tired of
being hunted down like a defenseless animal. And while you
might not give a rat's patootie, I want to know why Colonel
MacFarlane ordered Eliot Hopkins to kill us."

"The answer to that is patently clear. MacFarlane intended
to create yet another subterfuge that would shadow his actions
from the police." As he spoke, Caedmon sat down beside her.
"The first part of the plan was to have Hopkins kill us. At
which point, I suspect the unwitting museum director would
have been forced to put the gun to his own head and pull the
trigger."

Raising a hand to her head, Edie rubbed her temples, grateful she still had a temple to rub.

"This is insane. All of it. Eliot Hopkins pulled a gun on us. And when he didn't do as ordered, they killed him. That makes two men killed before my very eyes in as many days. And they would have killed us if we hadn't slogged across that creek." Raising her arms, she gestured to the ice-laden park. "So now what? I ask because this doesn't seem like much of a plan."

"I agree that we need to take a more proactive approach to the situation."

"Proactive? As in going on the offensive?"

"If you like."

A noticeable pause ensued, Caedmon refusing to elaborate.

"Just how are we going to pull that off?" Edie prodded.

"We know that Colonel MacFarlane is going after the Ark of the Covenant. And, assuming that Eliot Hopkins spoke the truth, I know where MacFarlane and his gang of cutthroats will be searching for the Ark."

Again, Caedmon failed to elaborate on the details, forcing Edie to needle him a bit harder. "So where are they going to put shovel to dirt?"

One side of Caedmon's mouth lifted in a bemused half smile.

"Of all places, England."

CHAPTER 30

"We're talking about a big island. Where exactly in England is the Ark of the Covenant hidden?"

"The 'where exactly' is a bit thorny," Caedmon replied. "If you recall, Eliot Hopkins spoke of an English crusader who supposedly discovered a gold chest on the Plains of Esdraelon.

He was referring to one Galen of Godmersham, a younger son who, like so many younger sons, went to the Holy Land to attain the fortune denied him by the circumstance of his birth."

"And did he find his fortune?"

"Indeed, he did, returning to England in 1286 an exorbitantly wealthy man. For centuries whispers and rumors rattled about, some claiming that Galen had uncovered the Spear of Longinus, others claiming he'd found Veronica's Veil." Leaning close enough to brush shoulders, he said in a lowered tone, "And then there are those who believe that not only did Galen of Godmersham discover the Ark of the Covenant, but that he transported the Ark to his home in Kent, whereupon he promptly buried the holy relic. Admittedly, there's scant evidence to prove or disprove the rumor, although that hasn't stopped a legion of treasure hunters from pockmarking the environs around Godmersham."

"Come on, Caedmon. Even you have to admit that the idea of some English knight just happening upon the Ark of the Covenant is hard to swallow."

"With your own eyes, you saw the sacred Stones of Fire. If the breastplate exists, why not the Ark?"

"Maybe I don't want the Ark to exist," she answered with her trademark candor. "If what you say is even partially true, the implications are immense. History altering, in fact."

"Do you think that hasn't crossed my mind?"

"Has this thought crossed your mind: right now, you've got nothing more solid than a rumor about some old knight. Lesson of the day? One crazy rumor does not a fact make."

"It's thin gruel, I admit, but many an extraordinary discovery has been made by men who were labeled harebrained. Most thought Schliemann mad when he went searching for Troy with only a battered copy of Homer as his guide."

Edie snickered, her breath condensing in the chill air. "Yeah, well, you know what they say about mad dogs and Englishmen."

"In defense of my countrymen, I should point out that Heinrich Schliemann was German born," Caedmon retorted, the argument having diverged into a petty tit-for-tat. "Since the Bible makes no mention of the Ark being destroyed, we must assume that it still exists. Although biblical scholars have long denied the rumors regarding Galen of Godmersham, there is a scholar at Oxford, a man by the name of Sir Kenneth Campbell-Brown, who has devoted his life to studying the thirteenth-century English crusaders. If there is any credence to the rumor of an English knight discovering a gold chest on the Plain of Esdraelon, Sir Kenneth would certainly know of it. And given all that has transpired in the last twenty-four hours, we must accept Eliot Hopkins's premise as a viable possibility."

Folding her arms over her chest, Edie stubbornly shook her head. "What we need to do is contact SAFE. The FBI. Somebody. Anybody. And let them know what's happening."

"And what precisely would you tell the authorities?" he countered. "That a murder occurred at the Hopkins Museum for which there is no body? Or perhaps we could regale the local constabulary with the tale of the fabled Stones of Fire? Given that the relic disappeared several millennia ago, I somehow doubt the police will believe that the relic was stolen from the aforementioned nonexistent corpse. In fact, if not for the dead man at the zoo, whose murder they will most assuredly accuse you of having committed, the police will label you a lunatic."

"I could take a lie detector test."

"And if your heart rate accelerated but a notch, your fate would be sealed."

Edie unfolded her arms, her sails not nearly so fulsome. "You could go to the—"

"If I come forward with my suspicions regarding the Stones of Fire or the Ark of the Covenant, my motives would immediately be suspect, the chaps at the FBI no doubt believing it a publicity stunt to garner more book sales."

"So what are you saying, that our hands are tied?"

"Most certainly not. We know that Colonel MacFarlane and his men are searching for the Ark of the Covenant. Furthermore, we have reason to believe that they'll be searching for it in England."

"Oh, you have got to be kidding!" Edie exclaimed, realization dawning in her eyes. "You're not really suggesting that we go to England and track down Stanford MacFarlane and his goons."

"Rest assured, I do not expect or desire your company."

"Ouch! That hurts," she retorted, having taken offense where none was intended. "Going to England in pursuit of the Ark of the Covenant is big. Huge. You've given this—what?— about thirty seconds of thought before making a decision."

"If you're accusing me of being rash, nothing could be further from the truth."

"Then how's this for being rash: have you thought about how you're going to pay for this little junket? As soon as you whip out a credit card, MacFarlane will be on to you like ugly on an alligator."

"I agree that an electronic funds transaction could easily be traced." He cleared his throat. Knowing there was but one way to clear the hurdle, he charged forward. "Which is why I thought to ask you for a loan." When Edie cast him a pointedly askance glance, he added, "I'm good for it, as you Yanks are wont to say."

"Well, here's another phrase we Yanks are wont to say: 'My way or the highway.' Meaning you take me with you or you don't see a dime of my money."

No sooner was the ultimatum delivered than an invisible Maginot Line loomed between them, both retreating into a wordless world of move and countermove. Ignoring him, Edie reached into the now-wet paper bag and removed a hazelnut biscotti. Behaving as though he didn't exist, she loudly chomped down on it.

"Why the sudden interest in pursuing my 'crazy' theory?" he asked, if for no other reason than to break the unnerving silence.

"I have my reasons. Look, I'm good with details. And let's not forget the old adage about two heads being better than just the one."

"Honestly, Edie, I don't think that—"

"I can be your research assistant," she interjected, unwavering in her persistence.

"I don't need a research assistant. Once I arrive in England, I have connections that—"

"Yeah, speaking of 'connections,' you told Eliot Hopkins that you could contact Interpol . . . making me wonder just what kind of shadowy connections you have."

Not seeing the sense in keeping it from her, he said, "I used to be an intelligence officer with Her Majesty's Secret Service."

Her eyes opened wide. "You mean like James Bond?"

"Hardly. During my tenure at MI5, I spent most of my time in front of a computer and very little time chasing after nefarious characters. Certainly none with an outlandish moniker."

"Well, that explains your supercharged street smarts," she remarked, seeming to take his confession in stride. "Yesterday I was truly stumped as to how a bookworm could so easily keep his cool when the bullets started to fly. In fact, there were a couple of times at the National Gallery when you looked like you were in seventh heaven."

"Trust me, that wasn't the case," he countered, not about to let her think otherwise.

"Whether you enjoy that kind of action or not, I still want to go with you."

Something in Edie Miller's brown eyes, a defiant expression, seized hold of him, refusing to let go. He was well aware that if they paid for their airline tickets with cash, it wouldn't prevent MacFarlane from discovering their destination. If MacFarlane managed to get ahold of the airline passenger manifold lists, he would soon discover they'd flown into Heathrow. Whereupon they would find themselves, once again, in a dangerous strait.

He raised his face heavenward. "'It's raining feathers,'" he conversationally remarked, the sleet having softened into a light snowfall. "Admittedly, it's not an original thought. The Greek philosopher Herodotus coined the phrase some twenty-four hundred years ago."

"I've got one for you: 'It's raining men.' The Weather Girls at the height of the disco era."

Caedmon sighed, thinking them an odd pair indeed.

"It would appear that our destinies are linked," he said, capitulating to her request to accompany him. For several long seconds, he stared at her. Although it was brief, he glimpsed a wariness in her eyes, at odds with her usual defiance. He intuited that Edie Miller's tough façade was akin to gold leaf. Rigid to the glance, but gossamer thin.

"You know, Caedmon, I'm a little uncertain about the agenda. Are you planning to stop MacFarlane from finding the Ark, or are you hoping to beat him to the punch?"

Thinking it best not to truthfully reply, he said, "For now, we must concentrate our efforts on stopping MacFarlane from finding the Ark."

"I agree. If the Ark is, as you claim, a weapon of mass destruction, it doesn't bode well that an ex–military man is actively searching for it."

He acknowledged Edie's spot-on observation with a brusque nod. "Just as worrisome, I suspect that MacFarlane is well funded, his stockpile of cash translating into a highly developed network of communications and logistics."

"So, in other words, it's going to be a whole lot like David going up against Goliath."

Caedmon kept silent, not about to point out that David, at least, had a slingshot.

CHAPTER 31

I will take revenge on my hateful enemies. I will sharpen my sword and let it flash like lightning.

Being a military man, Stan MacFarlane knew that another battle loomed on the horizon. Yet another chance to vanquish the enemy.

A lesson well learned in the trenches of Panama, Bosnia, Operation Desert Storm.

And, of course, Beirut.

Some said that was where he found religion. He preferred to think that was where his relationship with the Almighty began.

He still had vivid nightmares of that deadly October day when two hundred and forty-one Marines were taken out by a fanatical suicide bomber driving a water truck packed with explosives.

. . . the sickening stench of sulfur and burned flesh . . . a bellowing cacophony of pain and outrage . . . the frenzied rush to rescue the injured . . . the grievous task of finding the dead.

Amazingly, he'd survived the blast; his bunkmate not so lucky.

In retrospect, able to see with a survivor's clarity, he knew the attack had been the first sign that the End Times were near.

His wife, the treacherous Helen, left him within a year of his conversion, claiming spousal abuse. In the nine years of their marriage, he'd never laid a hand on the woman—although he'd been tempted to wring her loose-skinned neck with his bare hands during the divorce proceedings.

The judge, a pussy-whipped left-wing liberal, had given Helen custody of their son, Custis; Stan was allowed to see his son only on the weekends. Afraid Custis would turn into a mama's boy, he'd made sure his son joined ROTC while still in high school. Pulling a few strings, he'd been able to secure Custis a berth at Annapolis. Helen claimed that he'd bullied Custis into joining the Marine Corps, but he knew he'd done right by his son; the Corps made a man of Custis.

Who or what turned him into a weak-kneed coward was to this day a deep, dark mystery.

The official account claimed that after one deployment to Afghanistan and two to Iraq, Custis suffered from PTSD. Stan knew it wasn't post-traumatic stress disorder that caused his son to put the barrel of a loaded M16 rifle into his mouth. Stan knew that it was the barbarous infidels of Babylon who caused his only son to heed Satan's siren call. Men of God had a duty to battle the godless among them. Custis shirked his duty.

And would burn in the pits of hell because of it.

Soon after his son's death, he founded the Warriors of God, convinced that it was his duty to lead the army of the righteous, akin to King David leading the Israelite army as they conquered the Jebusites and Philistines. Or Godfrey of Bouillon leading the crusaders as they battled Muslim infidels in the streets of Jerusalem. And, of course, there was his personal hero, Thomas "Stonewall" Jackson, a deeply religious military man who refused to fight on Sunday and who led his men in prayer before each battle.

Today, despite his fervent prayers, the battle had yet to be won.

Part of his contingency plan had been to send in a sniper. In case the old man lost his nerve. No need to worry about the scion of one of America's great industrial families being gunned down in the middle of the National Zoo. The police would jump to the erroneous conclusion that a copycat killer, replicating the sniping spree that had gripped the nation's capital during the autumn of '02, was on the loose.

No doubt the funeral eulogies would wax poetic about Eliot Hopkins's generosity and great philanthropic spirit, making no mention of the many art thefts that had padded his museum collection.

The tributes would also not mention Eliot Hopkins's secret passion, the Ark of the Covenant.

Because of Stan's thorough planning, the biblical scholars and archaeology watchdogs would continue to lightly snore, unaware of a trespass.

When all the pieces were in place, only then would the world know of his divinely inspired mission. Right now, the world was on his timetable. It was early yet. Too early to reveal God's great plan. Although if the unbelievers had but eyes to see, they, too, would know that current global events had become an urgent call to arms from the Great Almighty.

Anxious about the upcoming mission, he hit the *Intercom* button on the phone console. "Any word on the flight plan?"

"I've just received the official approval, sir. You're wings up at thirteen hundred hours."

"Excellent," Stan said to his chief of staff before disconnecting.

Despite the fact that English food rivaled mess tent slop, he looked forward to greeting the new day in London. The Miller woman had set the schedule back a full twenty-four hours, and though he was frustrated by the snafu, he felt curiously uplifted, ready, willing, and able for the task he was about to undertake. Besides, in the larger scheme of things, Edie Miller and her consort were insignificant. Minor players in a drama penned by the Almighty twenty-six centuries ago.

He glanced at his watch. He had enough time to post his daily blog entry.

Seating himself at the desk, he used his two index fingers to type the opening Bible passage, a favorite from Psalm 11.

He will send fiery coals and flaming sulfur down on the wicked . . .

CHAPTER 32

"At this juncture I should probably mention that I'm not an adventuresome person. I like stability. Predictable, watch the same TV program every Monday night, stability. The only thing in my life that gets changed on a regular basis is the lightbulbs."

At hearing Edie's voice, Caedmon glanced away from the Oxfordshire scenery that passed in a limestone blur on the other side of the oversized coach window. Having touched down at Heathrow two hours ago, they were now en route to Oxford.

"How curious. You strike me as a most intrepid woman."

"Appearances can be deceiving."

"Indeed." He pointedly glanced at her attire.

Their clothes having taken a shabby turn for the worse after yesterday's foot race, they'd each purchased a new set of garments at the airport boutique. He'd selected tweeds, wools, and a beige anorak. Opting for more colorful plumage, Edie had chosen a yellow knit cap, a red military-style jacket replete with epaulets, and knee-high riding boots into which she'd tucked her denim jeans. While he resembled one half of a stodgy English couple come to town, she looked like a Mondrian painting come to life. He would have preferred that she select earth tones. Colors that faded into the winter scenery. Should an RIRA operative happen to catch sight of him, he would suddenly have two enemies to contend with rather than the one.

"Do you think MacFarlane and his goons will actually find the Ark of the Covenant?"

"It's an outside wager, at best," he replied. "Over the centuries many have searched—all in vain. Although if found, the

Ark of the Covenant would be the most astounding discovery in the annals of mankind."

Edie closed the Bible they'd purchased in the gift shop at Dulles airport. "It's been a while since I last read the Old Testament, being what you might call a New Testament kind of gal." She stuffed the King James Bible into the Virgin Airlines shoulder bag that they now used to convey their meager belongings. "Somehow I'd conveniently forgotten about all the death and mayhem associated with the Ark. Just now I was reading about the battle of Ebenezer."

"If memory serves correctly, Ebenezer was where the Philistines not only defeated the Israelites but managed to steal the Ark of the Covenant."

"And wasn't that a big mistake? Within hours of installing the Ark inside the Temple of Dagon, the Philistines discovered the statue of their deity smashed to smithereens. But, of course, that was nothing compared to the plague of boils that suddenly afflicted the entire city of Ashdod. In the ensuing panic, the Philistine king wisely decided to return his ill-gotten booty to the Israelites."

"At which point the Philistines loaded the Ark of the Covenant onto a cart and rolled it to the Hebrew town of Bethshemesh."

"Where, as you mentioned yesterday, fifty thousand residents were indiscriminately slaughtered because of a curious few who dared to peek inside the Ark." Edie's brow furrowed. "You know, I'm trying hard, but I just can't get a handle on an all-loving, all-forgiving God instigating that kind of brutality."

"I, for one, don't believe that God had anything to do with the Ark's devastating powers." Caedmon leaned back in his coach seat, crossing his legs at the knee. "Rather I believe that the Ark's power was entirely manmade. To comprehend its supposedly supernatural power, one must understand how the Ark was constructed."

"You said that the Egyptian bark was more than likely the prototype used by Moses."

He verified the statement with a quick nod. "I am certain of it. First, consider the materials used. Both bark and Ark were manufactured from gold. An enormous quantity of gold, to be precise."

"Well, gold is one of the most valuable metals known to man."

"More important, gold is an extremely dense metal that is chemically nonreactive. Although it can't be proved, some biblical scholars believe that the gold used on the Ark was nine inches thick."

"You're kidding? That would make for a *huge* hunk of gold."

"Indeed." Riffling through the shoulder bag, he removed pen and paper. Culling to mind the detailed descriptions given in the Old Testament, he managed to produce a fairly accurate rendition of the Ark of the Covenant.

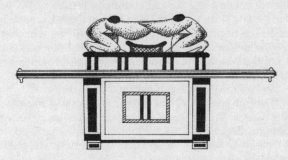

"As you can see, the gold box was covered with a lid known as the mercy seat."

Edie chuckled. "Not the hot seat?"

Caedmon smiled at his companion's wry remark. "The mercy seat was adorned with a matched pair of gold cherubim mounted on the lid. Mind you, these weren't the adorable putti that clutter the paintings of Peter Paul Rubens. The cherubim who stood sentry atop the Ark were fierce, otherworldly creatures, not unlike the winged figures of Isis and Nephthys that adorned many an Egyptian bark."

"Underneath all that gold, the Ark was made of wood, wasn't it?"

"Acacia wood, to be precise, the tree native to the Sinai Desert. In ancient times, such wood was thought to be incorruptible. Additionally, it would have acted as an insulator."

Her brown eyes opened wide, the realization having just dawned. "And gold is an excellent conductor. Since the acacia box was lined, inside and out, with gold"—using her hands, she made a sandwich, leaving several inches of air between her palms—"the Ark would have been an incredibly powerful condenser. And given all the dry desert air in the Sinai, I bet the darned thing would have packed a very potent electrical punch."

Despite her quirkiness, Edie Miller possessed a nimble mind; the woman was fast proving herself an enigma.

"Touching the Ark with one's bare hands would have resulted in instant death," he said, confirming her theory. "Moreover, the Old Testament is rife with tales of the Ark producing skin lesions on people who came into close proximity. Interestingly enough, recent research has verified that skin cancer is an occupational hazard of working near high-tension power lines."

"So how did the Israelites protect themselves?"

"The high priest wore specialized ritual clothing when handling the Ark, and the Stones of Fire was part of his protective wardrobe. Because the Ark built up an electric charge due to all the jostling while in transport, it was carefully wrapped in leather and cloth."

"Which acted as a protective barrier so that the guys stuck with carrying it wouldn't be tossed on their collective keisters," she astutely, if not, irreverently, remarked.

"Not that those calamities didn't occur. Despite the precautions, there are accounts of Ark bearers being tossed bodily through the air and a few blokes being killed outright." Caedmon pointed to the sketched drawing. "Now imagine that the wings on the two cherubim were hinged with leather and bitumen, enabling them to flap back and forth. The accumulated electric charge would not only have created visible sparks, it would have emitted strong electromagnetic pulses similar to Hertzian radio waves. Once charged, the Ark would have picked up strikes of lightning anywhere in the world. That, in turn, would have created an audible static."

"Like the crackling sound you get in between AM radio stations, right?"

"Precisely. And to the ears of the ancient Israelites that 'crackling' would have sounded like the voice of God. A careful reading of the Old Testament proves that the Ark of the Covenant isn't a literal deus ex machina. Rather it was envisioned and executed by Moses."

Edie stared at his sketched drawing, as though seeing the Ark of the Covenant in a new, and slightly disturbing, light. "Yeah, well, there's a whole legion of true believers who would disagree with you on that one."

Knowing she spoke the truth, Caedmon wearily nodded, having more than a passing acquaintance with the naysayers of the world.

A few feet away from where they sat, the coach's windshield wipers hypnotically swung to and fro like a metronome. Blinking, he fought off a seductive wave, having caught only a quick cat nap on the transatlantic flight.

In the distance he could see the honey-colored villages and rolling sheep pastures of Oxfordshire. From those pastures, limestone had been quarried and lugged to Oxford, where it had been used to construct some of the most stunning architecture in medieval England.

As the countryside passed in a wet blur, so too did his memories. He'd journeyed to Oxford by coach when he'd been a gangly lad of eighteen, his father too busy to accompany him. As the coach neared the city limits, he'd been in a tumult, his emotions ranging from anxiety to excitement to shame suffered on account of his father's indifference. Then, quite suddenly, those gut-wrenching emotions were superseded by a burst of exhilaration, his younger self staggered to have landed in the most famous university city in the world.

A sweet city with her dreaming spires.

"You mentioned that you went to Oxford," Edie remarked, making him wonder if she might not be a mind reader. "This will be like a homecoming for you, huh?"

"Hardly," he murmured, disinclined to reveal his tainted academic past. Particularly because she would find out soon enough.

Like most postgraduate students, he'd spent two years doing field research, after which he confined himself to his Oxford digs and commenced writing his dissertation. "The Manifesto," as he'd jokingly taken to calling it, had been an exhaustive examination of the influence of Egyptian mysticism on the Knights Templar. To his horror, the head of the history department at Queen's College publicly denounced his dissertation topic, claiming it a "harebrained" notion that could only have been opium induced. Not unlike the poetry of William Blake.

Such stinging criticism amounted to the kiss of death.

Finished as an academic, he left Oxford, his tail between his legs.

What a perverted bit of irony that he was, once again, en route to the fabled city of his youth. The gods must be chortling, gleefully rubbing their hands in anticipation.

Somewhat idly, he wondered what Edie would say if he were to inform her that Moses and the Knights Templar had been initiated into the same Egyptian mystery cult. He bit back an amused smile, certain his assertions would be met with a raised brow and a quick-witted rebuttal. Truth be told, he enjoyed their verbal jousts. Although she could punch hard, hers was an open mind.

He hoped that Sir Kenneth Campbell-Brown would be equally open-minded. If not, they would have journeyed to Oxford in vain.

As Edie peered through the coach window, he, in turn, peered at her. The straight brows gave his companion a decidedly serious mien wholly at odds with her exuberant personality. So, too, did the softness of her lips and the pale Victorian smoothness of her skin. When he first met Edie Miller, he'd thought her an unusual mix of Pre-Raphaelite beauty and quirky modernity.

Unthinkingly he raised a hand, cupping her chin between his fingers. Slowly, he turned her face in his direction. Startled, her eyes and mouth opened wide.

How bloody perfect is that? he thought as he leaned into her, about to ascertain if those wide open lips were as soft as they appeared.

Amazingly, they were.

Not having asked permission, he barely grazed his lips across her mouth, concerned she might balk at the trespass. For several seconds he played the gentleman, softly applying pressure, deepening the kiss in small increments. Until she murmured something against his lips. What, he had no idea; he only knew the incoherent utterance sounded incredibly sexy.

The male biological response not unlike a trigger mechanism, he shoved his tongue into her mouth. Then he shoved his hand to the back of her neck, effectively imprisoning her. Open-mouthed, he kissed her, wetly and deeply, doing all that he could to wed his lips to hers.

For several long moments he went at her like a madman, his hand moving from her neck to her back, pulling her that much closer to him, not stopping until her breasts were smashed against his chest.

Not stopping until he heard a horror-struck gasp from the across the aisle.

Abruptly, and somewhat awkwardly, he ended the kiss.

"That was unplanned and—forgive me if I acted inappropriately." His cheeks warmed at the butchered apology.

Wet lips curved into a fetching smile. "The only thing you did wrong was to end that kiss *way* too soon." Edie glanced out the window. "Looks like we just pulled into Oxford."

CHAPTER 33

Hoping she didn't appear too awestruck, Edie discreetly checked out the buildings that fronted High Street.

Everywhere she looked there were hints, some subtle, some in your face, of Oxford's medieval roots. Battlements. Gate towers. Oriel windows. And stone. Lots and lots of stone. Varying in shade from pale silver to deep gold. All of it combining in a wondrous sort of sensory overload.

"Where's the university?" she inquired, scrunching her shoulders to avoid hitting a group of midday shoppers who had just emerged from a clothing shop. She and Caedmon were en route to some pub called the Isis Room, where Caedmon seemed to think they would find Sir Kenneth Campbell-Brown.

Caedmon slowed his step as he gestured to either side of the busy thoroughfare. "Oxford University is everywhere and nowhere. Since leaving the bus depot, we've already passed Jesus, Exeter, and Lincoln colleges."

"We did?" Edie swiveled her head, wondering how she could have missed the three campuses. She knew that Oxford University was made up of several dozen colleges spread throughout the town limits. Having attended a downtown college herself, she assumed there would be placards and signposts identifying the various buildings. Clearly, she'd been working under a false assumption.

"Look for the gateways," Caedmon said, pointing to an imposing iron portal wedged in the middle of a stone wall. "They often lead to a quadrangle; most of the colleges were built to the standard medieval pattern of chapel and hall flanked by multi-storied residential ranges."

Edie peered through the iron bars. Beyond the gatehouse, she glimpsed an arched portico on either side of the quad.

"That's a formidable entrance. Guess it's meant to keep the little people out, huh?"

"Having spent an inordinate amount of time on the other side of those 'formidable' gateways, I always thought they were intended to keep the students from leaving. The college's way of cultivating a slavish devotion to one's alma mater." Edie wasn't certain, but she thought she detected a slight hint of sarcasm in his voice.

"Sounds like an academic Never Never Land."

"Indeed, it was."

"So, where are the Lost Boys?"

His copper-colored brows briefly furrowed. "Ah! You speak of the students. Michaelmas term ended last week, the vast majority of students having gone home for the holidays."

"Well that would certainly explain all the riderless bicycles," she said, nodding toward a crowded line of bikes parked in front of a stucco wall. Above the tidy line of bicycles, old posters flapped in the breeze, hawking an array of student activities. Debate societies. Drama societies. Choral societies.

Caedmon's gaze momentarily softened. "By their bicycles you shall know them," he murmured, his sarcasm replaced with something more akin to nostalgia.

Surprised by the sudden shift in mood, Edie surreptitiously checked out her companion, her gaze moving from the top of his thick thatch of red hair to the tips of his black leather oxfords. She was beginning to realize that Caedmon Aisquith was a complicated man. Or maybe she was just dense when it came to men. He'd certainly taken her by surprise with the killer kiss. For some idiotic reason, she'd assumed that because he was such a brainiac, he lived a monkish existence. *And wasn't that a stupid assumption?* Given the passionate smooch on the bus, he'd make a lousy monk.

Wonder what kind of lover he'd make?

Giving the question several moments' thought, she decided it was impossible to tell, the cultured accent acting like a smokescreen. Although the unexpected kiss most definitely hinted at a deeper passion.

Oblivious to the fact that he was being ogled, Caedmon turned his head as they passed an ATM.

"Though I'm sorely tempted to use the Cashpoint, it would undoubtedly lead Stanford McFarlane right to us."

"Don't worry. As keeper of the vault, I can assure you that there are enough funds to keep us afloat. At least for a little while." The airline tickets and new clothes had set them back a bit, but at last count she had nearly eighteen hundred dollars in the "vault."

"Being a kept man doesn't sit well with me. Bruised ego and all that."

She affected a stunned expression. "You're kidding, right? We've spent three days together and only *now* am I learning that you object to being my sex slave?" Playing the bit for all it was worth, she theatrically sighed. "Here I thought you were having the time of your life."

To her surprise, Caedmon blushed, his cheeks as red as Christmas berries. Raising a balled hand to his mouth, he cleared his throat.

"*Hel-lo*. I'm teasing. You're hardly a kept man," she assured him, amused by his embarrassment.

"Then how about spotting me two quid for a pint of lager?" Taking her by the elbow, Caedmon ushered her to a wood-paneled door. Above the door, a brightly painted sign emblazoned with the pub's moniker swung from a metal bracket.

"Be my pleasure, luv," she replied in a thick Cockney accent.

Not expecting the interior to be so dim, it took several seconds of squinting before her pupils adjusted, the room bathed in soft amber light. All in all, the joint was pretty much as she'd envisioned an English pub—wood-paneled walls, wood-beamed ceiling, and wood tables and chairs scattered about. Framed lithographs of British sea battles hung on the cream-colored walls, and a limp bouquet of mistletoe was tacked above the Battle of Trafalgar.

Her eyes zeroed in on the easel where a chalkboard listed

the day's menu. *Homemade lentil soup. Two-cheese quiche. Seafood salad.* She placed a hand over her abdomen, having long since digested the rubbery chicken cordon bleu that she'd been served on the transatlantic flight.

"Any idea what this Sir Kenneth character looks like?" she asked over the top of a very unladylike stomach growl.

"Ruddy cheeks, aquiline nose, and a pewter-colored mop of curly hair. Looks like a Devon Longwool sheep before the spring shearing. You can't miss him."

Edie scanned the crowded pub. "How about we divide and conquer? You take that side of the room and I'll take the other."

"Right."

A few seconds later, seeing a man of middling height with curly gray hair standing at the bar, Edie headed in that direction. Raising her hand to catch Caedmon's attention, she pointed to her suspect. For several seconds Caedmon stared at the man's backside, drilling the proverbial hole right through the older man's head. She wasn't certain, but she thought Caedmon straightened his shoulders before heading toward the bar.

Reaching the target a few seconds ahead of Caedmon, she lightly tapped the gray-haired man on the shoulder.

"Excuse me. You wouldn't happen to be Sir Kenneth Campbell-Brown?"

The gray-haired slowly man turned toward her. Although he was decked out in a brown leather bomber jacket, with a red cashmere scarf jauntily wrapped around his neck, he resembled nothing so much as a woolly ram; Caedmon's description had been right on the mark.

"Well, I'm not the bloody Prince of Wales."

"Ah! Still the amiable Oxford don much beloved by students and fellows alike," Caedmon said, having overheard the exchange.

Slightly bug-eyed by nature, Sir Kenneth became even more so as he turned in the direction of Caedmon's voice. "Good God! I thought you crawled into a hole and died! What the bloody hell are you doing in Oxford? I didn't think the Boar's Head Gaudy your cup of tea."

"You're quite right. In the thirteen years since I left, I've yet to attend the Old Members' Christmas dinner."

The older man snickered. "I suspect that's because your softhearted sympathies go out to the apple-stuffed swine. So, tell me, young Aisquith, if the pig is not your purpose, what bringeth you to 'the high shore of this world'?"

"As fate would have it, you're the reason why I'm in Oxford." Outwardly calm—maybe *too* calm given the older man's condescension—Caedmon redirected his gaze in Edie's direction. "Excuse me. I've been remiss. Edie Miller, may I present Professor Sir Kenneth Campbell-Brown, senior fellow at Queen's College."

Sir Kenneth acknowledged the introduction with a slight nod of his woolly head. "I am also the head of the history department, secretary of the Tutorial Committee, defender of the realm, and protector of women and small children," he informed her, speaking in beautifully precise pear-shaped tones. "I am also the man responsible for booting your erstwhile swain out of Oxford."

CHAPTER 34

"Mind you, that was long years ago," Sir Kenneth added, still addressing his remarks to Edie. Then, turning to Caedmon, "Water under the Magdalen Bridge, eh?"

Refusing to be drawn into that particular conversation—one could drown in a shallow puddle if led there by the woolly-headed don— Caedmon jutted his chin toward the far side of the pub. "Shall we adjourn to the vacant booth in the corner?"

"An excellent suggestion." Smiling, Sir Kenneth placed a hand on Edie's elbow. "And what is your pleasure, my dear?"

"Oh, I'll just have a glass of water," she demurred. "It's a little early for kicking back the brewskies."

"Right-O. An Adam's ale for the lady and a Kingfisher for the gent._I won't be but a second." Turning around, Sir Kenneth placed the order with a barmaid.

As he steered Edie toward the booth, Caedmon wondered how, after so many years, his estranged mentor remembered his preferred lager.

The old bastard always did have a mind like a steel trap.

Which meant he'd have to be on his guard to keep from ending up in the poacher's sack.

As they sidestepped a jovial group arguing the merits of the new PM, Edie elbowed him in the ribs. "You didn't tell me that you knew Sir Kenneth."

"Forgive the omission," he replied, failing to mention that the oversight had been quite intentional.

"You also didn't tell me that you were 'booted' out of Oxford. Geez, what else are you hiding from me? You're not wanted by the police or anything like that, are you?"

"The police? No." *The RIRA, yes.* Knowing he'd only frighten her if he disclosed that bit of unsavory business, Caedmon kept mum.

"So, what happened? Were you 'sent down,' as the highbrows on *Masterpiece Theatre* are wont to say?"

"No. I left on my own accord after it was made painfully clear to me by Sir Kenneth that my doctorate degree would not be conferred."

She glanced at the curly-haired don. "I'm guessing there's bad blood between the two of you, huh?"

"Of a sort. Although in England, we conduct our feuds in a chillingly polite manner," he replied, relieved when she didn't pry further. He'd been a cocky bastard in his student days, supremely confident of his intellectual prowess. He'd had his comeuppance. And preferred not to talk about it.

With a hand to her shoulder, he assisted Edie in removing her outerwear, hanging her red jacket on the brass hook embedded into the side of the wooden booth. That done, he removed his anorak and hung it on the sister hook. He then motioned her to the circular table that fronted the high-backed booth.

"Do you mind grabbing that basket of oyster crackers on the next table?" Edie asked as she seated herself, not in the booth, but in the Windsor chair opposite.

Caedmon complied with the request. Placing the snack basket in the middle of the table, he seated himself in a vacant chair just as Sir Kenneth, juggling a small tray, approached the table.

"Nothing like malt, hops and yeast to usher in a spirit of fraternal concord, eh?" A man of mercurial moods, Sir Kenneth had forsaken his earlier condescension for a show of bluff good humor. Drinks passed out, he seated himself in the booth. Surrounded on three sides by dark-stained wood, he looked like a Saxon king holding court.

Edie lifted her water glass. "I assume that I'm included in all that brotherly love."

"Most certainly, my dear." As Edie bent her head, Sir Kenneth slyly winked at him, Caedmon wanting very badly to bash him in the nose.

Although he hailed from the upper echelons of British society, Sir Kenneth wasn't averse to mucking about with the common man. Or woman—Sir Kenneth was particularly fond of the fairer sex. In a day and age when reckless behavior could get one killed, the man had a voracious sexual appetite. An appetite that had evidently not diminished with age. According to rumor, the provost had once remarked that Oxford might do well to return to the days of celibate fellows, if for no other reason than to keep roaming dons like Sir Kenneth at bay.

"So, tell me, young Aisquith, to what do I owe the pleasure of this most unexpected visit?"

Puzzled as to why his estranged mentor had twice referred to him by his old pet name, Caedmon shrugged off his discomfort. "We'd like to inquire about a thirteenth-century knight named Galen of Godmersham."

"How curious. I had an appointment yesterday with an American chap from Harvard. A professor of medieval literature interested in Galen of Godmersham's poetic endeavors."

Curious, indeed.

Caedmon immediately wondered if the "American chap" was an agent working for Colonel Stanford MacFarlane. Or was it mere coincidence that a Harvard scholar had been inquiring about an obscure thirteenth-century English knight? Sir Kenneth Campbell-Brown was the foremost authority on the English crusaders; it could be a coincidence. Although Caedmon had his doubts.

"What's this about poetry?" Edie piped in. "Are we talking about the same knight?"

His tutorial style having always been to answer a question with a question, Sir Kenneth did just that. "How familiar are you with Galen of Godmersham?"

Plucking several oyster crackers out of the basket, Edie replied, "I know him by name only. Oh, and the fact that he discovered a gold chest while crusading in the Holy Land."

"Ah . . . the fabled gold chest." His eyes narrowing, Sir Kenneth directed his gaze at Caedmon. "I should have known you'd be mixed up in that harebrained bit of business."

"I assume that the American professor expressed a similar interest in Galen's treasure trove," Caedmon countered, ignoring the gibe.

"If you must know, he never mentioned Galen's gold chest. The chap's field of expertise was thirteenth- and fourteenth-century English poetry. Recited reams of archaic verse between exhalations. Put me to bloody sleep, it did."

Even more curious, Caedmon thought, still pondering the significance of the meeting.

"Time out," Edie exclaimed, holding her hands in a T formation. "I'm totally confused. We're talking about a gold chest and you're talking about poetry. Is it just me or did we lose the connection?"

Sir Kenneth smiled, the question smoothing the old cock's ruffled feathers. "Because you are such a lovely maid, what with your raven elf locks and skin so fair, I shall tell you all that I know of Galen of Godmersham. After which, you will tell me why you are chasing after old dead knights."

"Okay, fair enough," Edie replied, returning the smile.

Not wanting Sir Kenneth to know the full extent of their interest in Galen of Godmersham, Caedmon fully intended to intervene when the time came to pay the debt. If mishandled, such knowledge could get one killed.

"As your erstwhile swain may or may not have told you, during the medieval period the entire Holy Land, or the Middle East as it is now referred to, was under Muslim control. Given that this was the land of the biblical patriarchs and the birthplace of the Savior, Europeans believed that the Holy Land should be a Christian domain. The centuries-long bloodbath that ensued has come to be known as the Crusades. No sooner was Jerusalem conquered by the crusading knights than the Church moved in, organizing religious militias to oversee their new empire.

"The two best-known militias were the Knights Templar and the Hospitaller Knights of St. John; the rivalry between the two orders was legendary," Caedmon mentioned, keeping his voice as neutral sounding as possible. The Knights Templar had once been a point of bitter contention between him and his former mentor.

"And it should be noted that the men who swelled the ranks of the Templars and the Hospitallers were anything but holy brothers," Sir Kenneth remarked, right on his coattails. "These were trained soldiers who fought, and fought mercilessly, in the name of their God. One might even go so far as to liken the two orders of warrior monks to mercenary shock troops."

On that point, Caedmon and Sir Kenneth greatly differed. Although he wasn't about to argue the point. He was there to learn about Galen of Godmersham, not to rekindle a long-standing dispute.

"As the crusading knights soon discovered, the Holy Land was rich pickings, and religious artifacts were sent back to Europe by the shipload," Sir Kenneth continued, folding his arms over his chest, an Oxford don in his element.

"Holy relics were a big fad during the Middle Ages, weren't they?"

"More like an obsession; many a pilgrimage was made to view the bones or petrified appendages of the holy saints. St.

Basil's shriveled bollocks. St. Crispin's arse bone. Such oddities abounded."

Beside him, Caedmon felt Edie's shoulders shake with silent laughter, his companion obviously amused by Sir Kenneth's bawdy humor.

"Christians in the Middle Ages were convinced that holy relics were imbued with a divine power capable of healing the sick and dying while protecting the living from the malevolent clutches of the demon world."

"Sounds like a lot of superstitious hooey." Indictment issued, Edie popped an oyster cracker into her mouth.

Sir Kenneth pruriently observed the passage of cracker to lip before replying, "While superstition did exist, the medieval fascination with holy relics was more than mere cultish devotion. Given that we live in a disposable society with no thought to the past and little for the future, it is difficult to comprehend the medieval mind-set."

"Guess you could call us the here-and-now generation," Edie remarked, seemingly unaware of the effect she had on the Oxford don.

"Indeed. But the generation that set forth for the Holy Land, donned in mail and armed with sword, full-heartedly believed that the land of their biblical forbears was a birthright. To these stalwart knights, biblical relics were a tangible link between the past, the present, and the unforeseen future. Thus the obsession with uncovering the treasures of the Bible."

"The most sought-after prize being the Ark of the Covenant," Caedmon pointed out, deciding to broach the subject in a roundabout manner. "No less a thinker than Thomas Aquinas declared that 'God himself was signified by the Ark.' Other Church fathers likened the Ark of the Covenant to the Virgin Mother of Christ."

"Ah, yes . . . *Faederis Arca*."

Edie tugged at his sleeve. "Translation, please."

Secretly pleased that Edie had turned to him, Caedmon replied, "It's the feminine form for the Ark of the Covenant. *Faederis Arca* was used to convey the religious belief that just as the original Ark had contained the Ten Commandments, the

Virgin Mary had contained within her womb the Savior of the world."

"So where does Galen of Godmersham fit into all of this?" Edie asked, proving herself a perceptive student.

"As with many younger sons with nary a prayer of inheriting, Galen of Godmersham decided to earn his fortune the old-fashioned way. That, of course, being the pillaging and sacking of the infidels in the far-flung Holy Land."

"Rape and ruin . . . the stuff of English history," Caedmon mordantly remarked.

Grinning, Sir Kenneth banged his palm against the table, setting half-filled glasses to rattling. "Ah! Those were the days, were they not?" Then, his voice noticeably subdued, he continued. "Both the Knights Templar and the Hospitallers were actively engaged in finding the Ark of the Covenant. As a Hospitaller, Galen of Godmersham would have joined the hunt. Ultimately, the knights' hunt proved the wildest goose chase known to mankind. But this is where our story takes an intriguing turn." Leaning forward, giving every appearance of a man taking a woman into his confidence, Sir Kenneth said in a lowered voice, "Although Galen of Godmersham did not uncover the goose, the lucky lad did happen upon a very fat gold-plated egg."

In like manner, Edie also leaned forward. "You're talking about the gold chest, right?"

Sir Kenneth nodded. "In 1286, while patrolling the region between Palestine and Egypt, Galen of Godmersham led a small contingent of Hospitaller knights through the Plain of Esdraelon. There, in a village called Megiddo, he—"

"Discovered a gold chest," Edie interjected. "But this is what I don't get"—she paused, a puzzled expression on her face—"if no one has seen this gold chest in nearly seven hundred years, how do you know the darned thing ever existed?"

"My dear, you are as mentally nimble as you are beautiful. I know because the local Kent records from the years 1292 to 1344 tell me so."

"Of course . . . the Feet of Fines," Caedmon murmured. When Edie turned to him, a questioning glance on her face, he elaborated. "The Feet of Fines was the medieval record of all land and property owned in England."

"And the Feet of Fines clearly indicates that Galen of Godmersham had within his possession a gold chest measuring one and a half by two cubits. The Feet of Fines also indicates that the gold chest was kept in Galen's personal chapel on the grounds of his estate. In addition to the gold chest, Galen owned a king's ransom in miscellaneous gold objects. *Objets sacrés*, as they are listed in the official records."

"So when Galen of Godmersham discovered the gold chest, he went from rags to riches, huh?"

The Oxford don nodded. "Like many a crusader, Galen of Godmersham profited from his tenure in the Holy Land. Although he seems to have had a generous streak. In 1340, he bequeathed to St. Lawrence the Martyr Church several *vestiges d'ancien Testament*."

"Old Testament relics," Caedmon said in a quick aside to Edie. Then, to his former mentor, "Bound by his vows of celibacy, Galen would have had no legal offspring. Who inherited the gold chest and all *objets sacrés* when the knight died?"

"While it's true that Galen of Godmersham had neither son nor daughter, it wasn't for lack of trying. No sooner did he return to England than Galen left the Hospitallers, taking up worldly pleasures with a vengeance."

"So who inherited the gold chest?" Edie inquired, playing the wide-eyed ingénue to perfection.

"That, my dear, is a mystery. A mystery that has confounded historian and treasure seeker alike. Bear in mind that when the plague struck in the middle of the fourteenth century, its effects were devastating; one-third of England's population succumbed. As you can well imagine, chaos ensued, and compulsory record keeping was thrown into a state of complete disarray. It has been suggested that Galen, who was nearing his eighty-fifth year when the bubonic plague reached the English shores, took the precaution of removing his precious gold chest from the family chapel in order to safeguard it from the looting rampage that followed in the plague's wake. Generations of treasure hunters have focused on Galen of Godmersham's deathbed burst of creative inspiration, the wily old knight having composed several poetic quatrains just prior to his death in 1348."

"Oh, I get it!" Edie exclaimed, nearly coming bodily off her chair in her excitement. "The clues to the whereabouts of the gold chest are contained within the poetic quatrains."

"Possibly," Sir Kenneth replied, refusing to commit. "Although Galen's verse is cryptic in nature, there is reference made in the quatrains to an *arca*."

"*Arca* being the Latin word for 'chest,'" Caedmon said, taking a moment to consider all that Sir Kenneth had divulged. If the clues to the gold chest's whereabouts were contained within the poetic quatrains, it would explain why a Harvard scholar had expressed an interest in those very lines of verse.

And if the scholar was in Stanford MacFarlane's employ, it meant the bastard had a twenty-four-hour head start in solving the centuries-old mystery.

"Is there any chance that the gold chest discovered by Galen of Godmersham was the Ark of the Covenant?" Edie unexpectedly inquired.

No sooner was the question posed than Sir Kenneth's woolly head swiveled in Caedmon's direction. "Is that your purpose in roasting me over the fire, so that you can chase after a myth?"

Caedmon opened his mouth to speak. But Edie beat him to the punch.

"We thought there might be a *slim* possibility that Galen of Godmersham uncovered the Ark of the Covenant."

"A fool's errand, my dear. The Holy Land fair brimmed with golden gewgaws, and more than one impoverished knight returned to England a wealthy man."

Undeterred, Edie said, "If Galen didn't discover the Ark of the Covenant, then—"

"I never said he didn't discover the Ark of the Covenant."

"But you just said—"

"I said that Galen of Godmersham discovered a gold chest. It has yet to be proved whether the gold chest is the much-

ballyhooed Ark of the Covenant. I am a scholar, not a conspiracy theorist. And as such, I deal in fact, not innuendo," the
older man brusquely asserted. As he spoke, he locked gazes
with Caedmon. A glancing blow. Then, his expression soften-
ing, he returned his attention to Edie. "Did you know there's
an old Irish legend that claims that not only did a band of
intrepid Hebrews take refuge on the Emerald Isle, but that they
brought with them the Ark of the Covenant? Supposedly
they buried the blasted thing under a hill in Ulster. Nearly as
preposterous an Ark tale as that of Galen of Godmersham discovering the Ark on the Plain of Esdraelon."

Just then the door of the pub opened and a gaggle of giggling women crossed the threshold, holding a birthday cake
aloft.

"It would appear that the lacy-frock brigade has taken
the field," Sir Kenneth dryly remarked. "Shall we continue the
conversation at Rose Chapel?"

Not bothering to wait for a reply—it being more of a sum-
mons than an invitation—Sir Kenneth rose to his feet.

Leaning toward him, Edie whispered in Caedmon's ear,
"He wants to go to *church*?"

"Not in the sense that you mean it. Sir Kenneth resides at
Rose Chapel."

"Just like a medieval monk, huh?"

Caedmon watched as Sir Kenneth appraised the cake bear-
er's backside.

"Hardly."

CHAPTER 35

Leading the way through the twisting labyrinth of narrow streets, Sir Kenneth came to a halt in front of a fan-vaulted entryway. "After you, Miss Miller."

Edie pushed open a wrought-iron gate. At hearing the spine-jangling squeak, she said, "A little WD-40 will fix that right up."

"My dear, I have no idea what you just said, but it sounded utterly delightful."

She forced her lips into a tight smile.

God save her from horny college professors.

Discovering that they had entered an ancient cemetery, a good many of the weathered headstones eerily tilted at a drunken incline, Edie unthinkingly leaned into Caedmon.

"Very creepy," she murmured, not wanting to disturb the dead.

"The scenery improves on the other side of the marble yard," he assured her, gently squeezing her hand.

A few moments later she breathed a sigh of relief at finding herself in a medieval knot garden. Taking the lead, his red cashmere scarf jauntily flapping in the breeze, Sir Kenneth guided them through the clipped boxwoods. Imagining the older man maneuvering through the circuitous route after a night spent at the Isis Room, Edie bit back a smile.

The knot garden navigated, they strolled through a small cluster of cedar trees and copper beeches.

Peering through the tree limbs, Edie's breath caught in her throat.

Lovely to behold, even dressed in winter's stark garb, Rose Chapel was constructed of rubbled stone, beautifully articulated with arched stained glass windows. Adjacent to the chapel was a three-story Norman tower that seemed out of place with its plain façade and arrow slits, tower married to chapel like a masculine/feminine yin/yang.

Stepping through an irreverently painted canary-yellow door, Sir Kenneth led them into a foyer. He removed his red scarf with a theatrical flourish, draping it around a marble bust of a bald-headed, beak-nosed man.

Who's that? Edie mouthed.

Pope Clement the Fifth, Caedmon mouthed back.

An older woman in a plain navy-blue dress—Edie placed her in the fiftyish range—scurried into the foyer. Any notion of the woman being Mrs. Campbell-Brown was instantly dispelled when she obsequiously bobbed her head and said, "Good day, Sir Kenneth."

Acknowledging the greeting with little more than a brusque nod, Sir Kenneth removed his leather bomber jacket and shoved it at the older woman. With a distracted wave of the hand, he indicated that Edie and Caedmon should do likewise.

"Soon after you left, sir, the Norway spruce was delivered," the housekeeper politely informed the master of the castle, her arms now laden with three sets of outerwear.

Sir Kenneth glanced at a beautiful, but bare, Christmas tree that had been set up at the other end of the foyer.

"Mrs. Janus has an annoying habit of stating the obvious." He gestured to the stacked boxes on the console table. "Please overlook the Christmas fripperies. Mrs. Janus also has an annoying habit of decking Rose Chapel with boughs of holly and streams of satin ribbon."

Not liking Sir Kenneth's high-handed tone, Edie walked over to the console table and carefully lifted a glass angel out of its nest of tissue paper. As she held it aloft, the gilt-edged wings caught the wintry light. "These are lovely ornaments," she said to Mrs. Janus, smiling.

"That particular angel came from Poland."

Without being told, Edie sensed that the Christmas holidays were particularly difficult for Mrs. Janus. Like many emigrants, she no doubt longed for the traditions of her native land. Taking care, Edie replaced the fragile angel in its box. "I'm sure it'll be a beautiful tree."

"The Christmas season is one of joy and remembrance," the housekeeper replied, casting a quick glance in her employer's direction.

"As is hot mulled wine," Sir Kenneth loudly barked. "And bring us some of those little tarts I saw you pop into the Aga."

Orders issued, Sir Kenneth led Edie and Caedmon down the hall. Playing the baronial lord, he swung open a paneled door and strode into a large, high-ceilinged room. About to follow him, Edie hesitated, taken aback by the stone grotesques that flanked the doorway.

"Is it my imagination or did one of those butt-ugly creatures just move its lips?"

"It's the play of light and shadow," Caedmon informed her. "Sir Kenneth's way of instilling fear into the hearts of all those who enter his sanctum sanctorum." Given what was clearly a grudge match between the two men, Edie wasn't surprised by Caedmon's sarcastic rejoinder.

At a glance, she could see that the sanctum sanctorum had originally been the main chamber of the chapel; the massive arched ceiling, stone floor, and stained glass triptych were the dead giveaway. Put all together, it made for an impressive sight. Assuming one ignored the half dozen cats snoozing in various places throughout the room. A nicked-eared feline, perched on top of a bookcase, drowsily lifted its head, the rest of the tribe taking no notice of the intrusion.

Trying not to gawk, she did a quick three-sixty. Some things, like the medieval torchères, looked right at home. Other things, like the modern wood shelving unit jam-packed with old records sheathed in clear plastic, looked conspicuously out of place in the medieval setting.

"I daresay that you are looking at the best collection of nineteen-fifties American rock and roll in the entire U.K.," Sir Kenneth remarked, having noticed the direction of her gaze. "The music of my youth, as you have undoubtedly deduced."

Edie also deduced that music wasn't the Oxford don's only

passion. On the wall nearest to where she stood hung a black-and-white poster of the 1930s movie siren Mae West, her curvaceous figure swathed in a satin evening gown. Beside the poster a large animal horn hung from a bright blue tassel, the hideous thing banded with engraved silver. All too easily, she could envision Sir Kenneth decked out in his red cashmere scarf and brown bomber jacket, swigging gin and tonics out of the loving cup like tap water from a spout.

"My dear, before you depart, you must have a look at my collection of incunabula," Sir Kenneth said, gesturing to a bookcase jam-packed with leather-bound volumes.

Put on the spot, Edie gave the bookcase a cursory glance, recalling a philosophy professor who'd once invited her to his house to look at his collection of Chagall prints. She sidled closer to Caedmon.

Sir Kenneth motioned to a pair of upholstered chairs positioned in front of a paper-laden desk, one stack of papers weighed down with a rusty astrolabe, another with a snow dome of the Empire State Building. Behind the desk, beautifully framed in gilt, hung a reproduction of Trumbull's painting depicting the signing of the Declaration of Independence.

"Sir Kenneth has a love of all things American," Caedmon whispered in her ear as he dislodged a dozing cat from his chair. "Do be on your guard."

"That's why you're here, Big Red," she whispered back at him.

Walking over to them, Sir Kenneth jovially slapped Caedmon on the back. "Middle age becomes you, young Aisquith." Then, turning his attention to Edie, he remarked, "When he first arrived at Oxford, he was a gangly-limbed lad with a thatch of unruly red hair."

Grinning, Edie gave Caedmon a once-over. "Hmm. Sounds cute."

"Ah! The lady doth have a penchant for redheaded buggers." As Sir Kenneth took his seat behind the desk, Edie heard him mutter, "Lucky bastard."

CHAPTER 36

At finding himself seated in Sir Kenneth's study, inundated with the twin scents of damp wool and musty leather, Caedmon experienced an unexpected burst of painful nostalgia.

Striving for an appearance of calm, he glanced at the stained glass triptych that overshadowed the room. A beautiful piece of medieval artistry, the three windows articulated that most famous of cautionary tales, the Temptation in the Garden.

Overtly phallic snake. A bright red juicy apple. Hands shamefully placed over fig-leafed genitals.

For some inexplicable reason, it reminded him of his student days at Oxford. Perhaps because, he, too, had dared to eat the fruit from the Tree of Knowledge.

And if he was the hapless Adam, Sir Kenneth Campbell-Brown could only be the conniving Lucifer.

Although in his impressionable youth, he'd cast his mentor in a far more exalted role.

A brilliant scholar, a rigid taskmaster, and at times a capriciously cruel bastard, Sir Kenneth demanded an unswerving fidelity from his students. In return, he gave his charges an unforgettable academic journey. Ever mindful that Oxford had its start when groups of young scholars gathered around the most illustrious teachers of the day, Sir Kenneth maintained the tradition, hosting weekly tutorials within the stone confines of Rose Chapel.

For nearly eight years, he and Sir Kenneth had maintained a close relationship. Not unlike a father and his son.

Initially, Sir Kenneth had approved his dissertation topic, intrigued by the notion that the Knights Templar might have explored the tombs and temples of Egypt during their tenure in the Holy Land. But when he dared to suggest that the Templars had turned their backs on Catholicism and become devotees of the Isis mystery cult, Sir Kenneth not only refused to countenance the notion, he took the backlash one step further, publicly ridiculing him for having "embraced rumors and passed them off as the truth."

It was as if he'd been mugged in the middle of a dark and rainy night.

Thirteen years later he turned misfortune to advantage, his derided dissertation paper becoming the cornerstone for his book, *Isis Revealed*.

Shoving aside the old memories, Caedmon cleared his throat, ready to embark on what would undoubtedly be a bumpy ride.

"Let us suppose for argument's sake that Galen of Godmersham did discover the Ark of the Covenant while on reconnaissance in Esdraelon," he carefully began, mindful that Sir Kenneth dealt in "fact, not innuendo." "Is there any evidence to support that particular supposition?"

Leaning back in his tufted leather wingback, his blue-veined fingers laced over his chest, Sir Kenneth's gaze narrowed; the old man was undoubtedly deciding whether to reply. With a noticeable lack of enthusiasm, he finally said, "There are a few shreds of historical data to support your supposition."

"Like what?" Edie piped in; subtlety was not her strong suit.

"As you undoubtedly know, theories have waxed and waned as to how and why the Ark disappeared. However, if one carefully shifts through centuries of biblical silence, the Ark's disappearance might possibly be laid at the sandaled foot of the Egyptian pharaoh Shishak, who invaded the holy city of Jerusalem in the year 926 B.C."

As his former mentor began to speak, Caedmon was reminded of the fact that Sir Kenneth never prepared for his tutorials, always speaking extemporaneously. And brilliantly.

Most who flew by the seat of their pants crash-landed midway in flight. Never Sir Kenneth Campbell-Brown; his lectures were legendary.

Caedmon turned to Edie. Filling in the gaps, he said, "Shishak's invasion occurred not long after Solomon's son Rehoboam inherited the crown of Israel. Because the northern tribes had recently broken away during a contentious power struggle, the Kingdom of Israel was left vulnerable."

"In other words, the opportunistic Egyptians swept down like vultures on roadkill."

Sir Kenneth laughed aloud, clearly amused. "Well put, my dear! Well put, indeed."

On the far side of the room, the study door suddenly swung open, the convivial mood interrupted by the heavy thud of rubber-soled shoes. Without uttering a word, the housekeeper, bearing a tray laden with Wedgwood and pewter, walked over to the tea table. Still silent as the grave, the stern-faced matron handed each of them a tankard of mulled wine and a dainty plate with two petite tarts.

Watching the housekeeper depart, Caedmon thought he recognized the woman, unable to fathom why any domestic would willingly suffer Sir Kenneth's mercurial ways for so many years. Clearly, the woman possessed the patience of Job.

"The blasted Aga has been running full throttle since the first of December. If I'm not careful, I'll pack on a stone before Twelfth Night."

Forgoing the beautifully incised dessert fork, Edie plucked the miniature tart off the plate with her fingers. "You were about to regale us with the story of Shishak's invasion of Israel."

"So I was." Choosing wine over sweets, Sir Kenneth cradled his tankard between his hands. "According to the book of Kings, in the fifth year of Rehoboam's reign, 'Shishak, king of Egypt, came up against Jerusalem: And he took away the treasures of the house of the Lord, and the treasures of the king's house; he even took away all.'"

"Meaning that the pharaoh stole the Ark of the Covenant!" When her exclamation met with silence, Edie's brows puckered in the middle. "Well, what else could it mean?"

"The Old Testament makes no mention of Shishak seizing the Ark. It merely records that the pharaoh managed to come away with five hundred shields of beaten gold."

"Solomon's famous shields," Caedmon murmured.

"Some biblical historians have theorized that King Rehoboam willingly handed over the five hundred gold shields as tribute to repay a debt of honor. Years earlier, the pharaoh had granted the wayward Hebrew prince asylum when his father ordered his assassination. All that internecine rivalry between family members is what makes the Bible such a jolly good read," Sir Kenneth said in an aside, broadly winking at Edie.

"Are there any historical records aside from the Old Testament that mention Shishak's invasion of Israel?" Caedmon inquired, wishing the other man would stay on point.

"The only other account is an inscription at Luxor inside the Temple of Amun-Ra. Per the inscription, after he attacked Jerusalem, Shishak apparently stopped on the Plain of Esdraelon, where he had a commemorative stele erected. The custom of the time mandated that Shishak show his gratitude to the gods by leaving behind a sizable offering. As with the tax man, one must always appease one's god. And to answer your next question, there is no record of what Shishak did with his ill-gotten gains once he returned to the capital city of Tanis."

"I thought the Ark was placed in Shishak's burial tomb. At least that's the theory put forth in *Raiders of the Lost Ark*," Edie conversationally remarked.

To Caedmon's surprise, rather than berate Edie for introducing a fictional movie plotline into the discussion, Sir Kenneth smiled. "You are absolutely charming, my dear. But you have jumped to an erroneous conclusion regarding Shishak and the Ark of the Covenant. As I earlier mentioned, there is no evidence that Shishak took the Ark."

"It stands to reason that if the pharaoh's army invaded Jerusalem, Shishak would have raided Solomon's Temple," Caedmon argued. "After all, the sole purpose for invading Israel was to come away with as much treasure as they could pocket."

"And what proof do you have that Shishak actually laid his greedy hands upon the much-coveted prize?"

"As you have already stated, there's no direct biblical evidence. However, it stands to reason that—"

"Rubbish! It does not stand to reason!" Sir Kenneth loudly exclaimed, punctuating his rebuttal with a banged fist. "Moreover, your assumptions are without warrant. You would be well advised, young Aisquith, to keep your fantastical deductions at bay."

Warning issued, the woolly-headed don surged to his feet, whereupon he strode to a nearby window. Despite the December temperatures on the other side of the glass, he threw open the window, letting in a burst of wintry air. The centuries-old grisaille glass caught the midday sun, cloaking the older man in a silvery gray nimbus.

"Reginae erunt nutrices tuae!" he hollered to the bare trees that bordered the chapel yard.

Edie's jaw nearly came unhinged, so great was her astonishment.

Having witnessed the performance many times before, Caedmon rose to his feet and walked over to the tea tray, snatching two pecan tarts from a Wedgwood plate. He handed one of the tarts to Edie. "'Queens shall be thy nursing mothers,'" he translated. "Taken from the book of Isaiah, it is the Queen's College motto."

Munching on his tart, Caedmon gazed beyond the woolly head at the window, espying the small stone terrace that overlooked the knot garden. In the blossoming profusion of Trinity term, Sir Kenneth liked to gather his favorites on the terrace. For some inexplicable reason, the memory of those lush spring days was especially poignant. And especially painful.

"I know Sir Kenneth would jump all over me if I suggested this," Edie said in a lowered voice, "but what if Shishak dumped the Ark of the Covenant at Esdraelon just like the Philistines dumped the Ark at Bethshemesh? Shishak might have done that if the Egyptian soldiers started to complain of tumors and lesions. Or, better yet, what if the pharaoh witnessed one or two of his soldiers being tossed in the air because of the electric current being produced by the Ark? I'd think that'd be reason enough to hide the Ark, say a prayer, and get the heck out of Esdraelon as quick as possible."

Thinking it a likely scenario, Caedmon reseated himself, the maudlin mood instantly lifted. "*You* are a woman after my own heart."

He also thought it probable that Shishak's appeasement offering was then happened upon by a crusading knight; the dimensions listed in the Feet of Fines for Galen's gold chest were an exact match to the dimensions given in the Old Testament for the Ark of the Covenant. And Esdraelon, the site where Galen of Godmersham discovered his gold chest, was where the commemorative stele had been erected by Shishak.

"Sir Kenneth said something about Galen being the proud owner of a number of *objets sacrés*. Are you thinking what I'm thinking, that Galen also happened upon a few of Solomon's shields?"

"It's not outside the realm of possibility that Shishak left a number of shields as a peace offering to the gods," Caedmon answered in a hushed tone. "Although I wouldn't broach the notion with our host."

"Gotcha."

Closing the window, Sir Kenneth strode back to his desk.

"Nothing like a full-throated bellow to clear one's mind, eh? You should try it, my dear. I suspect you have a fulsome pair of lungs." Pronouncement issued, he turned to Caedmon. "Although this has been a most entertaining discussion, young Aisquith, your original supposition is not unlike a fart in a wind tunnel. Ephemeral, at best."

"And thus 'a terrible beauty is born,'" Caedmon drolly murmured.

"You were always fond of literary flourish. Had you studied medieval literature rather than medieval history, you might have gone far."

"Rather late for such lamentations."

"Um, speaking of literary endeavors, I'm curious about the poems that Galen of Godmersham wrote prior to his death,"

Edie interjected, taking upon herself the thankless job of referee.

"Yes, I thought the two of you would be interested in Galen's poetry. The original quatrains are kept at Duke Humfrey's Library and do not circulate. But lucky for you, my dear, I've got a copy right here."

Still standing, he shuffled through a pile of papers on his desk. When Sir Kenneth didn't find what he was looking for, he impatiently riffled through the next pile. And then another, all the while muttering under his breath.

"This is unconscionable!" he angrily exclaimed, slapping a palm on top of the last pile searched. "Someone pinched the blasted quatrains!"

CHAPTER 37

As she did each and every year, Marta Janus carefully removed the tissue-wrapped ornaments from the packing crate. First she unwrapped the six handblown glass angels from her native Poland. Next she unwrapped the tartan-clad Santas. As always, she found the green-and-blue-plaid porcelain figures slightly grotesque. But Sir Kenneth was inordinately proud of his Scottish forebears, and so each year she hung the gaudy ornaments on the tree. One plaid Santa for each crystal angel.

Sir Kenneth always protested the dressing of the tree, claiming it a strange ritual for a woman who professed to be a devout Catholic. Marta simply turned a deaf ear. After twenty-seven years in Sir Kenneth's employ, she was no longer affected by his condescension. She'd built a wall around her heart. Brick by brick, the mortar so thick as to be impenetrable.

When she first arrived in Oxford, she believed Sir Kenneth

Campbell-Brown to be a kind and generous man. Although many intellectuals professed sympathy for the dissident movement, few were willing to take in a Polish refugee who spoke but a few words of English. Sir Kenneth had no such qualms. He pointed; she cleaned. For the first year they had no verbal communication whatsoever. And then one day she awoke to find handwritten signs taped to nearly every piece of furniture. Her grace period having abruptly expired, the lord of Rose Chapel expected her to master the English language. At first, it had been nothing more than a silly game of butchered phrases and garbled sentences. Then it went from game to something deeper, more complex; Marta was determined to prove her worth to the man who'd plucked her from the ashes of fear and uncertainty.

She had been one of the lucky few who managed to escape Poland, having paid an exorbitant fee to a "guide" who smuggled her out of Gdansk in the hull of a fishing vessel. Her husband, Witold, had not been so fortunate. Ensnared in the crackdown imposed by the Communist bosses, he'd been sent to prison for crimes against the state. He was a bricklayer by trade; his only crime had been to dream of a Poland free of Communist rule. Sentenced to ten years of hard labor, he lasted but three. Marta did not receive word of his death until he'd already been dead and buried sixteen months. She spoke of his death to no one. Not even Sir Kenneth, obeying what was an unspoken rule in Rose Chapel: *Never speak of matters of the heart.*

She supposed the rule came about because Sir Kenneth did not possess a heart. Or if he did, it was in rare evidence. In twenty-seven years, there were only two occasions when Sir Kenneth Campbell-Brown exhibited any sort of tender regard. The first occasion was when, having read of her plight in a local newspaper, he rang up the Catholic charity that had sponsored her when she first arrived in England, informing them that he would provide gainful employment for as long as need be. Nearly ten years would pass before the second occasion.

Although there were countless incidents in between— incidents that bespoke a decadent and depraved existence.

Many nights Sir Kenneth did not return to Rose Chapel. Many nights were spent in drunken revelry. One such night she happened upon two naked, giggling girls in the kitchen smearing butter on each other's bare breasts. Another night she went to turn down the bed, only to discover Sir Kenneth and a muscular black man committing an unspeakable act. Some nights she thought him the devil incarnate. Other nights, a beautiful Bacchus.

He'd certainly been beautiful that long-ago December eve, attired in a crisply tailored black tuxedo, his gray curls gleaming like polished pewter. He'd returned early from a party, claiming that it had been a "ghastly bore." Marta offered him a cup of mulled wine and asked if he would like to help trim the Christmas tree. He laughed at the invitation, but loosened his bow tie and helped nonetheless. He'd even steadied a chair so she could place a twinkling star atop the tree. But the chair wobbled and she accidentally fell into his arms. Before she knew it, they were rolling together on the recently vacuumed carpet, pulling at each other's garments like two crazed animals. She had not lain with a man in the ten years since she'd left her native Poland. In that impassioned instant, Sir Kenneth ceased to be the master of Rose Chapel. He was simply a man. *Forceful. Hard. Commanding.* She'd cried out, the pain so exquisite, she thought she would be torn asunder.

The next morning silence returned to Rose Chapel. Not unlike the first year of her tenure, Sir Kenneth did little but point and mutter. She did nothing but sweep and vacuum. No mention was made of the previous night's passion. Had it not been for the crystal angel smashed beneath the tree and Sir Kenneth's bow tie entangled in a tree limb, she could almost believe it had never happened. The broken angel went into the dustbin; the satin tie into her keepsake box.

One week later, on Boxing Day, when masters traditionally gave gifts to their servants, a small box wrapped in plain brown paper mysteriously appeared on her dresser. Inside was a hand-blown crystal angel. There was no card attached to the gift.

Each year the mystery angel was the first to be unwrapped. And each year, despite his protests and complaints, Marta trimmed a Christmas tree, forcing the master of Rose Chapel to remember their night of passion.

She'd long since given up any hope that Sir Kenneth's soul could be saved. For to have a soul, one must first have a heart. Heartless man that he was, she feared the day would come when she would be replaced with a younger woman. A woman whose hair had not turned gray, whose body had not gone flaccid. Marta feared what would become of her if she were made to face the wolves, penniless and pensionless.

But there was a way to avoid the wolves.

An American angel had come to deliver her from that which she most feared. She could now leave Rose Chapel on her own terms, her gray head held high.

It required but one phone call.

Reaching into her apron pocket, Marta removed the scrap of paper with the scrawled mobile phone number. For two days she'd carried the slip of paper in her pocket.

Staring at the mobile number, she hesitated. Uncertain what to do. Assailed with the memories of that long-ago December eve.

Like a woman lost in a dazzling white blizzard, Marta turned her gaze to the neat line of Christmas ornaments waiting to be placed upon the tree. In the kitchen, a buzzer noisily pealed. *Time to take the buns out of the oven.*

Marta turned away from the table with the neat line of ornaments. As she did, her hip jostled the edge of the table. One hideous blue-and-green Santa rolled to the edge, falling to the stone floor.

Marta stared at the broken bits of porcelain.

No longer uncertain.

CHAPTER 38

"Are you thinking what I'm thinking," Edie said in a lowered voice, "that the Harvard 'chap' stole the quatrains from Sir Kenneth?"

"Indeed, we are of like mind," Caedmon replied, the missing quatrains proof positive that Stanford MacFarlane believed Galen of Godmersham uncovered the Ark of the Covenant. It also proved that MacFarlane believed the Ark's whereabouts were contained within the lines of those archaic verses. A poetic treasure map, as it were. He and Edie had to move quickly.

"Sir, did you not say that Galen's poetry is housed at the Bod?"

Still shuffling through various piles of paper on top of his desk, Sir Kenneth glanced up. "What's that? Er, yes. The original copy of the quatrains is kept at Duke Humfrey's Library."

Duke Humfrey's Library was one of fourteen various libraries in the Bodleian system. Unless things had greatly changed, only matriculated students and researchers who'd obtained written permission could gain entry to Duke Humfrey's Library; the premises were strictly off limits to visitors. To circumvent the restrictions, MacFarlane's man had stolen a copy of the quatrains from Sir Kenneth.

"Is there any possibility that I might be able to examine the original quatrains?"

Sir Kenneth stopped in midshuffle. For several long seconds the older man stared at him from across the paper-strewn desk. Caedmon felt very much like a child expectantly awaiting a parent's decision about attending an upcoming football match.

"I could call the head librarian and ask that the two of you be granted a special dispensation to view the library's collection. But I warn you, Galen's quatrains are a linguistic puzzle tied with an encrypted knot."

Having assumed no less, Caedmon respectfully bowed his head. "I am in your debt, Sir Kenneth."

"Did you know, my dear, that young Aisquith graduated with First Honors?" Sir Kenneth remarked, abruptly changing the subject.

About to raise a tankard to her lips, Edie stopped in midmotion. "Um, no. Guess that makes Caedmon a really smart cookie, huh?"

"Indeed, it does. The smart cookie then went on to write a brilliant master's thesis on St. Bernard of Clairvaux and the founding of the Knights Templar. Later, when he went off to Jerusalem to conduct his dissertation research, I had every expectation that he would submit an equally brilliant dissertation."

The knot in Caedmon's belly painfully tightened.

Bloody hell.

This was the old man's price for granting the favor: to stuff his entrails with red-hot coals.

"As you have no doubt guessed, I was not up to the challenge. Nor did I meet Sir Kenneth's high standard for brilliance," he openly confessed, refusing to let his estranged mentor deliver the coup de grâce. Better a self-inflicted wound than to meekly be led to the scaffold.

"It didn't have to go that way. If you had come to me and discussed your plans before embarking half-cocked, I could have—"

"Is that what angered you, that I left the bloody nest without your consent, failing to obtain your highly esteemed academic opinion?" *Or were you angered that the son had deserted the father?*

Able to see that the sparks were about to catch fire, Edie

jumped to her feet. "We've sort of veered a little off track, don't you think?" Then, acting as though nothing untoward had occurred, she calmly walked over to the serving tray and snatched a pecan tart off the bone china plate. "Now, let me make sure I've got this straight, Sir Kenneth. You said that Galen of Godmersham had no children."

"That is correct."

"But since he left the Hospitallers when he returned to England, I assume that he was married." Holding the tart between thumb and forefinger, she slightly waved it to and fro as she spoke.

"Galen went to the altar not once, but thrice. No sooner did a spouse depart for the heavenly realm than Galen would find himself a young replacement. His last bride, Philippa Whitcombe, had been the daughter of the justice of the peace for Canterbury. When Galen died, Philippa promptly joined a cloistered order of nuns. One can assume that she did not suit to the married state."

About to take a bite of her sweet, Edie lowered the tart. "So who inherited the gold chest?"

"Ah! An excellent question, my dear." Walking over to the tray, Sir Kenneth plucked a mince tart from the near-empty plate. "Since the gold chest does not appear in any Feet of Fines record after 1348, one can infer that the gold chest was never uncovered. Not altogether surprising, given that there wasn't a single inhabitant of the godforsaken Godmersham who survived the plague."

"Meaning no one was left who had any recollection of ever seeing Galen's magnificent treasures," Caedmon murmured. For all intents and purposes, it was as though Galen's gold chest had never existed once the plague struck. With no Feet of Fines record for the intervening centuries, the mystery would be that much more difficult to solve.

"Okay, but what about the quatrains? How did they come to be discovered?" Edie asked, clearly as determined as he to glean information.

"Galen's estates remained in a state of ruin until the reign of the virgin queen Elizabeth. The new owner, a wealthy wine merchant by the name of Tynsdale, had the old chapel demolished to make way for a hammer-beamed monstrosity. It was during the demolition that the quatrains were discovered beneath the altar stone. Sir Walter Raleigh, a close acquaintance of the merchant, was the first to conjecture that the *arca* mentioned in Galen's poetry might refer to the Ark of the Covenant. He and Tynsdale scoured every inch of the property. To no avail, I might add. Not a century passed that some addlebrained treasure hunter didn't attempt to find—" Catching sight of his housekeeper poking her head through the study door, he stopped in midstream. "Yes, what is it?"

"A call, sir. From the provost's office."

Clearly annoyed by the intrusion, he waved her off. "The blasted relic's not working," he said by way of explanation, gesturing to an antique black telephone on the edge of his desk. "There's a telephone in the foyer. I won't be but a moment."

Caedmon rose to his feet. "The time has come for us to depart."

He wasn't certain, but he thought he detected a disappointed glimmer in the older man's eyes. Suddenly uncomfortable, he glanced at his wristwatch. "Duke Humfrey's Library is open until seven. If you could call ahead and make the necessary arrangements, we would be most appreciative."

"Yes, of course. My pleasure." As he spoke, Sir Kenneth escorted them to the foyer.

Out of the corner of his eye, Caedmon caught a glimmer of color. Turning his head, he could see that the once-bare Norway spruce now sparkled, richly colored glass ornaments glowing jewel-like among the dark foliage.

"Did you know that it was Queen Victoria's husband, the bewhiskered Albert, who introduced the Christmas tree to these shores? He had them all done up with edible fruit and little wax fairies." Sir Kenneth fingered a glossy green limb, a wistful look in his eye. "I told her to get a Scots pine, not a spruce. Blasted woman."

"I think it's absolutely gorgeous," Edie remarked.

"Yes, it always is." Turning his back on the tree, Sir Kenneth cleared his throat. "The Choral Society is singing Handel's *Messiah* at seven thirty. Perhaps you and Miss Miller would care to join me? There is nothing that compares to the sound of crystal voices lifted to the heavens. Quite moving. Even if one does not believe in the Christmas myth that's been spoon-fed to us by power hungry Church fathers, eh?"

Having obtained all that he needed from his old mentor, Caedmon shook his head. He'd had enough strained conversation for one day. "Thank you, Sir Kenneth. Unfortunately, we—"

"Yes, yes, I understand." Then, his right index finger pointing heavenward, like a man struck with an inspired idea, he said, "I've got just the thing. The crate arrived only this morning." Turning his back, he searched the boxes piled high on the console table. "Where is the blasted— Ah! There it is!" Reaching into a wooden crate, he removed a bottle.

"Merry Christmas, young Aisquith."

Caedmon hesitated a moment, instantly recognizing the label on the bottle of Queen's College port that the older man offered to him. *Collegii Reginae*. He well recalled the port decanter being passed between the senior fellow and his small band of favorites long years ago. Those were fond memories, unsullied by the later rupture.

With a brusque nod, he accepted the bottle. "And a Merry Christmas to you, Sir Kenneth."

The other man patted his stomach. "I don't know about 'merry,' but it shall certainly be filling, what with Mrs. Janus stuffing me with Christmas gâteau and pecan tarts."

Uncomfortable with the pleasantries, knowing they hid the bitter feelings that had earlier bubbled to the surface, Caedmon took Edie by the elbow. "Come. We must be on our way."

To his surprise, she disengaged herself from his grasp, stepped over to Sir Kenneth, and kissed him on his withered right cheek. "I hope you have a very Merry Christmas!"

Grinning like a besotted fool, Sir Kenneth followed them to the door. "And, in turn, I hope that you and young Aisquith uncover Galen's blasted box. If the gold chest is to be found, you are the man to find it." This last remark was directed to Caedmon.

Surprised by his old mentor's show of support, Caedmon said the first thing that came to mind.

"Thank you, sir. That means a great deal to me."

CHAPTER 39

Enraged, Stan MacFarlane snapped shut his cell phone.

Aisquith and the woman were in Oxford.

Although the *how* of it eluded him, the *why* was plainly evident. Somehow they'd managed to find out that the medieval knight Galen of Godmersham had uncovered the Ark of the Covenant while on crusade in the Holy Land. The museum director, Eliot Hopkins, must have passed that information on to Aisquith before his death.

"Do you want me to take care of it, sir?"

Stan glanced over his shoulder. He knew that former gunnery sergeant Boyd Braxton was anxious to make amends for the debacle in Washington.

"Sometimes it's in one's best interest to be merciful."

It took a few moments for the other man's befuddled expression to morph into an amused grin. "Oh, I get it, Colonel. Like Tony Soprano, you want to keep your friends close and your enemies even closer."

That being as good an answer as any, Stan tersely nodded. "Tell Sanchez to put a tail on Aisquith. I want to know the Brit's every move."

Turning on his heel, he strode down the low-ceilinged hall,

his booted footfall muffled by the well-worn Persian runner.
On either side of him hung gilt-framed landscape paintings.

*A tastefully appointed house for the discriminating trav-
eler.*

When he leased the house on the website, he hadn't given
a rat's ass about the décor. He only cared that the manor house
was located midway between London and Oxford at the end of
a half-mile oak-lined driveway. He needed a base camp to set
up operations. Oakdale Manor fit the bill.

Brusquely nodding, he acknowledged the armed sentry
standing ramrod straight beside the upholstered chair. The
Heckler & Koch MP5 clutched to the sentry's chest came courtesy of a sergeant major in the Royal Marines who routinely
padded his retirement account with illegal small-arms sales.

Passing the age-blackened doors that led to the formal dining room, he gave a quick, cursory inspection, verifying that
his highly paid contract worker was busy deciphering Galen of
Godmersham's archaic poetry. A postgraduate student enrolled
in Harvard's medieval studies program, the scraggly-haired
twenty-nine-year-old had jumped at the chance to pay off the
nearly seventy thousand dollars in student loans that hung over
him like a well-honed ax blade. Soft-spoken and effeminate,
the man put Stan in mind of a loose bowel movement. If not
for the fact that he possessed the arcane body of knowledge
necessary to decipher the fourteenth-century quatrains, he
would have cut the stoop-shouldered pencil dick after yesterday's meeting with the Oxford highbrow. For the moment,
however, he served a purpose.

Satisfied to observe the bespectacled scholar intently staring at his laptop, an eight-hundred-year-old map of England
spread out on the table beside him, Stan continued down the
hall to the kitchen.

For some reason the stone-floored country kitchen put him
mind of his grandmother's kitchen back home in Boone, North
Carolina. Maybe it was the green-mottled crockware that lined
the open shelves. Or the scarred wood-planked table that dom-
inated the center of the room. Whatever the reason, he could
envision his aproned grandmother standing at the oversized

gas stove frying up some freshly laid eggs with big slabs of salted ham.

Reduced to eating English slop, he cut himself a thick slice of bread from the loaf that'd been left on the table. Slathering it with plum jam, he carried it over to the casement window that overlooked the garden. Through the gnarled branches of dead wisteria that framed the outside of the window, he could see a fine-looking white horse frolicking in a distant field.

How much did Aisquith know?

Probably not much. That's why he was in Oxford consulting with the foremost expert on the English crusaders. How ironic that the two men were acquainted with one another. The intelligence dossier on Aisquith had made no mention of the relationship. Luckily, he'd had the foresight to buy off the housekeeper.

Still it was troubling to discover that Aisquith knew about the quatrains. Although given that he possessed the sole copy of the quatrains outside Duke Humfrey's Library and given that the library was only open to Oxford faculty and students, the Brit didn't have a prayer of examining the original codex. Without the quatrains, Aisquith was just pissing in a gusty wind.

He glanced at his watch.

It was 1331 local time.

He'd hoped to have the quatrains deciphered by now, his excitement mounting with each passing hour. No doubt this was how Moses felt when he crafted the Ark of the Covenant, placing inside it the two stones inscribed with the Ten Commandments. With the creation of the Ark, Moses had ushered in a new world order. The hinge of history had swung upon the Ark. And it would soon swing again.

Praise be to the Almighty! For the battle is the Lord's.

Although he knew that he had a tough fight ahead of him, he took solace in the knowledge that he would have at the ready the best weapon a soldier could have.

For twenty-five years he'd been readying himself. *Love of God. Purity of heart. Cleanliness of mind and body.* Those were the qualities of the Ark guardian.

Harliss, a burly ex-Marine, now a "consultant" with Rosemont Security, poked his head into the kitchen. "Sir, he's got something for you."

Knowing that "he" referred to the Harvard scholar, Stan headed for the dining room.

"What do you have?" he barked without preamble as he entered the room. The side chairs had all been pushed to one wall, enabling a free flow of movement around the large oval-shaped table. Several framed paintings were on the floor, propped against the same wall.

The scholar walked over and dimmed the overhead chandelier, a PowerPoint slide projected onto the now-pictureless dining room wall. Stan found himself staring at the four quatrains that Galen of Godmersham had composed prior to his death.

> The despitous Zephirus rood forth from Salomon's Cite
>   jubilant they sang
> But a goost forney followed as a tempest of deeth
> Repentaunt for his sins the shiten shepherd yeve penaunce
> Thanne homeward he him spedde the ill-got treasure on holy
>   stronders
>
> From Jerusalem a companye of knights in hethenesse they
>   ryden out
> Ech of hem made other for to winne on the heeth of
>   Esdraelon
> They bataille ther to the deeth the vertuous knight the feeld
>   he woone
> And ther-withal chivalrye he kepte wel the holy covenaunt
>
> This ilke worthy knight from sundry londes to Engelond he
>   wende
> Arca and gold ful shene he carried to the toun he was born
> With open yë he now did see the blake pestilence he wrought
> And whan this wrecche knight saugh it was so his deeth ful
>   well deserved

*Sore weep the goos on whom he truste for oon of hem were
   deed*
I couthe not how the world be served by swich adversitee
*But if a manne with ful devout corage seken the holy blissful
   martir*
*In the veyl bitwixen worlds tweye ther the hidden trouthe be
   fond*

"Just as you thought, this word *arca* is the key to deciphering the quatrains." Using a pointer, the younger man indicated the third quatrain. "*Arca*, of course, is the Latin word for 'chest.'"

Because the bespectacled nimrod hadn't told him anything he didn't already know, Stan made no reply. Although he'd provided his paid scholar with a high-speed Internet connection enabling him to hook into the world's best libraries, he'd parsed his words carefully, refusing to disclose the details of the mission.

By those who come near Me I will be treated as holy.

Not one to disobey God's dictates, Stan intended to do all in his power to ensure that the unholy did not cast their gaze upon the Ark. The scholar had merely been told that he and his men represented a consortium of art collectors trying to track down a medieval chest believed to have been buried in the mid-fourteenth century somewhere in England. If his Harvard-educated boy wonder wondered at the trio of armed guards, he'd been wise enough to keep his own counsel. Unbridled greed had a way of making a man turn a blind eye.

When no reply to his *"arca"* comment was forthcoming, the pasty-faced scholar nervously rubbed his hands together. "Slowly but surely, it's all coming together. I've got the first three quatrains more or less figured out, but I'm still trying to hammer out quatrain number four. Don't you guys worry. I'm guessing that I'll have this baby cracked in the next couple of hours."

"You've been deciphering the verses since late yesterday. I had expected some tangible results by now." Stan made no attempt to hide his annoyance; the scholar was unaware that he was working on a carefully crafted timetable.

"Hey, you can't rush these things. Although I can tell you that the four quatrains form a rectilinear allegory."

"What the hell does that mean?" Boyd Braxton muttered, staring at the scholar as though he were a turd on the bottom of his boot heel.

Smirking, the turd replied, "For those of us who never took geometry, I am referring to the four-sided geometric configuration known as a square."

CHAPTER 40

More slowly this time, Caedmon reread Galen of Godmersham's poetic quatrains.

"Admittedly, we are clinging to the thinnest of reeds."

Or the thinnest of reads, depending on one's take.

This wasn't the first time he'd been ensconced in the wood-paneled reading room of Duke Humfrey's Library, muddling his way through a thorny conundrum. In his student days, he'd spent countless hours in this very room seated at the very same table, medieval texts piled high.

Believing that a tidy work area elicited a similar tidiness in one's thinking, he organized the miscellaneous items that had been placed on the reading table. The librarian, no doubt spurred by Sir Kenneth Campbell-Brown's advance phone call, had been most solicitous in delivering the requested materials to their table. In addition to a leather-bound codex that contained a selection of fourteenth-century poetry, including Galen's quatrains, she had conveyed a slim volume that contained the Godmersham Feet of Fines records for the years 1300 to 1350. Paper, pencils, and cotton gloves had also been provided.

An exasperated frown on her face, Edie pointed a gloved index finger at the open codex. "Just look at this, will ya. It's written in Old English. Which is whole lot like saying it's written in a dead language."

Noticing that several library patrons irritably glowered, Caedmon raised a finger to his lips, reminding Edie that silence reigned supreme within the paneled walls of Duke Humfrey's Library. If one must speak, a muffled whisper was the preferred mode of communication.

"Actually, the quatrains are written in Middle English rather than the more remote Old English—thus enabling me to produce a fairly accurate interlinear translation."

"You're talking about a line-by-line translation, right?" Her voice had noticeably lowered. "When I was a graduate student, I wrote a research paper on the Wife of Bath. You know, from *The Canterbury Tales*. The paper was for a seminar class on women in the Middle Ages, and it darned near did me in."

Hoping to bolster her spirits, he patted her hand. "Don't worry. I'm certain that you'll survive the ordeal." Then, not wanting to dwell on the fact that an ordeal was by its very nature a trying endeavor, he reached for a pencil and a sheet of blank paper.

Although it'd been a number of years since he'd last translated Middle English, he managed to quickly work his way through the archaic spelling and phraseology with only a few missteps.

"Hopefully, this will make for more coherent verse," he said, pushing the sheet of paper in his companion's direction.

Lifting the handwritten sheet off the table, Edie held it at arm's length from her face. Lips silently moving, she read the translation.

The merciless west wind rode forth from Solomon's city
*   jubilantly singing*
But a ghost fire followed like a deadly tempest
Repentant for his sins, the befouled shepherd did penance
Then homeward he sped, the ill-gotten treasure left on holy
*   shores*

From Jerusalem, a company of knights rode out in heathen
  lands
Each of them tried to profit from the other on the field of
  Esdraelon
They battled to the death, the virtuous knight winning the field.
And with his show of valor, he kept the holy covenant

This same worthy knight went from sundry lands to England
He carried a chest and bright gold to the town where he was
  born
With open eyes he now saw the black plague that he wrought
And when the wretched knight saw this, his death was well
  deserved

The trusted goose sorely wept for all of them were dead
I know not how the world be served by such adversity
But if a man with a fully devout heart seek the blessed martyr
There in the veil between two worlds, the hidden truth be
  found

As she wordlessly lowered the sheet of paper to the table,
Caedmon discerned from Edie's frown that she was as befuddled by the translation as she had been by the original text.

"I suggest that we take the allegorical and symbolic references in turn. Phrases such as 'the merciless west wind,' 'the
befouled shepherd,' and 'the veil between two worlds' should
be thought of as pieces of code which have been strategically
placed within the quatrains. The key to solving the riddle will
hinge on how we decode the symbols contained within each
line of verse."

"And what if Galen loaded his word puzzle with a bunch of
mixed signals?" she asked, still frowning.

"Oh, I have no doubt that Galen deliberately inserted semiotic decoys into the quatrains. The medieval mind was quite
nimble when it came to inserting secret messages into seemingly innocuous text."

Edie stared at the handwritten sheet of paper. "Something
tells me that we're gonna need a CIA code breaker."

"Here, take this, for instance," he said, pointing to the first line of text. "'The merciless west wind rode forth from Solomon's city jubilantly singing.' I detect a bit of linguistic legerdemain at work. Clearly, this refers to the pharaoh Shishak leaving Jerusalem after successfully pillaging Solomon's Temple. Death then followed in the Egyptian's wake, the first quatrain ending with Shishak leaving the pilfered treasure behind as he and his army scurried back to Egypt."

Edie's eyes suspiciously narrowed. "Unless I'm greatly mistaken, you're actually enjoying yourself."

"Who among us does not enjoy the intricacies of a well-constructed word puzzle?"

"Well, me, for starters," his companion groused. "I'm more of a sudoku person. It's a number puzzle that— Never mind." She waved away the thought. "You know, the only reason we're sitting here in Duke Humfrey's Library is because we *assume* that when Galen of Godmersham composed his quatrains, he was actually leaving clues as to where he hid the gold chest."

"That is our base assumption," he said with a nod.

"Then I guess it's already crossed your mind that someone may have deciphered the quatrains and recovered the treasure long years ago."

"Since the cart has yet to pull the horse, we shall deal with that issue if and when it presents itself."

Edie smiled, a teasing glint in her eyes. "I think this is where I'm supposed to make a rude comparison between you and the back end of a horse."

Unable to help himself, he stared into those lively brown eyes. Since the earlier kiss on the Oxford coach, the air between them had become more sexually charged. He wondered if the storm would pass without fanfare. Or if they would be caught in a driving rain.

"Shall we continue?" Tapping the pencil on the handwritten sheet of paper, he redirected her attention.

Catching him by surprise, Edie snatched the pencil out of his hand. "This is just a guess, mind you, but I think Galen's puzzle is configured like a square."

CHAPTER 41

"In early fourteenth-century art, a chest or box of any sort was always depicted as a flat, one-dimensional square." Making no attempt to hide his condescension, the bespectacled scholar glanced at Boyd Braxton. "Something along the sophomoric lines of what you might draw if you were trying to depict a medieval chest. Once perspective was introduced into the artist's grab bag during the *quantocento*, all of that changed, of course. The *quantocento*, FYI, would be the Renaissance."

Arrogant little pissant, Stan silently fumed as he stared at the archaic verses projected onto the dining room wall.

Had the lank-haired weasel been under his military command, he would have kicked his scrawny ass between his narrow shoulders. At the moment, however, he needed the scholar's expertise. And cooperation. Although he suspected it would take a full measure and a half of self-control to keep his temper in check.

"To Galen of Godmersham's mind, a flat two-dimensional square would have been no different than the three-dimensional medieval chest your consortium is hoping to uncover. You guys following?"

Stan thought of how the Ark of the Covenant would have been illustrated in a church or cathedral during the fourteenth century. The weasel was right. More than likely, it would have been depicted as a plain four-sided square.

"Carry on," he ordered, not about to reply to the other man's question. Nor did any of his men reply. He'd told them point-blank that he'd ream each and every one of them with a piece of steel rebar if anyone let the words *Ark of the Covenant* slip past his lips.

"Now as far as deciphering this bear, I think the phrase in the first quatrain about 'Salomon's cite' refers to Galen being in Jerusalem on crusade. And in case you guys haven't figured it out yet, the first quatrain is also the first side of our metaphoric square."

Again, Stan remained silent. In truth, he didn't give a rat's ass about the first quatrain, assuming it referred to the pharaoh Shishak and *not* to Galen of Godmersham. That part of the story he was well acquainted with, because it was written in the Old Testament, 1 Kings 14:25, that Shishak "came up against Jerusalem" and that he then "took away the treasures of the house of the Lord."

What he was interested in were the cryptic messages contained within the next three quatrains. Hidden somewhere in those archaic verses, Galen of Godmersham revealed where he hid the Ark, the sacred chest that enabled God to dwell among men. And from which God would lead his holy army against the infidels in the last days.

Feeling his excitement rise, Stan glanced at the watch strapped to his left wrist.

Four days, nine hours, and twenty-six minutes until the start of Eid al-Adha, the Muslim religious festival.

Which meant he had four days, nine hours, and twenty-six minutes to find the Ark of the Covenant.

CHAPTER 42

"Ah, yes. A square. A spot-on observation," Caedmon enthused, smiling. "A quatrain is, after all, a poem with four lines."

"And Galen composed *four* quatrains," Edie added, the number four having been the giveaway.

"Not to mention that the Ark of the Covenant was usually depicted in medieval art as a four-sided square." Still smiling, Caedmon winked at her. "You must excel at sudoku. Now, to what end this metaphoric square?"

Pleased that Caedmon wanted her input, she gave it her best shot. "I think Galen was trying to compose a chain of custody for the Ark of the Covenant. And he begins the chain of custody right here in the first quatrain with the pharaoh Shishak taking the Ark from Solomon's Temple. From what Sir Kenneth told us earlier today, we know that the pharaoh left an appeasement offering, that is, the Ark, on the Plain of Esdraelon."

"Where it was happened upon some twenty-two centuries later by a roving band of Hospitaller knights led by Galen of Godmersham." He pointed to the second quatrain. "It would appear that the knights fought one another to the death over the treasure, and Galen was the lone man left standing on the field after the melee."

Lips pursed, Edie stared at the last line of the quatrain in question. "What does this mean, 'And with his show of valor, he kept the holy covenant'?"

"It probably means that Galen of Godmersham became the self-appointed guardian of the Ark."

"So, we're definitely on the right track, huh?"

"I believe so."

In all honesty, Edie didn't know how she felt about that. Although she was excited that they were working their way through the awkward medieval verses, she was at the same time uneasy about the whole thing. A little needling voice inside her head intoned the words, *Leave it be.* Over and over.

"And it's clear from the third quatrain that Galen took the Ark to England, specifically to the place of his birth, Godmersham," Caedmon continued, oblivious to her unease. "Correlating precisely with the information listed in the Feet of Fines property records. Now, *this* I find rather interesting," he said, pointing to the third quatrain. "'With open eyes he now saw the black plague that he wrought.'"

"It could be that Galen believed the Ark was responsible for the plague that hit England in 1348."

"He had ample reason to think so; the pustules that erupted on face and skin during the plague were uncannily similar to the lesions and boils that befell the Philistines. God's punishment for the theft of the Ark."

Caedmon's last remark made Edie wonder at the punishment for *finding* the Ark of the Covenant. Normally, she wasn't one to believe in curses or hexes, *but* . . .

. . . the evidence was damning. Literally. The Old Testament stories and Galen's quatrains both came stamped with the word *DANGER*. In big, bold, threatening type. Skull and crossbones included.

"Perhaps Galen hid the darned thing in the hopes that it would bring an end to the plague. Too bad he didn't have the Stones of Fire to protect himself."

Too bad they *didn't have the Stones of Fire,* Edie silently added, her unease now laced with fear. The type of fear that made one double-check all the door latches and sleep with a night-light.

"The last line of the third quatrain was probably composed while Galen was in his death throes," Caedmon blithely continued, unintentionally splashing gasoline onto the fire.

Knowing that the only way to combat fear was to take decisive action, Edie grabbed a sheet of blank paper.

"Okay, let's take our square analogy"—pencil in hand, she carefully drew a square—"and fill in the Ark's chain of custody as detailed by Galen in the quatrains."

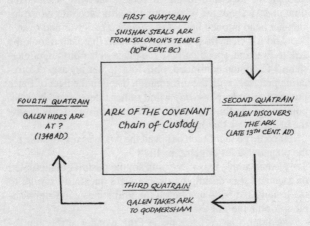

FIRST QUATRAIN

SHISHAK STEALS ARK FROM SOLOMON'S TEMPLE (10TH CENT. BC)

FOURTH QUATRAIN

GALEN HIDES ARK AT ? (1348 AD)

ARK OF THE COVENANT
Chain of Custody

SECOND QUATRAIN

GALEN DISCOVERS THE ARK (LATE 13TH CENT. AD)

THIRD QUATRAIN

GALEN TAKES ARK TO GODMERSHAM

"That's excellent." Clearly accustomed to being in a library, Caedmon managed to keep his enthusiasm to a hushed whisper.

"You know, you were absolutely right. Galen *did* use his four quatrains as a poetic cryptogram, with the Ark's current whereabouts encoded into the lines of the fourth quatrain."

She stared at the enigmatic fourth quatrain.

A trusted goose. A man with a fully devout heart. And the veil between two worlds.

"This would be a whole heck of a lot easier if Galen had simply drawn an 'X Marks the Spot' treasure map," she muttered, wondering if they'd finally hit a roadblock.

"Had he done that, the Ark would have been unearthed long centuries ago."

"While we're on the topic of finding the Ark, this might be a good time to mention that I'm starting to worry about Colonel MacFarlane having the Stones of Fire in his possession. You said it yourself: Not only was the breastplate a protective shield, but it was also used as a divination tool, enabling the wearer to communicate with God. Not unlike a two-way radio. If MacFarlane finds the Ark of the Covenant, he'd not only have the best intelligence device known to mankind, i.e. the Stones of Fire, but he'd have a very powerful weapon of mass destruction. You can't deny that it makes for a deadly duo."

For several long seconds, Caedmon held her gaze. "Then we'll do all in our power to ensure that doesn't happen." Although the words were quietly spoken, he had about him an air of fierce determination. For one brief, blurry second, she envisioned him decked out in chain mail, fighting to the death on the Plain of Esdraelon.

Returning his attention to the "custody box," Caedmon tapped his finger against the giant question mark on the fourth side of the square. "This is where we begin to tread murky water."

"Actually, this is where we need to call it quits," she matter-of-factly announced, unable to keep the jet lag at bay one second longer.

Sensing a run on her energy bank, her partner good-naturedly patted her on the back. "Come now. Time to brainstorm. Group dynamics and all that."

Needing to break up the party, she dolefully shook her head. "I need to refuel. How about we grab some pub grub? If I remember correctly, they're serving seafood salad and lentil soup at the Isis Room."

"Er, right. An excellent suggestion."

Not for one second was Edie fooled; she could see the disappointment in Caedmon's blue eyes. He might be able to pull an all-nighter, but there was no way she could tackle the fourth quatrain without some much-needed food. Followed by some much-needed sleep.

While Caedmon returned the leather-bound volumes and cotton gloves to the stern-faced librarian, Edie stuffed the sharpened pencils and notepaper into her tote bag.

A few minutes later, with Caedmon's protective arm slung

around her shoulders, they made their way along a crowded city sidewalk. Harried locals, heads ducked against a cold, wet wind, scurried alongside them. Casting a quick sideways glance down a deserted alleyway, Edie had a sudden, uneasy feeling, afraid that something malevolent, even deadly, lurked in the shadows.

CHAPTER 43

". . . at which time Galen of Godmersham succumbed to the Black Death, the great plague of 1348."

Pointer in hand, Marshall Mendolson underlined the last line of the third quatrain, having had no choice but to begin deciphering the verses. Guns at the ready, these guys were a tough crowd, the older dude with the buzz cut the scariest of them all. He wanted the goods, no two ways about it.

Marshall doubted the head dude even knew his name. Earlier he'd overheard one of his steroid-enhanced bodyguards refer to him as "the li'l Harvard prick."

"And the fourth quatrain, what of it?" his benefactor pressed, making no attempt to hide his impatience.

Marshall struck a thoughtful pose, doing a fair imitation of one of his favorite Harvard professors. "Hmm . . . good question." And one he had no intention of truthfully answering.

Did the Neanderthals really think they could outwit, outsmart, outplay a Harvard graduate?

It took only a quick, cursory reading of Galen's poetic verses for him to figure out that the *arca* in the third quatrain was an oblique reference to the Ark of the Covenant. *Not* the medieval chest the head dude had hired him to find. These guys wanted him to hunt down the Ark of the Covenant so they could cash in on it, his cut being a paltry seventy thousand dollars. After he paid off his student loans, there wouldn't be enough left for a Happy Meal at McDonald's.

Yeah, well, think again.

Jesus. The freaking Ark of the Covenant.

According to the Bible, the Ark could raze fortified cities, part seas, and kick some serious ass.

And if you believed *that*, he had some mountain property in Florida to sell you.

Although you didn't have to be a Bible thumper to know that the Ark of the Covenant was a treasure of immeasurable worth. As in more money than he could ever count.

Hello, Tahiti and a life of indolent leisure surrounded by bare-breasted island beauties.

Given that his mother had once sued the Fairfax County school board over the phrase *one nation under God* in the Pledge of Allegiance—the groundswell of religious fervor nearly swallowing Adele Mendolson whole—his finding the Ark of the Covenant would be friggin' ironic.

This one's for you, Mother.

"The 'goos' reference in the fourth quatrain is pretty straightforward," he answered after a long drawn-out pause, figuring some straight talk was in order, every good lie cloaked in the truth.

"You're talking about the goose that laid the golden egg, right?" This from the brawny bruiser named Boyd, the man straddling an expensive Sheraton chair like a lap dancer straddling a paying crotch.

"Very good, Sir Rambo. You go to the head of the class." A measured half beat later, he mockingly exclaimed, *"Not!"* At that moment he wanted nothing more than to smash the muscled behemoth's face into the wood-planked floor. As had been done to him by countless bullies in years gone by.

Knowing he could take the put-down only so far, he switched gears, once more the erudite Harvard grad. "In the medieval lexicon, the goose represented vigilance. And given the fact that Galen composed his quatrains just prior to his death, it specifically means vigilance *in* death."

Liking the sound of that, Marshall smiled, having just figured out how he could outmaneuver his benefactor.

"Line two of the last quatrain is simply a 'woe is me' com-
mentary on the plague," he continued, barely able to suppress
an excited grin. "That takes us to line three, which is an offhand reference to Saint—"

"I want to know where Galen hid his chest," the older dude
hissed, his eyes narrowing as he stared him down.

"Well, now, that *is* the sixty-four-thousand-dollar question,
isn't it?" Or a thousand times that amount.

It was all he could do not to break into song. Like the
bearded Tevye in *Fiddler on the Roof*. Except he really would
be a rich man. No "if" about it.

Stepping over to his laptop, Marshall clicked several keys,
projecting the next slide—a page from a nearly seven-hundred-
year-old document—onto the wall. "From the Feet of Fines
record, I discovered that Galen donated a hefty number of
golden objects to"—he snatched his handwritten notes from
the table—"St. Lawrence the Martyr Church in Godmersham.
That being the 'holy blissful martir' of the fourth quatrain.
Like most medieval men, Galen no doubt believed that he
could buy his way into heaven." Or bribe his way into heaven,
depending on your point of view. "Put it all together, my guess
is that Galen, quite literally, took the *arca* to his grave."

The older dude cogitated on that for a few seconds. Then,
obviously an anal sort who liked to verify the facts, he asked,
"Are you saying that the gold chest is buried in Galen of
Godmersham's tomb at St. Lawrence the Martyr Church?"

"Yup. That's as good a hypothesis as any." Seeing the flash of
annoyance on his benefactor's face, he hastily added, "It was the
custom of the time to wrap a corpse in linen, that being the 'veyl
bitwixen worlds tweye'—aka the veil between two worlds."

Marshall inwardly breathed a sigh of relief. Although
crafted on the fly, the lie had the ring of truth about it. Actually,
when the Ark had been housed in Solomon's Temple, inside
the Holy of Holies, a veil had been hung in front of it to keep
it hidden, the "veyl" in Galen's last quatrain referring to the
Ark, not a medieval death shroud.

Although the quatrains provided scant clues, he figured the Ark was really hidden inside the church under a statue of the martyred St. Lawrence. Or maybe behind a plaque or wall carving. Which is why he intended to steer the old dude and his three big bad bears away from the church building, focusing, instead, on the adjacent cemetery. Then, once his benefactor had given up the search, he would return on the sly to St. Lawrence the Martyr Church and lay claim to the prize.

A drum roll please . . .

"Galen of Godmersham's tomb . . . you're completely certain of this?"

"Certain enough," he retorted, not liking the way he was being raked over the coals.

A man clearly accustomed to giving orders, the older dude brusquely gestured to the paper-laden table. "Pack it up. We leave in ten minutes."

CHAPTER 44

"I don't know about you, but I'm not a big fan of dark and dreary weather," Edie grumbled. For the last few minutes she'd been standing guard at their hotel window, closely monitoring the courtyard below, relieved they weren't in a ground-floor room.

Relieved because her sixth sense told her that they were being watched.

Although given that she had zilch psychic ability, she couldn't rule out the possibility that her "intuition" was nothing more than an irrational fear.

Busying himself with placing pencils and paper on the small circular table that was tucked into the oriel window on the other side of the room, Caedmon glanced over at her. "Small wonder we English are such a gloomy lot."

"The Mahler doesn't help." Turning her head away from the window, Edie pointedly glanced at the small radio on the bedside table. The incessant sound of rain striking cobblestones competed with the ponderous strains of the Sixth Symphony in A Minor.

"Ah, but it doesn't hurt." Caedmon had earlier informed her that the drippy classical music helped him think. Something about musical notes and higher math.

Preferring rhythm and blues—Macy Gray was her favorite singer—Edie let it slide. There were worse faults than having questionable taste in music.

With a quick tug, she pulled the damask drapes across the window. That done, she glanced around the small hotel room. As had repeatedly happened since they checked in, her gaze landed on the king-sized bed decked out in a red-striped coverlet. Evidently a hotel room with two doubles was an unheard-of commodity in England; the front desk clerk had stared at her as though she were bonkers when she made the request.

She averted her gaze.

If she overlooked the bed—and it was darned difficult—the room had a warm, inviting feel to it. Ivory-colored walls were punctuated with dark wood beams and lots of pleated floral fabric. In a nod to the season, a ribbon-strewn garland hung above the entryway.

Again, she glanced at the bed.

"Yes, I know," Caedmon said, seeing the direction of her gaze. "Rather imposing, isn't it?"

"It's just that we're not . . . you know." She fought the urge to look away, the unspoken topic of sex having reared its tempting head.

Caedmon held her gaze a second too long. Although her dating skills were rusty, she had the distinct impression that he was silently asking. When no answer was forthcoming, he strode over to the foot of the bed. His jaw tightly locked, he placed a palm on either side of the mattress and—

—separated the bed into two twin-sized mattresses.

"Not certain what we should do about the bedding." He gestured to the mess he'd made of the red coverlet.

Acting on a hunch, Edie walked over to the armoire, opened it, and removed two sets of twin sheets. "We're in luck. There's a stockpile of twin sheets stowed away for this very emergency." She tossed the folded sheets onto the bed. "Don't worry. I'll take care of it later."

If he was disappointed, he hid it well.

"Afraid we'll have to share the loo. My Herculean powers don't extend beyond dividing the bed." Turning away from the mussed coverlet, he reached for the bottle of port. "For some reason, I feel oddly buoyed by our progress today. Like a medieval monk who's completed his daily chores and can now sit down to a jug of wine in the full knowledge that he has earned his simple pleasure." As he spoke, Caedmon inserted a corkscrew into the top of the bottle, having procured the implement from the front desk clerk.

A wet *plunk!* could be heard as the cork slid free from the bottle.

Holding a glass in each hand, he walked over to where she stood. "I apologize that the port isn't properly decanted. Since we're slumming it, we must make do." Then, smiling, "Careful. This stuff is dangerously gluggable."

Edie took the proffered glass. Returning his smile, she took a sip of the ruby-colored port. "Yum. This stuff *is* gluggable."

Caedmon laughed, the sound deep, rich, inviting. A lot like the port wine, it made her smile.

"Now, to the task at hand." He motioned to the oriel window and the small circular table. "Hopefully, we'll be able to yoke together the last four lines of verse."

Not sure how much help she would be, her brain working in slo-mo because of the jet lag, Edie seated herself at one of the two wingback chairs wedged into the projecting bay window. Having a funny feeling that the port wine wasn't going to help matters, she stared at the last four lines of translated text.

The trusted goose sorely wept for all of them were dead
I know not how the world be served by such adversity
But if a man with a fully devout heart seek the blessed martyr
There in the veil between two worlds, the hidden truth be
  found

Using her index finger as a pointer, she underscored the first line. "Undoubtedly, a thinly disguised reference to Mother Goose." Tongue literally in cheek, she winked at him.

All business, Caedmon circled the word *goose* with one of the sharpened pencils. "The words *goose* and *swan* were interchangeable in the medieval lexicon; the goose was symbolic of vigilance. In light of all that we know, that makes complete and utter sense."

"It does? Sorry, but I'm not following."

"Remember that Galen took upon himself the role of Ark guardian, vigilance *the* most important attribute of a sentinel."

"And let's not forget that the quatrains were also Galen's swan song."

Caedmon glanced at her glass, as if to silently inquire, *Just how much of that stuff have you had?*

Edie pushed her glass aside. "Sir Kenneth mentioned that everyone in Godmersham except for Galen's wife succumbed to the plague. So I'm guessing that's the gist of line two."

"That would be a correct assumption. As for the third line"—lifting his glass, Caedmon took a measured sip—"it's the typical admonition that one finds in any medieval tale."

"Only the knight who is pure of heart can seek the Holy Grail, right?"

"Mmmm . . . quite."

Slowly, he drummed his fingers on the wood tabletop, lost in thought.

A few moments later the finger tapping increased to a rapid *rat-a-tat-tat*.

"I take it that's a good sign."

"So good it makes my bollocks tingle," he bawdily replied, slapping his palm against the tabletop. "Unless I'm mistaken, the bloody 'blessed martyr' is none other than St. Lawrence the Martyr."

Edie searched her memory banks, the name vaguely familiar. It took a second for her to access the correct data file, the one about Galen donating a slew of sacred relics to the local church. "Oh my gosh! Galen hid the Ark at—"

"St. Lawrence the Martyr Church!" they exclaimed in unison, grinning at each other.

"According to the Old Testament accounts," Caedmon excitedly continued, underlining the last line of the quatrain with his finger, "when the Ark of the Covenant was placed inside Solomon's Temple, in the Holy of Holies, a veil was placed over the entrance to prevent direct access to that most sacred of holy relics. The expression 'beyond the veil' was thus coined because no one, not even the priests of the temple, could enter the sacred space."

"Which means that the last line is a direct reference to the Ark." When he nodded, she switched gears entirely. "Okay, when do we leave?"

"We don't have a coach schedule handy. However, I suspect we can be in Godmersham by early afternoon. Sooner if we secure an auto hire."

"Gee, I'm surprised that you don't want to leave tonight. It's only pouring down rain out there," she teased.

"Though I refuse to entertain the notion that MacFarlane may yet steal the prize, we need our rest."

On that point they were in complete agreement.

"Do you think the church is still standing?"

"Mmmm. Difficult to say. There were any number of churches and monasteries that were destroyed during the various wars of religion that raged for centuries across our little island kingdom. Tomorrow will be soon enough to ascertain if St. Lawrence the Martyr is intact."

"Even if it's still a going concern, we have no idea *where* on the church grounds the Ark is hidden."

"I never said this would be an easy venture." Scooting back his chair, Caedmon rose to his feet. As he walked over to the divided bed, one of Bach's melancholy cello suites droned from the radio. Edie thought it sounded like a slow-moving funerary march.

Ignoring the music, she surreptitiously watched as Caedmon snatched a cookie tin off the bedside table.

No doubt about it, Caedmon Aisquith was very much his own man, his quirky intellectualism strangely appealing.

When he headed back to the oriel, tin in hand, Edie could see that something was wrong; his expression was not nearly as ebullient as it had been seconds before.

"Uh-oh. What happened? You're no longer in a John Philip Sousa mood."

Caedmon handed her the tin of chocolate-covered cookies. "Here, tuck in."

"You're not going to have one?"

Waving away the cookie tin, he reseated himself at the table. "Something about the solution is too neat and tidy. Too bloody obvious."

"Maybe Galen wanted the solution to be obvious."

"Had that been his intention, he would never have gone to the trouble of writing the quatrains."

Her sweet tooth having also gone south, she shoved the tin aside.

"Yeah, I see your point." Bummed, she stared at the hand-written quatrain. "Maybe a not-so-neat solution will come to you in the morning."

"Or to you. Your chain-of-custody box showed a marked proclivity for analytical reasoning."

Her mood percolating a teensy bit, Edie smiled. "You liked that, huh?"

"It's one of many things that I like about you."

Caedmon's reply made her instantly regret the parting of the red bed.

"Well, what do you know? I like you too."

A great deal, in fact. Maybe more than she should, given that she knew so little about him. Other than the fact that he once attended Oxford, had worked for MI5, and recently wrote a book, she knew nothing about Caedmon Aisquith. A man of mystery was one thing. A man without a past was something else entirely.

But then, she'd not been very forthcoming herself.

"Caedmon, there's something that I've been meaning to tell you," she blurted without preamble.

His blue eyes locked onto hers.

Edie took a deep breath, bracing herself for the backlash.

"I lied to you."

CHAPTER 45

"Nothing here but a bunch of old bones."

At hearing that, Stan MacFarlane shone his Maglite into the exhumed grave where his aide-de-camp stood chest deep. Scattered at Braxton's booted feet were the mortal remains of Galen of Godmersham. And a whole lot of mud, the grave quickly filling with water. Earlier, the night sky had opened up, the rain coming down in horizontal sheets.

Stan next shone his flashlight into the face of the Harvard scholar, who stood shivering on the other side of the grave, the light beam casting a golden hue onto the driving rain.

"You told me it would be here."

"Based on the quatrains, I thought there was a likely possibility that the gold chest would be found in Galen's grave." His paid medieval expert, beginning to look like a wet rat, shrugged. "What can I say? We played the odds and lost."

"Could you have misinterpreted the quatrains?"

The scholar rubbed the back of his neck. "Hmm . . . it's possible, but . . . I really thought I correctly deciphered the verses. That's the tricky thing about Middle English, it's all about layered meaning. Hey, do you guys mind if I sit inside the Range Rover? I'm gonna catch my death if I stand out here much longer."

Tuning out the other man's whiny-ass complaints, Stan carefully considered his next move, knowing it was a move twenty-five years in the making. For it was twenty-five years ago that the archangels Michael and Gabriel had appeared to him soon after the blast in Beirut. Sent by God to pull him from the rubble.

The terror attack on the Marine barracks had been the first of the signs that the End Times were near.

Saved in body, and, more important, in spirit, he gave his life over to God's work. Not once had he shirked his duty, commissioned with the task of building God's holy army here on earth. What began as an informal prayer group in the first Gulf War had become a twenty-thousand-strong faith-based movement by the time the tanks rolled into Baghdad eleven years later.

Twenty-five years had come and gone, yet his mission was still incomplete.

God had something great and glorious intended for him.

But *only* if he uncovered the Ark.

The Ark was the key that would unlock the gates of the Millennial Kingdom.

The Ark was the weapon that would destroy the Muslim infidels.

Just as it had destroyed the Canaanites, and the Hittites, and the Jebusites.

"You know, I'm as stumped as you," the scholar droned, interrupting Stan's train of thought.

His attention snagged, Stan realized that the sentiment just expressed didn't ring true; the other man was too pat. Too well-rehearsed.

As though it were a gun aimed at point-blank range, Stan shone the Maglite at the scrawny man's face. Pupils quickly contracted into shiny black dots. "Why do I suddenly not believe you?"

"You're kidding, right?" The other man affected a theatrical look of stunned disbelief. "What reason would I have to lie? I need the cash to pay off my student loans."

"I can think of any number of reasons why you might lie to me." Stan continued to shine the light at the other man's face, as though he were boring a hole right through the middle of his forehead.

"Look, I thought for certain the Ark would be— I mean, the gold chest would be buried with Galen."

"What did you just say?" The beam of light drilled that much deeper.

"*Arca*. I said *arca*. As in 'Arca and gold ful shene he carried to the toun he was born.' Remember the third quatrain?"

The truth revealed, Stan stared at the scholar, contempt washing over him in undulating waves.

Sensing that the winds had suddenly shifted, the Harvard scholar nervously glanced at the parked Range Rover. No doubt trying to remember if the keys had been left in the ignition.

"You can't outrun a bullet," Boyd Braxton jeered, having climbed out of the exhumed grave.

Judge and jury, Stan pointed an accusing finger. "'And then shall the wicked be revealed, whom the Lord shall consume with the spirit of his mouth, and shall destroy with the brightness of his coming.'"

Surprisingly belligerent, the other man pointed a finger right back at him. "You're a fucking lunatic, that's what you are!"

"Unkind words for the man who holds your fate in his hands."

The Harvard scholar glanced at the Israeli-made Desert Eagle negligently held in the gunnery sergeant's right hand, belligerence now replaced with fear. Cowardly, sniveling fear.

"You're right, dude. Heat of the moment. Sorry. And just to prove that I'm still part of the team, I think I know where the Ark is hidden." The scholar jutted his chin toward the small church nestled on the other side of the cemetery. "When you guys did your earlier security check in the church, I caught sight of a very large marble plaque depicting the martyrdom of

St. Lawrence." Spreading his arms, the other man indicated an
expanse of some four feet. "I'm guessing that if we pry that
mother off the wall, we'll find the Ark hidden behind it."

"Pray that we do."

CHAPTER 46

"Back in D.C.," Edie clarified, not wanting Caedmon to think
that she'd recently lied to him.

"That would certainly explain the embarrassed blush you
wear."

"Actually, you've got it all wrong. I'm not the least bit embarrassed that I lied. I'm thoroughly ashamed." And, as he undoubtedly knew, shame was embarrassment on steroids.

"Did you lie about Padge's murder?"

"What!" Edie vehemently shook her head, the image of Dr.
Padgham's sprawled, lifeless body flashing across her mind's
eye. "No, of course not. I lied about my, um, family background."

Crossing his legs at the knee, Caedmon sat silent, waiting
for her to fill in the blanks. If he was upset or disappointed by
the fact that he'd been lied to, he gave no indication of it.

"Remember how I told you that my parents were killed in
a boating accident off the coast of Florida? Well, that story
was . . . well, it was a flat-out lie. I can't speak for my father,
but my mother never stepped foot in anything that ever floated
on the water."

She snatched a mandarin orange from the bowl on the table.
Hands shaking, she began to peel the piece of fruit, if for no
other reason than to give her suddenly sweaty fingers something to do. God, she felt lousy.

Unbelievably, she'd just told Caedmon Aisquith more about her childhood than she'd ever told another living soul.

"Did you tell the lie to elicit my sympathy?"

Edie stopped peeling.

"No! Absolutely not!"

Knowing why she told the lie, but not altogether certain why she suddenly wanted to tell the truth, Edie abandoned the orange and got up from the table.

Maybe she was sick and tired of going to bed with men under false pretenses.

Slowly, trying to collect her thoughts, she paced back and forth in front of the divided twin mattresses. Out of the corner of her eye, she noticed Caedmon finishing off the last dregs of his port wine.

She stopped pacing. Turning toward him, she said, "Were they still alive, there's not a single member of my family that I would be proud to introduce to you. I just . . . I just wanted a normal, sane, loving family. Was I so wrong in wanting that?"

Caedmon shook his head. "It is what we all long for."

"Yeah, it is, isn't it? But those weren't the cards I was given." Realizing how canned and melodramatic that sounded, she decided to just stick to the facts. No emotion. No drama-queen theatrics.

"Okay, here it is. The unedited version of the story is that my mother, Melissa, was addicted to heroin, and bad men, and playing the state lottery. And just so you don't jump to the conclusion that she was a horrible person, it wasn't completely her fault. She grew up in a very repressive fundamentalist household. Unfortunately, she fell in love with a Jewish boy in her geometry class. Pops didn't approve. So he kicked her out of the house. She was sixteen years old."

"I take it the ill-fated lover is your father?"

Edie derisively snorted. "Hmph! Don't I wish."

Wished because maybe her childhood would have unfolded differently had Jacob Steiner been her father.

"According to my mother, there was a freak car accident. A strong wind gust caused the vehicle to swerve into a tree. Jacob died; she survived."

"Is that when your mother turned to drugs?"

Edie nodded. "The grief nearly did her in. At least that's the excuse she gave for not being able to pull it together. Oh, every now and again, she'd clean up her act. In fact, she cleaned up real good. But then"—Edie snapped her fingers—"just like that, she'd start to reek of stale beer and vomit."

Which was about the same time that strange men started to show up, the thin walls of the trailer doing little to muffle the grunts and groans.

"I suppose I should mention at this juncture that my mother had no idea who fathered me. She thought it might have been 'the guy with the Harley.'" Using her fingers, Edie made a pair of air quotes. "But mind you, that's mere speculation."

Having just confessed to being illegitimate, Edie stared at the worn carpet beneath her feet. She could only imagine what Caedmon thought of her bio. He probably hailed from a snooty English household. Something straight out of *The Forsyte Saga*.

"It sounds as though your mother led a tragic life," he quietly remarked.

"Try tragically flawed. Anyway, it wasn't a long life. She overdosed on her twenty-eighth birthday. I found her sprawled on the floor of our trailer, the Allman Brothers song 'Sweet Melissa' playing on a secondhand tape recorder. They say that only the good die young, but—" She waved away the thought. "Never mind. I'm not really sure where I was going with that." She sat down on the edge of the bed, suddenly very tired.

"How old were you when your mother died?"

"Hmm?" She belatedly realized that Caedmon had asked a question. "Oh, eleven." *Eleven going on forty.*

"If you don't mind my asking, what happened to you when your mother died?"

Gnawing on her lower lip, Edie debated whether to tell him. But like a runaway train that couldn't put on the brakes, she went ahead and answered the question put to her.

"I was put into a foster home. There were five of us. Some older, some younger. The older ones knew the drill; the younger ones were clueless."

Caedmon's brow furrowed. "What drill? You've lost me."

"Lonny Wilkerson, my foster father, the man who signed a contract with the state of Florida agreeing to furnish me with a safe, clean, and healthy home, had a fondness for young girls."

"Bloody bastard! Don't tell me that he—"

"I have to tell you," she interjected. *Please, Caedmon. Let me tell my story. Let me give birth to this hideous memory. In the hopes that I can finally be free of it.*

"One night Lonny came into the room that I shared with the two older kids and he . . . he put his hand over my mouth, he pulled down my panties, and he . . . he raped me." As she spoke, she kept her eyes downcast. She didn't want Caedmon's sympathy. She didn't want his outrage. She just wanted a witness. "To this day I can't recall any of the details . . . it was too much to process. All I can remember is that it was painful, it was quick, and I was afraid I would suffocate."

Taking a deep breath, she glanced up at him. Just as she figured, his expression was equal parts anger and sorrow.

"That's all I remember," she said with a shrug. "That and the fact that it happened once a week for the next two months. When Lonny moved to a new girl, she promptly told the social worker what was happening and we were all moved to different homes."

Edie paused, battling the old recriminations.

"I should have been the one to expose that monster but"—she caustically laughed—"I was afraid of being abandoned. Of having to make a new start." *Yet again.*

"You were a child," Caedmon insisted.

She shook her head, unwilling to negotiate the point. "Anyway, to make a long story not nearly so long, a few years later a social worker took pity and went the extra mile to track down my maternal grandparents. I stayed with them until I was eighteen." And then, like her mother before her, she took a Greyhound bus out of Cheraw. Never to return.

Getting up from the table, Caedmon walked over to where she sat on the edge of the bed. Wordlessly, he sat down beside her, his hip brushing against hers.

"Don't get me wrong or anything. I'm not some emotionally scarred person who can't cope with the real world," she
matter-of-factly informed him. "I cope just fine."

"Yes, I know. But the old memories have a way of creeping
up on us when least expected."

Something in his voice made Edie think he spoke from
experience. Maybe his childhood hadn't been *Masterpiece
Theatre* wonderful after all.

"You trod the path to hell at a tender age. But somehow out
of the depths of that pain, you forged a new path for yourself."
As he spoke, Caedmon took hold of her hand. "You are a most
remarkable woman, Edie Miller."

"Remarkable enough that you want to go to bed with me?"
Turning her head, Edie looked him straight in the eye. "You
see, that's why I came clean. Every relationship I've ever had
has been wrapped in a lie. This time I wanted a clean slate."

Caedmon let go of her hand. "Are you sure that's what you
want, for the two of us to sleep together?"

Edie watched the conflicting emotions on Caedmon's face.
At times, and this was one of them, he could be too much the
gentleman.

"I came very close to climbing into bed with you the other
night. And just so you know, this isn't a puzzle that you can
reason your way through. It's just sex, okay?"

Seeing the uncertainty in his eyes replaced with desire,
Edie rose to her feet and stepped toward the nightstand.

Caedmon grabbed her by the wrist, stopping her in midstep.

"Where are you going?" There was a decided huskiness in
his normally cultured voice.

"I thought I'd switch off the lamp."

With a quick tug, he pulled her onto his lap.

"Leave the light on."

CHAPTER 47

Having verified that the gaping hole in the church wall was indeed empty, Stan wearily sat down on the nearest pew. The powerful Maglite cast an otherworldly glow onto the small parish church. Looking down from the adjacent stone walls, stained glass saints silently castigated him. His two men, one holding a sledgehammer, the other a pickax, stood at the ready, waiting for orders to be issued.

For the first time in twenty-five years, Stan worried that he might not be able to fulfill his obligations to God. With the Ark in his possession, he could change the destiny of the world according to God's holy plan. But first he had to find it.

I have to find the Ark.

Those six words reverberated in his head, like an emergency broadcast message playing on a continuous loop.

He pushed himself off the pew. A soldier of God would not, and could not, surrender.

As he stepped toward his men, he kicked aside several pieces of broken marble, the centuries-old bas-relief detailing the life of St. Lawrence destroyed in the excavation. The thick Saxon wall had not given up without a fight; nearly an hour of labor had been required to expose the glaringly empty stone cleft.

Stan straightened his shoulders, ready to fight the next battle. His rest would come when the mission was completed.

"Looks like we've hit another dead end, huh?"

Stan turned his attention to the Harvard scholar. Stoop-shouldered and shivering, he stood next to the pile of excavated stone.

"Yes, my thoughts exactly."

Suddenly intuiting that all was not right in the world, the scholar's gaze furtively moved from man to man. If it had not occurred to him before, it did now. He was outnumbered three to one.

"Hey, fellas! Why so grim? The clues are there, embedded in the quatrains. We just need to go back to the drawing board." When he received no reply, the scholar held his arms out, motioning to each of them in turn. "All for one and one for all, right?" When that received no reply, he tried a different tack. "I say we talk this over. All those in favor of peace talks, raise your hand."

Stan wordlessly stared at the scholar. The sniveling malefactor wanted to engage in pointless conversation in the hopes that they would shake hands, forgive their differences, and begin again.

"There is nothing more to be said."

Intuiting that the death sentence had just been issued, the scholar turned on his heel. Like a church mouse scurrying in the shadows, he ran toward the vestibule. Toward the oversized exit doors.

"You li'l fuckwad!" Dropping the pickax, Boyd Braxton reached for the .357 Desert Eagle secured in the holster under his arm.

Stan slapped a hand over the gunny's raised forearm, physically barring him from shooting the fleeing scholar.

"Not in the house of God," he sternly ordered.

"Yes, sir!"

Both of his men, their weapons drawn, raced from the church in pursuit of the scholar, who had betrayed them.

In no particular hurry, knowing the prey would soon be quarried, Stan headed for the double doors at the back of the church. Tomorrow morning the denizens of the small hamlet of Godmersham would wonder at the jumbled pile of marble and stone. Teenage vandals would be blamed. No doubt an endless slew of bake sales would be held to pay for the damage.

Stuffing his Maglite under his arm, he reached into his pants pocket and removed a gold money clip. He quickly unpeeled three Franklins and shoved them into the wooden slit of the collection box.

Amends made, he stepped outside, pleased to note that the rain had finally tapered to a manageable drizzle. In the adjacent cemetery, he saw a bobbing pinpoint of red light. The laser beam from the gunny's pistol. He headed in that direction.

Trapped en route to the Range Rover, the scholar now stood before Galen of Godmersham's exhumed grave, his arms raised in a show of surrender.

"'God swiftly traps the wicked,'" Stan murmured.

Boyd Braxton placed the barrel of his Desert Eagle against the other man's temple. "I think we're gonna have to rename him Mister Twinkletoes."

"Do you guys have any idea the sentence for murder?" the scholar wheezed, his arms unsteadily wavering in midair. Like bedsheets flapping in the breeze.

"I answer only to God's law," Stan replied. Then, giving the scholar an opportunity to atone for his depraved existence, "'Except ye repent, ye shall die in your sins.'"

"Hey, I didn't do anything wrong! You're the guys sneaking around, breaking into churches, carrying guns. I'm just a debt-ridden grad student trying to make an honest—"

"Man up! For you are soon to meet your Maker."

"Christ! Don't do this! I'm begging you to—" The soliloquy was cut short by a mewling whimper.

"Whew! Somebody needs a Depends," Boyd Braxton muttered, the scholar having lost control of his bowels.

Disgusted, Stan nodded at the former gunnery sergeant. "Kill him. He is an abomination unto the Lord."

A single shot reverberated in the night.

Like the tolling of a church bell.

"Now *that's* convenient," the gunny remarked, gesturing with his gun barrel to the nearly headless body crumpled in the bottom of the exhumed grave. Stuffing the powerful pistol into his holster, he bent at the waist and retrieved a shovel. "All in a day's work, huh, sir?'

"God derives no pleasure from the death of the wicked. Neither should you."

His faith renewed, Stan knew that Eid al-Adha was four days away and counting. Time enough to find the Ark.

Like the good Marine that he was, he had a contingency plan.

"Has Sanchez checked in yet?" Sanchez was the man tasked with surveillance.

"About three hours ago, sir. Aisquith and the woman are holed up in an Oxford hotel room. Sanchez snagged the room next to theirs. Since there's an adjoining door between the two rooms, he's keeping an eye on the pair with a peephole video camera."

"I want hourly status reports. If the Brit so much as sneezes into a snot rag, I want to know about it."

CHAPTER 48

"Leave the light on."

His request, not hers.

Believing the sex act a give-and-take exchange, Edie had wordlessly complied.

The golden glow from the bedside lamp illuminating their every move, they had undressed one another, fingers and hands slightly trembling. Both of them succumbing to an awestruck hesitancy. A bashful sort of voyeurism as more and more flesh was revealed. *Torso. Breast. Pelvis. Thigh.* Until they finally faced one another, completely, and disarmingly, naked. In that moment, she became acutely aware of her own body. Her breasts brushing against her inner arm. Her puckered nipples.

The slight quiver in her knees. It'd been three years since her last lover. She wondered if she measured up.

"You are lovely."

Pleased with the compliment, Edie stepped forward, coming within arm's reach of Caedmon. Needing to make contact, she ran her hands over his chest, surprised to discover that he had the lean, tight build of a younger man.

Moving closer, she pressed her mouth against the pulse at the base of his throat, able to feel the blood course through him with each rapid beat of his heart.

He was nervous.

For some strange reason, that excited her.

Bending her head, she lathed his nipple with her tongue. Teetering slightly, Caedmon moaned her name, the cultured accent nowhere in evidence.

Taking the lead, she slowly backed him to the mussed and divided bed. When the backs of his knees hit a twin mattress, she shoved him to a seated position. She then straddled his hips.

Caedmon's hands glided along the tops of her thighs, up the sides of her rib cage, before finally stopping at her breasts. A nipple popped between the V of his fingers. It was a lurid, but strangely beautiful sight. She was glad they'd left the light on.

Intuiting what she wanted, his hands slid to her waist. His eyes having turned an iridescent shade of blue, he helped her find the right angle.

"Ready?"

"Set, go," she replied.

A second later, with her hands stabilized on his chest, she started to move. Gripping her thighs, Caedmon groaned, the guttural sound competing with the strident piano chords in the background.

Edie clenched her muscles. Then released. The movement merited another groan. Caedmon's grip tightened. *Go faster.*

She came. Quickly. Powerfully. Caedmon held her gaze, silently pleading with her to keep moving. Reaching behind her, she touched him. Then watched as he shuddered, his eyes rolling to the back of his head.

The crisis past, Edie fell forward, crash-landing against his torso. Tears in her eyes, she struggled to catch her breath. With her damp cheek nestled against his equally damp one, she softly laughed.

"I don't know about you, but I now have a whole new appreciation for classical music."

CHAPTER 49

Caedmon raised a hand to his mouth, stifling a yawn.

"Sorry. I'm a bit knackered. Last night was—" He laughed softly. "No need to tell you. You were there."

Walking alongside him as they made their way down High, Edie nudged him in the ribs. "Was I ever."

With their paltry belongings stuffed into the Virgin Airways shoulder bag, they checked out of the hotel immediately after breakfast. The plan was to take a coach to Heathrow, and from there to hire a vehicle for the drive to Godmersham; they were presently en route to Gloucester Green. The hotel clerk had informed them that the airport coaches left Gloucester Green every twenty minutes. Caedmon and Edie agreed that St. Lawrence the Martyr Church might well prove a false lead.

He glanced at his watch. Thirty minutes past seven. It explained why High Street was nearly deserted. Smiling, Edie pressed closer. Returning the smile, he silently acknowledged that desire was born in the one who desires. Like most men in the initial throes of lust, he wondered if he fancied Edie a bit *too* much, his thoughts frequently settling upon her.

The events of the previous evening had unraveled so quickly, he could only cull them to mind in flashes. The quiet hum of rain pounding against the window pane. The not-so-quiet hum of guttural moans and lusty sighs. Round one had ended in an exhausted tangle. Round two had been more subtle, more seductive. They'd eaten mandarin oranges in bed, Edie squirting the juice onto his lower abdomen then lapping it up with her tongue, a mass of curly hair falling to either side of his hips. Unable to control himself, he'd grabbed her head and pushed her lower.

The pleasure that ensued had been near unbearable.

"You're smiling. Broadly, I might add. Just what the heck are you thinking about?"

"Hmm?" He glanced at his companion, imagining breasts like smooth melons, legs falling open to expose an overripe fig. "I am contemplating the most erotic fruit bowl imaginable," he replied.

Edie laughed; the woman was no prude. "I hear tell you guys have one of those thoughts every ten seconds. Amazing that you ever get anything accomplished."

"A penciled list greatly helps."

She laughed all the harder.

As he'd already discovered, understanding Edie Miller was one thing, sorting her out another thing altogether. Her early life had been one of abuse and betrayal. And unfathomable pain. Yet somehow she persevered.

Simply put, he was awed by her strength.

"What if we actually find the Ark of the Covenant hidden at St. Lawrence the Martyr Church?" Edie inquired out of the proverbial blue. "Have you given any thought as to what we would do with it?"

In truth, he'd given it scant consideration, focusing, instead, on deciphering the quatrains.

"I mean, do we hand it over to a museum? Or do we give it to a church or synagogue?"

"Perhaps we should wait until we find the Ark before consigning it to a second party," he evasively answered.

"Or maybe you intend to keep the Ark for yourself," she

pressed, refusing to let the matter drop. "Fodder for your next book."

"Bloody hell! I must have talked in my sleep."

"I'm serious, Caedmon. So far, you've refused to give me a satisfactory answer as to why we're on this insane quest."

"I believe you've just hammered the nail square on the head. It is a quest, is it not? Like a knight of old, I seek knowledge and enlightenment."

"Oh, puh-*leeze*." Her voice fairly dripped with derision. "Henceforth, Sir Gawain, I would appreciate it if you gave me a straight answer rather than a canned sound bite."

Caedmon inwardly cringed at the comparison. In later Grail legends, Sir Gawain, possessed of a singular arrogance, failed to grasp the holy import of the quest. He suspected that Edie had purposely plucked the name from the Round Table cast.

"All I'm saying is that we need to give this a little forethought before rushing off like a pair of fools into the great unknown. And what about MacFarlane and his holy warriors?" She stared at him, clearly apprehensive. "What happens if we run into them while wandering around in Godmersham?"

Although most fringe groups were all mouth and no trousers, he knew MacFarlane's group to be the exception to the rule.

"Rather than succumbing to fearful scenarios, let's concentrate on finding the blasted Ark."

A pronounced silence ensued. Uncomfortable, he feigned an interest in the passing shop windows.

"We can always go to the police," Edie suggested, the first to break the unnerving quietude.

"And promptly be accused of two murders we didn't commit." He forcefully shook his head. "We can't go to the authorities unless the situation absolutely warrants it."

"And who gets to make that call, you or me?"

"We're a team, are we not?" As he spoke, he slung an arm around her shoulders, marrying trunks, hips, and thighs, one to the other. "'She winters and keeps warm her note,'" he murmured into her ear, reciting the lyric from an old English song.

Edie wrapped an arm around his waist. Turning her face upward, she smiled. "Yeah, I'm with you. I much prefer to make love than war."

CHAPTER 50

Oh, man, he wanted to fuck her.

So bad his johnson had been standing on end for the last couple of hours. Ever since, with his peephole video camera shoved against the hotel room door, he'd had a front-row seat on what turned out to be an unbelievable fuck fest.

At first he'd been pissed that he'd been given the graveyard surveillance shift. Small wonder Sanchez had been grinning when he relieved him of duty. Who the hell would have thought the curly-haired bitch had the moves of an experienced whore? It'd been all he could do not to hump himself against the adjoining hotel door like a Pakistani raghead in an Islamabad alleyway.

The colonel was fond of saying, "When lust hath conceived, it bringeth forth sin. And sin, when it is finished, bringeth forth death." The Bible verse helped keep his lusts in check. Usually.

Placing a hand over his crotch, Boyd Braxton rearranged his equipment.

A shopkeeper hauling a bucket of flowers behind a plate glass window glared at him. He glared right back and continued on his merry way, Aisquith and the woman one block ahead of him. The streets were practically empty of pedestrian

traffic, so shadowing them was a piece of cake. Besides, the
redheaded Brit was too intent on whispering sweet nothings
into the bitch's ear to even realize he had a tail on his six.

On account of the audio surveillance, he knew they were
headed to the local bus depot. His job was to head them off at
the pass, grateful for the chance to redeem himself after the
goat-fuck four days ago in D.C.

He adjusted his stride, quickening the pace.

As he did, his heart excitedly pounded against his breastbone.

He couldn't wait for the takedown. Knowing it would happen in ten, nine, eight . . .

CHAPTER 51

Craning her neck to examine a storefront window display, Edie
caught a sudden flash of movement reflected in the plate
glass.

She turned her head. First stunned, then shocked.

It was Dr. Padgham's killer. No more than twenty feet behind them.

Without thinking, she pivoted on her booted heel, placed
both hands on Caedmon's shoulder and shoved him as hard as
possible. Right off the curb and into High Street.

"Caedmon, run!" she screamed at the top of her lungs, realizing too late that she'd pushed him directly in front of an oncoming vehicle.

Car horns blared. Tires screeched.

Deciding that Caedmon would be safer in the roadway than
in the killer's line of fire, she took off running, sparing a quick
glance over her shoulder.

As hoped for, the killer, forced to choose between the two of them, decided to pursue her rather than Caedmon.

Up ahead, Edie caught sight of an aproned man pushing a wheeled handcart loaded with cardboard boxes. A second later, he disappeared into a building that fronted High Street. Without thinking, she followed the delivery guy, surprised to discover that the entry led to an indoor shopping arcade, its narrow corridors snaking out in several directions. As if he'd vanished into a big, black hole, the delivery guy was nowhere in sight.

Not so Padgham's killer; the behemoth had followed her into the shopping arcade.

Edie willed her legs to move that much faster as she veered down a deserted corridor. All of the shops were closed, their darkened windows decked out in Christmas greenery. *Pet supplies. Home accessories. Jewelry. Leather goods.* It all passed in a blurry flash.

Hearing a heavy footfall directly behind her, Edie, frantic, grabbed a carousel of Christmas cards that had been wedged into the doorway of a closed gift shop. With a yank, she hurled it to the ground, spilling the cards willy-nilly onto the floor. Roadblock erected, she kept on running.

A second later, she heard a muttered curse. Then a crash. Evidently, her assailant had slipped on a greeting card.

Good. She hoped the bastard broke his neck.

Catching sight of what looked to be plucked and trussed birds hanging from a wall, she ran in that direction, making a sharp left when she reached the poultry shop. The course adjustment took her down a different corridor, this one well lit. Several shops—a greengrocer, a coffee emporium, and a butcher—were actually open for early-morning business, although paying customers were few and far between. And the ones that were afoot gave no notice to the harried woman running past.

On the periphery of her senses, she became aware of an almost nauseating swirl of fused scents—Stilton cheese, ground coffee, fresh meat. As though a hundred years of smells had coalesced into one uniquely weird odor. She opened her mouth and gulped down a breath of air.

Which is when she ran headlong into a pimply-faced, tat-tooed youth carrying a wooden box of iced fish.

"Silly cow!" the teen bellowed as iridescent fish and white blobs of crushed ice arced through the air, pelting him on the head and shoulders. A scatologically detailed rant immediately ensued.

Managing to stay afoot after the collision, Edie muttered an apology as she sprinted forward. Her energy flagging, her leg muscles now protested each and every forward stride. And she didn't have to turn her head to know that her assailant was fast closing in on her, the collision with the fishmonger voiding whatever gains she'd made.

No more than ten yards away, Edie saw what looked to be an exit; the lock bar across the steel door made her think it was intended for emergency use only. Fast running out of options, she raced forward. Slamming her palms onto the metal bar, she pushed for all she was worth.

The door swung open.

A heartbeat later, she emerged into a narrow alleyway. At a glance, she could see that there wasn't a soul in sight, only a cluster of parked delivery vans.

"Don't even think about it, bitch!"

Hearing that gravelly-voiced command, Edie spun around. The moment she opened her mouth to scream, her assailant slapped a hand over her mouth as he grabbed a fistful of hair. With one strong-armed tug, he yanked her toward him.

Slamming into his chest, Edie tried to jerk free. Anticipating the move, he let go of her hair and cinched a hand around her wrists. Maliciously smiling, he yanked her arms above her head, pulling her onto her toes. With few defenses left to her, Edie tried to bite down on the hand that covered her mouth. His smile widening, her assailant pushed all the harder, mashing her lips against her teeth. Blood gushed into her mouth. Still grinning, he shoved her between two parked delivery vans, ramming her against a limestone wall. Completely out of sight.

Unable to use her hands, Edie tried to knee him, but discov-

ered she couldn't move her lower body; her assailant's hips
and thighs were pressed flush against her own.

Oh, God! She was completely immobilized against the
wall.

"I've got a little gift for you," the behemoth hissed as he
crudely and repeatedly shoved himself against her pelvic bone.
"Nice, isn't it?"

Edie stared into his face—noticing the heavy shadow of
whiskers, the flared nostrils, the thick lips—noticing everything and anything in a desperate attempt to block out what he
was doing to her.

Still thrusting his hips, he licked her face, his tongue moving from her jaw to her temple. "Baby girl, I'm gonna split ya
right in two."

Like salt on a wound, old memories flashed in front of her
eyes.

Terror quickly turned to rage.

This time she'd fight back! No way in hell would she let this
animal rape her.

Writhing, squirming, Edie did everything she could to free
herself.

But it was like fending off the monstrous devil-dog Cer-
berus.

Her assailant grunted. "You want it bad, don't you,
bitch?"

Belatedly realizing that her struggles excited him, Edie
went still.

Within seconds the dry-humping ceased.

"Fucking cock tease!" Crisscrossed vessels bulged on either side of his head. Ready to blow.

Able to feel that he'd gone soft, Edie contemptuously
snorted against his hand. Her would-be rapist removed his
palm from her mouth. Fist balled, he reared back his arm.

Closing her eyes, Edie braced herself for what she figured
would be a bone-crushing blow.

It never came.

Instead her assailant loudly grunted as he rolled away from

her. Edie opened her eyes, surprised to see blood pouring down
the side of his face, gushing from those crisscrossed vessels.
She was even more surprised to see Caedmon standing a few
feet away, a broken bottle gripped in his right hand. Lurching
forward, she ran to his side.

A tense stalemate ensued.

Then, like the coward he was, the bloodied behemoth scurried down the alley. Edie saw what looked to be a gun protruding from his waistband. She and Caedmon stood silent, watching
him depart. When he reached the end of the alleyway, he vanished.

"Did you see that? He had a gun! Why didn't he use it?"

"He may yet." Caedmon tossed aside the broken bottle.
Edie could see that he was furious.

"How did you find me?"

"I simply followed the swath of destruction that followed
in your wake." As he spoke, Caedmon glanced up and down
the alleyway, his eyes settling on a deliveryman who'd just
exited the market.

"The upended box of fish was an accident."

"Tell that to the fishmonger. Come on! We're wasting
time!" Grabbing her by the elbow, he steered her toward a
black service van, the words *Morton & Sons* emblazoned on
the side panel in a fancy Edwardian script. Exhaust fumes
snaked from the muffler.

Caedmon reached for the chrome handle on the back door.

"Get in!" he brusquely ordered. "Before the driver
takes off!"

Edie glanced inside, surprised to see a row of trussed fowls
swinging from a metal rod.

"You're kidding, right? There's no way I'm hitching a ride
with a bunch of dead birds."

"Don't make me put my boot to your arse."

Having been manhandled enough for one day, Edie wordlessly climbed into the back of the van.

CHAPTER 52

Positioning himself near the rear of the lorry, Caedmon shoved his foot against one of the double doors, ensuring that they wouldn't be locked inside the refrigerated vehicle. As the lorry took off, the door gently bounced against the sole of his shoe.

"How long do we have to stay cooped up in the chickenmobile?" Edie grumped, her head and shoulders slumped to avoid being broadsided by the swinging fowl overhead. She held his wadded handkerchief to her mouth, blotting the blood from a cut lip.

"We remain in the lorry as long as I deem it necessary. And the birds in question are geese." Bound for Christmas tables all across the shire.

He spared Edie a quick glance, still furious about her foolhardy sprint through the Covered Market; the woman had more blasted moves than the Bolshoi Ballet.

Bloody hell. She'd nearly got herself killed.

Had he not arrived in time, she would have suffered a grievous injury, the goon's fist on the verge of making contact with her cheekbone.

"I figured he'd take you out first," Edie explained. "That's why I pushed you into the street. To cause a diversion."

And to ensure that the assailant chased after her, not him.

Good God, but he wanted to throttle her.

"Like the repentant thief crucified beside our Lord, you are quick on your feet. But that doesn't mean that you made a wise or reasoned decision," he chastised, not in a forgiving mood. Then, dreading what her answer might be, "Did he harm you in any way?"

"I wouldn't go so far as to say he violated my person, but he did take a few liberties."

"Bloody bastard!"

"It was nothing. Trust me. Other than a cut lip, I'm fine."

Caedmon stared into Edie Miller's brown eyes and saw the scared, vulnerable child she once had been. He fought the urge to pull her to him, worried that he might say something utterly asinine.

Evidently suffering from no such qualms, Edie crawled toward him, nearly losing her balance when the lorry made a sudden left turn. He snatched the bottom of the door with his hand, preventing it from swinging wide open. Despite the anger, he stretched out his free arm, cradling her face in his hand.

"It's cold in here," she complained, nestling alongside him.

Caedmon gently rubbed his thumb over her swollen lip. "Thank God you're all right."

"What now?"

"Taking any form of public transportation is out of the question, as MacFarlane's men will undoubtedly be monitoring the coach depot and the train station. Therefore we'll remain in the lorry until we've safely departed Oxford. Hopefully, we'll be able to find a sympathetic motorist willing to take us to London."

"Maybe we should notify the authorities."

"It's not as though we can have the villain brought to book. And given your rampage in the market, should you contact the police, you'd probably end up an overnight guest of the Thames Valley Authority."

"So where does that leave us?"

"Floundering about like two—"

"Geese," she interjected, staring at the trussed birds swinging overhead.

"I was about to say two landlocked mackerel, but I suppose a pair of frightened geese would suffice."

"No. I'm talking about the first line of the fourth quatrain." Snatching the airline bag, she unzipped it, removing the folded sheet of paper with the translated quatrains. "Here it is," she said, underscoring the line as she read aloud. "'The trusted goose sorely wept for all of them were dead.' Do you remember I told you that I once wrote a research paper on the Wife of Bath from Chaucer's *The Canterbury Tales*?"

He nodded, wondering where this particular projectile would land.

"Well, the swinging geese overhead reminded me of a line from the prologue to that particular tale. Mind you, it's been more than ten years, so I'm paraphrasing big-time, but Chaucer wrote, 'Nor does any grey goose swim there in the lake that, as you see, will be without a mate.' In fact, the whole premise of my paper was that women in the Middle Ages *had* to wed. Or join a nunnery. Those were the only two options available."

Admittedly baffled, he raised a brow. "Your point?"

"I just remembered that in medieval literature the word *goose* always refers to the good housewife. Yesterday, you said that the goose was a symbol for vigilance. And you're right. Who in the medieval world was more vigilant than the good housewife? I suspect no one ever considered the possibility that the quatrains were written by *Mrs.* Galen of Godmersham, Philippa being the 'trusted goose.'" She folded her arms over her chest, theatrically rolling her eyes. "Male chauvinism at its academic best."

"I admit that your theory about Philippa has rich possibilities. However—"

"Think about it, Caedmon. How would an eighty-five-year-old man hide a heavy gold chest? What do you want to bet that Galen's dying wish was an urgent plea to his much younger wife to hide his precious *arca* from the looters rampaging the countryside during the plague? Sir Kenneth told us that everyone in Godmersham perished from the plague."

"Save Philippa," he murmured, her premise beginning to ring with perfect pitch. "And once her husband was dead, Philippa hid the gold *arca* somewhere on the grounds of St. Lawrence the Martyr Church."

"Actually, I've got a theory about that, too," Edie countered, surprising him yet again.

"Brains *and* beauty. I am totally bewitched."

Edie playfully hit him in the arm. "Hey, you forgot to mention the brawn." Then, her tone more serious, she continued, "I'm beginning to think that we got the martyr part of the quatrains all wrong."

"I take it that you refer to the third line of the last quatrain?"

"Correct. 'But if a man with a fully devout heart seek the blessed martyr' does *not* refer to St. Lawrence the Martyr. At least I don't think it does. I'm thinking it refers right back to the goose."

"I'm not following your argument." Unhindered by ego, he didn't care who exposed the truth; only that it be found.

"Okay, we now know that the goose refers to Philippa, the good housewife," Edie replied, ticking off her first point on her pinky finger. She next moved to her ring finger. "Per Sir Kenneth, Philippa was the daughter of the justice of the peace for Canterbury." She delineated the next point on her middle finger. "And Canterbury, as you know from having read Chaucer, is where medieval pilgrims journeyed—"

"—to see the sight where the archbishop, Thomas à Becket, was killed in 1170 by Henry the Second's henchmen," Caedmon finished, well acquainted with the historical incident, the murdered archbishop a victim in the conflict that raged between church and state. "Within weeks of the murder, wild rumors began to circulate throughout England, those who came into contact with the bloodied vestments of the now-dead archbishop attesting to all sorts of astonishing miracles. Soon thereafter, the Catholic Church canonized Thomas à Becket as a *martyred* saint."

"And thus the cult of St. Thomas was born."

With perfect clarity, Caedmon knew that Edie was absolutely correct. When they originally deciphered the fourth quatrain, they misread the clue. As Philippa no doubt intended.

Edie leaned against the metal wall of the lorry, a satisfied smile on her lips. "It makes perfect sense, doesn't it? Philippa, entrusted with hiding the Ark, takes it to the only place other than Godmersham that she has any familiarity with, that being the town of her birth, Canterbury."

"Mmmm." He mulled it over, still sifting through the pieces. "We don't know that Philippa actually hid the Ark in Canterbury," he said, well aware that Edie had a tendency to hurl herself at a conclusion.

"Of course we know that Philippa hid the Ark at Canterbury. It's right there in the quatrains. 'There in the veil between two worlds—'"

"'He will find the truth.' The truth, not the *arca*," he quietly emphasized. "Which may be an encrypted way of saying that we'll find our next clue at Canterbury."

Clearly disgruntled, Edie sighed. "And here I thought this was going to be easy. Okay, any ideas where in Canterbury we should look?"

More accepting of the roadblock put before them, he didn't waste his time with peevish laments, having assumed from the onset that they would traverse a crooked path.

"Thomas à Becket was murdered inside the cathedral. I suggest that as a starting point for our search." As he spoke, the lorry slowed to a stop.

Caedmon peered out the rear door and saw that the driver had pulled into a car park with a roadside café. Hopefully, they would be able to hitch a ride to London from one of the dozen or so motorists parked in the lot.

"I believe this is our stop."

CHAPTER 53

"You might be interested to know that these medieval walls were built atop an older Roman foundation, the original village dubbed *Durovernum Cantiacorum*."

As they strolled across the ancient stone battlements that rimmed the town of Canterbury, Edie was relieved that she and Caedmon had reverted to their earlier camaraderie. She wasn't altogether certain, the male beast a difficult one to decipher, but she thought Caedmon had gotten angry back in the alleyway because he hadn't been able to adequately safeguard her from MacFarlane's goon.

Which raised a disturbing question . . . *if the goon had a gun, why didn't he use it?*

Able to see in her mind's eye a massive pair of shoulders, the scary buzz cut, and a rivulet of blood zigzagging down a throbbing temple, Edie shuddered.

"Cold?" Caedmon solicitously inquired, draping an arm over her shoulder.

Shoving the frightening image aside, she wordlessly snuggled closer to him. Although she couldn't be 100 percent certain, she didn't think that they had been followed. After hitching a ride to London, they caught a train out of Victoria Station, the trip to Canterbury taking only ninety minutes. The train station being located on the outskirts of town, they were now en route to the cathedral.

With a damp breeze raggedly sawing at her backside, Edie flipped up the collar on her coat. Overhead the clouds hung low in the sky, casting a dreary shadow.

Taking a quick peek at the town map they'd picked up at the train station, Caedmon ushered her to the left, past the remains of an old tower that she guessed had once been attached to an equally old church.

"All that remains of St. George's Church," he remarked, "the tower having somehow weathered the travails of time and history."

"Although it looks like most of the town fared pretty well." She gestured to the neat line of half-timbered structures that fronted the narrow street. "I feel like I'm walking through a medieval living history museum."

"Indeed the inns, taverns, and shops are little changed from the days of Chaucer, all still vying for the traveler's coin."

Like Oxford, the town was dressed in its Christmas finery, fairy lights merrily twinkling behind storefront windows. But Canterbury had about it a magical air that the staid Oxford had lacked. Probably on account of its fairy-tale appearance.

As they walked along Mercery Lane, the pavement teemed with tourists, the modern-day pilgrims undeterred by the chilly weather. With each footstep, Edie was very much aware that she walked in another woman's footsteps—none other than Philippa of Canterbury. Like most medieval women, Philippa's life story had been written at birth. A man's life in the four-teenth century was recorded on vellum, enabling changes to be made. But a woman's life was struck in stone. Unchangeable.

As they neared the city center, the thorny spires of the ca-thedral began to fill more and more of the skyline. To Edie's surprise, she began to experience a sense of agitated excite-ment. Caedmon evidently felt it too, taking her by the hand as they approached a massive three-story gatehouse. Bedecked with tiers of medieval shields and a contingent of stone angels, the Savior stood front and center, welcoming saint and sinner alike.

Caedmon led her through the arched portal. "Christ Church Gate . . . the physical divide between the secular and the sa-cred."

Emerging from the portal, Edie caught her first glimpse of Canterbury Cathedral.

"Wow," she murmured, the cathedral so immense as to be downright daunting—one of those perpendicular Gothic structures purposefully constructed for maximum impact. Everywhere she looked, there were towers and spires and statues.

"Wow," she again murmured, having yet to emerge from her dumbstruck state.

"We approach as did the medieval pilgrims, awed and bedazzled," Caedmon remarked. "Of course, the magnificence of Canterbury is not surprising, this being the mother cathedral for the Church of England."

"More like the mother ship," Edie muttered, still overwhelmed by the sheer size of the place. "This is gonna take days. Particularly since we don't even know what we're looking for."

"But we know that whatever it is, it's located inside the cathedral. And I suspect the clue has something to do with the Ark of the Covenant."

"But the clue could be anything. A piece of sculpture, a painting, a bas-relief. *Anything*. It could even have something to do with Thomas à Becket," she added. "After all, he is the 'blessed martyr,' right?"

"I believe that Thomas is merely a peripheral character, little more than a reference point to direct us to Canterbury. For it's this colossus of stone and glass"—raising his arm, Caedmon motioned to the cathedral—"that played a pivotal role in Philippa's daily life before she left for Godmersham. Moreover, she—"

Caedmon abruptly stopped, in midsentence and midstep. Wordlessly, he stared at the exterior façade of the cathedral. Like a man transfixed.

"What's the matter?" she asked, grabbing him by the upper arm.

"The clue is embedded in neither sculpture nor painting nor bas-relief." He turned to her, a beatific smile upon his lips. "It is embedded in glass. Stained glass, to be precise. Arguably one of the greatest artistic achievements of the medieval world, it was the first modern medium of direct communication; complex ideas could be transmitted in a pictorial format." His smile broadened. "Not to mention that stained glass acts a 'veil between the two worlds.'"

Edie stared at the dark panes of glass that fronted the southern façade of the cathedral.

"Stained glass was intended as a barrier between the secular world existent in the city streets," Caedmon continued, "and the sacred world contained within the cathedral. Illuminated by light, the first of God's creations, stained glass can come to life before one's very eyes."

As though an affirmation from on high, a church bell sonorously tolled.

"Come, Miss Miller. Destiny beckons," Caedmon remarked, ushering her toward the main entrance.

Following on the tailcoats of an American tour group, they entered the elaborately carved doors at the western end of the church. Immediately they were assaulted by the twin scents of incense and flowers and the twin sounds of clicking camera flashes and a Midwestern twang.

"Above you, in what is known as the West Window, you will see a brilliant example of medieval stained glass," the American tour guide expounded, in what was obviously a canned speech. "The sixty-three glass panels, which depict various saints, prophets, and kings, are just a drop in the bucket to what you're gonna see on the tour; the cathedral boasts hundreds of glass panels. Make no mistake, folks, *this* is one of the cultural treasures of Europe."

Along with everyone else in the group, Edie peered upward.

"Oh, God." She groaned, stunned. "It's gonna be like finding a holy needle in a sacred haystack."

Placing a hand to her elbow, Caedmon led her away from the tour group. "Admittedly, we have a daunting task ahead of us."

Edie craned her neck, taking another gander at the sixty-three glass panels on the West Window.

"You think?"

CHAPTER 54

His neck inclined at an awkward angle, Caedmon stared at the top register of the stained glass panel, the blaze of color near dazzling, casting what could only be described as psychedelic patterns of light onto the cavernous gloom of the gothic interior.

Les belles-verrières, he silently mused. Certainly more beautiful glass than one man and one woman could reasonably absorb in a single day. But mindful of the fact that MacFarlane might have correctly deciphered the quatrains, he and Edie forged onward.

Some two hours into the search, they now stood in the Corona, a semicircular chapel originally built to house the relics of St. Thomas à Becket. Despite the fact that they had methodically examined dozens of stained glass panels created before the mid-fourteenth century, thus far they'd seen no images or references to the Ark of the Covenant.

As he swayed slightly on his feet, the colorful windows having a hypnotic effect, several lines of Bible verse came to mind. "'I will lay thy stones with fair colors, and lay their foundations with sapphires. And I will make thy windows of agates, and thy gates of—'"

Edie raised a hand, preempting him in midsentence. "Enough already. I am totally and completely Bibled out. Trying to decipher these stained glass windows is an awful lot like learning a foreign language. Except we don't have the Berlitz tapes. And you spouting verses from the Good Book does not help matters."

"Understood," he contritely replied.

Though Caedmon was at an advantage, having studied medieval iconography while at Oxford, the symbolism and didactic meaning contained within the Canterbury windows was, to the modern observer, not unlike a foreign language. Although it was a language well known eight hundred years ago. Illiteracy was the norm during the Middle Ages, so stained glass enabled the faithful to learn the stories of the Bible in an easily accessible format, thus making medieval stained glass a picture book for the masses.

Ignoring the painful crick in his neck, he continued to study the glass panels, forcing himself to examine only those images specific to the Old Testament. *Moses consecrating Aaron. The ascent of Elijah. Samson and Delilah.*

As they continued to the next group of glass panels, he caught sight of a leather-clad blur out of the corner of his eye. The size and heft of the blurred figure were similar to that of the assailant in Oxford; he slowed his step. Almost instantly, his heartbeat escalated, goose bumps prickling his skin. He knew this feeling. He'd had had it any number of times when he worked for Her Majesty's service. Something in Denmark most definitely stank to high heaven.

Muscles tightening, he slowly turned to face the enemy.

It took but an instant to verify that the "enemy" was simply a tourist. Though the robust physique was similar, the facial features were completely off cue.

Bloody hell, but he was on edge.

And had been since the incident on High Street.

"Is something the matter?" Edie inquired. "All of a sudden, you're looking awfully tight around the jaw."

"No, no, nothing is the matter," he assured her, taking her by the elbow and steering her toward the aisle of the cathedral choir. To one side of them, massive columns supported incised stone arches; on the other side, stained glass windows beautifully gleamed.

"Ah! The famed Typology Windows," he announced, effectively changing the subject. Knowing that the Typology Windows had been created prior to the thirteenth century, he angled his head to examine the upper panes of glass, ignoring the bolt of pain that traveled from his nape to the base of his spine.

Edie elbowed him in the ribs. "Explanation, please. In case you've forgotten, I'm a novice at this."

"Typology was a tool often used in the Middle Ages to certify the legitimacy of the New Testament with stories taken from the Old," he explained. "A typical example would be the tale of Jonah and the whale. According to the Old Testament, Jonah remained within the whale's belly for three days and three nights."

"Prefiguring Jesus being entombed for the same length of time," she astutely commented.

"Precisely. Usually, the stories were paired, one to the other, thus reinforcing a particular theological point through the manipulation of biblical imagery."

"Thought control at its very best."

He winked at her. "How else does one control the masses?"

"Hey, look, it's Noah and the Ark!" she exclaimed, pointing to a half-roundel. Placing a hand to her mouth, she stifled a burst of laughter. "Yeah, I know, wrong ark. Although at this point, I'm happy to see *any* ark."

Not nearly so enthused, Caedmon led the way to the next panel. Again, he began the slow process of identifying each and every biblical figure, his gaze systematically beginning at the top and moving downward. A monumental window, the panel was divided into seven horizontal registers, each register containing three separate scenes. When he came to the fifth register, he did a double take.

"Bloody hell . . . I think I found it."

Edie's eyes slowly panned the length of the window, opening wide when they hit upon the telltale image. "Oh my gosh! It's a four-sided gold box."

"Actually, it's *the* four-sided gold box. None other than the Ark of the Covenant." Barely able to contain his excitement, he had an overwhelming urge to laugh aloud, to raise his voice to the heavens and whoop with joy. Instead, he pulled Edie into his arms, hugging her close. "We found it," he whispered in her ear. "We actually found the bloody thing.'"

Disengaging her right arm, Edie excitedly pointed to the

window in question. "Did you notice the two baby geese in the basket?"

He nodded, certain they'd found the very panel that Philippa intended them to find. The scene, *The Presentation of Christ*, detailed the well-known New Testament story of Mary and Joseph presenting the infant Jesus to the high priest in the temple at Jerusalem. Two seemingly innocuous items within the scene fairly screamed at him: Joseph carrying a basket that contained two goslings, and Mary, holding the baby Jesus aloft, standing before the Ark of the Covenant.

"Yesterday you and Sir Kenneth were rambling about the medieval comparisons between the Mother Mary and the Ark of the Covenant. Is this what you were talking about?"

Deciding not to take issue with the "rambling" charge, he nodded. "It was a religious concept known as *Faederis Arca*. No less a theologian than St. Bernard of Clairvaux explicitly compared the womb of Mary to the Ark of the Covenant; for as the Ark contained the Ten Commandments, so Mary carried the New Covenant within her womb."

"The symbolism of the Old Testament reinforcing the New Testament."

"Precisely."

Clearly excited, Edie yanked the Virgin Air bag off her shoulder. Unzipping it, she hurriedly riffled through its contents, removing her digital camera.

Excitement was soon replaced with a crestfallen expression. "It's a dead dog," she muttered, showing him the darkened display. "And as you know, the digital camera has yet to be invented that will run on a drained battery." She glanced at the exit door located on the far side of the nave. "I could run out and buy some new batteries at one of the souvenir shops."

Caedmon checked his watch. "I don't know if you'll have enough time. The cathedral is set to close in twenty minutes. The digital photo will have to wait until the morning."

"Do you *really* want to wait that long? Yeah, we found the window, but now we have to figure out what it means. And to do that, we'll gonna need a picture."

"I agree. However—"

She put a staying hand on his chest. "Don't move. I'll be right back."

Obediently standing by, he watched as Edie rushed toward the northwest transept. When she disappeared from sight, he returned his gaze to the stained glass panel. As he stared, spellbound, the distinctive scent of incense wafted through the chill air. It suddenly occurred to him that here, within the confines of one of the world's great cathedrals, where man-made bread daily became God's flesh, anything was possible.

Turning away from the panel, he watched as Edie returned with a bespectacled, long-haired young man in tow. "This is William. He's agreed to do a quick line drawing of the stained glass window."

A man of few words, William removed an artist's sketch pad from his satchel. Paying them scant attention, he negligently leaned against a nine-hundred-year-old column and began to draw.

"I earlier noticed him sketching the St. Thomas Memorial inside the transept," Edie explained.

"Ah! A budding artist."

"More like a budding con artist," she replied, lowering her voice to a hushed whisper. "He refused to put pencil to paper for less than fifty bucks. Since we need an image in order to decipher the window, I agreed to his terms."

The silent seconds ticked past. Caedmon anxiously checked his watch, hoping the young artist completed his masterpiece before the docents herded them to the nearest exit.

"What happens if we actually find the Ark?" Edie asked, staring at the four-sided gold box in the glass panel.

I've asked the same question myself, love.

And still he didn't have an answer. Only a mounting sense of excitement.

The Ark of the Covenant.

Truly, the stuff of dreams.

Having yet to utter a word, the art student ripped a sheet of white paper from his sketch pad. Paper in hand, he walked over to where they stood and silently handed Edie the drawing he'd made. She, in turn, handed him a small wad of American bills. Transaction concluded, she politely thanked him for his services.

"This better be worth fifty dollars," she muttered under her breath as William wordlessly took his leave.

Caedmon examined the drawing, pleased with the result. "I'd say it's bang-on perfect."

Thrilled that all was going well, Caedmon watched the play of colored lights as they bathed Edie's smooth complexion in shades of blue and gold. Unthinkingly, he said the first thing that came to mind. "Fancy a quick bonk?"

Her eyes opened wide. "What? Here? In the middle of Canterbury Cathedral?"

So rapidly did she put the brakes on his suggestion, Caedmon could almost smell the stink of burning rubber. Although her lack of enthusiasm did little to dampen his ardor. "We earlier passed a dimly lit niche on the other side of the choir."

"Are you crazy? In case you haven't noticed, O horny one, we're in a cathedral."

That being the stuff of fantasies, he smiled. "Nothing the Almighty hasn't seen countless times before." Then, determined to win her over, "Come on, Edie. Surely you can spare me a moment of your time?"

"Not with all the angels and saints watching from on high, I can't." She pointedly glanced at a haloed figure in a nearby stained glass panel. "But just so you don't think me a complete killjoy, I might be amenable to being bonked in a hotel room."

Hearing that, Caedmon grabbed her by the hand, hastily making his way to the exit. "We passed a guesthouse on Mercery Lane. If we hurry, we can be between the sheets within the half hour."

CHAPTER 55

"It's not the Savoy. But then again it's not the almshouse," he'd drolly remarked, surveying their modest accommodations.

Edie glanced at the iron bedstead. "What now?"

"A drink, I think. No, better yet, let's skip the pleasantries and get right down to it, shall we? In the prone or upright position? Your choice, love."

Giving it a moment's thought, she picked the latter. . . .

* * *

Trousers refastened, Caedmon bent down and retrieved a pair of lacy knickers from the threadbare carpet. Somewhat sheepishly, he handed them to Edie. His embarrassment stem-

ming from a decided lack of finesse, he glanced at the un-
mussed bed.

He could do better. He *would* do better.

He'd always considered himself a considerate lover. But for
some inexplicable reason he'd acted on his animal urges, behaving like a testosterone-driven oaf.

"I just need to, um, you know, freshen up." Her cheeks
flushed, Edie pointed to the adjoining bathroom.

"Er, right."

A few moments later the bathroom faucet opened, followed
by a muttered complaint about the lack of hot water. Unable to
find a vacant room at an accredited B&B, they'd been forced
to take lodgings at a small guesthouse, the only available room
being in the garret. In an attempt to add some charm to the
claustrophobic space, both the walls and the steeply pitched
ceiling had been papered in a blue toile, the prancing maids in
farthingales and the sad-faced Pierrot straight out of a Watteau
canvas.

"Shall we have a go at the stained glass window?" he inquired when Edie returned.

"Sounds like a plan. Since there's no table to sit at, how
about we pull that pine bench over to the side of the bed?"

Caedmon obediently fetched the bench in question, the two
of them sitting side by side on the mattress, their shoulders
lightly touching. In front of them, spread across the bench, was
the sketched drawing of the stained glass window, the handwritten copy of Philippa's quatrains, a blank sheet of paper,
and two sharpened pencils.

"When deciphering code, 'no stone unturned' is the best
rule of thumb," he instructed. "Prison is full of thieves and
murderers."

"No kidding. Your point?"

He smiled at what was fast becoming her familiar refrain.
"Look for the obvious. Every link in the chain is somehow
relevant."

"Well, the two geese in the basket are pretty obvious, don't
you think?"

"Indeed. But what is the significance of the pair? We know that one of the geese represents the good housewife Philippa. But what of the other?"

Edie shrugged. "I have no idea. But the fact that Philippa purposely led us to Canterbury Cathedral makes me think she may have given the Ark to the church. Not to mention, the scene in question details the Holy Family inside the Temple of Jerusalem."

For several seconds, he pondered the notion. Though the idea had merit, something about it didn't ring true.

"'I know not how the world be served by such adversity,'" he said, reading aloud from the quatrains. "It's clear that Philippa attributed the plague to her husband's ill-gotten treasure. Good Catholic woman that she was, Philippa would not have burdened the church with that same 'adversity.'"

Getting up from the bed, Edie walked over and retrieved the Virgin Air bag from the room's one and only chair, a lumpy Marquise reproduction upholstered in the same pattern as the wallpaper. She removed a metal nail file from the zippered pocket.

"I broke a nail."

Intuiting that she was in no mood to decipher the drawing, Caedmon moodily stared at the pine bench. In truth, he wasn't at all surprised by her lack of enthusiasm, the day's events having no doubt taken a heavy toll on her.

"Will you be spending Christmas with your family?"

Caedmon's head jerked, caught off guard by Edie's unexpected query. Although he knew she'd eventually inquire about his private life, he'd foolishly hoped it wouldn't happen anytime soon.

"My father died some years back. But even when he was alive, we were never big on the holidays, and Christmas fell by the wayside when I was a young lad. I suspect the lack of holiday cheer came about because there was no woman in the household. My mother died in childbirth," he added, anticipating her next question.

"This is the first you've made mention of your family."

"My father and I had what you might call a strained relationship. A strict taskmaster, he eschewed frivolities of any sort." *Such as "hanging the stockings by the chimney with care."*

"He sounds like a real hard-ass."

"Actually, he was a solicitor."

Edie laughed aloud. "Sorry. It's just the way it came out. It sounded . . ."

"Absurd?" The old wounds not nearly as painful as they'd once been, he managed a half smile. "Yes, in retrospect there was a certain absurdity to our relationship."

"Absurdity aside, I bet your father was proud of you. Going to Oxford and everything."

At hearing that, Caedmon derisively snorted. "Hardly. When I left Oxford, the shame of it killed him."

"Don't you think you're exaggerating just a *weensy* bit?" With thumb and index finger, she indicated a "weensy" unit of measure.

Shoving the pine bench aside, he rose to his feet. There being few places to roam, he walked over to the fireplace. The act of confession an uncomfortable one, he turned his back to her.

"Within days of my Oxford debacle, I was summoned to St. Anselm's Hospital, where my father was undergoing tests for an intestinal complaint." Able to see the sterile white room in his mind's eye, he frowned, the vividness of the recollection unnerving. "My father wore a light blue hospital gown; it was the first time I'd ever seen him in a garment that had not been properly pressed." He glanced over his shoulder at her. "A most dignified man, my father."

Although she made no reply, he could see that he had a captive audience; Edie was leaning forward in the chair.

"The morning sun was shining through the window adjacent to my father's hospital bed, casting upon him a soft light, making him appear as a kindly older gentleman. An aged putti, I irreverently thought at the time."

"So what happened?"

"Something that was years in the making." He turned and faced his confessor. "At this juncture I should mention that I spent the first thirteen years of my life fearing the bastard and the next thirteen loathing him because of that fear."

"Did he physically abuse you?"

He tersely shook his head, disavowing her of the notion. "No. In fact he never laid a hand on me, not in anger nor affection. His was an emotional abuse, a systematic shunting that left little doubt he rued the day that I was born. On those few occasions when he did take notice of me, it was always with a critical eye."

"I'm guessing it all came to a head when you went to visit him in the hospital."

Caedmon nodded. "No sooner did I arrive than my father informed me of precisely how much it had cost to support my studies at Oxford. He then point-blank told me that he expected due recompense. With interest, I might add."

"You're kidding, right?" Her stunned expression was near comical.

"I told the old bastard to bugger off. That said, I took my departure, perversely pleased with myself for finally standing up to him. Twelve hours later his doctor rang me up, notifying me that my father had unexpectedly died from an embolism."

"How did you feel about that?"

The question was so typically American, their culture grounded in the visceral, that he should have anticipated it. Should have, but didn't.

"If you're asking if I felt complicit in my father's death, I did not. Although, admittedly, I've spent an inordinate amount of time trying to understand my father's motives." He shrugged, indicating that it had been a futile endeavor. "All I know is that my father had a singular inability to love."

Good God! Did he really just say that?

Horrified, he self-consciously cleared his throat, refusing to meet Edie's disarmingly direct gaze.

"Maybe he did love you; he just didn't know how to express it."

"To know the man was to know better."

Getting up from her chair, Edie walked toward him. "I think your father was an idiot for wasting his life the way he did. It's what Herman Melville referred to as the 'horror of the half-lived life.' So, what about the rest of your life? Have you ever been married? Do you have any kids?"

Caedmon stared at the threadbare carpet, the conversation having veered into uncomfortable territory, his unsavory past about to rear its ugly head. The ghost of his murdered lover, Juliana Howe, lurked in the near vicinity. If he told her about Jules, he'd also have to tell her about his murderous rampage in the streets of Belfast.

Arms crossed over his chest, he listened as the mantel clock relentlessly ticked off each passing second with an air of funerary gravitas.

Edie placed a hand on his forearm. "Look, whatever it is that you're afraid to tell me, I'll understand. Really, I will."

Angry that he'd been shoved into a tight corner, he moved away from her. "You'll understand? Correct me if I'm wrong, but you first made my acquaintance four days ago. Barely enough time to know how I take my tea, let alone understand me." He snatched his anorak from the nearby wall hook. "There's a curry house several blocks down the street. I'm going to get some takeaway."

CHAPTER 56

Edie yanked the black turtleneck over her head, tossing it onto the wood toilet lid. Placing her hand into the claw-footed tub, she swirled the sudsy water, testing to make sure she had the right mix of hot and cold. Evidently, it had yet to occur to the Brits that a single faucet was a whole heck of a lot better than dueling hot and cold water taps. But as she was quickly learning, the Brits were a strange and curious lot.

Unhooking her bra, she let it drop onto the linoleum floor. At seeing the small hickey next to her nipple, she smiled, remembering. Caedmon had surprised her with his passion, morphing into a lusty alpha male the moment he removed his wools and tweeds. A lot of things about Caedmon surprised her. The way he would dunk a cookie into his coffee cup then immediately apologize, as though he'd committed the gravest of sins. His almost boyish exuberance when it came to anything even remotely esoteric. His insistence on opening doors and preceding her down the steps. His sweetness. His tenderness. His unrelenting resolve when it came to the Ark.

God, he could be a hard-ass. She suspected that he took after his father more than he realized.

Yeah, she'd pushed him. But he'd pushed back even harder. Short of killing a man in cold blood, she'd understand whatever deep, dark secret he kept under lock and key. She was certainly no saint.

What she needed to do was back off. Enforce a *Don't Ask, Don't Tell* policy. When he was ready, when he felt more comfortable with the relationship, he would open up.

Clothes removed, she walked over and shut off the taps. Tentatively, she stuck a big toe into the tub. Then, a hand braced on either side of the claw-footed tub, she slowly sank into the frothy water, having found a half-used bottle of lemon-scented bubble bath.

"Perfect," she crooned, her tensed muscles finally relaxing. She stared at the pitched ceiling, the light from the adjoining room turning the surface a pretty shade of cotton-candy pink.

She reached for the washcloth she'd earlier draped over the curved lip of the tub.

"'Deck the halls with boughs of holly, fa-la-la-la-la, la-la-la-la.'"

Belatedly realizing that it was one of those songs that wore better after a couple of glasses of eggnog, she switched gears, instead humming "The Little Drummer Boy" as she soaped up the washcloth.

Raising her right leg out of the water, she washed it from toe to knee.

Again, her thoughts turned to Caedmon. Christmas had to be a difficult time of year for him given that his father—

"Getting all cleaned up to do the dirty, huh?"

At hearing that deep-throated voice, Edie swung her head toward the open bathroom door.

Oh, God. It was him.

CHAPTER 57

Stunned to find her Oxford assailant negligently leaning against the doorjamb, Edie thought her heart would explode.

Overcome with fear, she helplessly gripped the sides of the tub.

"And in case you got any notions about screaming or hollering or complaining to the management, you might want to reconsider," the intruder drawled, slowly pulling a gun from the waistband of his military-style cargo pants. "The two of us are gonna do this nice and quiet."

Edie stared at the dark lump of steel clutched in his meaty hand. She didn't know much about firearms. But she knew a silencer when she saw one. He could kill her in cold blood and no one in the guesthouse would be the wiser. Just like he'd killed Dr. Padgham at the museum. Just like he'd probably killed God knows how many people.

Gun in hand, he strolled over and retrieved her bra from the floor. As he did, Edie noticed the surgical tape on the side of his head. Evidently, he'd had to have sutures after Caedmon hit him with the broken bottle. Like he wasn't scary enough already; the little pieces of white tape made him look like a turbo-charged Frankenstein.

Holding her bra up to his face, the behemoth read the inside tag. "Thirty-four C. *Nice.* They ought to fit my hands just perfect."

Hearing that, Edie wanted to puke.

"H-how d-did you find me?" she nervously stammered, hoping that if she changed the subject, she could somehow change his intentions.

Grinning, he dropped the bra. "Amazing how you can hunt down a person anywhere in the world with a microdot tracking device and a Palm Pilot. And the beauty of it? It doesn't cost more than two hundred dollars. That's the good thing about them chinks and how they mass-produce everything on God's green planet. Keeps down the cost of running surveillance."

"That's why you attacked me in Oxford, so you could plant a tracking device on me."

"Aren't you the clever bitch?" He gaze slowly moved down her soap-covered body, stopping at her quivering breasts.

Edie sank deeper into the mound of bubbles, her head being the only thing that remained above water. If she could have, she would have squeezed herself right down the drain.

"He's going to be back. Any minute now. So you better leave while you still have the chance." She pointedly glanced at his sutured skull, hoping to drive home her point.

"Ooh, I'm quaking in my boots. Besides, I've got my doubts about your redheaded honey returning any time soon. Last I saw him, he was sitting at the corner bar, downing a cold one. So, it looks like it's gonna be just me and you, sweet tits. But after what I saw last night, I think you can handle it." Lewdly grinning, he winked at her. "I got last night's fuck fest on video. Hot. Real, real hot." Reaching down, he cupped his crotch with his free hand, pursing his thick lips in an exaggerated air kiss.

"I'm going to be sick," Edie moaned, leaning over the side of the tub, gagging.

"The fuck you are!"

Charging forward, her would-be rapist grabbed her by the hair. Lemon-scented water splashed onto the floor as he yanked her up and out of the tub. Arms flailing, Edie reflexively slammed her balled fist into the bandaged wound on the side of his head.

"Fucking shit!" he bellowed, instantly releasing his hold on her.

Edie seized her chance, running into the other room.

A weapon. She had to find a weapon.

Her eyes quickly darted from the floor lamp to the bed to the lumpy chair.

The metal nail file.

Oblivious to the fact that she was stark naked, she lunged toward the fake Louis XIV chair. That was where she'd been sitting when she filed down her broken nail.

From behind her, she heard the thud of heavy boots.

Where the hell was the nail file?

She shoved her hand alongside the seat cushion, her search coming to an abrupt end when a muscled arm snaked around her waist, yanking her away from the chair. Frantic, she tried to twist free, but it was as though she had a giant vise grip clamped around her midsection.

"Think again, cunt," her assailant snarled, lifting her bodily off the ground. Pivoting, he tossed her onto the bed, the iron frame noisily clanging against the wall. Edie immediately rolled to her right side, but anticipating the move, he grabbed her by the ankle, pulling her back to the middle of the bed.

"Don't move," he ordered, pointing the gun at her heart. "Or there won't be anything left of your left titty."

Not so much as twitching, Edie braced herself, certain a bullet would slam into her chest at any moment.

When it didn't happen, she released a pent-up breath, wordlessly watching as her would-be rapist clicked the safety on his weapon. That done, he placed it on the mantel. Completely out of reach.

Cracking his knuckles, he walked toward the bed. "In case you're wondering, I can kill you with my bare hands as easily as I can shoot you."

Edie didn't doubt for one second that he spoke the truth.

Intently staring at her, he placed a knee on the foot of the bed. In the next instant, he had her pinned beneath him. His harsh breath hit her full in the face. Edie figured he had a good hundred pounds on her.

Unable to move, barely able to breathe, she mutely stared at her assailant.

She had only two choices: submit or fight. Either way, when all was said and done, she figured she'd end up dead.

At that thought, Edie heard a buzzing in her ears, the rapist-cum-murderer's rough unshaven face blurring at the edges.

Submit, a voice in her head ordered.

Submit and you might live.

If you live, you can snatch the gun on the mantel.

And if you get the gun, you can blow him away.

Her mind made up, Edie clenched her jaw and stared at the ceiling.

Finagling his hand between their hips, the monster unbuttoned his pants. In the same instant his cell phone vibrated; Edie could feel the pulse against her bare hip.

"Fucking shit."

Removing his hand from between their two bodies, he reached for the vibrating phone clipped to his waistband. "Not a word," he warned, supporting himself on his elbows.

Relieved to have some of his weight removed, Edie obediently nodded.

"Braxton. Yes, sir, I got her." He frowned, his brows drawing together in the middle. "No, sir, she's all right . . . yes, sir . . . I'll have her there in fifteen minutes."

Disconnecting the call, he snapped his cell phone shut and reclipped it on his waistband. Muttering some of the most foul-mouthed profanities she'd ever heard, he pushed himself to his knees, clamping a hand around her upper arm as he did so. With no explanation as to what he was doing, or why he was doing it, he pulled her off the bed.

Edie had no idea who had been on the other end of the line. And she didn't much care. She only knew that she'd been given a reprieve.

His hand still wrapped around her upper arm, he dragged

her over to the mantel, retrieving his gun. He then shoved her through the open bathroom door.

"Get dressed," he ordered, gesturing to the messy pile of clothes on the toilet seat.

Bending at the waist, Edie picked up her discarded bra. "Can I at least dry off? I'm still wet."

"Bitch, do I look like I care?"

CHAPTER 58

Without a doubt, he'd been a pompous ass.

Ashamed of his earlier actions, Caedmon hoped that a heartfelt apology would smooth the rough waters. If it didn't, he would woo Edie with Parsi lamb and cardamom pudding.

He glanced at the brown takeaway bag clutched in his hand, hoping the peace offering would lead to improved relations. And that improved relations led to something decidedly more intimate. More romantic.

As he climbed the well-worn treads that led to their garret room, he wondered if the day would ever come when he could make a full confession. When he could freely and openly tell Edie about the pain of love lost, of vengeance sought and claimed, of the eventual emergence from an alcohol-induced fog. He thought that because of her own travails, she would understand. Maybe even forgive.

"And a warm, fuzzy hug would be nice, too," he said aloud, chortling.

Still laughing as he reached the top of the stairs, the chuckle caught in his throat.

The door to their room had been left ajar.

Afraid of what he would find on the other side of the door, he slowly pushed it all the way open, entering the room. At a glance, he could see that a violent ruckus had taken place. Almost immediately his gaze landed on the large dark spot that stained the tousled coverlet. Setting the brown bag on the dresser, he walked over to the bed. His heart painfully thudding against his chest, he placed his hand on the wet spot, then breathed a sigh of relief. It wasn't blood.

Edie Miller was still alive.

Not as well as she could be, but most definitely alive.

And for that, God, I do indeed thank you.

Out of the corner of his eye, he spied the Virgin Air bag on the floor next to the bed, upended, emptied of its contents. He next surveyed the room, searching for a ransom note.

There was none. He didn't need a scrawled scrap of paper to know Edie had been kidnapped because they wanted him.

Stunned by the well-executed abduction, he went into the bathroom, heading straight for the sink. Turning on the cold water tap, he rinsed his face.

He knew the drill: wait until further instruction. Eventually, he would be contacted. If their plan had been to kill Edie, they would have left her corpse behind as a warning. But there was no sprawled, blood-splattered body. Her abduction was simply a means to an end.

He reached for the neatly folded bath towel and dried his face.

Taking deep, measured breaths, he walked back to the bedroom. Again, he inspected the premises, searching for anything that could be used as a weapon. When the time came to confront his foes, he didn't want to stand before them defenseless. His gaze alighted on the upholstered chair. The chair where Edie had earlier sat, filing a broken nail.

Having no recollection of her returning the file to the Virgin Air bag, he walked over to the chair. The file not being in plain view, he slid his hand around the chair cushion. Frustrated when he came up empty-handed, he removed the cushion from the chair.

There, betwixt two stale chips and a piece of hard candy,

dully gleaming in the lamplight, was the nail file. Though it was hardly a well-honed broadsword, it would have to do.

He replaced the chair cushion.

Bloody hell, but he wanted a drink. Needed a drink to—

Not on your life, old boy. You face the enemy head-on. No armor. No weapon to speak of. Only your wits.

And a burning desire to save the woman he'd come to think of as his own.

Lowering himself into the lumpy Marquise chair, he inhaled the exotic scents of cardamom and cumin mingled with that of lemon-scented water.

Waiting . . .

CHAPTER 59

"I mean you no harm," Stanford MacFarlane said as he ushered her into the room.

Edie snorted, the memory of her near rape all too vivid. "Yeah, and British beef is safe to eat."

As she spoke, she glanced around her prison, taking in what appeared to be an old millhouse, the metal cogs and wheels of the original machinery still in place on the other side of the room. She could hear water running beneath the floorboards and figured the millhouse was located on a stream or brook.

Next she turned her gaze to the man standing across from her. She gauged Stanford MacFarlane to be in his mid- to late fifties, the graying buzz cut with the sharply defined widow's peak being the dead giveaway. At one time he was probably handsome, but years spent in the sun had turned age lines into deeply incised creases, giving him a stern, gnomelike visage. A man of medium height, he had an erect military posture, with an air of command that bordered on the egomaniacal. She figured that right about the time he started to toddle, folks got out the garlic when they saw him coming.

"Just answer me this . . . what are you going to do if you actually get your hands on the Ark?"

"That's between me and the Almighty," MacFarlane replied.

"What if the Ark of the Covenant turns out to be nothing more than a gold-plated box?"

MacFarlane smiled. "And God said to Moses, 'Let them make me a sanctuary, that I may dwell among them.'"

Realizing that he considered the Ark some kind of God box, Edie decided to try a different approach. "There's no question in my mind that you're a God-fearing man. Which means that we have a lot in common. You may not know this, but I go to church every Sunday and . . . well, I don't have to tell you what the Bible says about mercy and compassion. 'Blessed are those who are pure in heart: for they shall see God,'" she recited, tossing out a Bible verse of her own, figuring the only way to fight fire was with more of the same.

Hearing that, MacFarlane's gaze narrowed. "Like many of your ilk, you've hijacked the Bible in order to put forth your left-wing, feel-good agenda. The carjacker will not steal your vehicle if you show some compassion. Nor will the killer pull the trigger as he is an intrinsically good man."

And the rapist will not brutalize his victim if shown loving-kindness. Yeah, right.

Turning away from her, MacFarlane walked over to the nearby kitchenette; the stone-walled room was a big open space with matching sofas on one side, a dining room table in the middle, and a kitchen on the opposite end. She watched as he pulled two clean mugs from a shelf. He then opened two packets of instant cocoa. That done, he poured hot water from a carafe.

Even as he handed her one of the mugs, he glared at her. A dark, impassioned glare that sent a chill down her spine. She didn't dare refuse the cocoa.

"I know you and your kind, Miss Miller. You think that by putting your carcass in the pew every Sunday, God will look kindly upon you, that perfect church attendance will equal a free pass into heaven."

"You've got me mixed up with some other person. Personally, I think it's important for . . ." She searched for the right word. ". . . the *betterment* of one's soul to engage in good works, Christian charity being the touchstone of—"

"Spare me the secular soliloquy. As if volunteering at some inner-city soup kitchen will gain you entry into heaven. Faith, not deeds, will secure you a place among the righteous."

"Don't you mean the self-righteous?" she retorted.

"You and your kind are an anathema unto the Lord."

"Then we clearly worship two different gods."

"At last, something we can agree upon."

And as Edie knew full well, it was an agreement based on a bitter divide.

Truth be told, she was taken aback at how much Stanford MacFarlane reminded her of Pops; her maternal grandfather had held to a very conservative interpretation of the Bible. At the time she'd thought it a stifling interpretation. But when espoused by a man like MacFarlane, it went from stifling to scary. Put a black robe on him and Stanford MacFarlane would have made the perfect Spanish inquisitor.

"Speaking of a free pass into heaven, if you think that finding the Ark is your stamped ticket, think again," she said, refusing to go quietly into the funeral pyre.

About to raise his mug to his lips, MacFarlane lowered it. For several seconds—seconds that conjured images of burning bodies—he stared at her.

"Unlike you, I will die and rise with the Old Testament saints." Then, as though he'd simply made a passing comment about the weather, he calmly took a sip of his cocoa.

Edie stood silent.

There was no way to argue with a zealot. The years spent with Pops had taught her that; the memory still weighed heavy. Like a giant millstone on her heart.

Out of the corner of her eye, she caught sight of a gossamer strand of cobweb dangling from the wood-beamed ceiling. Staring at it, she suddenly felt very much like the fly ensnared in that deceptively beautiful web.

But unlike the ensnared fly, she had an out. *Caedmon.*

Above all else, she knew he would come. If not to rescue her, then to find the Ark.

CHAPTER 60

Hearing a sonorous knock, Caedmon turned in his chair. The guesthouse proprietor, a florid-faced Welshman, stood in the doorway, no doubt baffled as to why the door had been left ajar. Simply put, he had not seen a need to close it.

"You've got a call," the other man announced, clearly annoyed at having had to climb four sets of stairs to convey the message. "You can take it at the front desk." Announcement made, he took his departure.

Caedmon rose to his feet. As he walked toward the door, he glimpsed the sketched drawing of the Canterbury window, along with the handwritten translation of the quatrains. Both left in plain sight on the wooden bench. A stark and painful reminder that Edie's abduction had everything to do with the Ark of the Covenant.

Knowing he would have need of both, he retrieved the two sheets of paper, slipping them inside his anorak pocket. That being the only thing of value in the room, he trudged after the proprietor, closing the door behind him.

A few moments later, standing at the rough-hewn counter that masqueraded as a front desk, Caedmon lifted the heavy handset of an old-fashioned telephone. "Go ahead. I'm listening," he said, refusing to engage in the hypocrisy of a civil greeting.

"I do hope you're having a pleasant evening," the American male on the other end smoothly, and hypocritically, said in turn.

"Sod off! Is she still alive?"

"You know that she is."

"I know no such thing. If we are to continue the conversation, I require proof of life."

"You're hardly in a position to make demands."

"I am not demanding," Caedmon countered in a calmer tone, reining in his unruly emotions. "I am requesting, as a show of good faith, you give me proof that Miss Miller is, indeed, your captive."

The request was met with silence, and then Caedmon could detect a muffled command being issued.

Then, a few seconds later, "It's me, Caedmon. I'm . . . I'm all right."

At hearing Edie's voice, he glanced heavenward.

She was alive.

"Have they harmed you in any way?"

"No, they—"

"Satisfied?" her captor snarled into the phone.

"Yes, I'm satisfied. What must I do to ensure her safe return?"

The other man chuckled, obviously amused by the question. "Find me the Ark of the Covenant, of course."

Caedmon fell silent.

Hearing the proviso so bluntly spelled out—in clear, concise, unequivocal terms—made him acutely aware that Mac-Farlane might very well be asking the impossible. For nearly three thousand years the Ark had remained hidden. Naught but a legend. Many before him had tried—and failed—to find it. Somehow, against impossible odds, he had to succeed.

His stomach muscles painfully cramped; he was afraid that the challenge might prove insurmountable.

Knowing the negotiations would come to a horrible end if such doubts were hinted at, let alone verbalized, he strove for a confidence he didn't feel. "Do I have your word that when I find the Ark, Edie Miller's life will be spared?"

"My word is my bond," the other man promptly replied. "As soon as we hang up, I want you to leave that rathole of a hotel and head three blocks south. Turn left at the telephone booth on the corner. There's an alley halfway down the street. My men will be waiting for you. Don't try anything foolish. If you do, the woman dies. And, trust me, it won't be a pleasant death."

Instructions issued, the call was unceremoniously disconnected.

For several long seconds Caedmon stared at the telephone, events unraveling at a faster pace than he would have liked.

Needing to be on his way, he banged his palm against the silver bell on the counter. When the Welshman appeared, he slid his hand inside his coat pocket and removed his billfold. "I would like to check out."

The proprietor suspiciously stared at him. "Where's the missus?"

"She has gone ahead without me."

Bill paid in full, he left the guesthouse and proceeded south as directed, his progress slowed by an almost impenetrable fog, the gray mist as dense as Irish oatmeal.

On his right, he passed a pub, its yellow light spilling onto the pavement. Earlier in the evening, he'd glumly sat in that same pub, staring at a full pint of lager. Knowing alcohol would do nothing to resolve the unsettled business with Edie, he'd handed the glass to an inebriated local before wordlessly slinking out.

Had he not succumbed to a moment's weakness, the abduction might have been thwarted.

Caedmon shoved the thought aside. He couldn't change the past. He could only affect the here and now.

As he made his way through the dense fog, sound became muffled to such an extent that he couldn't discern whether a honking vehicle was to his left or to his right. The alarming scene was so cinematic, he wondered if MacFarlane had somehow magically conjured the foul weather on command, such notions reminding him anew that all he had at his command was the nail file hidden beneath the leather insole of his right oxford.

Again, he rehearsed the plan in his mind's eye. *A jab to the eye. A deep puncture to the neck.* If used correctly, the metal file could become a deadly weapon. He'd killed before. He could do so again.

Approaching a red call box, he turned left as he had been instructed. When he came to the alleyway, he made another left. At the end of the deserted lane, he sighted two men leaning against a parked Range Rover.

MacFarlane's bully boys. Dicey characters, the both of them.

Though he had no concrete evidence, Caedmon assumed that MacFarlane recruited his mercenaries straight out of the U.S. military. Special Forces, more than likely.

"Good evening, gentlemen," he said, touching his fingers to an imaginary hat brim.

Neither man acknowledged the greeting, although one of them pushed himself away from the vehicle and stepped toward him. Without being asked, Caedmon raised his arms, grasping the back of his head with his clasped hands. The other man impersonally patted him down, searching every crevice where a weapon might be concealed.

Search concluded, Caedmon slowly lowered his arms.

"Strip off your clothes."

"I beg your pardon?"

"You heard me—strip off your clothes." To ensure that the order was obeyed, the other man pulled aside his jacket lapel, revealing a holstered gun.

Bang goes the smarty-smarty plan to use the nail file.

There being nothing he could do but comply, Caedmon removed his anorak, dropping it onto the ground. Then, giving every indication that he was a man with nothing to hide, he toed off his right leather oxford, purposely kicking it in his escort's direction.

The subterfuge worked; his surrendered shoe warranted little more than a disinterested glance.

As he divested himself of his garments, he noticed that the thick fog provided a surreal modicum of privacy.

Naked, he stood before his captors. He couldn't think of a time when he'd felt more vulnerable. "I know. I should probably be more diligent about my exercise regimen."

Neither man responded, although the one with the holstered weapon did reach inside his jacket pocket. Removing a dark length of fabric, he tossed it at Caedmon's bare chest.

"Put on the blindfold."

"Such measures seem a bit draconian, don't you think?"

Evidently not draconian enough; the other man's response was quick and unpitying. Removing the gun from its holster, he stepped forward, smashing the revolver butt against the side of Caedmon's head.

A myriad splash of color, like a Jackson Pollock abstract, instantly flashed behind his eyes.

An instant later, the colors bled together, turning a deep, dark inky shade of black.

CHAPTER 61

Lucidity still beyond his grasp, Caedmon shuffled into the room, clutching his wool jumper and various undergarments to his chest. He heard himself nattering on about something. George Eliot and *The Mill on the Floss*. Or some such nonsense.

He tried to focus, but couldn't contain his flyaway thoughts. Couldn't stop the ringing in his ears.

Bloody hell, but his head hurt.

"Caedmon! Are you all right?"

He turned, his vision still blurred.

"I'm fine," he lied, uncertain to whom he spoke.

He blinked several times, willing the particulars to come into focus. They came in bits and bobs. *Two parallel worry lines between two equally worried brown eyes. Long curly hair. A red bruise on a pale cheek.*

"Edie . . . thank God . . . are you all right?" He immediately realized that it was an asinine question; he could see that she wasn't.

"I'm fine."

Hearing her automatic reply proved that they were woven from the same piece of fabric.

His vision clearing, he surveyed what was obviously the first floor of an old millhouse. All around him he saw solid eighteenth-century construction. Shuttered windows. Wood-planked floors. Thick stone walls. It was a prison from which there would be no escape, even if he could somehow disable his adversaries, of which he counted four. He wondered which of the quartet was responsible for the bruise on Edie's cheek; any one of the brutes appeared capable of hitting a defenseless woman.

"Caedmon, what did they do to you?" Edie worriedly inquired, barred from approaching by an older man who had a hand manacled around her upper arm.

As though he were caught in one of those bizarre dreams in which he was naked and everyone else was fully clothed, he belatedly realized that while he was attired in trousers, shirt, and shoes, he held in his hands jumper, pants, and socks. Mercifully, his trousers were zipped, although his shirt was completely unbuttoned.

"I was subjected to a somewhat thorough body search. Needless to say, I feel a bit violated."

"I hope my men weren't too rough," the older man remarked, mirthlessly smiling. "I ordered them to go easy on you."

Assuming the gray-haired man to be none other than Stanford MacFarlane, Caedmon summoned an equally humorless smile. "No need to sound the alarm. Your boys merely tapped the claret." He wiped his hand under his bloodied nostrils, his armed escorts having come damn close to breaking his nose. "I shall live to fight another day."

"As you can well imagine, I have several questions that I'm hoping you can answer for me."

"Mmmm. I believe this is where I'm supposed to say, 'I want my solicitor,'" he deadpanned.

"First and foremost, where is the Ark of the Covenant?"

Knowing that Edie's life was very much at stake, he truthfully replied, "I have no idea. Although I'm certain that if we put on our team bonnets, we can uncover its location."

"That's what the last scholar I enlisted said to me . . . right before his death."

Out of the corner of his eye, he saw Edie put a hand to her mouth, horrified. In truth, he felt a bit queasy himself at hearing of his predecessor's demise.

"I'm not a bloody psychic. I'm an academic. And as such, I must insist that you give logic a chance to put on its pants. That said, in my anorak pocket, you'll find a sketched drawing which I believe may be of some interest."

Properly enticed, MacFarlane walked over to the thug in possession of his anorak. Removing two sheets of folded paper from the front pocket, he first examined the translated quartets, then the sketched drawing of *The Presentation of Christ*.

"Before I get to the drawing, I should tell you what we've learned to date. We now know that the quatrains were not written by Galen of Godmersham." MacFarlane's head jerked, the man clearly thunderstruck. "Rather they were written by Galen's third wife, Philippa of Canterbury."

"You're certain of this?"

"There is no doubt in my mind."

MacFarlane chewed on the morsel for several seconds. "And what about St. Lawrence the Martyr?"

"Another red herring," Caedmon replied, suspecting the other scholar's fate had been sealed with that particular mistranslation. "The 'blessed martyr' in question is Thomas à Becket. Which led us to Canterbury Cathedral, where we discovered a stained glass window."

MacFarlane stared at the sketched drawing, like an addict staring at a full needle.

"As to the specifics of the window, one must bear in mind that it was created by an artisan with a very different set of cultural references. From a semiotic standpoint, deciphering the window is akin to peering through a dark lens. Complex theological tenets, historical fact, and archaic language structures are all jumbled together in that one seemingly innocuous drawing. Admittedly, it will take time to sort out the various strands." Seeing the displeased expression on MacFarlane's face, he hastily added, "However, we have reason to believe that the two geese in the basket are significant."

"What makes you think that?"

"Because one of the geese represents Philippa herself, in the medieval guise of the good housewife. Unfortunately, we have yet to decipher the meaning of the second goose."

"When will you have it deciphered?"

"When I am sufficiently rested." Caedmon stood his ground, knowing that if he didn't, there would be precious few roots to cling to. Then, gesturing to Edie, he said, "We both require bed and board."

The added caveat was more for Edie's sake than his own. He could see it in her strained expression; she was utterly exhausted. If an opportunity arose to escape, she would need to be sufficiently rested to turn opportunity to advantage.

MacFarlane impatiently tapped his watch crystal. "If the Ark of the Covenant is not in my hands in sixteen hours' time, I'll kill the woman."

Although the proceedings had thus far proved civil, Caedmon recalled the old proverb advising the unsuspecting diner to use a long spoon when supping with the devil.

"I will do all in my power to find the Ark," he assured his adversary.

MacFarlane locked gazes with him, a barely contained

malevolence lurking beneath the controlled expression. "Behave like a guest and you'll continue to be treated as such. Am I making myself clear?"

"As a bell."

CHAPTER 62

"I don't know about you, but I've had enough chips for one day," Caedmon grumbled.

"And guys with big guns and things that go bump in the night." Edie squinted, there being only a small glimmer of light shining through the locked door. MacFarlane's twisted idea of "bed and board" was a small storage closet and a couple of bags of soggy fries.

"But on a bright note, we shall be lulled to sleep by the babbling brook that runs beneath the mill."

Edie made no reply; a damp chill oozed up from the floorboards on account of that same babbling brook. Already she could feel the ache in her joints.

"By the by, I've got your metal nail file hidden under the insole of my shoe."

"I can top that . . . I've got a thousand dollars stuffed inside my boot. After the attack in Oxford, I was worried someone might steal the Virgin Air bag." Her thoughts running every which way, she abruptly changed gears. "There's something I need to tell you . . . I have intimate knowledge of Stanford MacFarlane."

"Indeed?"

"Not that I have biblical knowledge of the man," Edie quickly amended. "But I do know the heart of Stanford MacFarlane."

"And how is that?" There was no mistaking the interest in his voice.

"My maternal grandfather was something of a religious zealot. If not cut from the same bolt of cloth as MacFarlane, Pops was certainly cut from a similar one." She caustically laughed, the memory an unpleasant one. "My grandfather believed that freedom of religion extended only to other fundamental Christians."

"Being a young girl, I'm surprised that you weren't, er—"

"Indoctrinated? Having been raised by a mother who repeatedly told me that she would clean up her act, and who repeatedly failed to make good on the promise, made me a hard sell. Deep-seated trust issues, I suppose." She readjusted her legs, the dark space a tight fit for the two of them. "Having sat through all those Sunday sermons, I know that men like my pops and Stanford MacFarlane lie awake at night, consumed with visions of a global theocracy."

She paused a moment, recalling the earlier one-on-one conversation. "Although I get the feeling that, unlike Pops, MacFarlane thinks of himself as some sort of Old Testament patriarch."

"One of those unsavory bastards who prays before the bloodletting, hmm?"

Edie shuddered. "He's probably praying as we speak."

Putting an arm around her shoulder, Caedmon pulled her close. "As long as there's a chance of finding the Ark, you will be safe. MacFarlane knows that if he harms you in any way, I'll refuse to comply with his wishes."

"You don't actually trust him to keep his word, do you?"

It being too dark in the closet for her to discern Caedmon's features, she sensed rather than saw his sardonic smile.

"In my experience, trusting one's enemy is a fine art."

In the same way that she sensed the smile, Edie suddenly sensed its disappearance.

"It's my fault that you got dragged into this mess. I should never have agreed to—"

Edie put a hand over his mouth, *sshhing* him. "Since meeting you at the National Gallery of Art, everything that I've done—and I mean *everything*—from coming to England to making love to riding in the back of that refrigerated truck, I've done of my own free will. We're in this together, Caedmon. And don't for one second think that we're not. There was no way that either of us could have known they'd place a tracking device on me."

"Are you saying that the punch-up at the Covered Market was merely a feint? Bloody hell. I should have seen that one coming. From the onset, MacFarlane has remained one step ahead of me."

Hearing the self-recrimination in his voice, she thought a change of subject in order. "We now have less than sixteen hours to figure out the meaning of those two geese in the basket. All we know is that one of the geese represents Philippa." She sighed, well aware that it was a very brief allotment of time. "I wish we knew more about Philippa. Other than the fact that she married Galen and she joined a nunnery, we've got precious few clues."

"The nunnery . . . that's it. You, Edie Miller, are bloody beautiful!"

Without warning, Caedmon began to loudly bang on the closet door with his balled fist.

"What the hell's goin' on in there?" came a deep-throated voice on the other side of the locked door.

"Tell MacFarlane that I know where the Ark is hidden."

CHAPTER 63

Onward, Christian soldiers, Caedmon silently mused, realizing that each of the four armed men gathered around the table wore a Jerusalem cross ring on his right hand.

"And you're absolutely certain that the two geese depicted in the stained glass window will lead us to the Ark of the Covenant?" MacFarlane gestured to the Canterbury drawing that lay on the tabletop.

Seated in front of a laptop computer, Caedmon stopped typing, taking a moment to glance at his adversary. He knew that he served but one purpose. Once he fulfilled that purpose, he would no longer be in a position to safeguard Edie.

Surreptitiously, he glanced at the locked closet door on the far side of the room.

Somehow he had to devise a suitable enticement, a bargaining chip, that he could use to garner Edie's freedom. Until then, he would merely reveal enough to whet MacFarlane's voracious appetite. But not so much that he lessened his overall worth. Stanford MacFarlane had to believe that without him, he would never find the Ark.

"As I mentioned earlier, one of the geese symbolizes Philippa in her role as the good housewife to her husband, Galen of Godmersham. After Galen's death, Philippa joined a nunnery, where she lived out her remaining days. With that in mind, I believe that the second goose also represents Philippa; nuns are often referred to as the bride of Christ. Or the good housewife of Christ, as it were."

MacFarlane took a moment to digest the crumb just tossed to him. "What does Galen's widow being a nun have to do with anything?" he asked, his eyes narrowed with suspicion. He'd already been led down a false path by one man. Clearly, he was not about to venture forth without a proper road map.

"It's possible that Philippa took the Ark with her to the nunnery." He jutted his chin at the Oxford University search engine that he'd pulled up on the Internet. "Hopefully, I'll be able to find out which order Philippa joined. Although it may take some time, as there were scores of now-defunct religious orders active in the fourteenth century."

"Time is the one thing I've got in short supply."

As he waited for the search results, Caedmon couldn't help but wonder at MacFarlane's impatience to find the Ark. It made him think that the self-styled Warriors of God were operating under some sort of deadline.

But a deadline for what?

Though he was tantalized by the ancient mystery that had beguiled such luminaries as Newton and Freud, he was keenly aware that lives had been ruthlessly taken; MacFarlane's obsession with the Ark knew no bounds.

"Ah! We have a hit," he announced, pointing to the computer screen. "According to a fourteenth-century document called the *Regestrum Archiepiscopi*—"

"Can the Latin," MacFarlane snarled.

"Right." Properly chastened, he decided to dumb down all relayed material. "What you are looking at is the Archbishop of Canterbury's registry of nunneries compiled in the year 1350. That being two years after the plague, I suspect the archbishop was very keen to take a head count. Since most folk in the Middle Ages rarely traveled more than thirty miles from the place of their birth, I'll first search for Philippa in the Kent listings."

As he scrolled the register, Caedmon knew that he was operating on nothing more than a strong hunch. A hunch that if proved wrong could have tragic results.

"There she is," he murmured. "Philippa, widowed wife of Galen of Godmersham, is listed as a member of the Priory of the Blessed Virgin Mary. According to the entry, she entered the nunnery with a dowry worth approximately—"

"Just tell me where the priory is located," MacFarlane interrupted.

"It is located in the hamlet of Swanley, southeast of London."

MacFarlane turned to the behemoth with the sutured head. "Pull it up on the GPS."

Using a small stylus that looked ridiculous in his oversized hand, the brute began pecking away on a handheld device.

"I've got it. It's at the intersection of highways M20 and M25," he announced, passing the handheld computer to his superior.

MacFarlane studied the computer-generated map. "You were right. Swanley is exactly thirty miles from Canterbury. Which means we can be there within the hour."

Caedmon vetoed the idea with a shake of the head. Knowing that MacFarlane was a man willing to punch above his own weight, he calmly pointed out the obvious. "If we traipse around a medieval priory in the middle of the night, we might very well be confronted by the local constabulary. Particularly if the nunnery is listed on the Heritage Trust. Given the delicate task at hand, we will be better aided by the light of day than the gloom of night."

MacFarlane stared at him, long and hard.

"We hit the road at first light," he said at last. Then, his gaze narrowing. "But if you're thinking about sidestepping me like that li'l Harvard pencil dick, you think again, boy."

Although he took exception to being called "boy" Caedmon kept his ire in check. "Bear in mind that Swanley may simply be where we find the next clue."

"What are you saying, that this is going to turn into some sort of scavenger hunt?"

"If you wish to hide a tree, you must hide it in a forest. We won't know if the Priory of the Blessed Virgin Mary is the forest we seek until we can properly examine the site."

"Well, you better hope to God that it is the right forest."

At hearing that, Caedmon intuited what would happen should they not find the Ark. It was an intuition that involved slit throats and bodies buried at the low-water mark.

CHAPTER 64

Dawn arrived, damp and gray, the passenger windows on the Range Rover still ice-rimmed. The cold went right through Edie, causing her teeth to loudly clatter—though she suspected that fear had as much to do with her teeth clacking as the outside temperature.

Rudely awakened only a short time earlier, she and Caedmon had been ushered into the backseat of the waiting vehicle. Seated in front of them was the driver, Sanchez, a sullen man given to muttering in Spanish, and his copilot, Harliss, a southerner with an accent so thick he might as well have been speaking in Spanish. Both men were armed. And both had made it very clear that they would not hesitate to use their weapons.

Leading the pack in a second Range Rover were Stanford MacFarlane and his right-hand man, Boyd Braxton. To Edie's relief, she'd had little to no contact with the hulking brute since the attempted rape. Knowing that Caedmon had enough on his plate, she'd made no mention of the near miss.

"Didn't you say something about swans and geese being interchangeable in the medieval lexicon?"

"Hmm?" Clearly lost in thought, Caedmon tore his gaze away from the window. "Er, yes, I did say that."

"Making it all the more likely that this place Swanley is where we'll find the Ark."

"Actually, I have no idea if the Ark is hidden at the nunnery. The Priory of the Blessed Virgin Mary may simply be where we find the next clue."

Jealously she watched as MacFarlane's henchmen passed a thermos filled with hot coffee back and forth between them.

"My feet feel like two blocks of ice," she complained in a lowered voice, pointedly glancing at the pair of green wellies she'd earlier been issued.

Caedmon, decked out in an identical pair of boots, commiserated with a nod. "The English Wellington was designed to keep the foot dry, not warm. Although we'll be glad of them should we have to traipse through a damp field."

Edie didn't bother to point out the obvious—that a full-speed sprint through that same damp field would be next to impossible in the clunky rubber boots.

They'd driven through the postdawn gloom for approximately twenty minutes when Edie sighted the first road sign for Swanley. As they approached the town limits, she was surprised that Swanley looked a whole lot like any American residential suburb, the outskirts littered with strip malls and fast-food eateries.

How were they going to find the Ark in the midst of so much suburban sprawl?

"Don't worry. The priory is located in the outlying countryside," Caedmon remarked, correctly guessing at her thoughts.

As if on cue, Sanchez exited from the superhighway, veering onto a two-lane country road. Peering out the window, she'd forgotten how simple things—trees in the distance, brown pastures, stone farm fences—could exude a stark cinematic beauty; the contrast between the countryside and the nearby town was like midnight and high noon.

Up ahead, MacFarlane's Range Rover came to a halt, pulling to the side of the road. Sanchez pulled in a few feet behind.

"Is this the place?" she asked, not seeing anything in the rural landscape that even remotely resembled a medieval nunnery.

"I believe so," Caedmon replied. "MacFarlane plotted the course on a computer navigation system. Although we'll probably have to trek across a field or two to reach our destination."

Harliss opened the passenger door. "Get out." Gun in hand, he ushered them toward the other vehicle while Sanchez unloaded several large, bulky canvas packs from the Range Rover's cargo bin.

As MacFarlane huddled his men, she and Caedmon were ordered to stand to one side. She could see that Harliss had a handheld GPS receiver, which all four men intently studied. Although she tried to listen in, she could catch only a few snippets—*avenues of approach . . . terrain features . . . obstacles . . . reconnaissance.*

"They're treating this like some sort of military operation," she whispered to Caedmon.

"Apparently so."

"Making us the enemy combatants, huh?"

Too busy scanning the surrounding area, Caedmon made no reply.

"Move 'em out," MacFarlane gruffly ordered.

Sandwiched between two pairs of armed men, she and Caedmon moved with the pack in a northeasterly direction. In front of them about two hundred yards in the distance was a dense grove of trees. As they trudged across the field, Edie wondered if Philippa of Canterbury had had any notion of the deadly train of events she would someday trigger with her quatrains.

More than likely she had.

Why else would the noblewoman-cum-nun have gone to such lengths to hide her dead husband's gold *arca*? Philippa had survived the horror of the plague and no doubt blamed the Ark for the deadly wave that swept across England.

Last night Caedmon had informed her that Philippa belonged to the Gilbertine Order, an order of nuns founded in England. In a span of only six years, Philippa had risen through the priory ranks, eventually becoming the cellaress, a position in which she oversaw all of the food production. A capable woman with a flair for management, she could have easily arranged for the Ark of the Covenant to have been brought to Swanley. Maybe she let her fellow nuns in on the secret. Because they lived a life devoted to religious worship and contemplative prayer, there was little fear that the secret would be revealed to nosy outsiders.

Holding the GPS receiver in his right hand, Harliss led them through the grove of trees, the gnarled leafless limbs like so many arthritic hands.

Just beyond the bare boughs, Edie glimpsed a stone wall.

"I see it!" she exclaimed, raising her right hand and pointing, inexplicably excited. "It's on the other side of the grove."

"Roger that," Harliss responded, leading them toward to the right.

A few moments later, they entered a clearing.

Edie quickly glanced from side to side.

"Oh God . . . it's been destroyed."

CHAPTER 65

Stunned, the six of them stood rooted in place.

"What the fuck happened?" Braxton muttered, expressing what everyone in the group was no doubt thinking. All that remained of the Priory of the Blessed Virgin Mary was three stone walls punctuated with arched windows; tangled strands of dead ivy cascaded from the glassless openings.

"It looks like it was hit by mortar fire." This came from MacFarlane, his leathery cheeks flushed with what Edie assumed to be barely contained rage.

"My guess is that the Priory of the Blessed Virgin Mary was destroyed during the Tudor reign," Caedmon quietly remarked. "In 1538, Parliament, at the behest of Henry the Eighth, issued an official edict known as the Dissolution of the Monasteries. The new law enabled Henry to confiscate all property owned by the monastic orders. Aided by an overzealous population who hoped that church riches would trickle into their greedy hands, the king's men demolished many a monastic building;

the lead in the roofs was removed and the stone reused for secular building projects."

Edie stared at the eerie remains: the gouged Gothic shell that opened heavenward, the sheaves of ice-laden grass, shimmering jewel-like. Perhaps it was the early-morning mist, but she could have sworn that a ghostly imprint of incense and candles and prayerful chants still lingered.

She turned and glanced at Caedmon, conveying a silent question: *What if the next clue had been embedded in a piece of stained glass that had been smashed to smithereens centuries ago?*

With an almost imperceptible shake of the head, he warned her against voicing the query aloud. He then pointedly glanced at Stanford MacFarlane.

Edie got the message, loud and clear. If MacFarlane thought the game was over, she and Caedmon would be killed on the spot. No matter what, they had to maintain the pretext that it was still "game on."

Startled by a sudden screech, Edie reflexively turned her head.

There, perched on the branch of a leafless tree was a raven, loudly cawing.

Although not a superstitious person by nature, she considered the raven a very bad omen.

CHAPTER 66

"Not to worry," Caedmon announced, affecting a tone of bluff good cheer. "The fact that the priory was destroyed will not impede our progress in the least. In fact, it will make the task at hand far easier to execute."

"Do you think I suddenly went loco? There's nothing here," MacFarlane argued, gesturing to the empty space abutting the three stone walls.

"Ah! 'They have eyes, but they do not see.'"

"And what does King David have to do with anything?"

Knowing that he needed to produce a rabbit from his top hat, Caedmon replied, "The good king's observation is most apropos. For though the untrained eye sees nothing but overgrown grass and three stone walls, the trained eye sees the nunnery as it once stood."

Several seconds passed in terse silence.

"Go ahead. I'm listening," MacFarlane said, rather grudgingly.

Relieved that he'd passed the initial audition, Caedmon cast Edie a quick, reassuring glance.

Don't worry, love. I can do this. I can buy us the time we need.

He gestured to the meadow adjacent to the stone walls. "If you care to join me, I would like to take what the archaeologists call a 'field walk.' Since we don't have the benefit of an aerial photograph, by slowly walking the site, we should be able to detect slight fluctuations and anomalies in the ground surface. These fluctuations and anomalies will enable us to piece together the perimeter boundary of the original nunnery. Once we've done that, we'll be in a much better position to know where to begin the search."

Although MacFarlane nodded his assent, a silent addendum was included—the gadabout had better produce some tangible results.

The rabbit trick suddenly becoming that much more difficult, he commenced the tour by saying, "First, a quick primer in monastic layout. The majority of medieval priories followed a standard prototype of three buildings, usually two stories in height, arranged in a U shape. This U-shaped configuration would have abutted a church." Caedmon gestured to the three stone walls. "As you can see, the demolished church is all that remains of the Priory of the Blessed Virgin Mary."

"If I'm imagining this correctly, the church and the

U-shaped buildings would have enclosed some sort of court-yard," Edie remarked.

"Quite correct. The garth, or cloister as it is more commonly called, was the large open space within the enclosed buildings. The cloister was primarily used for gardening and the interment of the dead."

A definite spark of interest in his eyes, MacFarlane clearly recognized the possibilities that the cloister presented. "I'm guessing that no one would have thought twice about a deep hole being dug inside the enclosed courtyard."

"We are of like mind. Furthermore, only nuns and novices were permitted inside the cloister, thus making it the perfect place for Philippa to bury the Ark of the Covenant." Arms spread wide, Caedmon gestured to the vacant meadow that moments ago MacFarlane had been so quick to dismiss. "Here, Philippa could have safeguarded the Ark from the outside world while at the same time keeping a watchful eye on it. Shall we begin our stroll around the cloister?"

Taking the lead, he walked to the other side of the small meadow, MacFarlane on his heels, Edie and the henchmen also in tow.

"This, I believe, is where the refectory would have been situated," he said, gesturing with his hands to an area of over-grown weeds and tangled grass. "The refectory was, as you undoubtedly know, the dining hall where all meals were taken."

". . . aka the penguins' mess tent," one of the henchmen snickered.

Ignoring the jibe, Caedmon marched forward approximately fifteen meters. "And this would have been the *lavatorium.*"

"The wash area, right?"

He nodded at Edie. "That's correct." He then walked another fifteen meters. "Here would have stood the kitchen area."

"And just how is it that you know all of this?" MacFarlane suspiciously asked, glancing back and forth between the last two areas delineated.

Caedmon knowingly smiled, about to divulge how he'd

pulled a rabbit out of thin air. "If you'll look carefully, you'll see a slightly raised furrow." He pointed to the ground. "That is what's known as a kitchen midden. Or what the layman might refer to as a buried trash heap. And if you were to search the *lavatorium*, you would see a depressed furrow rather than a raised furrow."

"Caused by centuries of running water," Edie correctly deduced.

"Satisfied?" He directed the question to the man who held their fate in his hand.

Again, MacFarlane glanced back and forth between the "kitchen" and the *"lavatorium."* Appeased, he jutted his head at the small meadow. "Keep walking."

Caedmon continued with the tour. "Across from us, on the other side of the cloister, would have been the nuns' dormitory. And directly opposite the church would have been the chapter house and abbess's quarters." Raising his arm, he motioned in four separate directions. "With each of the four nunnery buildings accounted for, we can now extrapolate the cloister boundaries."

MacFarlane surveyed the area in question. "And you're certain that the Ark would have been buried somewhere within the cloister?"

Caedmon hesitated, the question inherently a tricky one. "I have strong reason to believe that Philippa would have deemed the cloister the safest place to hide the Ark. Although where in the cloister, I couldn't begin to speculate."

To his surprise, the admission garnered an unconcerned shrug. Turning to his men, MacFarlane commenced to give orders.

"Sanchez, I want you on the metal detector. Gunnery Sergeant, you've got the GPR. And, Harliss, you're on guard duty." The orders met with a deferential chorus.

His input no longer needed, Caedmon was ordered to stand beside Edie, the two of them placed under the watchful eye of the unintelligible southerner. A man prone to toothy grins that conveyed a dark malevolence, Harliss let it be known that he had disabled the safety mechanism on his H&K MP5 machine gun. "Meanin' I can shoot y'all all the sooner," as he had so obligingly informed them.

Scanning the landscape, Caedmon could sight no avenue of escape, no farmhouse that he and Edie could run to; the Priory of the Blessed Virgin Mary was situated in a remote milieu. If they could somehow make their way to the country lane where the Range Rovers were parked, they might be able to flag down a passing motorist. But getting to the roadway amid a hail of bullets was a remote possibility at best.

Which left only one viable option: He had to disarm one of MacFarlane's henchmen.

No easy feat, given that all three men were sturdily constructed and no doubt knew how to comport themselves.

"What's going on?" Edie asked, nudging him with her elbow. Sanchez's sweep of the cloister already underway, the ground was littered with several small flags.

"Each time his metal detector finds any buried metal, the device beeps. Whereupon the spot is marked with a flag, the color of which designates the type of metal detected."

"Oh, I get it. So, I'm guessing that gray is for silver, orange is for bronze, black is for lead, and yellow is for gold."

He nodded. "Since a metal detector can't fully identify the buried object, Braxton will use ground-penetrating radar to survey all areas that tested positive for gold. The working assumption is that the Ark of the Covenant was indeed made of pure gold."

Edie raised a quizzical brow. "Radar? You mean like the guys in the airport tower use?"

"Not exactly. Rather than sending radio waves into the air, these waves are directed into the ground. The electronic signals then bounce back into a receiver." He nodded toward the small laptop computer that Braxton had set up on top of the GPR receiver. "A computerized map will be generated based on the density and position of the returned signals. It should enable them to determine the size and depth of any buried object."

"Normally, I'd say, 'Way cool,' but I've got a funny feeling this ground-penetrating radar is going to make or break us."

Caedmon made no reply, having reached the same conclusion.

Worried about their immediate future, he wordlessly stared at Edie. At the curls covered in a bridal veil of morning mist. At the mottled purple bruise on her right cheek. He thought that she resembled nothing so much as a bedraggled street urchin. Something straight out of Dickens. Brave and vulnerable in the face of danger.

"I've got something!" Braxton suddenly hollered.

At hearing that, Caedmon inwardly breathed a sigh of relief. "I'd say we're bang on target." Then, his interest getting the better of him, he called out, "May I have a look?"

When MacFarlane nodded his assent, Harliss happily did the honors of escorting them over to the laptop computer, prodding them forward with a negligently held machine gun pointed at their backs.

"I'm getting a whole bunch of little unidentified objects," Braxton said, pointing to the computer screen.

Caedmon studied the monitor; the computer-generated image resembling nothing so much as a black-and-white photograph of the moon. And the dark side of the moon at that.

He tapped his finger at several small spots on the computer screen. "I believe these are miscellaneous stones left hither and yon when the nunnery was destroyed. But this looks promising," he said, pointing to what appeared to be a large, solid object buried some two meters below the surface.

"Whatever it is, it's a big mother. Sir, you want me to dig it up?"

A definite gleam in his eyes, MacFarlane nodded.

Moments later, pickax in hand, the behemoth began swinging like a brigand in search of gold doubloons, no thought given whatsoever to properly excavating the site, of carefully slicing away section by section in order to recover any historic artifacts that might be nestled in the soil. For these men, there was only *one* artifact of any import.

While Braxton attacked with his pickax, Sanchez assisted with a hand shovel, the two men making fast work of it. Donning a pair of knee pads, MacFarlane perched himself on the edge of the hole. His gaze intent, he peered into the deepening chasm, putting Caedmon in mind of a large bird of prey about to swoop upon its quarry.

Overhead the clouds bumped and collided, fusing together and releasing a cold drizzle on their uncovered heads. The light sprinkling soaked MacFarlane's gray hair, the spiky tufts clinging to his head like a skullcap. Seen in profile, he resembled a fierce Celtic warrior come to life. Although Caedmon suspected the reality was far worse than anything produced by that warlike race of men.

"Yeah, boy! We got it!" Braxton jubilantly shouted.

Sanchez heaved himself out of the hole and rushed over to one of the canvas equipment bags, retrieving a length of rope. He tossed the coiled length at his digging partner.

Edie slipped her hand into his. "I can't believe it . . . they actually found it," she whispered.

As Sanchez and Braxton pulled their find to the surface, Caedmon held his breath, about to set his gaze on the most sought-after relic in the history of mankind.

It could have been mine, he jealously thought. *Had I but played the game differently.*

After several loud grunts and a muttered curse, the box was hauled out of the hole.

Its appearance was met with a stunned silence.

"I don't think it's made of gold," Edie said, garnering a damning glare from Stanford MacFarlane.

"No, it isn't made of gold," Caedmon concurred. "A lesser metal. Bronze perhaps. Difficult to say what's under all the grime." Moreover, the box was secured on the outside with a large lock for which there was no key.

Braxton ran the back of his hand over his dirt-smudged brow, still panting from his labors. "Maybe the Ark is inside."

"Open it," MacFarlane ordered.

With one strong-armed swing of the pickax, the behemoth broke the lock.

His jaw tightly clenched, his gaze resolute, MacFarlane threw back the lid. Everyone stared wide-eyed at the uncovered treasure trove.

Everyone save for Stanford MacFarlane.

"What are *those*?" MacFarlane pointed an accusing finger at the golden objects that filled the box.

Extending a hand, Caedmon lifted a finely wrought candlestick out of the chest. Next, he examined a bejeweled gold chalice.

"These are the altar vessels from the destroyed church," he said, running his hand over an exquisitely fashioned paten. "No doubt the nuns had advance warning that the king's men were en route to the priory. I imagine they hid these vessels so they wouldn't be confiscated." He gestured to the gold objects. "Not exactly a king's ransom, I admit, but still valuable. You should have no problem finding a buyer for—"

"I'm not interested in earthly profit," MacFarlane interjected. "My reward will come in the next life." Turning his head, he pointedly set his gaze upon Edie. Then, like an Old Testament patriarch of old, he very quietly and calmly said, "Kill her."

The order of execution given, the behemoth raised his pickax.

Caedmon lurched forward.

But anticipating the move, Harliss and Sanchez seized hold of him, barring him from intervening.

"No!" he shouted, violently struggling to free himself.

Not like this! God in heaven, not like this!

CHAPTER 67

"Last night you gave me sixteen hours to find the Ark of the Covenant! I have forty minutes left!" Caedmon yelled, twisting and straining to free himself from his burly captors.

MacFarlane stared at him as he considered the appeal put before him—Michelangelo's stern-faced Moses come to life.

"Colonel MacFarlane, I know you to be a man of your word," Edie husked, her eyes flooded with tears, every limb in her body quivering with fright. "Please give Caedmon a chance. Without him, you'll never find the Ark."

Pondering it later, Caedmon decided that it was this last caveat that held sway, Edie having cannily played upon Mac-Farlane's obsession. Specifically, his fear of never obtaining the object of what was fast proving a most unnatural desire.

Mollified, MacFarlane curtly nodded. "You have exactly forty minutes. If you don't want to see Miss Miller's head split open like a Fourth of July watermelon, you *will* find the Ark of the Covenant." He dismissively glanced at the gleaming altar vessels in the still-open trunk. "I'm not interested in digging up any more golden trinkets."

With a stay of execution issued, Braxton lowered the pickax. Glancing at Edie, Caedmon battled a strong desire to bend over and retch.

It'd been close. With one mighty swing, the behemoth would have punched a gaping hole right through her skull.

"I'll find your bloody gold box," he muttered, glancing at his watch, the countdown having already begun.

Christ. Forty minutes to find something that had been buried long centuries ago.

The clock ticking away like a blasted gong, he ignored the stricken expression still plastered on Edie's face. With precious few minutes left, they had to stay focused on the task at hand. To that end, he slowly turned full circle, studying the wintry landscape that surrounded the cloister. Leafless trees. Dead grass. The pillaged walls of the chapel.

There was something here that he wasn't seeing. *But what?*

In the distance he heard a loud honking sound. A swan searching for its mate.

Bloody hell.

"Swans and geese," he murmured, wondering if the answer to Philippa's riddle could really be so simple. Hoping to curry favor, he turned to MacFarlane. "In the medieval lexicon, the two words are interchangeable, one and the same. And if you'll recall, there were two geese depicted in the Canterbury window, symbolizing the fact that swans and geese mate for life."

The older man's brow furrowed. "I'm not following."

"The name of this place is Swanley. In the Middle English of the fourteenth century, a ley was a meadowland."

"I got the clue!" Edie exclaimed, realizing the significance of the place name. "The word *Swanley* would roughly translate as 'swan meadow.' Meaning that we need to start searching for a meadow. Or some swans. Or maybe even both."

The furrow in MacFarlane's forehead deepened. "What kind of bullshit are you trying to pull? Swans swim on the water. They don't flap around on a grassy field," he bristled, gesturing to the surrounding dell.

"I will be the first to admit that it's a nonsensical word combination. But that doesn't detract from the fact that it is highly significant. In the quatrains, Philippa referred to herself as the 'trusted goose.' At Canterbury, we discovered a stained glass window in which the Ark of the Covenant was depicted along with two geese in a basket. Now we find ourselves here at Swanley. Trust me. It *does* mean something." He turned to Harliss, the keeper of the GPS navigation device. "Is there a lake or pond in the near vicinity?"

Given the go-ahead from his commander, the muscle-bound lackey consulted his handheld device. "Yeah, I got a body of water about two hundred meters east of here."

"Then I suggest we proceed to said location with all due haste."

When no objection was raised, he motioned to Harliss to lead the way. Sanchez remained behind at the cloister to pack up the equipment. Braxton, the pickax jauntily swung over his left shoulder, a powerful Desert Eagle pistol clutched in his right hand, pulled up the rear.

As they trooped toward the new destination, bare branches rustled in the damp breeze. Whispering. Warning.

"Please tell me that I've got more than thirtysome minutes

to live," Edie said in a lowered voice, furtively glancing at MacFarlane.

"You need to firm up," he answered in an equally hushed tone, not wanting her to dwell upon that very narrow allotment of time. He knew from experience that it was best to deal with variables that one could command rather than obsess on something beyond one's grasp.

"Yeah, yeah, I know. I need to stand tall. Or stand my ground. Or some silly cliché." Though she appeared outwardly composed, Caedmon detected an underlying note of panic in her voice.

Worried that Edie might succumb to her fear, he reached over and squeezed her hand. "An opening will present itself. It always does. And when that happens, we must seize the moment. No time for second-guessing, right?"

The pep talk having taken hold, she nodded her head, a vengeful gleam in her brown eyes. Caedmon suspected that she, too, entertained a gruesome fantasy that involved a certain behemoth and a very sharp pickax.

A few moments later they arrived at a fish pond that he estimated to be a good ten acres in size. Toward the center of the pond was a spit of land. *The swan meadow.* In the middle of the small isle, a simple stone cross had been erected. It appeared to have taken root long centuries ago.

"This is looking really, *really* good," Edie said, clearly relieved at seeing the cross. "The fish pond would certainly have come under Philippa's domain as the priory cellaress. Do you think she had the cross placed in the middle of the island as a signpost?"

Caedmon shook his head, disavowing her of the notion. "I suspect the cross was erected before the construction of the priory. However, Philippa would certainly have recognized its significance. As with the Ark of the Covenant, the cross is a point of direct communication between heaven and earth." He cast a quick sideways glance at MacFarlane, the older man intently staring at the lone cross. As though it were some sort of mystical beacon.

He'd made his case. *Thank God.*

"It could very well be that before the priory was built, this site was used as a religious shrine," he continued. Then, gesturing to the surprisingly clear, glassy surface of the pond, he said, "Undoubtedly the fish pond is fed by a natural spring. Such springs were often dedicated to a local saint."

"Making this a holy site, right?"

Caedmon nodded. "And that would have made the isle a fitting place for Philippa of Canterbury to hide the most sacred relic in all of Christendom." He gestured to a quartet of small skiffs moored to the nearby bank. "I doubt the local anglers will mind if we make use of their vessels. That said, we should set sail. Groups of two, I think."

MacFarlane walked over and inspected the small rowboats bobbing on the water. "Gunnery Sergeant, I want you to row across with the woman. Harliss, you wait for Sanchez to arrive with the equipment. Aisquith and I will take the lead." Orders given, he untied one of the boats, brusquely gesturing for Caedmon to precede him into the vessel.

"Hopefully the old girl is seaworthy," Caedmon muttered as he took hold of the oars and began the laborious business of rowing toward the isle.

MacFarlane made no reply, his unblinking gaze set upon the limestone Lorelei that stood sentry in the middle of the isle.

For the next several minutes the only sound shared between them was the creak and groan of wood oars repeatedly slicing through the chill water and the occasional honking of the resident swans. The rain had stopped and wispy tendrils of white vapor hovered over the surface of the water, wrapping the pond in a cloying embrace.

No sooner did the prow of the boat butt against the small isle than MacFarlane disembarked, the older man hurriedly sloshing through the calf-high water that lapped the grassy shoreline. Clearly impatient, he motioned for Caedmon to secure the fishing boat to a clump of nearby bushes. A few moments later, Edie and the behemoth docked beside them. Together the four of them made their way to the cross.

Well aware that he had only eighteen minutes left on the

clock, Caedmon fingered the worn stone. If a clue had been carved into the cross, the rain gods and wind zephyrs had long since made certain of its erasure.

Undeterred, he walked around to the backside of the cross. As he did, he detected a rigid, nonpliable surface beneath his right wellie. Curious, he sank to his knees, shoving aside the overgrown grass.

"What are you doing?" MacFarlane hissed, hunkering beside him.

"There's something embedded in the ground. I think it's a. . . . yes, a plaque of some sort. Do you have a handkerchief or a piece of cloth? I need to wipe clean the surface."

MacFarlane gestured to the behemoth, wordlessly ordering him to remove the black knit cap that he wore on his head.

Cap in hand, Caedmon began to vigorously rub at what looked to be a bronze plaque some ten inches square, with years of dirt accumulated on the incised surface. As he worked, a shadow fell over him. Glancing up, he saw Edie hovering over his right shoulder, an anxious look on her face. She knew, as did he, that her life still hung in the balance. That the decision as to whether she lived or died could very well hinge on the strangely placed bronze plaque. Fear being a powerful motivator, Caedmon rubbed that much harder.

It took several minutes of determined polishing to reveal a single line of Latin script.

As he stared at the plaque, Caedmon's heart thudded against his breastbone, utterly staggered by that solitary line of Latin. Like a man who'd just seen a ghost flit past.

"Hic amicitur archa cederis," he murmured, as though it were a magical incantation.

"What does it mean?" MacFarlane demanded, shouldering him out of the way so that he could examine the plaque.

Caedmon took several deep breaths, collecting himself. "It reads, 'Here is hidden the Ark of the Covenant.'"

CHAPTER 68

"The corpus delicti is about to be uncovered. But not by me," Caedmon murmured, standing close enough to Edie that she could feel his body heat. That and his complete and utter anguish at not being the one to uncover the Ark of the Covenant.

She sidled closer to him, a cold breeze setting her teeth to clattering.

Standing a few feet from where Braxton and Sanchez swung and shoveled in unison, they could see that the excavation was already well under way, the stone cross upended in the frenzy that ensued after Caedmon translated the bronze plaque. Believing the inscribed plaque to be no different from a giant X inscribed on a treasure map, MacFarlane's men hadn't bothered with running a ground scan, clearly of the consensus that the Ark of the Covenant was buried beneath the cross.

"Incredible to think that it's been nearly seven hundred years since someone last set eyes on the Ark of the Covenant," she remarked, if for no other reason than to keep her terror at bay. According to her watch, there were six minutes left to find the Ark. "I now know how Galen of Godmersham felt when he found the Ark on the Plain of Esdraelon."

"If you'll recall, he had to fight two other knights to the death for possession of the relic." Like her, Caedmon intently stared at the deepening hole. "However, if it means coming away with our lives, I will gladly forfeit all claim to the prize."

"Somehow, I don't think you have much say in it. Which still leaves the matter of battling the terrible trio." Having had to endure several minutes of fear-inducing threats when

Braxton rowed her over to the isle, the man a blunt instrument in search of a victim, she was acutely aware of the fact that they were outgunned and outnumbered. "I'm not much of a military tactician, but I'm guessing that being out here literally in the middle of nowhere is not to our advantage. Even if we could sneak over and untie a boat, there's no way we can row to shore fast enough." At least not fast enough to elude the bullets that would fly from multiple weapons all being fired simultaneously.

"Like you, I fear that Philippa's fish pond will become a watery grave should we attempt to escape."

"So, where does that leave us?"

"In a very dire strait," Caedmon quietly replied, not one for sugarcoating the truth.

Out of the corner of her eye, Edie noticed that MacFarlane had carefully removed several items from the canvas equipment bag that Sanchez had hauled to the isle. Unzipping what appeared to be a waterproof garment bag, he took out a long, flowing white robe and some sort of striped apron. Unconcerned that he had two avid onlookers, he unbuttoned and removed his rain slicker. Raising his arms, he pulled the robe over the top of his cargo pants and military-style sweater. Over that, he donned the apron, belting it at the waist.

Attired in the strange-looking garb, he next opened a padded container from which he removed a gem-studded item that Edie instantly recognized.

She nudged Caedmon in the ribs. "Look, it's the Stones of Fire."

With an air of rehearsed solemnity, Stanford MacFarlane donned the gold breastplate.

"What in the world is he doing?" she whispered out of the corner of her mouth, suddenly wondering if, in addition to being dangerous, their adversary might well be deranged.

"Unless I am greatly mistaken, he's preparing to view the Ark of the Covenant. Which is why he's attired in the garb traditionally worn by a Hebrew high priest."

Edie squinted her eyes, the breastplate not quite as she remembered it. "It looks as though MacFarlane had the twelve stones reset in a new gold setting. Maybe it won't work and he'll get blasted to the fire pits of hell. Just like the Nazis in *Raiders of the Lost Ark*."

"According to the Bible, it was the twelve stones, not the gold breastplate, that afforded the high priest the necessary protection to interact with the Ark."

MacFarlane, wearing what could only be called a patronizing sneer, approached them.

"Steadfast faith and the Stones of Fire will ensure my safety," he announced, evidently having overheard Caedmon's last remark. "For just as the Ark was constructed per God's specific instructions to Moses, so, too, the Stones of Fire. As you undoubtedly know, the twelve stones of the holy breastplate were God's gift to Moses, the first guardian of the Ark."

"Implying that you have appointed yourself as the new guardian of the Ark," Caedmon replied.

"I am the *ordained* guardian of the Ark."

"Mmmm . . . how very interesting." Folding his arms over his chest, Caedmon mirthlessly smiled; Edie sensed that he was about to hurl the only weapon left to him—his superior intellect. "Were you aware of the fact that the Stones of Fire once belonged to Lucifer?"

MacFarlane's eyes narrowed, his angry expression nearly comical.

"Ah! I can see that you are familiar with the tale," Caedmon blithely continued. "Then you undoubtedly know that contained within the pages of the Apocrypha, those being the twelve books omitted from the Protestant Bible, the story is recounted of how God presented to his favorite, the beautiful and arrogant Lucifer, the Stones of Fire. Proudly Lucifer did wear the breastplate as a symbol of his esteemed status amongst the heavenly host." Tilting his head to one side, Caedmon examined the gem-studded relic. "Curious to think the same breastplate that you now wear once adorned the Prince of Darkness."

In unison, MacFarlane's three subordinates glanced at the Stones of Fire. Edie could see that Caedmon's remarks unnerved more than one man among them.

If they could flip one of them, they might have a shot at escaping with their lives.

Although Braxton was loyal to a fault, she thought Harliss or Sanchez might be persuaded to change team colors. Assuming she and Caedmon could push the right buttons.

Hoping the relic's infamous lineage would create some dissension in the ranks, Edie asked the obvious. "What happened to the Stones of Fire when Lucifer was cast out of heaven?" As she spoke, she noticed that all three of MacFarlane's henchmen turned an attentive ear.

"The Stones of Fire then passed to the archangels Michael and Gabriel. Not only did they share joint custody of the breastplate, but it is their two images that supposedly adorn the lid of the Ark." Picking up the game ball, Caedmon pointedly glanced at Braxton, Harliss, and Sanchez before turning his attention to MacFarlane. "Do you think it's safe for your boys to come into such close proximity to the Ark? Unlike you, they have no protection should a tragic accident occur."

"Yeah, I hear tell that skin cancer can be difficult to treat," Edie piped in. "And as far as I know, there's no cure for the plague." Seeing Sanchez's slack-jawed expression, she decided to push the fear factor for all it was worth. "Oh, and let's not forget about those poor guys at Bethshemesh. Not a pretty story, let me tell ya."

Craning his head, Caedmon peered into what now appeared to be a five-foot-deep hole, directing his comments to Braxton and Sanchez. "Did your commander mention that the Ark of the Covenant is, in fact, a weapon of mass destruction, once used to slaughter the enemies of Israel? My own theory is that the Ten Commandments were inscribed upon pieces of radioactive—"

"Lies! Every last word of it!" MacFarlane bellowed, his face having turned a distinctly unhealthy shade of madder red.

Nervously gripping the shovel handle, Sanchez came to a standstill. "But, sir, what if—"

"Keep digging!"

"Yes, sir!" Sanchez replied, applying spade to dirt with a renewed vigor.

Realizing the momentum had just swung the other way, Edie's shoulders slumped. "So much for converting one of the faithful."

"There is a reason why they are called true believers," Caedmon replied. Though he didn't show it, she knew that he, too, was dismayed by the almost-win.

At hearing a loud metallic *clunk!* MacFarlane rushed over to the hole.

"Sir, we just hit some sort of metal box," Braxton excitedly declared.

Edie swallowed back a nugget-sized lump of fear.

"I think they may have actually found the bloody Ark of the Covenant." Like a man possessed, Caedmon intently stared at the excavated hole.

Repeating the procedure from the cloister, Sanchez fetched the length of coiled rope, and he and Braxton cinched it around the buried object.

MacFarlane, smiling indulgently, turned his attention to Caedmon. "Do you by any chance know the meaning of the words *apocalypse* and *tribulation?*"

If Caedmon thought the question odd, he gave no indication. "Apocalypse is taken from the Greek word *apokalupsis*, meaning 'revelation.' And tribulation is from the Greek *thlipsis*, meaning 'affliction.' Did I pass?"

MacFarlane's smile broadened. "No, you did not. Because like most, you have no concept of the *power* that is inherent in those two words, the prophetic *truth* that those two words reveal. Most people think of Judgment Day as a fairy tale that can never come to pass."

"I take it that you think differently?"

"'And I will plead against him with pestilence and with blood; and I will rain upon him, and upon his bands, and upon the many people that are with him, an overflowing rain, and great hailstones, fire, and brimstone.'"

Listening to the verbal joust, Edie started to get a very bad feeling in the pit of her painfully cramped stomach.

Apocalypse. Tribulation. Judgment Day.

She'd heard those words before. Long years ago when

she'd been made to sit silently while her grandfather nightly read aloud from the dog-eared family Bible.

End Times prophecies.

The Bible, both Old and New Testaments, was full of it. When she was a young girl, those stories of disease, famine, and global warfare had terrified her.

But what did the End Times prophecies have to do with the Ark of the Covenant?

CHAPTER 69

"I know that Bible verse . . . it's from the book of Ezekiel," Edie murmured.

Knowing that Edie had been force-fed a biblical diet during her teenage years, Caedmon turned to her. At a glance, he could see that she was distressed by MacFarlane's recitation.

"I didn't take you for being a woman versed in the prophecies," MacFarlane dismissively replied.

Edie shrugged. "My grandfather held to the same End Times belief, absolutely certain that Ezekiel's war, as he called it, loomed on the near horizon."

"Then you undoubtedly know that the ancient prophecies are a gift from God. A light in the midst of the spiritual malaise that is so prevalent in our day and age. Long centuries ago, the prophet Ezekiel clearly spelled out God's battle plan to save mankind from the forces of evil that lurk on the near horizon." MacFarlane spoke with a proprietary air, as though imparting a great and wondrous secret.

"Which merely proves what I've thought all along . . . that biblical prophecy is too often used to justify the hate-filled agendas of warmongers like yourself." Edie's normally pale cheeks were flushed with vivid color; Caedmon was well aware that, for her, the argument had a personal dimension. "Many fundamental Christians believe that the verses of Ezekiel contain a detailed plan for the invasion of Israel by an alliance of foreign countries," she continued, addressing her comments directly to Caedmon. "It's what known as the Battle of Gog and Magog. Furthermore, they believe that this battle will be fought during the last days."

The last days.

By that he supposed that Edie referred to the much-ballyhooed apocalypse. The end of the world as we know it. As in bend your knees and kiss your arse good-bye.

Was MacFarlane's obsession with the Ark of the Covenant somehow intertwined with an apocalyptic vision? God help them if it was; history was full of men who had proclaimed that the end of the world was near at hand. In almost every instance, those "visionaries" left only pain and misery in their wake.

"I'm curious about this so-called Battle of Gog and Magog," Caedmon said. If he'd learned anything during his tenure with Her Majesty's government, it was that information was a form of power. Sometimes the only power one had over one's enemies. "Where precisely will the conflict take place?"

"The great battle will be fought in the mountains of Israel," MacFarlane replied.

"I see." Caedmon mulled the disclosure, his curiosity piqued. "And who will be involved in this clash of titans?"

His nemesis answered, "The prophet Ezekiel clearly writes of an alliance of nations from remote parts of the north known as 'the land of Gog.' This alliance will come under the leadership of the ruler of Gog, also known as Magog, and will include the princes of Rosh, Meshech, and Tubal."

Caedmon silently considered what, to the uninitiated ear, was so much gibberish. "I assume that Rosh refers to the tribe of Ros, an ancient group of people believed to have inhabited the region of modern-day Ukraine and Russia." When MacFarlane nodded, he next said, "So presumably this northern alliance will be composed of former eastern bloc countries."

"Many of which, such as Kazakhstan and Tajikistan, are Islamic nations," Edie pointed out.

Islamic nations fighting a cataclysmic battle within the borders of Israel.

The stew pot had considerably thickened.

"According to Ezekiel, Magog's army will be supported by the nations of Persia, Cush, and Put." This came from Edie, who was fast proving herself a font of biblical information.

"Iran, Sudan, and Libya, if my ancient history serves me correctly." Caedmon took a moment to mull over what he'd been told thus far. Then, finding a glaring inconsistency with the prophesized scenario, he said, "Let's assume for argument's sake that the Ezekiel prophecy does foretell of a Russian-led invasion of Israel; what possible reason would Russia have for initiating such a war?"

MacFarlane stared at him as though he'd asked a simpleton's question. "Economic and political instability are reason enough, don't you think? Israel is, after all, the Silicon Valley of the Middle East."

"And don't forget that there's a wealth of minerals to be mined in the Dead Sea, as well as the untapped oil reserves within Israel's borders," Edie piped in, her remarks leaving Caedmon unsure of whether she believed the apocalyptic tale. "Given that both Russia and Israel have nuclear weapons in their arsenals, the end result will be catastrophic."

"I must confess that it's not an improbable scenario; the Middle East is a volatile region," Caedmon admitted in response to Edie's last remark. "Although if that particular conflict ever manifests, it will be orchestrated by man, not God. The world's thirst for oil is unquenchable, and Russia is undoubtedly concerned by the extreme lengths that the U.S. has gone to in order to secure a foothold in the Arab world. The Iron Curtain may have fallen, but the old rivalry still lingers."

"The prophet Ezekiel describes the battle to come in clear, concise terms," MacFarlane said with a manic gleam in his eyes. "One has only to read the daily newspaper to know that the prophesized Battle of Gog and Magog can come at any time."

Unconvinced, Caedmon folded his arms over his chest.

"Prophecy is always a slippery slope to navigate. Although I'm curious as to who you think will be the victor if this unholy conflagration were to occur."

"Why, Israel, of course. And that victory will assure Jews and Christians alike that God is still in their midst, as he was in the days of old when he dwelled among them during the forty-year trek through the wilderness. With victory, a new temple will be erected in Jerusalem. Once it is constructed, the Ark of the Covenant will be restored to its rightful place."

The Ark of the Covenant . . . finally, they had come full circle.

Caedmon glanced at the trio of men busily engaged in hauling their treasure trove out of the hole. Time was not on his and Edie's side. And it was certainly against them if the excavation turned up anything other than the sought-after prize.

"Why are you telling me all of this? Aren't such disclosures akin to letting the cat out of the biblical bag?"

MacFarlane took a step in his direction; Caedmon was surprised to see a look of entreaty on his face.

"I have a reason for sharing the prophecy with you . . . I want you to join us in our holy cause. The Lord always has need of good, stalwart men ready to fight his battle."

CHAPTER 70

". . . As with Paul on the road to Damascus, you have a chance to redeem yourself. Read the prophecies for yourself and you will see that I speak the truth."

Astonished that the offer had even been made, Caedmon stood silent for several seconds. That is, until cynicism got the better of him.

"Ah, yes, 'the sure word of prophecy,'" he drolly remarked, quoting another Church father, St. Peter.

"I know you to be a man searching for meaning in his own life and in the world around him."

"Though that may be true, I'm not a malleable soul ready to latch onto the first prophet who offers a ready-made curative to life's travails." Purposefully he held MacFarlane at bay, knowing that if he committed too soon, he would show his hand.

"Your words imply a deep-seated fear. I can take that fear from you." MacFarlane expansively gestured to the three men industriously working to haul their treasure trove aboveground. "My Warriors of God know no fear."

"He's feeding you a load," Edie exclaimed, grabbing him by the arm. As though she feared he might step across the imaginary line that had been drawn between them and their nemesis. "I've read the Ezekiel prophecies, and do you know what I think? I think Ezekiel was a madman, a doomsday prophet who would have been on lithium and a very short leash had he lived in the twenty-first century. One of his so-called visions actually tells of how he came upon a pile of dry bones in the desert and supposedly breathed life into those same bones, creating a mighty army. Maybe I'm the crazy one here, but that sounds like the kind of delusional prophecy that would be spouted by some homeless guy pushing a shopping cart."

Eyes narrowing, Stanford MacFarlane contemptuously glared at Edie.

Hoping to smooth the rough waters, Caedmon cleared his throat. "Although I won't go so far as to speculate on Ezekiel's mental state of mind, I know that many of the Old Testament authors wrote metaphorically, never intending their verses to be literally interpreted by later generations."

"This I know above all else," MacFarlane countered in an acid tone, "not only will the divine revelation given to Ezekiel come to fruition, but the Battle of Gog and Magog *will* be fought. Only those who put their trust in the Almighty will escape the coming doom. And those who take up arms against the soldiers of Magog will be doubly blessed. When the battle is fought and won, the Ark of the Covenant will be restored to its rightful place within the new Temple. Repent and you will live eternally. Turn your back on the Lord and you will be damned."

"But why ask me to join your ranks? It's been years since I last stepped foot in an Anglican church."

"We can use a man with your specialized talents."

Something in the offhand compliment gave Caedmon pause, leaving him with the distinct impression that MacFarlane knew about his tenure with MI5. Such skills would certainly appeal to a man like MacFarlane. Although he had a small army at his disposal, there was a world of difference between a soldier and a trained intelligence officer.

"I would be happy to join your ranks. However, there is a condition attached to my acceptance . . . you must free Miss—"

"Don't do it, Caedmon!" Edie screeched over the top of him.

"—Miller. Needless to say, the point is not negotiable," he added, hoping to check Stanford MacFarlane. And to check Edie as well. To that end, he cast her a stern glance, wordlessly ordering her to cease and desist.

"The woman knows too much. She can't be trusted to keep quiet," the other man uncharitably replied.

"I trust her implicitly. Is that not enough?"

"She is a degenerate vessel, unworthy of your consideration. My offer does not include the woman."

Visibly rigid with the force of his contempt, MacFarlane glared at Edie. Loathing incarnate. Throughout history, men such as Stanford MacFarlane had voraciously condemned the female sex, blaming them for the ills of the world. He'd always thought the loathing stemmed from a deep-seated fear of woman's innate wisdom.

With a heavy heart he offered Edie a silent apology.

Knowing that monsters, by their very nature, were devoid of mercy, he said, "Your offer puts me in mind of a medieval inquisitor attempting to convert a hapless heretic. Regardless of whether the heretic repented, it usually ended badly. For the heretic, that is."

"I can see that your eyes are jaded. That you aren't fit to gaze upon God's glory." His contempt having mutated into a stern-faced rage, MacFarlane turned to his men. "Harliss, prepare the tabernacle!"

"Yes, sir." Like a marionette on a string, Harliss unzipped one of the oversized equipment bags.

Unable to look Edie in the eye, well aware that he had lost his only opportunity to save her life, Caedmon was surprised when she leaned her head against his shoulder.

"When the end comes, at least we'll be together," she whispered.

"Yes . . . we will be at that."

"Any idea what they're up to?" She jutted her chin at the folded stacks of material that Harliss had removed from the zippered bag.

"A badger skin, a length of blue cloth, and a tightly woven veil were traditionally wrapped around the Ark whenever it was in transport. I suspect the three layers created a primitive form of nonconducting insulation. Clearly, MacFarlane intends to play the game by the book."

"That being the Good Book, huh?"

"Indeed. Although the scriptures have a way of becoming distorted beyond recognition when spouted by a man like MacFarlane."

Curiosity superseding his dread, Caedmon watched as the other two members of the trio hauled a large metal box out of the earth. A quick mental calculation proved that the box was large enough to house the Ark of the Covenant. As he'd done at the cloister, Braxton opened the lock with a mighty swing of his pickax.

His movements slow and reverential, Stanford MacFarlane opened the lid.

Although he craned his neck, Caedmon could see nothing more than the dull glimmer of gold. A gold *what*, he couldn't say. What he could see, however, was the awestruck expression affixed to the face of each of the four men gathered around the open box. As though they'd just wandered into Aladdin's cave.

"'And there was seen in his temple the ark of his testament and there were lightnings, and voices, and thunderings, and an earthquake, and great hail,'" Stanford MacFarlane loudly intoned.

"Don't forget the drizzle," Edie muttered under her breath. "And the fog," she added a moment later when Harliss set off a smoke bomb, completely obscuring the proceedings from their view.

"The Hebrew priests used to shroud the Ark in a thick blanket of incense to keep it hidden from curious onlookers." As he spoke, Caedmon squinted and strained, but the smoke barrier was impenetrable.

A few seconds later, Harliss emerged from the smoke. Two sets of plastic flexi-cuffs dangled from his fingertips. "I've got a restraining order for you two."

"Will you at least tell us if the Ark of the Covenant was uncovered?" he asked, desperate to have a definitive answer.

"Oh, yeah," the other man slowly replied, the bedazzled expression returning to his unshaved, rawboned features. "The two angels on top of the gold box were the telltale clue."

Hearing that was like hearing an unexpected boom of thunder; Caedmon slightly swayed on his feet.

They had actually found the Ark of the Covenant.

Knowing it was futile to resist, he stood motionless as Harliss bound his hands together, his mind unable to wrap around the enormity of the find.

Softly humming a jaunty tune, Harliss ripped a piece of duct tape from a roll. "Wouldn't want to disturb the neighbors," he said with a mean-spirited cackle as he slapped the length of tape across Caedmon's mouth. That done, he bound and gagged Edie in a similar fashion.

"We got orders to row you two to shore and take you to a remote location. The colonel says it wouldn't be right to kill you in the same place where we found the Ark."

CHAPTER 71

For the second time that day, the specter of death hovered over
Edie's shoulder. But this time, unlike those petrified moments
when she'd stood shaking beneath the sharp point of Braxton's
pickax, she'd had time to prepare for her death; Harliss and
Sanchez had loaded them into the Range Rover and taken them
to a remote location some ten miles east of Swanley. Somewhere toward the sea; Edie could discern the tang of salt in
the air.

In the distance, she heard the outraged screech of a seagull.
The thunderous roar of a jet engine. Familiar sounds. Probably
the last sounds she would hear.

At least she'd lived longer than her mother.

She turned and glanced at Caedmon, who, duct tape strapped
to his mouth, hands bound in front of him, stoically stared
at the passing scenery. She wondered if he, too, had used the
time to take stock of his life. He could have saved himself back
on the isle. But he didn't do it. Instead, he tried to garner her
freedom. From a madman, no less. Although she was furious
with him for passing up his one and only chance, she thought
she might just love the brave, quixotic Englishman.

Harliss, again relegated to being the copilot, peered over
the headrest. "Soon you two will be sleepin' with the angels.
The colonel is fond of sayin' that 'the judgments of the Lord
are true and righteous altogether. More to be desired are they
than gold . . . sweeter also than honey and the honeycomb.'"

*Oh, yeah. A bullet to the back of the head. How sweet was
that?*

Still leaning over the back of his seat, Harliss reached into
his jacket pocket and removed a pack of filterless Camels. "I'd

offer you one, but . . ." Chortling, he shook a cigarette free. He then flipped open a silver lighter. Taking a drag, he blew a perfect smoke ring into her face.

Inhaling the smoke through her nostrils, Edie gagged. Beside her, Caedmon twitched, his muffled protest sounding as though he were attempting to speak under water.

Seemingly oblivious to the psychodrama, Sanchez steered the SUV onto what looked to be a deserted farm road; the Range Rover lurched from side to side as they slowly proceeded down a rutted lane. They'd gone approximately a half mile when Sanchez put on the brakes and cut the engine.

Edie and Caedmon simultaneously turned and looked at one another.

I'm sorry, Caedmon.

As am I, love.

Craning his head from side to side, Harliss gave an approving nod. "This looks as good a place as any. Don't know that anyone's been down this road in a good long while." He turned to his partner. "What do ya think?"

"I think I gotta take a crap," Sanchez blurted, releasing his seat belt.

"Jesus! A body could tell time by your bowel movements."

"Shut up and get me the wipes out of the glove compartment."

A few seconds later, diaper wipes in hand, Sanchez ambled toward a clump of trees. Harliss, a half-smoked Camel sticking out of the corner of his mouth, opened the passenger's-side door and got out of the SUV. Slamming the door shut, he stretched his back, then walked around to the front of the vehicle. Leaning against the hood, with his back to them, he proceeded to finish smoking his cigarette.

No sooner were they alone than Caedmon urgently nudged her with his elbow. Having gotten her attention, he nodded toward his anorak pocket before shooting her a meaningful glance.

The metal nail file.

When they'd been issued the rubber Wellington boots

earlier that morning, Caedmon had managed to remove the file from his discarded oxfords, hiding the file in his coat pocket. Because he'd already been subjected to a thorough body search, the working premise was that they wouldn't search him a second time. Edie could see that with his hands bound in front of him, he wouldn't be able to retrieve the file. But her hands, although similarly bound, were much smaller.

Quickly she flipped open the flap on his pocket, shoving her fingers into the opening. It took only an instant for her to remove the file from Caedmon's pocket.

Now what? she silently asked.

Caedmon wordlessly indicated that he wanted her to pass him the file.

A few seconds later, with the metal file tightly grasped between his interlocked fingers, he motioned for her to use the file to cut through her plastic flexi-cuffs.

It took several moments of frantic sawing back and forth before the plastic finally gave way.

Her hands freed, she immediately reached up to remove the strip of duct tape from her mouth. Beside her, Caedmon tersely shook his head, silently commanding her *not* to remove the gag. Uncertain why he wanted her to keep the tape in place, she grabbed the file out of his hands; they had a narrow window and she wasn't about to waste any time second-guessing him.

Tightly gripping the nail file between her clenched fists, she held steady while Caedmon roughly sawed through his flexi-cuffs, freeing himself at the exact moment that Harliss flicked aside the tail end of his cigarette.

Hurriedly Caedmon snatched the file from her. Then, his hands lying inert in his lap, he stared straight ahead. Now understanding the reason for not removing the duct tape, Edie struck a similar pose.

With the tape in place, they created the illusion of still being bound.

Harliss, softly humming to himself, walked around the front of the Range Rover. With one hand he retrieved the gun shoved into the back of his waistband while with the other hand he reached for Caedmon's door handle.

Edie tensed. Completely in the dark as to what Caedmon intended to do, her heart beat a painful tattoo.

An instant later, Caedmon's door swung open.

"Okay, boys and girls. Time to say hello to the hang—"

In a quick peripheral flash, Edie saw Caedmon violently shove his shoulder against Harliss's right hand, slamming the southerner's wrist against the metal door frame; the unexpected motion caused Harliss to drop his gun.

"Fucking shit! I'm gonna—"

Nail file grasped in his hand, Caedmon raised his right arm, slashing downward in a smooth arc.

A split second later, blood splattered onto the passenger window. A thick, red Rorschach blotch. Then a bloodcurdling scream of agony.

Harliss fell to the ground, his legs convulsively twitching. Once. Twice. Before he went eerily still, his booted feet awkwardly splayed.

Caedmon ripped the piece of duct tape off his mouth. "Don't look!"

The caution came an instant too late.

Horrified at seeing the metal nail file protruding from the sprawled man's eye socket, Edie yanked the tape from her mouth, spraying the back of the front seat with yellow stomach bile.

"Quick! Get out of the vehicle!" Caedmon ordered. "Sanchez will be here any second."

Operating on autopilot, Edie reached for the doorknob, stumbling out of the SUV in an ungainly heap. Turning her head, she saw that Caedmon had exited on his side and was hunched on the ground, searching for Harliss's weapon.

Just then, a barrage of bullets peppered the Range Rover.

Edie screamed, instinctively throwing herself to the ground. Peering under the vehicle, she saw Sanchez slam an ammunition clip into his weapon as he charged toward them. She also saw Caedmon grab Harliss by his shoulders, using the lifeless man as a shield.

Another *rat-a-tat-tat* of gunfire rang out.

Edie slammed a balled fist into her mouth, hoping, praying that Caedmon—

Reaching her side of the Range Rover, Caedmon immediately released his hold on the bullet-riddled corpse, the human shield having no doubt saved his life. Crouched beside the SUV's hood, he began firing Harliss's retrieved weapon.

"Search his pockets for an ammo clip!"

Edie quickly crawled over to the dead southerner. Forcing herself not to look at the nail file protruding from his eye socket, she shoved her hand into Harliss's jacket pocket.

"All I've got is the GPS receiver and a cigarette lighter!" she hissed at Caedmon, frantically wondering how long he could keep Sanchez at bay. A quick peek over the top of the SUV verified that the other man had taken up a firing position behind the tumbled remnants of a stone fence.

"Damn! I'm out of bullets," Caedmon muttered, tossing the gun aside.

Suddenly catching a whiff of a very familiar scent, Edie glanced at her feet, surprised to see liquid pooling at her feet. "Oh, God! He pierced the gas tank! We've got to get out of here!"

Snatching the GPS receiver and cigarette lighter out of her hand, Caedmon shoved them into his anorak pocket.

"Keep low!" he whispered, cinching a hand around her elbow. "We don't want Sanchez to know that we're on the move. Hopefully, he'll maintain his defensive position long enough for us to escape."

But to where? Edie wondered, seeing nothing but overgrown fields in every direction.

They'd gone no more than twenty yards when Sanchez resumed firing his weapon. Placing a hand on her shoulder, Caedmon shoved her to the ground.

"On your belly," he ordered, flinging himself beside her.

Side by side, they lay hidden in the tall grass.

Every limb in her body shaking, as though in a palsied state, Edie watched as Caedmon removed the used piece of duct tape from his coat pocket. Along with Harliss's sterling silver cigarette lighter.

"What are you planning to—"

"Shhh!"

Terrified, Edie watched as Caedmon flicked on the lighter, the blue flame jauntily moving to and fro. He then wrapped the salvaged strip of duct tape around the lever so that the flame wouldn't go out. Edie noticed that the initials *USMC* were engraved on the side of the lighter.

Putting a finger to his mouth, Caedmon wordlessly warned her to be silent; the admonition was totally unnecessary, as fear had rendered her speechless.

Narrowing her gaze, she watched as Sanchez crept away from the stone wall. Bent at the waist, his gun held between his hands, he slowly approached the Range Rover.

Edie held her breath, suddenly realizing what Caedmon intended to do.

In no apparent hurry, Caedmon waited until Sanchez was within a few feet of the SUV. His expression steadfast, he rose to his knees, cocked his arm back and—

—hurled the lighter toward the Range Rover.

An instant later, a huge blast erupted and the Range Rover exploded into a ball of fire.

Jubilant, Edie slung an arm around Caedmon's knees. "Oh, God! Do you think we're actually gonna get away?"

Caedmon crookedly smiled; Edie could see that he, too, was joyfully relieved. "To paraphrase that oddly named American chap, we're not done for until the fat lady sings."

"I've never been able to sit through a Wagner opera."

"Nor I. But on the off chance that Sanchez survived the blast, we need to find a safe haven."

More concerned with speed than stealth, they clumped through the dried stalks of winter grass.

CHAPTER 72

They'd wandered nearly a mile when they came upon an abandoned stone farmhouse. From its derelict appearance, the house had been vacated long years before, there being more than a few missing panes of window glass.

"Now what?" Edie asked, glancing around the ramshackle farmyard and seeing only a jumble of weeds and tall grass.

Caedmon surveyed the area. "Search the house for weapons. Knives, scissors, an old hunting rifle, anything you can lay your hands on. I'll search the outbuildings for some sort of conveyance."

"You actually know how to hot-wire a car?"

"In theory. Assuming I can find a serviceable vehicle."

Rising up on her tiptoes, Edie leaned over and kissed him on the cheek. "Here's hoping the practical application comes off without a hitch."

Having been issued her orders, she rushed toward the front stoop. The door sat crooked in the jamb; it took some jostling of the knob and a very determined shoulder shove to coerce it open. Ignoring the dust mites, cobwebs, and heavy odor of mildew, she scanned the foyer, her gaze finally alighting on a solitary golf club protruding from a tall metal milk jug. Thinking it as good a weapon as any, she grabbed the eight iron.

She then felt her way down the dark hallway, the light switch producing nothing but a dull click, and soon found herself in a primitive kitchen. The grimy window above the dry sink produced enough light for her see that vermin had had the run of the place. More than one cupboard door was ajar, and containers of boxed food had been ripped open. In an apparent feeding frenzy, a bag of sugar and a box of salt had been torn asunder; a small white pile of each sat on the kitchen counter.

She hurriedly began opening drawers, hoping to find a kitchen knife that had been left behind.

To her dismay, the search turned up nothing more deadly than an ice cream scoop and a rusty can opener.

Seeing an old-fashioned telephone mounted on the wall, she rushed over and grabbed the heavy handset.

Damn. Dead air.

As she hung up the phone, the wood planks near the doorway softly creaked.

"You didn't really think that someone would abandon the house but leave the phone connected?"

At hearing that slightly accented voice, Edie spun on her heel, the golf club slipping through her fingers and clattering onto the wood floor.

Her heart caught in her throat.

Standing across from her, holding a gun that was aimed at her chest, was Sanchez. Not only were his face and clothes blackened with soot, but blood freely poured from a jagged wound on his upper cheek, the skin having been flayed in the car blast.

Edie stood unmoving. Like a frog in a warming cauldron.

"Hope springs eternal," she told the unsmiling gunman, striving for a calm she didn't feel. To keep her hands from noticeably shaking, she reached behind her, gripping the edge of the countertop.

"Where's your redheaded lover boy?"

"We got separated after the blast," Edie lied, knowing Sanchez would be out for vengeance, the old "eye for an eye" taking on a whole new level of meaning.

The sound of a car door being slammed echoed across the farmyard.

Sanchez cocked his head, then shrugged. "Can't start a car with a dead battery. What a bitch, huh?"

As he spoke, Edie inched her hand toward the salt pile that she'd earlier seen on the counter. "Yeah, what a bitch," she retorted, tossing a handful of salt at the gaping wound on his face.

Rearing his head back, a thunderbolt in reverse, Sanchez loudly bellowed.

Pushing herself away from the counter, Edie charged down the hall toward the open front door.

No sooner did she clear the doorway than she ran headlong into Caedmon. In his right hand he held a small ax; in his left he had what looked to be a long-handled garden hoe.

"Sanchez is in the kitchen!" she breathlessly exclaimed. "And he's got a gun!"

She saw the muscles in Caedmon's jaw clench and unclench, saw the feral gleam in his eyes. This was the man who had mercilessly taken out his foe by jamming a nail file into his skull.

Wordlessly, he shoved the ax into his pocket. Then he wrapped his free hand around her upper arm and took off running; Edie could barely keep pace with his long-legged stride.

They'd gone no more than a hundred yards when shots rang out, a half dozen of them in rapid succession. Caedmon dodged toward a large stone outbuilding. Kicking open a wood-planked door, he shoved her inside.

Edie squinted, surprised to see a huge chain with an ominous hook at the end of it dangling from a ceiling beam.

"It looks like some kind of torture chamber."

"Close enough," Caedmon muttered, dragging her across the dimly lit room. "It's an old abattoir."

"What's an abattoir?"

"A slaughterhouse."

CHAPTER 73

The place does have a decidedly charnel house feel to it, Caedmon thought as he hurriedly ushered Edie across the abattoir.

Hopefully not a harbinger of things to come.

Shouldering open a rickety door, he motioned Edie through. A second later, they emerged into another dimly lit room, this one with a high-pitched ceiling and an arched window set into the gable. Heavy chains dangled from the rafters. Elaborate cobwebs adorned all four corners. Overhead, a pair of sparrows flew through the broken panes of glass, the abandoned abattoir having evidently become a makeshift aviary. The menacing space would have made a black-robed inquisitor feel right at home.

Quickly, knowing he had but a few moments to set the trap, he shoved Edie toward a rusty metal cart, that being the only piece of "furniture" in the room.

"Get yourself behind the cart. And for God's sake, don't move," he tersely instructed.

Satisfied that she was out of sight, he placed the long-handled garden hoe on the floor near the door, the blade pointing upward. In what he hoped would be Sanchez's direct path. Then, removing the ax from his pocket, he positioned himself in a dark, cobweb-strewn corner.

Knowing he would have but one chance with the dully honed ax, he waited.

A few moments passed in tense silence. Then, as though scripted, the door to the cavernous room creaked open.

In the next instant, Sanchez, looking like a battered chimney sweep, slowly entered the room, gripping a semiautomatic pistol in his right hand. A powerful weapon, it could blow a man's head clean off his shoulders. Two steps into the room, Sanchez came to a standstill, scanning for the slightest hint of movement.

Don't move, Edie. For the love of God, don't even think about moving.

Caedmon held his breath, hoping that the other man didn't glance downward, the hoe innocuously set some six feet from his booted right foot.

Tightening his grip on the ax handle, he mentally envisioned the attack. A practice run. Having bowled many a cricket game while at Oxford, he first imagined hurling the ax in a straight-armed delivery. Knowing he wouldn't get the desired height, he replayed the scenario in his mind's eye, this time with bent elbow.

He spared a quick sideways glance at the cart, relieved to see that Edie had faded into the shadows. His gaze then ricocheted back to Sanchez, who had taken a tentative step forward.

He calculated the other man to be three steps from the up-turned blade of the hoe.

Then two steps.

One step.

As planned, the instant that Sanchez's booted foot landed atop the blade, the hoe handle flew upward, hitting him square in the face. Like a child's top, Sanchez unsteadily wobbled. With the element of surprise now on his side, Caedmon stepped out of the shadows and hurled the ax toward the other man's chest.

A dust-laden beam of light from the window glinted off the spinning ax blade.

Instinctively Sanchez twisted, his arm protectively shielding his heart, parrying the blow as best he could.

The dull blade caught him on the right bicep, slicing deep. But not deep enough; Sanchez grunted as he grasped the ax by the handle and yanked the blade out of his arm. His eyes glazed, but still cognizant, he searched the room, a gun in one hand, the bloody ax in the other.

Seeing Caedmon standing in the corner, he narrowed his gaze.

Slowly, in no apparent hurry to kill his quarry, Sanchez aimed the powerful pistol at a point somewhere in the middle of Caedmon's head.

There being nothing he could do to stop the bullet from reaching its intended target, he defiantly stood his ground.

Smiling, Sanchez pulled the trigger.

A dull click.

The smile having suddenly vanished from his lips, Sanchez pulled the trigger a second time. Again, the only sound was the hollow click of the firing pin.

Sanchez was out of ammunition.

With a muttered oath, he dropped the gun. Then, in a quick blur, he was on Caedmon, swinging his arm, the ax blade aimed at his soft underbelly, the man clearly of a mind to eviscerate him. Caedmon leaped sideways, the blade missing him by a scant inch.

Out of the corner of his eye, Caedmon saw Edie lurch to her feet.

"You bastard!" she screamed. Wild-eyed, she grabbed a chain from a nearby wall hook and began swinging it over her head like a medieval mace.

Endowed with enviably quick reflexes, Sanchez pivoted in Edie's direction.

Which is when Caedmon lifted his left foot off the ground, ramming his wellie into Sanchez's kidneys. The well-aimed kick propelled the other man several feet, smashing his head into an array of metal instruments hanging from the wall. The ax slipped through his fingers, falling to the floor.

Not giving his foe time to recover, Caedmon rushed forward. Securing one hand against the back of Sanchez's skull and the other against his spine, he rammed the brute's head against the metal cart.

The rickety walls of the abattoir shook with the impact.

Sanchez, a stunned, owl-like expression on his face, rolled into a fetal ball. A moment later, he opened his lips. To speak or scream, Caedmon knew not. The only thing emitted from his gaping mouth was a bright red trickle of blood. A second later his body shook with a mighty spasm, his feet convulsively jerking. Caedmon suspected that the other man's brain battled on, still sending fight-or-flight messages to his limbs, his brain refusing to accept the inevitable, refusing to lie down and quietly die.

Edie turned her head, unable to watch Sanchez in his death throes.

A few seconds later, Caedmon placed a comforting hand on her shoulder.

"He is gone. Where to, I can not say. Although I suspect he will be refused entry to the heavenly realm."

Edie glanced at the sprawled corpse. Deprived of that bit of animating spirit called the soul, bulging muscles were flaccid, eyes open wide in a ghoulish stare.

"I need to get out of here." Pushing him aside, Edie staggered toward the door.

Going down on bent knee, Caedmon quickly searched through Sanchez's pockets. The search concluded, he followed Edie out of the abattoir.

Silently they stared at the wreck of a farm. On the wet breeze Caedmon heard the creak and groan of rotted wood. In the distance, a dilapidated shutter rattled against an equally dilapidated window frame.

"Now what?"

"If we are to steer the ship through the dense fog, we must remain calm," he told her.

"Couldn't you have come up with a more uplifting cliché?"

"Sorry. My brain is a bit mashed." He showed her the cell phone that he had discovered in Sanchez's coat pocket.

"Do you think MacFarlane will give chase?"

Caedmon thought about it for a moment before finally shaking his head. "He has the Ark. That is all he cares about."

CHAPTER 74

Surely in that day there shall be a great earthquake in the land of Israel, so that the fish of the sea, the birds of the heavens, the beasts of the field, all creeping things that creep on the earth, and all men who are on the face of the earth shall shake at My presence. The mountains shall be thrown down, the steep places shall fall, and every wall shall fall to the ground.

Opening the storage compartment in the middle of the SUV's console, Stanford MacFarlane stowed his well-worn Bible; the words of the prophet Ezekiel never ceased to inspire him.

Beside him in the driver's seat, his gunnery sergeant muttered under his breath, complaining yet again about having to drive on the left side of the road. Stan ignored him. They would be in Margate soon enough. A small fishing boat docked at the harbor would enable them to bypass British customs.

Again, he craned his neck, his eyes alighting on the well-padded shipping crate placed in the Range Rover's cargo hold.

The Ark of the Covenant.

It had taken more than twenty years for him to find that most sacred of relics. His search ordained by God, he had tracked down every lead, every rumor, every crackpot theory regarding the Ark; his search had taken him to the distant corners of the globe. *Ethiopia. Iraq. Southern France.* One by one, each theory had been discredited, leaving only the quatrains of the medieval knight Galen of Godmersham.

Again, he glanced at the shipping container, experiencing a tingling sensation. As though his entire body were enveloped in a static electric field.

The Lord was near at hand! He could feel it!

For it was at the Ark that God, made manifest, had appeared to Moses. The Ark not only embodied the Almighty, it was the symbol of God's promise to His chosen people. Nothing had changed. It was now as it had been then. Adorned with the Stones of Fire, he, too, would be able to speak with the Almighty. Just as Moses had conversed with God in the wilderness.

That heady thought gave rise to a vision in his mind's eye; Stan could hear the blast of trumpets and the clang of cymbals, the shouts and cheers, a throng of men joyfully singing hosannas. As though thirty-five hundred years had come and gone in the blink of an eye.

All praise to God the Almighty!

He knew full well that God's plan for mankind had been formulated in the Garden of Eden and that it would end with a new paradise where those worthy of God's blessings would enjoy a thousand years of peace and prosperity. Finally, the rest well deserved, the warriors would put aside their bloody weapons and lie side by side with the meek and gentle lamb.

With astounding clarity, the prophet Ezekiel had seen the crimson future that would proceed the golden dawn.

Stan did not doubt that Ezekiel's prophecy would soon unfold, taking an unprepared world by storm. The future was already written, prophecy the gift that God gave to quell man's fear in the face of the dark and violent nights that were to come.

And when Ezekiel's prophesized war finally came, sinful man would have no doubt as to God's existence.

Those would be dark days. Days that would push humankind to the limits of their endurance. But those who refused to traffic with the enemy would be reborn in the new world to come. A time of rest for the people of God. When the deserts of the earth would be made fertile and when the Dead Sea would no longer be dead. Ezekiel foretold of how those waters would be stocked with the very fish that would feed the new kingdom of God.

A thousand years of peace. Time for an old warhorse to at long last take his rest.

Reaching into his pocket, Stan removed his BlackBerry, quickly typing out a numeric code with his thumbs. Double-checking each digit, he sent the text message, knowing it would simultaneously reach members of Rosemont Security Consultants stationed in Europe and the Middle East. Battle orders issued, he returned the device to his pocket.

As they approached the Margate town limits, Stan thought of the Englishman and his harlot. Their execution was well deserved, and he felt no pity for them. Instead, a wave of hatred washed over him. Hate was good. Cleansing even. Hate enabled a man to slay the infidel and slaughter the sinner.

He would put his hate to good use in the days to come.

CHAPTER 75

"I know this is going to sound crazy, but I'm actually sad," Edie confessed, taking the proffered coffee cup from Caedmon's outstretched hand. "Angry, but sad. I mean those two guys were a couple of homophobic misanthropes in dire need of some sensitivity training. But watching them die was—" She broke off and stared at the narrow roadway that fronted the public bench.

Coffee cup in hand, Caedmon seated himself beside her. He, too, gloomily stared at the main thoroughfare that ran through the middle of the small seaside port of Gilchrist.

Knowing that the local constabulary would be drawn to the plumes of black smoke produced by the Range Rover explo-

sion, and that, in turn, would lead them to at least one dead
body, he'd used the pilfered GPS receiver to plot a course in
the opposite direction from the charred ruins. Although exhausted, they'd tramped through deserted farmers' fields,
eventually arriving at their present location. Unwelcoming in
the way that small clannish enclaves tended to be, Gilchrist
had about it the distinct scent of salt and dead fish, the town's
only saving grace being that it had a coach depot. Assuming
one could call a metal-covered bench situated only six feet
from the roadway a proper depot.

Raising the paper cup to his lips, Caedmon took a sip of the
horrible-tasting brew that he'd purchased at the fish-and-chip
shop across the way. According to the reticent fellow behind
the counter, the afternoon coach to London was due to arrive
in forty minutes.

"It's never easy to witness the extinction of a life," he
replied, also haunted by the deaths of Harliss and Sanchez.
"Try as one might to erase the memory, it leaves an imprint on
your soul."

"Not for MacFarlane or his men." Raising the plastic lid,
Edie took several swallows. Only to grimace a few seconds
later from the bitter aftertaste. "They wholeheartedly believe
that when they pull the trigger, they're doing God's work."

"Somehow I doubt that MacFarlane's God would have
much truck with those of us who long for peace, not war."

Sighing, Edie wrapped her free arm around his waist, leaning her head on his shoulder. "I don't know about you, but
I'm in desperate need of a group hug."

As am I, love. As am I.

The web of life was fragile, indeed, and he hoped this day's
atrocities would quickly recede from Edie's memory. Hoped
she could forget what she'd witnessed. And forgive what she'd
seen him do. As soon as they reached London, he intended to
call in a favor from an old chum at MI5 and have her placed in
an out-of-the way safe house. Some place where Stanford
MacFarlane and his assassins could never find her.

Edie inclined her head away from his shoulder. "What do
you think MacFarlane plans to do now that he has the Ark?"

"The first order of business will be to get the relic out of Britain. If he's discovered with the Ark on English soil, not only will the bloody thing will be confiscated, it will be sent directly to the British Museum." Where it would draw larger crowds than the Rosetta stone, the Elgin Marbles, and the Sutton Hoo treasure combined.

He removed the nicked GPS receiver from his anorak pocket. "It'll take a few moments to initialize," he informed her as he hit the *Power* button. He held the receiver aloft to get a satellite fix on their position. A few seconds later, glancing at the small display screen, he said with a teasing smile, "Ah, we are exactly where we should be."

Edie halfheartedly returned the smile. "Since I have yet to correctly program the TV remote, I'll have to trust you on that one. But isn't the GPS receiver a bit superfluous? I mean, we're here already and we know where 'here' is located."

"On the contrary. Given that this is a handheld computer with satellite capabilities, untold information could be stored on the device." Using the *NAV* key, he accessed a database file of saved maps. "Now, isn't this interesting. A number of maps were recently downloaded. According to the list, there are maps for Oxford, Oxfordshire, Godmersham, Swanley, and—" He stared at the list, stunned.

"Come on, Caedmon. I can only hold my bated breath for so long."

"And Malta," he replied, turning the receiver in her direction.

"Malta?" Tapping her pursed lips, she stared at the display screen. "Although world geography isn't one of my strong suits, I seem to recall that Malta is a spit of an island located in the Mediterranean Sea. Do you think that's where MacFarlane is headed?"

"Given that the list of maps perfectly corresponds to Mac-Farlane's known movements in the last seventy-two hours, we must assume that Malta is his intended destination." And how very ironic, given that the diminutive isle had once been home to the Knights of St. John, the same order of warrior monks to which Galen of Godmersham had been an initiated member.

"Isn't Malta where St. Paul was shipwrecked while en route to Rome?"

"Hmm? Er, yes," he answered, interrupted from his reveries. "As a crossroads between Africa and Europe, the island has hosted many a famed and infamous personage during its turbulent history."

"But why would MacFarlane take the Ark to Malta?"

Caedmon shrugged, admittedly at a loss. "The dreams of a madman are difficult to decipher."

"I'm guessing that getting the Ark out of England is going to be an even more difficult feat, what with airport security having tightened considerably in recent years."

"Which is why Stanford MacFarlane will no doubt transport the Ark via a shipping vessel. An innocuous boat leaving port in the dead of night sounds about right." As he spoke, the mobile phone in his pocket began to shrilly beep.

"What's that?"

Caedmon shoved his hand into his anorak pocket and removed the mobile he'd taken from Sanchez. He glanced at the digital display.

"Unless I'm greatly mistaken, we've just been given Stanford MacFarlane's next chess move," he said, showing her the flash message.

104-13-94-38-35-17-89-62-122-57-19-97-33-26-42-109-86-
70-40-9-53-2-119

"Well, will ya look at that? It's some sort of a text message sent by an unnamed person at Rosemont Security Consultants. Although I don't know that I would call it a text message per se, since it appears to be nothing more than a numeric list."

"A *coded* numeric list, I daresay." Caedmon suspected that Stanford MacFarlane maintained contact with his troops with flash messages sent via mobile phones. A brilliant means of communication in the satellite age, enabling MacFarlane to simultaneously issue battle orders to followers across the globe.

"If only we had the encryption code," he murmured.

"Do you think the encryption has anything to do with the map of Malta that we found on the GPS receiver?"

"Mmmm . . . difficult to say." His gaze ricocheted between the receiver and the mobile. "Probably not, given that Harliss was the only one of MacFarlane's men to carry a satellite receiver. I suspect that MacFarlane moves his chess pieces very carefully across the board, revealing the master plan in dribs and drabs."

"Where do we begin the hunt?"

"In Malta. However, from this point forward, there is no more 'we.'"

When Edie heard that, her brown eyes furiously gleamed. "So, in other words, you're planning to dump me and chase after MacFarlane on your own."

"Rather than 'chase after MacFarlane,' I intend to retrieve the Ark." Getting up from the bench, he walked over to the nearby trash receptacle and tossed his coffee cup into the plastic-lined can.

He had no delusions as to the difficulty of the task he'd set for himself. Tracking down MacFarlane and actually confiscating the Ark of the Covenant would more than likely prove an impossible, if not deadly, undertaking. But try he must. The GPS receiver had proved a godsend. Now, at least, he knew where to hunt for his nemesis.

Grabbing him by the wrist, Edie urged him to retake his seat on the bench. "I know you're worried about me. That said, going after the Ark isn't a one-man job. You're going to need all the help you can get to vanquish MacFarlane and his Warriors of—"

"I can't take you with me."

"Why not?"

"Because I don't have time to potty-train you."

"Why, you arrogant bastard!" She leaped to her feet. "I'm not some Bond girl along for the ride. I'm your partner. And in case you didn't get the memo, I am a full and equal partner."

Caedmon stared at her, unable to take his eyes off the long

corkscrew curls that blew about her flushed face. Also unable to quash the memory of her standing beneath an upraised pickax.

"'In the world you *will* have tribulation,'" she continued. "John sixteen. A Bible verse that Stanford MacFarlane, no doubt, holds near and dear."

"And a frightening prospect it is."

"Yes, it is frightening. Which is why I'm going with you to Malta. Unlike you, I completely understand MacFarlane and his radical beliefs. For five years, I was fed a steady diet of Ezekiel and the End Times prophecy."

"After today's primer in apocalyptic belief, I should be able to manage."

"What you heard was just the tip of the iceberg. Think of me as your very own expert in Christian fundamentalism. Besides, we're a team. We have been from the very beginning. So, short of knocking me unconscious, there's nothing you can do to stop me."

"Very well," he murmured.

If she wondered at his ready acquiescence, she gave no indication. "Okay, now that we've got that settled, what's the game plan?"

"Simply put, to grab MacFarlane by the Old Testament and squeeze very, very hard."

CHAPTER 76

Caedmon took a deep breath of the invigorating sea air. Bracing his hands on the deck railing, he stared at the rolling blue Mediterranean waves that danced in the lemony light of early morn. It was the same sea that Odysseus once sailed en route to battle the Trojans.

Standing beside him, her cheeks tinted red from the breeze, Edie also deeply inhaled. "Other than a Potomac River dinner cruise, this is the first time I've ever been on a big boat. I think I like being on the open sea." A mischievous smile playing about her lips, she winked at him. "Could be because I was a lady pirate in a past life; what do you think?"

"I think I'd rather be in an airplane roaring high above the sea," he grumbled. "Too many of these blasted ferry boats have sunk in recent years. Not to mention that traveling by ferry is a damn slow way to get from point A to point B." Point A being Naples and point B their final destination: Malta.

"Yeah, but given that it's the dead of winter, flights into Malta are few and far between. This will actually get us to our destination six hours sooner than if we'd waited for the next available flight. Which you would know if you'd ever watched *The Amazing Race*. So stop griping."

"I have been doing quite a bit of that, haven't I?"

"Understandable. You're under a lot of stress."

Truly an understatement. Already, the old paranoia had set in. The niggling fear that an unseen enemy would lurch from the shadows. Danger and treachery but a heartbeat away. If allowed to run rampant, fear could quickly become a man's worst enemy. More dangerous than the brute with a gun.

Because of his intelligence training, he knew the drill—always use cash, refrain from using one's real name, and never, ever sleep in the same bed two nights in a row. Simple enough if not for having Edie in tow. With her Pre-Raphaelite beauty, she garnered attention wherever she went.

Short of knocking me unconscious, there's nothing you can do to stop me.

An ultimatum. One he didn't much care to ponder.

"You've got two very big creases in the middle of your brow. Care to share your worries?"

"I was thinking about the Ark and the poor blokes at Beth-shemesh," he lied, not about to confess his true thoughts.

"And you're concerned that when we commandeer the Ark from MacFarlane, it may gobble us whole."

"Mock me if you will, but the Ark *was* once used as a supercharged weapon of mass destruction," he informed her, still hoping she would have a change of heart and return to the mainland.

"Eons ago. Which means there's nobody around who knows how to activate the ancient electromagnetic technology that once powered the Ark. To operate a piece of machinery, you need an instruction manual. And that manual, whether it was written down or passed verbally from father to son, has long since vanished. In other words, the Ark has lost its *oom-pa-pa*. So no need to worry about it exploding in our faces or anything like that."

"That's not the danger I fear. As a tool of propaganda, the Ark could be used to convince millions of God-fearing people that the so-called End Times are truly upon us."

Her eyes focused on the sprightly waves in the distance, Edie plaintively sighed. "Yeah, that has me worried, as well," she conceded. "Though God may not be fooled by MacFarlane's false piety, a whole lot of good, well-intentioned people will eat up his prophetic ramblings. But enough said on that topic, huh?"

Pronouncement made, Edie turned away from the water. Leaning against the railing, her arms folded across her chest, she stared at him. Quite unabashedly. Although they shared the vessel with countless passengers, there was something inherently intimate about the wind, the water, the warmth that radiated between their two bodies, all of it countermanding the cool satin chill of the winter's day.

Caedmon sidled closer.

After Jules died, he'd had a few casual relationships, unwilling to take another chance. Which is why it made no sense, with the Ark hanging over his head like the blasted sword of Damocles, that he would now want the very thing he'd studiously avoided.

Bloody hell. He was daft to think they could make a go of it. They didn't even live on the same continent.

In truth, he didn't know how he felt about Edie Miller. He'd not had time to analyze his feelings. He only knew it was akin to coming out of a tube station and suddenly finding himself in a strange and unfamiliar location.

"Christ! I need a blasted map," he muttered.

"I beg your pardon?"

"Nothing." He waved away the thought. "A bit of nonsense."

And it was nonsensical. He was forty. A man of middling years. He'd long since put such emotions behind him, a cheery forever after being the hope of one's youth. Not one's maturity. *And yet . . .*

Edie slid her hand behind his head, pulling him close. "Wanna go back to our room?" she asked, rising up on tiptoe, giving him no time to reply.

It took but a second for the unexpected kiss to turn decidedly passionate.

"I think you know the answer to that," he murmured against her lips.

Taking her by the arm, he strode down the gangway; Edie had to jog to keep up with his hurried pace. It took only a few moments for them to reach their room, his hand shaking as he inserted the key into the lock. He wasted no time dragging her inside, slamming the door shut behind them.

CHAPTER 77

It was a moment of quiet intimacy. Of murmured endearments. Life slowed down to its simplest, most lovely, facet.

In the midst of the quietude, Edie felt a spark. She snuggled closer to Caedmon, burrowing her head into the crook of his bare shoulder. This was not the first time she'd felt the spark, and she wondered if anything would come of it.

Could anything come of it?

On paper, she gave their relationship the shelf life of a carton of milk. If that. They were simply two sexually healthy people caught up in the excitement of the moment. Although, glancing at the small clock mounted to the wall, she could see that the excitement had lasted quite a few hours.

"You do know that this . . . this attraction is nothing more than a primitive urge," she said, propping her head on his chest.

"Perhaps it must be primal, stripped of all civility, in order for us to put aside our preconceived notions of what should and shouldn't be."

Hmm . . . it sounded as though he'd given their relationship more than a passing thought.

"And maybe Freud was right about there being no such thing as pure unadulterated love. Maybe there's sexual need and nothing else," she countered, testing him.

"I suspect that Freud was an impotent bugger who wouldn't have known love if it had slapped him in his bearded face. Let's not analyze it. Let's simply accept it, whatever it is, as a beginning. Tentative and tenuous, perhaps, but a beginning nonetheless."

She smiled; Caedmon had passed the test with flying colors.

"Agreed. But if you think I'm one of those women who'd settle for a man just because he puts down the toilet seat, think again."

"Point taken. Although I hope you'll reward me with several bonus points for being so considerate."

"Change of subject," she announced. "I'm curious as to what would have happened if you had stayed at Oxford and received your doctorate?"

"You mean how would my life have unraveled?" When she nodded, he said, "In a very typical fashion, no doubt. I would have received a college appointment, most likely at Queen's. At which point my life would have become a steady stream of tutorials, committee meetings, and university functions."

"You know, I'm one of those people who believe that things happen for a reason. Personally, I don't think you were meant to live such a sheltered life. Just look at Sir Kenneth Campbell-Brown. Okay, the man is brilliant, but he's also a confirmed alcoholic bachelor. You were meant for a better life."

Smiling, Caedmon brushed his lips against hers. "At the mention of the path not taken, I feel strangely glad-hearted."

"Me, too."

"Bloody hell," he abruptly exclaimed a half second later. "How do terrorists communicate with one another?"

Surprised by the unexpected question, she lifted a shoulder. "Beats me. Although I suspect the answer is not messenger pigeons."

"In a sense, that is the correct answer in that they communicate via the Internet," he informed her, his blue eyes excitedly gleaming. "Which enables them to freely pass messages to cells and operatives all over the globe. Perhaps MacFarlane and his Warriors of God are no different."

"Okay, suppose that's true. How does the instant text message on Sanchez's cell phone fit in? I thought *that* was how MacFarlane was communicating with his men."

"When we first received the flash message, I thought that a communiqué had been encoded into the numeric list and that an encryption key would be needed to decipher the message. But what if the numeric list *is* the encryption key?"

"Sorry, I'm not following." Edie propped her head on her hand.

"Knowing he can't be too careful when sending messages across the globe, MacFarlane might very well have devised a two-pronged mode of communication. The first prong being the numeric list that was sent to Sanchez's mobile phone."

"And the second prong?"

"Mind you, this is mere speculation, but the second prong,

or piece of the puzzle, might be the Warriors of God Web page."

"You're talking about the Web page that we checked out back in D.C., right?"

Caedmon shrugged. "As I said, it's merely a working theory. All bones, no meat."

"So let me make sure I've got this straight," she said, still uncertain how all the pieces fit together. "You think there might be a message encoded in the Warriors of God Web page and that this message can only be *decoded* using the numeric list from the text message."

"There's only one way to find out. Unless I'm mistaken, the ferry boat is equipped with Inmarsat."

"What's that?"

"A mobile communications system that enables Internet access while at sea."

Throwing back the sheet, Edie swung her feet to the floor. "Well, what are we waiting for?"

CHAPTER 78

"Doom and gloom of the worst sort, eh?"

Sitting side by side in front of the ship's computer monitor, Edie and Caedmon stared at the Warriors of God home page.

"'When the Warriors of God battle the dark forces—will you be ready for this holy Revolution? Will you be a Patriot marching under God's golden banner'?" Edie read aloud from the computer monitor. Unnerved by the apocalyptic "announcement" that was prominently displayed on the screen, she shuddered. "You don't really think there's a secret message buried somewhere in this so-called announcement, do ya?"

Leaning back in his chair, Caedmon slowly tapped his index finger against his chin. Several seconds passed in contemplative silence before he finally said, "My guess is that MacFarlane has used a simple alphanumeric substitution cipher. Since his flash message was intended for mass consumption, I doubt that he would employ too elaborate a cipher."

"The old KISS rule, huh?" Seeing Caedmon's quizzical expression, she smiled. "As in 'Keep it simple, stupid.'"

Amused, Caedmon chuckled. "Clearly, we are of like mind. Employing the KISS rule, I propose that we consecutively number each letter and punctuation mark in MacFarlane's hate-filled diatribe."

Pencil in hand, he carefully wrote out the "announcement" on a sheet of paper. Then he sequentially numbered each letter and punctuation mark.

While Caedmon busied himself with laying out the cipher, Edie nervously glanced over her shoulder; the ship's Internet computer was set up in the very public club room. A few tables away a middle-aged quartet played cards. From the cigarette butts overflowing the table's only ashtray, she guessed that they had been playing for some time. About twenty feet away, an older well-dressed man and his much younger male companion were huddled together in front of a soft drink machine. And on the other side of the club room, a harried mother openly breast-fed her infant.

"I'll have you know that this is the same cipher that won you Yanks your independence, the words *revolution* and *patriot* being the dead giveaway."

Her eyes opened wide. "You're kidding, right?"

"Not in the least. Created by Benjamin Franklin, this particular alphanumeric cipher was used to code messages shuffled back and forth between the Continental Congress and sympathetic French diplomats. Would you like to do the honors?" Caedmon offered her the pencil.

Taking the implement, Edie first glanced at the alphanumeric chart that he had created from MacFarlane's Web page.

W	H	E	N		T	H	E		W	A	R	R	I	O	R	S		O	F		G	O	D	B	A	T	T	L
1	2	3	4	5	6	7	8	9	10	11	12	13	14	15	16	17	18	19	20	21	22	23	24	25

E T H E D A R K F O R C E S — W I L L Y O U B E R
26 27 28 29 30 31 32 33 34 35 36 37 38 39 40 41 42 43 44 45 46 47 48 49 50

E A D Y F O R T H I S H O L Y R E V O L U T I O N
51 52 53 54 55 56 57 58 59 60 61 62 63 64 65 66 67 68 69 70 71 72 73 74 75

? W I L L Y O U B E A P A T R I O T M A R C H I N
76 77 78 79 80 81 82 83 84 85 86 87 88 89 90 91 92 93 94 95 96 97 98 99 100

G U N D E R G O D ' S G O L D E N B A N N E R ?
101 102 103 104 105 106 107 108 109 110 111 112 113 114 115 116 117 118 119 120 121 122 123 124

Then she glanced at the list of numbers from the text message.

104-13-94-38-35-17-89-62-122-57-19-97-33-26-42-109-86-70-40-9-53-2-119

"Wish me luck."

Caedmon having done all the work, it only took a few moments for her to write out the deciphered message.

dome of the rock eid al-adha

Neither of them said anything; Edie was not altogether sure what, if anything, the message meant.

"The Dome of the Rock is the big gold-leafed Islamic shrine that sits on top of the Temple Mount, right?"

"Unquestionably the most famous silhouette on the Jerusalem skyline," he confirmed; Edie could detect a husky catch in his voice.

Something was wrong. That much was readily apparent.

"MacFarlane's message means something to you, doesn't it?"

Still staring at the decoded message, Caedmon slowly nodded. "I now know why Stanford MacFarlane and all of his followers wear the Jerusalem cross ring. As you, no doubt, recall, the Jerusalem cross was the symbol adopted by the medieval crusaders when they conquered the Holy City in the eleventh century." The entire time he spoke, he stared at the decoded message.

"And why do you think that's significant?" she prodded, not altogether certain that she wanted to know the answer.

"Because Jerusalem was only theirs for the briefest of interludes; the Muslim caliph Saladin retook the city in 1187." Suddenly resembling a sad-faced crusader from a medieval woodcut, Caedmon turned his head and looked at her. "Clearly, MacFarlane has taken upon himself the crusaders' cause."

"I don't understand. What cause?"

"Like the crusaders of old, MacFarlane and his men intend

to conquer the holy city of Jerusalem, their first military target being the Dome of the Rock."

At hearing that, her jaw slackened. "When? How?"

"I have no idea as to the *how*. As to the *when*, it is obvious that they intend to launch their attack on the Islamic holy festival of Eid al-Adha. Which, unless I'm greatly mistaken, begins on December the eighth."

"But"—she did a quick mental calculation—"that's less than two days away."

CHAPTER 79

"Giving us a narrow window of opportunity."

As he spoke, Caedmon was acutely, *painfully*, aware of the play of opposites. Good and evil. Love and hate. *Life and death.*

"So, what exactly are you saying—that MacFarlane intends to destroy the Dome of the Rock on December eighth?"

"It does fit in with all of his apocalyptic posturing. And there's a certain irony in his selection of holy days, Eid al-Adha being the Muslim Day of Sacrifice, commemorating the day when Abraham intended to sacrifice his beloved son Ishmael to prove his love to Allah. The Dome of the Rock marks the precise location of where the sacrifice was to have taken place. It's also the spot where the Prophet Muhammad ascended to heaven—making the Dome of the Rock the third-holiest site in all of Islam."

"Right behind Mecca and Medina."

He nodded, staggered by MacFarlane's dark vision. *Eid al-Adha.* The Day of Sacrifice. The day when Muslim worshippers would be packed onto the Temple Mount. Ten thousand strong.

"Maybe we need to dial back a bit. I mean, the encrypted message doesn't *specifically* mention anything about destroying the Dome of the Rock," Edie pointed out, playing devil's advocate.

"But MacFarlane did unequivocally state that he intends to install the Ark of the Covenant in the newly constructed Temple," he countered. "And I think it no coincidence that the Dome of the Rock sits on the very site where Solomon's Temple once stood."

"Solomon's Temple?" Edie gave him a long wordless stare, her pupils contracting into microdots. As though she, too, suddenly realized the magnitude of the encoded message. "Oh, God . . . I didn't know," she murmured. "That changes everything."

"The terrible thing about the truth is that sometimes you find it. Not only is the Temple Mount a holy site for the three major religions of the world, but over the centuries, it has been the most fought-over piece of real estate in the world." Fraught with bloodshed, carnage, and internecine rivalry, the history of the Temple Mount was a fantastical tale almost too violent to be believed.

"I know that in 1967, during the Six-Day War, the Israelis captured the Temple Mount."

"Although in an attempt to appease their Muslim neighbors, the Israelis permitted the Waqf, or Islamic Trust, to continue to act as the official administrators of the holy site."

"So while the Jews have sovereignty over the Temple Mount, the Muslims maintain control of it."

"And, as you undoubtedly know, this arrangement has been a point of contention between several generations of peace negotiators." A heaviness in his heart inspired him to say, "Not for the first time have I wondered if the world would have been a better place had Solomon's Temple never been constructed, the site being one of the most volatile spots on the planet."

Slumping slightly in her chair, Edie stared at the innocuous sheet of lined notepaper.

Caedmon also stared at the deciphered message, stunned anew. "And now a madman has arrived on the scene, wholly intent on destroying the Dome of the Rock so he can build a Third Temple. With the Ark in his arsenal and a well-trained army at his disposal, he could easily bring about a series of events that mimic the events foretold in the Old Testament. Thus fulfilling Ezekiel's prophecy."

"We can't let that happen," Edie whispered, her body rigid with the strength of her emotion. "I don't know if you're aware that for some time now there's been a strengthening alliance between Jewish and Christian fundamentalists."

"Birds of the same dark feather," he uncharitably remarked.

"Old Testament prophecies are shared by both religions. Which means that MacFarlane might possibly have allies inside Israel who would be more than willing to help him destroy the Dome of the Rock."

Caedmon shook his head, the scenario having just become that much more frightening.

"Fanatical Christians working in league with fanatical Jews to incite the fanatical Muslims of the world. Incite any of the three and you have global instability. Incite all three and you have the makings of the next world war."

Knowing that many a war had been ignited by the collective frenzy of which they spoke—the Middle Ages had been one big bloodbath of blind faith—Caedmon turned his head and stared at the churning water visible through the picture window on the other side of the club room.

They couldn't get to Malta fast enough.

CHAPTER 80

Caedmon glanced up from the map spread before him on the bar counter.

A vacancy having come open at the last minute, he and Edie were seated at the Dragonara Hotel bar waiting for the maid to finish cleaning their suite. To his surprise, Valletta, the capital city of Malta, was quite the convention center; their seaside hotel was currently hosting a large gathering of British plastic surgeons. Because Malta had at one time been part of the British Empire, it was a popular destination with his countrymen. He'd purposefully selected the Dragonara in order to fade into the crowd. If a desk clerk or bellhop was questioned as to whether an Englishman had checked into the hotel, the reply would be "Yes, the hotel currently has two hundred English guests."

Before returning his attention to the map, Caedmon surreptitiously glanced at the mirrored wall behind the bar, having resorted to old behaviors, scanning each and every bar patron, running mock scenarios in his head, trying to discern who among them would go in for the kill. He would have preferred sitting at an innocuous table in the back of the room, but the overflow of plastic surgeons swilling predinner drinkies had forced them to grab two stools at the bar.

"You know, I've been meaning to ask, is there really a big rock inside the Dome of the Rock?"

Caedmon nodded. "In fact, the rock, known in Hebrew as the *Shetiyyah*, is believed to be the foundation stone of the world. Before it was stolen by Shishak, the Ark of the Covenant rested on top of the *Shetiyyah*."

The bartender, a swarthy fellow with an amiable disposition, placed a tonic water and a cola in front of them. Then, with a practiced flourish, he presented Edie with a plate full of fried calamari and a small dish of quartered lemons.

"*Grazzi,*" she replied in Malti, the response earning her a toothy grin.

Out of the corner of his eye, Caedmon watched as Edie squeezed a lemon, not on her squid, but into her cola. He continued to watch as she pursed her lips around the end of a fuchsia-colored straw. He well recalled how her lips had clamped around him earlier in the day.

Careful, old boy. Now is not the time for prurient thoughts and adolescent longings.

With a renewed focus, he stared at the GPS receiver, continuing the business of transferring the coordinates that he'd discovered in the database file onto a local topographical map with the aid of a map ruler. In the event the GPS batteries died a sudden death, he wanted a hard-copy backup.

"From where I'm sitting, Malta doesn't look like that big of an island."

"Approximately three hundred square miles. About the size of the Isle of Wight." He plotted the last set of coordinates. "Ah! I think I've got a location." Excited to have made such fast work of it, he pointed to a small jut of land off the southwest coast of Malta.

Edie squinted as she peered at the map. "Calypso's Point," she read aloud. "Geez, it's no bigger than my front yard. What do the dark wavy lines mean?" She pointed to the contour lines that distinguished a topographical map from the run-of-the-mill motorist map.

"It means we'll have to scale a cliff wall. Although there's a road leading to the point, we must assume that MacFarlane will have the roadway closely guarded."

He signaled the bartender to step over. When the young man approached, he swiveled the paper map in his direction. "Are you by any chance familiar with a place called Calypso's Point?"

The bartender barely glanced at the map. "*Iva,* I know it well. It used to be a hideout for the Barbary pirates until the

knights defeated them. But"—he expressively shrugged—
"why would you want to go there? It's uninhabited. You will
find only seabirds and the ruins of St. Paul's *torri*."

An abandoned tower . . . how interesting. No doubt a signal
tower once used by the Knights of St. John.

"Actually, it's the sea birds that I wish to see," he glibly
lied, turning the map back in his direction. "I am something of
an amateur bird watcher. Would you happen to know anyone
who would be willing to take us to the point by way of
the sea?"

"My brother-in-law has a fishing vessel. I am sure he could
be persuaded to take you there. Assuming the price is right."

"He has but to name it, the only stipulation being that I
would like to depart later this evening."

If the young man thought it odd that someone would go
bird watching in the dead of night, he gave no indication,
scribbling his brother-in-law's phone number onto a cocktail
napkin.

Their business concluded, the bartender turned and waited
on a portly surgeon who loudly raved about the "jolly good
pasties."

Relieved that the logistics were taken care of, Caedmon
neatly folded the map. That done, he slid map and ruler into
his anorak pocket. With one more task to attend to, he glanced
through the glass doors that fronted the entrance to the bar, able
to see across the lobby into the so-called business center.
One of the hotel amenities was the free use of a desktop
computer, a fax machine, and a color copier. For the last twenty
minutes, the computer had been commandeered by a Suffolk
surgeon.

"Is he still there?"

"If you're asking if I can still see the chap's tonsured pate,
the answer is yes."

"Why do you need a computer, anyway? We got everything we needed from the ferryboat computer. Or at least
I thought we did."

"I need the computer because I intend to put together a dossier for the British consulate. If by tomorrow morning we

haven't returned to the hotel, the dossier will be sent to the consulate office here in Valletta. From there, it will be forwarded to British Intelligence. Hopefully, the lads at Thames House will be able to succeed where we failed."

"You're talking about your old buddies at MI5, right?"

He nodded. "One doesn't need the Delphic Oracle to know that Stanford MacFarlane won't relinquish the Ark without a fight."

"And a deadly fight, at that," Edie murmured; Caedmon could see that she was still distressed by the encoded message they had earlier deciphered. For several seconds she stared at her cola glass, the only sound being the dull *clink-clink* as she continued to swirl her straw.

Quite abruptly, she set the straw adrift.

"I keep thinking about that proverb, 'Everything has an end.' And I can't help but wonder . . . is this the beginning of the end?"

His thoughts running a similar course, Caedmon cast his gaze at the second set of French doors, which opened onto a terrace; the hotel was set on a scenic perch overlooking the water. The sun had already begun its descent into the sea, creating a glorious explosion of tangerine and magenta. So beautiful, it was almost painful to watch. To his right, the baroque city of Sliema, a burnished maze of stone façades, rose up as if spawned from the sea.

How did he get himself into this mess? More important, how had he gotten Edie so deeply involved in it?

At first it had been simple academic curiosity. *The Ark of the Covenant.* If he could find it, if he could lay his hands upon it, he could prove himself worthy of the man who'd overseen his ouster from Oxford. Prove to his long-dead father that—

"I'm afraid," Edie said, her tremulous voice breaking through the silence. "What if we can't stop him? We were powerless to stop him from walking away with the Ark."

Turning his head, he peered into Edie's sad brown eyes. "Although MacFarlane may best us, we're not as powerless as you seem to think. Knowledge has a power all its own."

"It's the guns and bullets that have me worried."

"They can only kill you. But knowledge lives on."

Placing a hand on his knee, she leaned toward him. "So does this," she whispered, brushing her lips against his.

CHAPTER 81

Like a miser counting pennies, the crescent moon stingily cast a jaundiced light upon the choppy sea. Its lantern extinguished, the small fishing vessel steadily made its way toward the barren chunk of limestone in the distance. *Calypso's Point.* The captain, a wizened salt who spoke no English, stood at the helm. Having been amply compensated for his services, he had turned a blind eye to the peculiarities of the voyage.

Caedmon glanced at Edie, only the pale oval of her face visible in the inky darkness; both of them were garbed in dry diving suits with matching black hoods.

"You know, maybe we *should* let British intelligence handle this," Edie said in a hushed voice. "It's not too late."

Seated across from her, he leaned forward, resting his elbows on the top of his thighs. "Until MacFarlane actually steps foot inside Jerusalem, there's little that British intelligence or Mossad can do to stop him. Those chaps don't hold much truck with doomsday prophecies. And though the intelligence agencies will do all in their power to prevent a terrorist act from occurring on the Temple Mount, they won't be able to act until they have material proof that MacFarlane intends to commit the unthinkable. I, however, am no longer bound by such dictates."

"Yeah, but short of killing Mac—" She slapped a hand over her mouth. A second later, she lowered it. "That's exactly what you're intending to do, isn't it?"

"In order to destroy a serpent, one must decapitate it."

"But what if the snake turns around and bites you?"

Rather than answer the question put to him, he instead said, "I think you should return to Valletta with the captain."

"I told you once already, you'll have to knock me unconscious to stop me from going with you to Calypso's— What's happening?" she hissed, clearly startled.

"No need for alarm. The captain has merely cut the engine."

"So this is our stop, huh?" She stared at the remote and off-putting promontory that loomed above the small vessel.

Caedmon peered upward. The limestone cliff rose approximately two hundred meters above the sea. "Yes, I know. It has a decidedly Gothic aspect." As he spoke, he stepped over to the side of the boat, his neoprene booties softly smacking against the deck. Edie followed in his wake, dashing his hope that she'd have a change of heart at the last.

"Right. Let's get to it," he said, swinging his leg over the side. A second later, he plunged into the cold sea, grateful they had only a short distance to traverse.

Treading water, he watched as Edie jumped ship and proved herself an able swimmer.

A few minutes later, shivering from the cold and breathing heavily from their exertions, they emerged onto a spindly strip of land that was strewn with chunks of rock that had fallen from the cliff face. At a glance, Caedmon could see that the fishing vessel had already begun its homeward voyage, the captain not bothering to confirm whether they had safely landed.

Removing her hood, Edie jutted her chin at the imposing sea cliff. "Without climbing gear, I don't know how we're going to get up that sucker."

"I have it on good authority that there's a narrow trail not far from here." That authority being none other than the hotel bartender, who had laid claim to ascending the cliff on many a youthful outing. Something of a local rite of passage.

He swung a rubberized rucksack off his shoulder. Opening it, he removed yet another watertight bag, from which he removed a coil of wire, a sheathed diving knife, a green laser light, two torches, the GPS receiver, the topographical map, and two pairs of athletic shoes. Inventory verified and double-checked, he unzipped and removed his dry suit. Like Edie, he had worn black hiking attire beneath his suit.

"Guess it's time for the final reckoning, huh?" Although Edie attempted a brave smile, she fell woefully shy of the mark.

"Yes, I'm afraid that the time has come."

Rearing back his arm, his right hand balled in a fist, he delivered a quick, precise blow to the side of Edie's head.

Instantly, her eyes rolled backward, Caedmon catching her as she pitched forward in an unconscious heap. KO'd by the ghost fist that she never saw coming.

Very gently he laid her on a bed of saltwort, using the empty rucksack as a pillow for her head. He then placed a torch in her lax hand. If he didn't return before she came to, or if he didn't return at all, she would be able to signal for help.

Still on bent knee, he leaned forward and softly kissed her on the lips.

I'm sorry, love. You gave me no choice.

CHAPTER 82

Unable to stop what had become an almost compulsive behavior, Stan MacFarlane again glanced at the innocuous shipping container on the other side of the tower room.

Before permitting the Ark to be packed for transport, he'd spent hours gazing upon it. Awestruck. For someone accustomed to the severe austerity of a Baptist church, the Ark had about it an almost pagan beauty. From the fierce pair of winged cherubim mounted on the gold lid to the strange and incomprehensible symbols incised on all four sides, it bespoke an ancient and holy heritage. A time when Moses led the Hebrew children to the land promised to them by God.

Anxious, he pushed his folding chair away from the camp table and reached for the pair of night-vision goggles. NVGs in hand, he walked over to the square-cut opening on the other side of the circular room. The tower had once been used by the Knights of St. John to monitor sea travel. This night, it served the same purpose, as Stan watched for the luxury yacht that had set sail from Israel earlier in the week. Owned by Moshe Reznick, a Knesset member and cofounder of the Jerusalem-based Third Temple Movement, the yacht would briefly anchor in the bay, pick up its precious cargo, then make the return trip to Haifa. From there, the Ark would be transported to Jerusalem. Stan and his gunnery sergeant, Boyd Braxton, would accompany the Ark on its sea voyage. The rest of his men would fly into Ben-Gurion Airport. Christian tourists making the pilgrimage to Jerusalem.

The yacht was due to arrive within the hour.

There were many who would argue that having been uncovered, the Ark should be placed in a museum. But there was only one place for the Ark, that place having been ordained by God. *The yet-to-be-built Third Temple in Jerusalem.*

Once constructed, the Third Temple would stand for a thousand years. As foretold by the prophet Ezekiel.

Stan was being aided in his endeavors by the members of the Third Temple Movement: Jews who fervently believed in the prophecies foretold by Ezekiel, certain that out of the ashes of the great Battle of Gog and Magog, a new Messiah would step forth.

Although some Christians condemned the Jews, accusing them of having killed the Savior, he knew that Jesus had himself been a Jew. As had been his parents. And all his forebears. Each and every member of the first Church had been a Jew. The Jews were the Chosen People, the custodians of the First and Second Temples, the original guardians of the Ark of the Covenant. And in the great battle to come, the Jews would prevail, fulfilling the destiny envisioned for them by Ezekiel.

Hearing a high-pitched chime emanate from his laptop computer, Stan lowered the night-vision goggles and walked back to the camp table.

Praise be. The much-anticipated e-mail from his comrades at the Third Temple Movement.

Seating himself in front of the laptop, he quickly pulled up the missive.

"It's beautiful," he whispered, examining the architectural blueprint that had been forwarded to him. "Absolutely beautiful."

The construction plans for the Third Temple.

Based on the precise description given by the prophet Ezekiel—cubits having been converted to feet and inches—the temple would be constructed on the same parcel of sacred land where the First and Second Temples once stood. When completed, it would rival the beauty of even Solomon's fabled marvel.

Only two more days.

Two days until Eid al-Adha. The Muslim Day of Sacrifice. The day when two million Muslims would be gathered at Mecca. And when those two million infidels learned that the Dome of the Rock in Jerusalem had been destroyed, they would go on a violent and bloody rampage. That rampage would incite them to take up arms against Christians and Jews. To become the fierce and bloodthirsty army of Gog. As foretold by the prophet Ezekiel.

A battle between Good and Evil would ensue.

But this time the crusaders *will* be victorious.

With the destruction of the gaudy and heathenish Dome of the Rock, the beloved Children of God would finally be delivered from the Islamic tyranny, the gold-plated shrine having been built over the exact site where Solomon's Temple once stood. For the first time in eight hundred years, God's sacred parcel, the Temple Mount, would again be a place of holy worship.

Obliterating the Dome of the Rock from the Jerusalem

skyline had been planned to the last detail; the Muslims had actually simplified the mission op. For years now the Islamic Trust, the supposed caretakers of the Temple Mount, had turned a blind eye to the six-hundred-foot-long bulge in the southern wall. Given its present condition, the ancient foundation wall was already in a severely weakened state. With the insertion of a few carefully placed IEDs, the wall *would* come tumblin' down, bringing with it the newly built al-Marwani mosque that had been constructed on the southern end of the Temple Mount. In the ensuing chaos, his demolition experts would then be able to set a ring of high-powered explosives around the exterior perimeter of the closely guarded Dome of the Rock.

The old bait and switch.

The infidels would never know what hit them.

With the second explosion, the path would literally be cleared for the construction of the Third Temple.

Only then could the Ark of the Covenant be returned to its anointed place within the Holy of Holies. Only then could the Ark become the vehicle through which heaven and earth become one. And only then could a new covenant be made between man and God, paving the way for a holy kingdom that would prosper for a thousand years. A true theocracy where nonbelievers would be judged swiftly and harshly. One Christian nation under God.

"Sir, the sentries just made their rounds and have given the all clear."

Stan glanced at his gunnery sergeant, who stood in the doorway. The sitrep did little to allay his fears. So far, the lanky Englishman had proven a worthy adversary, somehow managing to kill two of his best men. Though he was certain that Aisquith had no way of knowing the Ark had been brought to Malta, he couldn't forget that the man had done what many before him had tried and failed to do—he'd found the Ark of the Covenant.

"Keep me posted."

Snatching the night-vision goggles, Stan walked over to the

window. Elbows braced on the limestone sill, he returned his gaze to the sea.

One if by land, two if by sea.

He chuckled, amused by the thought. Like the founding fathers, he, too, was about to launch a revolution. One of biblical proportions.

CHAPTER 83

Hurriedly Caedmon made his way up the treacherous path cut into the side of the limestone cliff, grateful for the faint light shed by the cluster of stars overhead. Particularly because he couldn't risk using the torch. At least not until he had reached the summit and surveyed the area. MacFarlane would undoubtedly have sentries posted. Men who would not hesitate to shoot at a stray beam of light.

His forty-year-old knees aching from the strenuous ascent, he was very much aware of the fact that he no longer had the power and might of Her Majesty's government behind him. He was on his own. The lone and hungry wolf.

He snorted, amused by the thought.

In sheep's clothing, I daresay.

Huffing slightly, he reached the top, the top being a treeless, rocky plateau. About two hundred meters to the northwest, he could discern the outline of St. Paul's tower, the only visible landmark on the barren escarpment. Once, long centuries ago, the Knights of St. John had used the tower to signal ships at sea. Wishing he had a pair of night-vision goggles, he thought he saw what looked to be a large military transport truck parked beside the tower.

MacFarlane could possibly have the Ark stored inside St. Paul's tower. Out of sight from prying eyes. Or stowed inside the truck, ready for transport.

Standing motionless, he scanned the rocky terrain, searching for a telltale sound or a blurred bit of motion. Something to indicate that he was not alone. That others lurked in the shadows.

A good two minutes passed before he saw a faint flicker, little more than a pinprick of light.

A burning cigarette.

The target sighted, he set forth.

As he navigated his way across the bramble-strewn escarpment, his thoughts turned to the Knights of St. John, who for nearly three centuries had patrolled those same craggy heights, safeguarding their domain from Turkish corsairs. During the Great Siege of 1565, sixty of those stalwart knights had defended the fort at St. Elmo against a Turkish force numbering eight thousand strong. Perhaps this night, history would repeat itself.

Lord, he hoped so. The thought that he might never again set his gaze upon Edie Miller's face left him bereft.

He quickly shoved the wayward thought aside, turning his attention to the man negligently leaning against a large slab of limestone, a lit cigarette dangling from the corner of his mouth.

And an H&K MP5 submachine gun cradled against his chest.

Though it was difficult to see in the murky shadows, Caedmon assumed the man's finger was on the trigger and that the safety had been disengaged.

Coming to a standstill, keeping to the shadows cast by the limestone outcropping, he slid the five-inch diving knife from its sheath. The hilt securely grasped in his right hand, he inched forward, hoping the sentry didn't suddenly spin around. Praying he didn't inadvertently kick a loose stone. To his dismay, he saw that the other man had a communications device protruding from the side of his head.

If the sentry so much as whimpered, the game would be over before it even began.

Caedmon slowed his breathing. An age-old trick to calm one's nerves.

Then, having come to within two feet of the sentry, he lunged forward.

In one smooth, surefooted motion, the movement ingrained from his long-ago training, he grasped the other man from the rear, clasping a hand over his mouth as he yanked his head back, exposing the jugular vein and carotid artery. First he slashed. Then he ripped.

Warm blood gushed from the opened artery.

A silent kill.

As the sentry dropped to the ground, Caedmon shoved his finger into the weapon's trigger guard and yanked the H&K MP5 out of the dying man's grasp, knowing that a spent round would be his undoing.

Sliding his arm through the submachine gun's shoulder strap, he crouched beside the now-dead sentry, relieving him of the radio equipment, the device both a blessing and a beast. Although he'd be able to monitor sentry movement in and around the tower, when the dead sentry failed to report in, MacFarlane and his cutthroats would know they had an enemy in their midst.

CHAPTER 84

Edie sat up and hacked, the frigid sea air scalding her lungs.

Damn Caedmon Aisquith.

Her head ached. Her body ached. And, not unexpectedly,

her heart ached; Caedmon hadn't trusted her to pull her weight. *So what did he do?* He cut her adrift. No warning. No discussion. Just wham-bam, thank you, ma'am.

Rolling onto all fours, she awkwardly shoved herself to her feet. She glanced at her left wrist. *No watch.* Because the cheapo Timex wasn't waterproof, she'd left it behind at the hotel.

She wondered how long she'd been out. Hopefully not too long.

With a groan, she bent at the waist, snatching the flashlight.

"How considerate," she muttered, wishing her AWOL partner had instead left her a bottle of aspirin.

Knowing the anger wouldn't get her off the desolate strip of beach, Edie tilted her head back and peered upward, the sea cliff like an impregnable fortress wall. One that she intended to ascend. Just a few months ago she'd mastered the rock wall at one of D.C.'s largest sporting-goods stores.

So, I'm good to go.

Furtively, she searched the rocky shoreline, recalling that Caedmon had said something about a nearby path. Switching on the flashlight, she followed the footprints that he'd left in the sandy soil, tracking them about forty feet.

Right to the trailhead.

Afraid the flashlight might attract unwanted attention, she flipped it off, securing it in one of the elasticized loops on the waistband of her hiking pants. Hands free, she carefully began the steep climb up the incised stone steps. She wondered if it was the Barbary pirates or the Knights of St. John who had undertaken the painstaking chore of carving what amounted to a staircase into the side of the sea cliff. No doubt Caedmon would have been able to pull that particular factoid out of his hat. Had he been there.

Damn him, anyway. The man actually thought that he could take on the doomsday prophet all by himself. MacFarlane would fight him tooth and nail. And his loyal followers would use far deadlier weapons.

That thought spurring her on, Edie glanced behind her and

saw that she was only at the halfway mark. Her breathing noticeably labored, she struggled to keep on climbing, stunned to realize she was pathetically out of shape.

Finally, sheer willpower coming to the fore, her leg muscles having long since turned to rubber, she reached the summit. With nothing she could do about the burning scrape on the palm of her hand, she wiped the blood as best she could against her pant leg.

At a glance, she could see that she was standing on a flat-topped ridge. A pitiless place that in the light of day probably resembled nothing so much as a big asteroid. Only the faint whiff of rosemary indicated that it could actually sustain some sort of vegetative life.

In the distance she saw a tall, circular tower. That being the only building in sight, she headed in that direction.

As she got closer to the tower, she saw a large canvas-covered truck parked outside. It was the kind of vehicle one might see on a military installation. Hoping it wasn't loaded with armed soldiers, she headed toward it. Trying to keep as low a profile as possible, she hunched over, running in a crouched position. The way people scurried about in the movies.

She hadn't gone far when she saw a bear of a man emerge from the tower and head toward the truck.

Boyd Braxton.

Terrified, Edie came to an abrupt halt. Needing a weapon, and needing one quick, she snatched a jagged rock from the ground.

Give me strength, God.

The same kind of strength that had enabled Samson to slay a thousand foes with the jawbone of an ass.

Edie glanced at the harmless-looking rock clutched in her hand.

If *only* she had the jawbone of an ass.

CHAPTER 85

Pondering his next move, Caedmon stared at the watchtower that loomed a hundred meters away. Absently, he stroked the smooth metal of the H&K MP5, wondering if a little shock and awe wasn't in order. That would certainly ensnare MacFarlane's attention.

And, no doubt, would get him killed in the bargain. Without ever having set eyes upon the Ark.

No, he needed a far more subtle tactic. An unexpected trap. Something that would lure MacFarlane's men away from the tower where he presumed the Ark was being stored, enabling him to sneak inside and decapitate the serpent. And maybe, if he was lucky, he could then exit the tower with none of the bully boys the wiser. The wily fox outwitting the ferocious pack of hounds.

But how best to create the necessary diversion?

If he were anywhere else in the world, he would start a fire. However, other than a few windblown brambles, there was no combustible tinder to be had. He did have the portable laser light, a last-minute purchase. Perhaps he could do something with that.

Like a man mesmerized by a dangling crystal, he continued to stare at the tower. The Ark of the Covenant was near at hand. Yet completely unattainable.

Had Stanford MacFarlane deciphered its secrets? Had he donned the Stones of Fire, stood before the Ark, and communed directly with God?

"We've got a breach on the northwest quadrant. Somebody just tripped the security laser."

Hearing that disembodied voice in his earpiece, Caedmon's breath caught in his throat.

Edie.

He scanned the promontory, searching for that familiar, curly-haired silhouette, knowing he had to find her before MacFarlane did.

CHAPTER 86

Standing as still as a Grecian marble, Edie surreptitiously watched as Boyd Braxton threw back the canvas tarp on the military-style truck and swung open the tailgate. She assumed that he was about to unload something. Or else he was getting the truck ready *to be* loaded. Whichever scenario it was, it had to have something to do the Ark. Of that she was certain.

Taking deep measured breaths, she continued to watch Braxton, curious as to why he suddenly pressed a finger to his ear. Just before he pulled his gun out of its shoulder holster, turned on his heel, and took off running.

Something had spooked the man. But what could possibly have—

Oh, God! They'd found Caedmon.

Swiveling her head back and forth, squinting to better see in the murky shadows, she searched the rocky promontory.

It was like searching the dark side of the moon.

Belatedly realizing that it really was a whole lot like being on the moon in that there was no place to hide, she began to shiver.

A few moments later, four men emerged from the tower,

carrying what looked to be a large shipping container. Two other men, stubby machine guns at the ready, followed in their wake.

Without being told, Edie knew that the Ark of the Covenant was inside the shipping container.

Her heart painfully thudding against her breastbone, she watched as it was loaded into the back of the truck. That done, the two armed guards took up a position on either side of the vehicle, the four load bearers returning to the tower.

Slowly, she backed away from her observation post.

She'd taken no more than three tentative steps when a large hand was slapped over her mouth, an unseen assailant bodily lifting her off the ground.

CHAPTER 87

"Keep your hair on!" a distinctly English voice hissed in her ear. "We don't want to alert them to our position."

Releasing his hand from her mouth, Caedmon stepped in front of her; Edie was surprised to see a machine gun strapped to his chest. A disgusted look on his face, he snatched the rock that she still had clutched in her hand.

"First they would have to know that we're here before—"

"They do know!"

Cinching a hand around her upper arm, he unceremoniously pulled her to the ground, the two of them squaring off in a low squat.

"Have you lost your bloody mind?" His warm breath hit her full in the face. Not bothering to ask permission, he yanked one of her hands to his face. The palm of her scraped hand was smeared with blood.

"Don't say it. I'm here. Deal with it."

"I can render you unconscious at any moment, so kindly do not tell me what I can or cannot do."

"That reminds me . . . did you have to hit me so hard?"

"Be thankful it was me doing the hitting and not one of MacFarlane's thugs. And before you rail at me further, I had no choice in the matter. You were the one who issued the ultimatum." For several seconds he stared into her eyes. Then, raising his left hand, he gently caressed the side of her face. "I am truly sorry, Edie, that I hurt you." Both his features and his voice had noticeably softened.

"My feelings are more hurt than anything else. Mainly because you didn't trust me enough to—"

"I trust you with my life. And I will do all in my power to safeguard yours." He removed his hand from her cheek. Taking her by the elbow, he urged her to stand upright. "You are to follow my lead. No harebrained heroics or I *will* stuff my kerchief in your lovely mouth before binding you hand and foot."

"If you did that, I wouldn't be able to tell you that they loaded the Ark into the back of that big truck. Oh, and how about giving me a weapon?"

Reaching into his pocket, he removed something that resembled a capped ink pen. "Here."

"What am I supposed to do with this?"

"Shine it directly into an assailant's eyes. I don't have time to explain the laws of photonics, except to say that it will instantaneously induce a state of temporary blindness. So please be sure that the business end is pointing away from you when the light is activated."

Edie reluctantly took the portable laser light. "I was hoping that you might give me your diving knife, seeing as how you managed to find yourself a machine—"

Just then, she heard a sound—the friction of rubber on stone—emanating from a booted footfall.

Frantically, she glanced at Caedmon.

Amazingly calm, he put his left index finger to his lips, cautioning her to silence, while at the same time he placed his right index finger on the trigger of the submachine gun strapped across his chest.

Suddenly, surprising Edie with his quickness, he pulled off a lightning-fast one-eighty spin.

"Drop your weapon and remove the headset! Now!"

Realizing his pistol was no match for Caedmon's mightier weapon, Boyd Braxton obediently put his pistol on the ground, kicking it in Caedmon's direction. That done, he yanked off the headset and, snidely smiling, tossed it several feet away. "You didn't want that, did you?"

Afraid the headset might have an open mike, Edie strode over and forcefully smashed the heel of her shoe against the communications device.

The smile instantly vanished from the behemoth's face. Stepping past him, Edie noticed that the crisscrossed bandages on the side of Braxton's head surreally gleamed in the darkness. Sutures courtesy of Caedmon and a well-aimed bottle. She returned the snide smile.

Braxton took a threatening step in her direction, his right hand balled in a fist.

"Touch her and I'll gladly add a kilo of lead to your current body weight."

At a glance, Edie could see that it was no idle threat. In fact, she was beginning to realize that Caedmon Aisquith never made idle threats. He was one of those men blessed with incredible follow-through.

"She's got you wrapped around her little pinkie, doesn't she?" Braxton snickered. "Guess you know by now that she's a real prick tease, huh? Hell, my pecker has been standing on end since I first set eyes on the curly-haired bitch."

His shoulders visibly relaxing, Caedmon slyly smiled at Braxton . . . just before he reared back and kick-boxed him in the crotch.

Sounding a lot like a braying donkey, the behemoth dropped to his knees, clutching his testicles with both hands.

"I trust that has relieved the condition." Caedmon turned to Edie. "My apologies."

About to say *For what?* Edie instead went slack-jawed, horrified at seeing a quartet of men who had suddenly, and very silently, materialized, as though from thin air. Shoulder to shoulder, they stood in a united front some ten feet behind Caedmon.

The Four Horsemen of the Apocalypse come to life.

Before she could shout a warning, a spotlight was switched on, illuminating the entire area.

"You would be well advised, Mister Aisquith, to drop your weapon. Very, very slowly," came the addendum order.

Calmly, not so much as peering over his shoulder, Caedmon unclipped the leather strap that held the submachine gun to his chest. Holding the weapon in his left hand, his right hand held aloft so it could easily be seen, he slowly bent at the waist, placing the weapon on the ground.

Stanford MacFarlane stepped forward. Retrieving the submachine gun, he handed it to Boyd Braxton.

"Here, boy. You look like you could use this."

Still doubled over and gasping for breath, Braxton straightened just enough so he could aim the weapon directly at Caedmon's chest.

Unthinkingly, Edie grabbed MacFarlane by the forearm, knowing that he was the only man present who could stop Braxton from pulling the trigger.

"One Christian to another . . . don't let him do it," she begged, ready to throw herself at his booted feet if that was what it took to save Caedmon's life.

"You are not a Christian woman!" MacFarlane bellowed, his face twisted in an ugly sneer. "You are a harlot!"

CHAPTER 88

"And you are a disgusting stain on a snowy white bedsheet," Caedmon snarled at MacFarlane, words the only weapon left to him.

Unaccustomed to insubordinate words or deeds, the colonel appeared apoplectic. Like an Old Testament prophet on the verge of an aneurysm.

"I want him searched before he's killed," MacFarlane barked at one of his men.

The situation having spiraled completely out of his control, Caedmon stood motionless while a muscular man with a shaved pate roughly patted him for weapons. The torch he tossed aside; the GPS receiver and diving knife he handed to his overlord. MacFarlane quickly perused the confiscated items before giving them to yet another of his men for safe-keeping.

Still gasping to draw breath, Braxton gracelessly rose to his feet, instantly transforming from a wounded bear to a menacing mountain of a man. "Let's just say I ain't gonna miss you when you're gone."

Having known all along that this was how it might possibly end, Caedmon defiantly stared his executioner in the face. As he did, Goya's famous painting *The Third of May* flashed across his mind's eye; bloodshed and violence were the chain that inevitably linked one historic epoch to the next.

"Turn your head, woman," MacFarlane commanded. "Unless you have a predilection for bloodshed."

"You kill him, you kill the messenger!"

Hearing that, Caedmon swung his head in Edie's direction. *The messenger?*

What in God's name was she up to? A subterfuge, clearly, but not having been briefed, he had no idea of the nature or direction of the lie. Relegating him to the role of hapless passenger.

Refusing to be bullied into submission, Edie startled every man present, including Caedmon, when she next said, "And something tells me that you'll want to hear what MI5 has to say. They know all about your planned terrorist attack on the Dome of the Rock. Lucky for you, they want the Ark of the Covenant, which is why they're willing to broker a deal. But all bets are off the table if you gun down Caedmon Aisquith. The Queen's men don't like it when you kill one of their own. In fact, they would take it very personally if any harm came to him."

Although MacFarlane stood in the shadows, Caedmon could see that the older man didn't appear the least bit surprised to learn of his connection to MI5.

Bloody hell. Edie's stratagem might actually work. No doubt Stanford MacFarlane, like most Americans, stood in awe of the mighty Five.

With a brusque wave of the hand, MacFarlane motioned Boyd Braxton to stand down. His eyes narrowing, the behemoth lowered the submachine gun. Then, snarling like a rabid animal, he brazenly toggled his index finger over the trigger, wordlessly relaying a very stark message—with the mere press of a finger, he could instantly end Caedmon's life.

Having no control over Braxton, Caedmon turned his attention, instead, to his commanding officer. Well aware that the best falsehoods were those crafted from the truth, Caedmon did just that. He told the truth. "Since last we met, I've used my time wisely. With Miss Miller's able assistance, I put together an in-depth intelligence dossier."

"Complete with photographs, maps, you name it," Edie embellished, spinning yet another outlandish lie on her improvised loom.

"You're going to have to be more specific than that." As MacFarlane spoke, the muscles in his jaw began to spasmodically twitch.

"As Edie mentioned, Thames House has been apprised of your plan to destroy the Dome of the Rock two days hence on Eid al-Adha," Caedmon replied, having quickly cobbled together what he hoped was a plausible scenario. "And, to answer your next question, Five has already contacted their Israeli counterparts. The moment you enter Israel, Mossad will very painfully tighten the noose around your neck. The Israelis do not take kindly to terrorists in their midst."

"And the deal?" Other than a tightness in his jaw, MacFarlane gave no visual clues as to whether he believed the tale thus told.

"The deal is simple: Surrender yourself to British authorities and you will be assured humane and civilized treatment. Reject the offer and you will be at the mercy of Mossad. I understand their interrogation tactics are particularly brutal."

"In case you've forgotten, I'm an American citizen," MacFarlane declared, as though that gave him some sort of carte blanche.

"Do you think that will matter to the Israelis? To them you are merely a terrorist intent on destroying the most holy site in all of Jerusalem."

The tic in MacFarlane's jaw became more noticeable. "And what of the Ark?"

Beginning to think he might actually pull off a bloodless coup, Caedmon said, "It must be turned over to Her Majesty's government. Were it not for the fact that you have the Ark of the Covenant in your possession, you would have been thrown to the Israeli wolves as a matter of course." Caedmon glanced at this wristwatch: 10:20 P.M. "If you have not surrendered yourself to the British consulate by twenty-three hundred hours, the deal will be rendered null and void." Of course, he had no way of knowing if, at this late hour, anyone was on duty at the consulate. He would cross that rickety bridge when he came to it.

A terse silence ensued, the only sound being a soft *rat-a-tat-tat* as Braxton drummed his fingers against his weapon stock. Caedmon purposely refrained from looking at Edie, knowing that any communication, even a silent exchange of glances, would be closely scrutinized; MacFarlane was in the process of separating the wheat from the chaff.

"Since the beginning, I wondered if you would contact British intelligence," MacFarlane finally said after what seemed an interminable silence. "But knowing the power that the Ark holds, something told me that you'd want to keep MI5 out of the loop. Why? Because I assumed that like most men, you would want the Ark of the Covenant all for yourself. It's the reason why Galen of Godmersham made no mention of his extraordinary find to his brethren, the Knights of St. John, even though he was duty-bound to do just that. Instead, he lugged the Ark back to England, where he promptly hid it from prying eyes." MacFarlane took several steps in Caedmon's direction, the tic in his jaw no longer in evidence. "So I have to ask myself . . . what makes you a better man than that brave knight?"

Caedmon shrugged. "I was faced with a crisis that Galen of Godmersham never had to confront."

"And what crisis might that be?"

"How best to prevent the destruction of the Dome of the Rock. Brave knight though I am, I am but an army of one," he drolly added, hoping to recapture the momentum. "And so I had no choice but to contact Thames House. Better the British Museum have the Ark of the Covenant than a man bent on destroying the world." Even before the words passed his lips, Caedmon knew them to be the truth, silently damning himself for not contacting Five. For thinking that he, like Galen of Godmersham, could keep the Ark all to himself.

And when the wretched knight saw this, his death was well deserved.

How apropos; the cryptic line from the quatrains finally made perfect sense to him.

"Mark my words, doomsday will soon be upon us. And when it comes, we will slay the beast of perfidy with divine revelation." As he spoke, Stanford MacFarlane compulsively twisted the silver Jerusalem cross that he wore on his right ring finger. Caedmon suspected the ring was his anchor. A constant reminder of the big picture.

Seeing that repetitive motion, he feared the scales had just tipped. And in the wrong direction.

Edie, who had heretofore remained silent, pointed to the string of lights visible from a vessel that had just entered the bay in the distance. "Doomsday is coming, all right. Dressed in commando black and wielding some awesome firepower. You guys have only got a few minutes left to surrender peaceably." Wearing her bravado like a new suit of clothes, she donned a cocky grin.

Good God. The woman was taking her cues from a Hollywood script.

Without warning, MacFarlane stepped over and grabbed Edie by the hair, yanking her against his chest. Although she valiantly tried to twist free, he wrapped her curly locks around his fist as he pulled her head back at an awkward angle, exposing her neck. He then held out his free hand, palm up. "Give that me that diving knife."

Suddenly realizing the other man's intention, Caedmon lurched forward.

Only to be pistol-whipped in the side of the head by one of MacFarlane's men.

Knowing he could do nothing to save Edie if he was dead, he stood immobile. Edie, evidently sensing that she couldn't escape, had suddenly stopped resisting.

"You know, boy, I've got a funny feeling that you and this curly-haired harlot are lying to me." MacFarlane, his face twisted in a sneer, locked gazes with him. "Now, I know that you're a trained intelligence officer. So I'm going to assume that you have the mental fortitude to stand by while I hold a gun to your pretty woman's head." As he spoke, he lightly ran the knife blade along Edie's cheek. "But do you have the stomach to watch the flesh flayed from her bones in long bloody strips?"

Although her neck was stretched taut as a bow string, Edie tried to shake her head. Tried to caution him not to reveal that there would be no commandoes dressed in black coming to the rescue.

A brave woman. But, more importantly, a beloved woman.

"As earlier stated, I did, in fact, compile a dossier outlining everything that has occurred since Jonathan Padgham's murder," he confessed, the match lost, his queen taken. "Included in the report is a detailed threat assessment of your planned attack on the Dome of the Rock."

"Where's the dossier?"

"It is in the vault of the Dragonara Hotel." Having carefully planned for just such a moment, Caedmon then presented what he hoped would be their Get Out of Jail Free card. "If Edie and I have not returned to the Dragonara Hotel by eight o'clock tomorrow morning, the dossier will promptly be delivered to the British consulate. From there, it will be forwarded to Her Majesty's intelligence service. You are a clever enough man to realize that it would be advantageous to keep us alive. Now, would you please be so kind as to relax your grip on Miss Miller's hair?"

MacFarlane unwound a palm's length of hair. Just enough so Edie could move her neck, but not enough for her to escape.

"How do I know that you're telling me the truth?"

"As with your belief in Old Testament prophecy, you must take it on good faith that I am."

MacFarlane unwound Edie's hair from his fist. Muttering something about "lying harlots," he forcefully shoved her aside. Opening his arms, Caedmon caught Edie, clutching her to his chest.

"You and the harlot have a reprieve."

Without asking, Caedmon knew that he and Edie would be accompanied to the Dragonara Hotel by one of MacFarlane's men. Once there, they would be forced to retrieve the dossier from the hotel vault and give it to their escort. After which, they would promptly be executed.

All told, the reprieve would amount to no more than a few hours. Not unlike watching the killer shark from the glass-bottomed boat, knowing all the while that the vessel would soon capsize.

Hearing the mobile phone clipped to MacFarlane's belt shrilly ring, Caedmon watched as the other man took the call, turning his back on the assembled group. A few moments later, he turned to his second-in-command, the gargantuan Boyd Braxton.

"Call in the troops. We're ready to set sail."

Edie frantically tugged on his sleeve. "The boat that just sailed into the bay, I bet that's how they're getting the Ark out of Malta," she hissed in his ear.

"I suspect you're right."

"The harlot is right," MacFarlane verified, having overheard the exchange. "Not only is my mission ordained by the Almighty, but God is acting through me. How else do you explain that after three thousand years, the Ark of the Covenant has been reclaimed?" His eyes sparkling with an inner fire, he smiled, confirming Caedmon's suspicions that Stanford MacFarlane was quite mad, the man suffering from a full-blown messiah complex.

"Yeah, well, I wouldn't be measuring for the drapes just yet," Edie taunted. "If you think for one second that the good, sane, decent people of the world will stand by and let you and your misguided followers start the next world war, think again."

"God spoke through the prophet Ezekiel, making his will known to mankind. I will see to it that his orders are carried out."

"No greater sacrilege is known under the heavens than to take upon one's shoulders the mantle of God," Caedmon quietly informed their nemesis. "Men like you not only diminish the human spirit, you diminish the very nature of God."

"Soon enough you and your whore will learn what comes of sleeping with the devil," MacFarlane retorted. Then, pointing an accusing finger, "'But evil men and imposters will grow worse and worse, deceiving and being deceived.' Gallagher, take them away!"

The bald-headed underling, with a semiautomatic pistol capably held in his right hand, stepped toward them.

"At least we bought ourselves a little bit of time," Edie whispered.

Caedmon glanced at the yacht in the bay. "Yes, but what of the rest of the world? For them the doomsday clock still ticks."

CHAPTER 89

"'. . . If you warn the wicked, and he does not turn from his wickedness, or from his wicked way, he shall die for his iniquity.'" As he spoke, their guard, the bald-headed Gallagher, motioned Edie and Caedmon to take a seat on a nearby slab of limestone.

Caedmon plunked down on the raised flat stone. "Good God, but I've had enough apocalyptic nattering to last a lifetime."

Wordlessly, Edie sat next to him, knowing it would be a lifetime cut down in its prime if they didn't figure out a way to escape their captor.

Approximately a hundred yards away, Edie could see that MacFarlane and his crew were quickly piling into the military-style transport truck. The same truck into which they'd earlier loaded the Ark of the Covenant. She assumed that the plan was to drive the truck to a boat launch at the bottom of the sea cliff. They could then transport the Ark from shore to yacht via a small motorboat.

From there it would be clear sailing. All the way to Israel.

That thought enraged and terrified her all at once. But it was an impotent rage. And an equally impotent fear. There was nothing she or Caedmon could do to stop the ancient prophe-

cies from being fulfilled. With the End Times hanging over
them like an ominous shadow, the voice of reason had become
eerily silent. Instead, she'd reverted to being the terrified child
who feared the death and destruction that was part and parcel
of God's wrath.

"Caedmon. . . I'm afraid. I don't want it to end. Not the
world. Not any of it," she lamely murmured, unable to put her
feelings into words. At least not words that made any sense.

He placed an arm around her shoulders, pulling her close to
him. "As the Irish are fond of saying, 'At least we had the
day.'" Edie intuited that he was speaking of their earlier love-
making onboard the ferryboat.

Knowing they didn't have much time left, she took her fill
of him. The thick red hair. The lean, rangy physique. The beautiful blue eyes. The relationship over before it ever began.

"I've given it a lot of thought, and I've decided that it's
more than mere physical lust," she informed him, speaking in
a low whisper.

"Do I detect a deathbed confession?"

"You know, gallows humor has always eluded me."

"Then perhaps we need to get off the scaffold and shine
some much-needed light."

"Yeah, but—" She stopped, suddenly realizing what Caedmon was alluding to.

The portable laser light.

Caedmon had said that it could temporarily blind a man.

Edie surreptitiously placed her hand on top of her jacket
pocket. The penlike device was still there. In all of the pandemonium, no one had thought to search her for weapons. Not
that anyone would consider something resembling a Bic pen
much of a threat.

"Be ready," she whispered in a hushed voice, certain that
when the time came, Caedmon would know what to do.

A few seconds later, Gallagher reached into his breast
pocket and removed a crumpled pack of Marlboro cigarettes.
Next he patted the front of his cargo pants, searching for a
match. Or a lighter. It didn't much matter because it gave Edie
an opportunity to slide her hand into her jacket pocket, all the

while praying that their captor's gaze didn't land on her slow-moving hand.

Her fingers wrapped around the laser light. Quickly, she found the small on/off switch. In the same place where you'd expect to find the clip on an ink pen. She removed the pen from her pocket.

Gallagher's bald head suddenly swiveled in her direction.

"Hey, bitch! What the hell are you doing?"

"Bringing you to Jesus!" she retorted, aiming what she hoped was the business end of the laser at Gallagher's face.

A thin ray of green light immediately burst forth, hitting Gallagher first in one eye, then the other. Instinctively, he raised his arm to shield himself from the lens-burning beam of light.

"Quick! Turn it off!" Caedmon hissed, snatching her by the forearm to get her attention. The abrupt motion caused the light beam to shoot heavenward, making it appear as though the thin green light actually touched the marmalade moon that hovered thousands of miles above the earth.

Edie flipped the switch into the off position.

Like a striking viper, Caedmon lurched forward, his right hand thrusting outward, his fingers wrapping around the barrel of Gallagher's gun. One quick, strong-armed twist and the gun was loosened from the other man's grip. The pistol now in his possession, Caedmon used it to violently bludgeon Gallagher on the skull. An instant later, Gallagher went limp. Grabbing him by the scruff of the neck, Caedmon lugged him behind the slab of limestone. Out of sight. That done, he unclipped Gallagher's cell phone from his belt.

Edie furtively scanned the area, terrified that the scuffle, which lasted only a few seconds, had been observed.

Mercifully, she heard no alarm being issued; MacFarlane's men were still clambering into the back of the truck.

"Is he . . . ?" She jutted her chin at the man sprawled on the other side of the limestone slab.

Caedmon tersely shook his head. "But pray the bastard doesn't awake any time soon."

Taking her by the elbow, Caedmon quickly shepherded her

toward the convoy truck. Not only did they keep to the shadows, but they kept a low profile, both of them hunched at the waist.

About fifty yards from the truck, Caedmon yanked her behind a scraggly clump of dried vegetation.

"Our objective, our *only* objective, is to prevent the Ark from being loaded onto that yacht in the bay. If that happens, it will be lost forever. I mean this, love . . . no heroics." As he spoke, he lightly grasped her by the chin.

"Do you think we've actually got a chance?"

"So long as our escape from the hapless Gallagher goes undetected. Their success is not yet a fait accompli."

"If they do find Gallagher, they're gonna turn on us like a pack of wolves."

Still holding her by the chin, Caedmon stared at her. Taking a deep breath, he said, "The bloodletting, if it comes, will be voracious. And altogether pitiless."

CHAPTER 90

"I don't know about you, sir, but I can't wait to blow the Dome of the Rock to kingdom come." Fully recovered from his earlier injury, Boyd Braxton positioned himself behind the steering wheel of the 6×6 convoy truck.

"'Vengeance *is* mine, sayeth the Lord,'" Stan replied, well aware that in the eleventh century, the Muslim infidels had attempted to destroy the tomb of Jesus; the reprisal was long overdue. "Gunny, do you know what the word *Islam* means?"

"No, sir. Can't say that I do."

"It means 'submit.'"

Submit or die.

As always happened when he pondered the true meaning of the infidel's faith, Stan felt a hot rage surge upward from the base of his spine, his temples pounding with the force of his hatred.

"As God is my witness, I will never be conquered by those people. Never."

"I hear ya, sir!" Braxton banged his balled fist against the steering wheel. "We'll teach those ragheads a lesson! Every last one of 'em!"

Pleased with his subordinate's exuberance—the Lord always looked with favor upon those who executed their duty with a glad heart—Stan slammed shut the passenger door. In the back of the truck, all nine of his men were present and accounted for. The Ark would be well guarded. To a man, they would unflinchingly lay down their lives to protect the holy relic. Although it was doubtful that they would encounter any resistance. The Englishman had readily admitted that British intelligence was ignorant of their plans. And according to the yacht's captain, the voyage from Haifa had been uneventful.

Soon, in God's name, he would prevail. Then, on the battlefields of that most holy of lands, he would triumph. The Ark of the Covenant was the key to victory. As it had been in the days of old when it was used to bring down the walls of mighty Jericho. *And so it shall come to pass.* The prophecies of Ezekiel were a roadmap to success.

With the last obstacle removed, nothing could stop him. Not the peaceniks. Not the left-wing secularists who railed against religion. Not the passive wusses at the UN. Not even the stalwart Englishman who had proved such a formidable foe.

Respect for one's enemy, however, only went so far; Stan was well aware that there was a special hell for men like Caedmon Aisquith and his degenerate harlot. Soon they would discover that God's fire was inextinguishable. The flames of hell burned eternally bright.

And the serpent will be cast into the bottomless pit . . . so that he should deceive the nations no more till the thousand years were finished.

Out of the corner of his eye, Stan saw a shadow approach. The shadow belonged to Rostov, his communications expert. He rolled down the window on the truck.

"What is it?"

An anxious glint in his eyes, the other man said, "We've got a problem, sir. Gallagher isn't answering his cell."

The muscles in Stan's belly painfully tightened. He took a deep breath, striving for a calm he didn't feel.

As he silently begged for divine guidance, he envisioned in his mind's eye the Tree of Life, not seen since the expulsion from Eden, blossoming atop the Temple Mount.

Blessed with that calming vision, he turned to his communications expert. "Get in the back." He then turned to his trusted subordinate. "We're gonna find 'em and run 'em down."

"Yes, sir!"

CHAPTER 91

Ignoring the vibrating mobile phone clipped to his waistband, Caedmon urged Edie to keep moving; the convoy truck was no more than thirty meters ahead of them.

"Maybe you should answer it," Edie whispered, clearly unnerved by the incoming call. "Otherwise they'll know something's up."

Well aware that the end result would be the same regardless of whether he answered the mobile, Caedmon made no reply as they continued to creep along at a quick but cautious pace.

A few moments later they approached the stone watch-tower. The wood-planked door stood wide open; MacFarlane's men hadn't bothered with locking up before they departed the premises.

Time being a commodity in short supply, Caedmon yanked Edie into the building's protective shadow, where the two of them huddled close. He peered around the corner, verifying that the truck was still parked on the other side of the tower.

"I want you to go inside and, if at all possible, lock yourself into a room. Then I want you to use Gallagher's mobile to ring the authorities. Understood?" When she nodded, he handed her the now-silent mobile phone. "Tell them that you're an American tourist and that you were earlier abducted from your hotel room. Make no mention of the Ark of the Covenant."

"What about you?"

"I am off to slay the dragon," he deadpanned. As he spoke, he checked the clip on the Glock. Sixteen rounds. *Thank God.* He only needed three bullets. One to blow out a tire on the convoy truck. One to take out Stanford MacFarlane. And a third bullet to fell the behemoth.

Hit those three targets, and chaos would ensue.

With chaos, all of MacFarlane's well-laid plans would come to a crashing halt. The dreams of a madman finally put to rest.

He motioned to the door of the watchtower. "In you go."

"But—"

"No buts," he interjected, placing a hand over her mouth. With the other hand, he gently pushed her through the open doorway. Then, hoping she would heed his command, he pulled the door shut.

Stay safe, love.

His right arm cocked at the elbow, the Glock clutched in his hand, Caedmon wended his way around the perimeter of the tower; his plan was to approach the truck from the front rather than the rear, enabling him to take out the cab passenger, the driver, and one of the front tires. In that order. And in quick succession.

The plan was brazen. Reckless, even. But it was the only option left to him. Under no circumstance could he permit MacFarlane to leave the isle alive. Too much was at stake. Too many lives in the balance.

Suppressing the innate fear that arises in any life-and-death situation, he ventured forth. The truck was no more than twenty meters away, just beyond the curve of the building.

Suddenly, he heard the roar of an engine. Blinked at the near-blinding beam of a headlight. The truck was on the move.

He fought the instinctive urge to fire his weapon.

He needed a clean shot. If he botched it, all would be lost.

Knowing he had but seconds to launch his attack, he charged out of the shadows, coming at the truck from an angle to avoid being caught in the headlights. He refused to entertain the thought that in the contest between man and machine, machine almost inevitably won.

Arms locked in a firing position, he found his first target— Stanford MacFarlane—took aim, and fired.

"Shag it!" he muttered; the Glock had jammed. He pulled back the slide on the top of the pistol.

Suddenly, the clatter of machine-gun fire erupted all around him.

Caught in a corona of bullets, he quickly chambered a round, shock and anger hitting him in equal measure.

A heartbeat later, shock instantly mutated into fear as he saw a shaky shaft of green light being aimed at the truck's windshield.

CHAPTER 92

"Jesusfuckingchrist! I can't see!" Boyd Braxton hollered, raising his arms to stave off the green light beam. "I can't see a damn—"

The truck swerved. Jerking to the right. Then the left. A few seconds later, it began to lose speed.

"Put your foot on the gas pedal!" Stan yelled over the top of his gunnery sergeant's foul-mouthed screams. "We *must* fulfill the prophecy! Do not give in to your fears!"

Averting his head from the burning light, Stan leaned over the top of his gunny and grabbed the steering wheel, knowing that fear was the tool of the devil. Fear was what he'd felt that long-ago night in Beirut. When his best friend, his comrades, his CO were ripped to shreds by an Islamist's bomb. When he stood shaking in the bomb's aftermath, snot driveling from his nose, piss puddling at his feet. Afraid to grab his weapon and take action. Afraid to do anything other than drop to his knees and beg God's mercy.

That was when the angels came to him. Gabriel and Michael. The same two angels who adorned the lid of the Ark. They took his fear from him, asking only that he take up the Lord's fight.

And every day since, he had done just that.

This day would be no different.

For he knew no fear.

He had complete and certain faith in the sanctity of his mission.

The same faith that had led Abraham and Moses in their darkest hour. The same faith that had compelled David to face his mighty nemesis Goliath.

*You come at me with a sword and spear. I come to you in
the name of the Lord!*

Those were words to live by. Words to die by.

"The battle for the Temple will soon be upon us! Praise be
to the Lord!" he joyfully shouted, retaking control of the truck,
steering it straight toward the green beam of light.

CHAPTER 93

Caedmon ran full speed toward the pencil-thin, erratic green
glow.

"Turn it off!" he shouted, able to see that MacFarlane had
taken control of the careening vehicle. Able to see that he was
steering the truck directly toward the source of the light
beam.

Edie turned her head in his direction. With her curly hair
wildly blowing all about her, she looked like one of the Furies
in pursuit of the wicked among them.

Her expression resolute, she shook her head, refusing to
move out of the path of the oncoming convoy truck.

He pumped his legs and arms all the faster, afraid he
wouldn't reach her in time. Afraid she would meet her end in
a most hideous fashion. *Afraid.*

He only had a few seconds, the whole of the world reduced
to his pounding heart, the *rat-a-tat-tat* of automatic-weapon
fire, the roar of the powerful engine.

She was just a few feet away.

He could do this.

He could save—

In the next instant, he was airborne, diving toward her, his
arms and legs stretched taut.

His heart in his throat, Caedmon plowed into Edie with a thudding impact, knocking her off her feet and out of the truck's pathway. The laser light knocked from her hands, its beam frenetically arced through the night sky before harmlessly plummeting to earth. Limbs tangled together, the two of them rolled across the rocky terrain, the inhospitable surface providing no leaf or blade of grass to soften the impact.

With no time to inquire as to injuries, he rolled to his knees. His finger on the trigger of the Glock, his arms locked in a firing position, he prayed that he had successfully cleared the jam.

The truck now moving away from him, he took aim at the rear tires, permitting himself one deep, calming breath before he fired six shots in quick succession.

His aim true, he hit the new targets, blowing out both rear driver's-side tires, the truck abruptly fishtailing, wildly swaying from side to side as Stanford MacFarlane lost control of the mammoth two-and-a-half-ton vehicle. As the truck headed toward the steep cliff that overlooked the sea.

The gun limply hanging from his hand, Caedmon stood motionless, watching in disbelief as the truck went over the side of the cliff.

For the briefest of seconds the red taillights eerily twinkled in the darkness before disappearing from sight. A sonorous *Boom!* was soon followed by a sudden burst of bright light, the ensuing explosion illuminating the heavens. A surreal swan song for a madman and the coveted Ark of the Covenant.

All was vanity and grasping for the wind, he dazedly thought even as his stomach roiled.

Edie ran to his side, throwing herself into his arms.

"Oh, God! I can't believe what I just saw!"

"Nor I," he whispered, holding her tight.

CHAPTER 94

As though trapped in a dream from which he could not awake, Caedmon surveyed the wreckage. The explosion having been seen for miles, rescue workers, naval marines, law enforcement personnel, and local fishermen had descended in an excited swarm onto the rock-strewn beach.

The official crash site.

Like many he'd seen over the years, this one had all the familiar trappings—yellow tape, black smoke, smoldering hunks of twisted metal. At a glance he saw that no man could have survived so horrific a blast. Although that didn't deter the local police divers, who plopped salmonlike from the starboard side of a nearby vessel, aided in their search by powerful underwater torches that cast an otherworldly glow onto the dark sea.

"He thought he could walk on water," Edie, standing beside him, quietly intoned. "Boy, was he ever wrong."

"The din is silenced. At least for the moment. Perhaps now the voices of tolerance and compassion can finally be heard."

"Or, put another way, God works in mysterious ways."

"Mmmm," he noncommittally grunted, unable to see God's hand in the violent events that had earlier transpired.

Since the crash, he and Edie had kept very much to the sidelines. *Two curious, but innocent bystanders.* To ensure that they weren't caught in the police dragnet, he had informed the local officials that they were simply a honeymooning couple who "got the wild notion into our heads to spend a romantic night at the ancient tower." And though they had heard the thunderous explosion, they "had no bloody idea what caused it." Coitus interruptus, and all that. The lie took, the police not favoring them with so much as a second glance.

"Deheb! Deheb!" a grizzled fisherman exclaimed as he charged through the surf, excitedly pointing to a rivulet of molten gold visible in the soot-colored sand.

Staring at that telltale stream, Caedmon felt like a battle-wearied and defeated knight come home from the wars.

The Ark of the Covenant had not withstood the fiery blast. *He had failed in his quest.*

What was left of the sacred Ark of the ancient Israelites was slowly being washed out to sea.

He contritely glanced heavenward. *I gave it my all.*

But his all had not been good enough.

Feeling the shameful sting of tears, the crash site suddenly turning into a nightmarish blur, he abruptly turned his back on Edie. She'd seen enough this night. She didn't need to see a grown man break down and cry.

"I need to relieve myself," he muttered, adding yet another lie to an ever-mounting heap. With a quick parting wave of the hand, he headed for the far end of the rock-laden beach, removing himself from the excited melee and contorted scraps of smoldering steel.

His vision still slightly blurred around the edges, he flipped on his torch. *So I don't unman myself further by breaking my bloody neck,* he irritably thought as he navigated over and around the tumbled rocks that had, over the years, flaked away from the imposing sea cliff. Like so many orphaned children.

Emotionally and physically drained, he seated himself on a flat-topped boulder. Elbows braced on his thighs, head supported between his hands, he glumly stared at the gently rolling waves.

"How could I have been so arrogant to think that—" He stopped in mid-castigation.

Espying a shiny glint out of the corner of his eye, he bounded off his perch and scrambled over several large boulders, maneuvering onto his stomach so he could better see the golden object wedged between two mammoth pieces of limestone.

He shone his torch into the deep crevasse.

An instant later, his breath caught in his throat.

Bloody hell.

There, upended at an awkward angle, was an incised golden lid, measuring approximately two and a half by four feet.

The lid to the Ark of the Covenant. What the ancient Hebrews called the mercy seat.

Affixed to the top of the lid were two winged stern-faced figures. The cherubim, Gabriel and Michael. *I will meet with thee and will commune with thee from above the mercy seat, from between the two cherubim which are upon the Ark.*

Without a doubt, it was the most spectacularly beautiful thing he'd ever seen.

"God does truly work in mysterious ways," he murmured, well aware that the cherubim were traditionally associated with the primal element of fire.

How ironic that the two winged figures survived the fiery blast.

Utterly bedazzled by the find, he stretched out a hand to touch the beautifully incised lid.

Just as quickly, he withdrew his arm, suddenly recalling the fate of the hapless men of Bethshemesh. Worried that a residual spark of the Ark's awesome power might still inhabit the golden lid, he rolled onto his back and gazed heavenward, silently asking, *begging*, permission.

Instead of a heavenly dispensation, he instead saw the sins of his life flash in quick succession across his mind's eye like so many cue cards.

"Oh, shag it," he irreverently cursed, rolling back onto his belly and shining his torch into the crevasse.

Teeth clenched, he shoved his hand into the rocky fissure and committed the unthinkable—he placed his hand upon the lid of the Ark of the Covenant.

When nothing untoward occurred, he slowly inched his fingers along the rim, able to detect some sort of etched ornamentation. He adjusted the angle of the torch, enabling him to inspect a small incised figure that had the body of a man and the head of a falcon.

"I don't believe it."

"What are you doing?" a voice behind him inquired.

At hearing Edie's worried tone, he sat upright. "Come, have a look." He extended a hand to help her onto the boulder. Then he directed the torch beam at the golden lid.

"It's the lid to the Ark of the Covenant!" she exclaimed, nearly coming bodily off the boulder.

"Yes, that's what I thought, as well," he replied, knowing that he was about to burst a very inflated bubble. "Do you see that row of markings on the rim?"

She scooted a few inches closer to the crevasse. "Uh-huh."

"Those are Egyptian hieroglyphics." Reaching into the crevasse, he pointed to a line of incised characters. "This is a rough translation, mind you, but I believe the etched inscription reads, 'Ra-Harakhti, Supreme Lord of the Heavens.'"

Edie immediately snatched the torch out of his hand and directed it into the fissure, evidently needing to verify for herself. "But . . . I don't understand . . . why are there Egyptian hieroglyphics on the Ark of the Covenant?"

"Because it's not the Ark of the Covenant. Rather it is an Egyptian bark."

"An Egyptian bark," she parroted, clearly stupefied. "But—are you absolutely certain?" she demanded; the woman was a hard nut to crack. "And what about the two angels on top?"

"Isis and her sister Nephthys, I suspect. As you may recall, the ancient Egyptians were the originators of a sacred chest known as a bark. Furthermore, I believe the Egyptian bark was the prototype used by Moses in creating the fabled Ark." He took the torch from her shaking hand. "It would seem that Galen of Godmersham uncovered an Egyptian bark, not the Hebrew Ark of the Covenant."

Tears silently cascaded down Edie's cheeks. Soon followed by an unexpected burst of raucous laughter.

"Bloody hell!" she loudly bellowed.

At hearing the spot-on impersonation, Caedmon grinned.

"Come here, love."

CHAPTER 95

As she stepped onto the hotel room balcony, Edie pulled the two halves of her terry-cloth robe closer together and tightened the belt; there was a damp, but invigorating chill in the air. Overhead, a few stars were still visible, shimmering specks of light flung haphazardly across the predawn sky. Glancing heavenward, she sighed, always amazed by the breathless expectancy that heralded the arrival of each new day.

"Enchanting, isn't it?" Caedmon said as he joined her on the balcony. Having just gotten out of the shower, he was attired in an identical fluffy white robe. He handed her a teacup and saucer.

Catching a heady whiff of bergamot, Edie smiled. "The Earl Grey is much needed and much appreciated. And, yes, it is enchanting," she agreed as she seated herself at the small bistro table set up in the corner of the balcony.

So enchanting, she wasn't altogether certain she wanted to leave. At least not yet. After the violence of the night just passed, she needed some downtime. Some stress-free, kick-off-your-shoes, sleep-till-noon, I'm-not-answering-the-telephone downtime. She didn't know, however, whether Caedmon would be joining her. Other than a brief discussion regarding what time the hotel breakfast buffet opened, no mention of the future had been made.

Caedmon seated himself next to her. Suddenly nervous, Edie stared at the horizon, the sky now tinted a soft pink. Like the inside of a seashell. On the wharf, a few industrious fishermen were already out and about, tossing huge nets onto whimsically painted skiffs.

"When I was little, I used to think that the stars went into hiding once the sun came up. Of course, being older and wiser—well, actually, I'm not exactly certain what happens to the stars come daybreak, so just forget I even brought it up," she said, waving away the silly thought, belatedly realizing that she was rambling.

"When I was a young lad, I used to wonder what alchemical mix created the rainbow," Caedmon remarked, his English accent sounding more clipped than usual; Edie wondered if he wasn't a little bit nervous himself.

"The mysteries of the universe. Seems we were both intrigued at an early age."

"By the by, I sent an e-mail to my old group leader at MI5," Caedmon said, changing the subject. "Told him that I caught wind of a plot to destroy the Dome of the Rock on the upcoming Muslim holy day. Trent is a good man. He'll see to it that Mossad and the Israeli public security minister are contacted."

"You don't think that—"

"No, no," he quickly assured her. "I'm just dotting my *i*'s, as they say. The possibility that MacFarlane had a contingency plan is rather remote. He seemed very much the micromanager."

Edie fiddled with the delicate handle on her teacup, hesitant to broach the next topic. "You haven't said anything, but . . . I know you're disappointed. That it wasn't the Ark of the Covenant."

For several long moments, Caedmon stared at the early-morning activity on the bay; Edie was unable to gauge his thoughts. Or his mood; the small pucker on his brow made her think that he was wrangling his way out of a quandary.

Finally, taking a deep I've-come-to-a-decision kind of breath, he redirected his gaze toward her. "You wrongly assume that I no longer aspire to find the Ark."

"But I just thought that—" At a sudden loss for words, she stared at him.

"It's still out there. I'm certain of it. Still waiting to be discovered. Still waiting to bear holy witness to an eternal truth that is beyond mortal man's comprehension."

"'Thou, silent form, dost tease us out of thought as doth eternity.'"

Smiling, Caedmon took a sip of tea. "How did you know that Keats is my favorite poet?"

She shrugged. "I didn't. It just seemed"—again she shrugged—"apropos. So, gosh, this is—wow. Guess you can tell I'm kind of speechless, huh?" Crestfallen, she had a sudden urge to glug down one of those tiny bottles of scotch from the room's minibar.

"The Knights Templar believed that Ethiopia was the secret resting place of the Ark of the Covenant, the holy relic having been spirited out of Jerusalem by Menelik."

"Menelik?"

"Yes, Solomon's illegitimate son by the Queen of Sheba. There are several passages in Wolfram's *Parsifal* that intimate as much. The stuff of legends, eh?"

"As I understand it, the Ethiopian highlands are quite lovely." She wondered if she should wish him luck with his life now or wait until the taxi pulled up to take him to the airport. "And, of course, it would make an interesting topic. You know, for your next book."

"My thoughts exactly. Although . . ." One side of his mouth quirked; the man was clearly amused by something. "I will have need of a photographer. You wouldn't happen to know anyone who would be interested in the assignment?"

"Well, now that you mention it, I do know a photographer who's currently available. Would this be, you know, a strictly professional relationship or . . . ?" She very purposefully crossed her legs at the knee, her robe gaping open to reveal a bare leg well-toned from Pilates.

Caedmon openly stared, proving what she already knew— that under the English veneer lurked a man of deep passions.

"You do know that I've always been fascinated by valiant women."

"A valiant woman and an adventuresome man. We make quite the pair, don't we?"

"Quite." Then, his jaw tightening, Caedmon figuratively locked horns with her. "And given your valiant behavior with that green laser light, you should be bent over and given a thorough whacking. You came damned close to getting yourself killed."

"Funny, but you don't strike me as an S-and-M type of guy."

"Just find me a man who doesn't enjoy being spanked by a beautiful woman."

Edie burst out laughing, having to slap a hand over her mouth to keep a mouthful of tea from spewing onto the bistro table.

Balancing his elbows on his thighs, Caedmon leaned toward her. "What is it that you want from your life, Edie?"

The question, unexpected and to the point, surprised her. "Well, like most people, I want security, happiness, a sense of belonging."

"I can give those to you."

"Are you sure? I mean, we sorta got flung together."

Blue eyes twinkling, Caedmon grinned. "I am quite certain."

Hearing that, Edie decided to dive in, as well. "Since we're on the subject, I suppose the time has come for me to confess that I'm absolutely crazy about you. You're intelligent, witty, well mannered, and considerate. Everything a woman could possibly want in a man."

"Might I point out that you didn't include *handsome* in your litany of attributes."

"I was saving the best for last." Edie raised her teacup. Holding it aloft, she clinked rims with him. "Here's to finding the Ark."

"And if not the Ark, then the secret of the Knights Templar."

"And if not the secret of the Templars, then—" She pointedly glanced at the oversized bed in the middle of their hotel suite.

Caedmon also glanced at the bed, its coverlet invitingly turned down. Getting up from the table, he placed a hand on her elbow, urging her to her feet.

"Let the adventure begin."

Don't miss the international bestseller

THE
LAST
POPE

by Luís Miguel Rocha

Vatican City, 1978: On September 29, the world awakens to news of the shocking, sudden death of Pope John Paul I, elected only thirty-three days earlier.

London, 2006: Journalist Sarah Monteiro finds a mysterious envelope stuffed in her mailbox. Inside is a list of unfamiliar names and a coded message.

Drawn into a vortex of terrifying double crosses and terror, Sarah soon learns that the contents of the envelope hold the key to unveiling corruption beyond anything she has ever known—a plot that implicates not only unscrupulous mercenaries and crooked politicians, but also princes of the Church itself . . .

"Exciting...Thriller fans will enjoy *The Last Pope*."
—BookReview.com

"Fascinating."
—*USA Today*

M497T0909

BEHIND EACH SECRET IS A TRUTH.

BEHIND EACH TRUTH IS A SACRIFICE...

ON THE FIFTH DAY
A. J. Hartley

The mysterious death of a Catholic priest has been met with suspicion by his brother, Thomas Knight—and the grave silence of church authorities. All Thomas knows is that his brother died in the Philippines, the last stop of an international trek researching the history of Christian symbols. But Thomas and curator Deborah Miller aren't alone in retracing the priest's perilous and labyrinthine path. Their every move is being shadowed by a fanatical cabal of agents who are desperate to hide the astonishing secret Thomas's brother stumbled upon—and willing to kill to keep it buried in the shadows of history forever.

"Terrific plotting, first-rate suspense.
On the Fifth Day is a ripping good read."
—Kathy Reichs

penguin.com

Don't miss the page-turning suspense, intriguing characters, and unstoppable action that keep readers coming back for more from these bestselling authors...

Tom Clancy
Robin Cook
Patricia Cornwell
Clive Cussler
Dean Koontz
J.D. Robb
John Sandford

Your favorite thrillers and suspense novels come from Berkley.

penguin.com

M14G0907